Song
of
Gabrielle

The Woman
Who Loved Two Men

by John Anthony Miller

i

Taylor and Seale Publishing, LLC.
Daytona Beach Shores, Florida

ISBN: 978-1-950613-74-8
Copyright 2020

Taylor and Seale Publishing, LLC.
2 Oceans West Blvd. Unit 406
Daytona Beach Shores, Florida 32118
marycpub1@gmail.com.
386-481-0502. 386-760-8987

Books can be bought at
amazon.com
Barnes and Noble
Books-A-Million
and wherever fine books are sold

To buy in bulk for schools, museums, and organizations, please contact Taylor and Seale Publishing for special discounts

Printed in the U.S.A.

Dedication

For family – and all that's most important

Acknowledgement

Special thanks to Donna Eastman at Parkeast Literary

and to Dr. Mary Custureri

and Dr. Melissa Shaddix

at Taylor and Seale Publishing

Prologue

Normandy, France in the year 1316

As the sun sank into the sea, darkness draped the Normandy coast. Black clouds swollen with moisture rolled across the cliffs that thrust upward from the shore, promising rain or sleet or whatever God might bring to a land ravaged by war.

I shifted the satchels upon my back, their weight making me weary. One held my belongings, a tunic more tattered than that which I wore, a skin of water that was close to dry, and fragments of verse from books long forgotten, while the other housed the lute I used to earn my keep as I traveled town to town, telling tales and singing songs. I eyed the storm as it came ashore and the terrain that sprawled behind me, ensuring that I was alone on the ridge, safe from the bands of English soldiers who roved the countryside. A sharp wind whipped up from the sea, and I pulled my cloak about my neck, trying to keep warm. I had to seek shelter to avoid a night that might kill as easily as the enemy whom I now tried to avoid.

I walked along a dirt lane worn by wagon wheels, indented by horses' hooves, as it rose and fell with the cliffs that rimmed the Normandy coast. I scanned all directions in search of shelter, if only for rocks or trees to shield me from the wind and rain. I could see a village to the south, the church steeple announcing the town it anchored, still an hour or more away. But as I came to the top of a crest, I saw a cottage that hugged the coast, a convent sitting beside it.

I quickened my pace, my bags heavier, my legs more tired with each step. A few drops of rain began to fall, a cold drizzle that bit my hands and face, and I turned away from the wind and looked to the ground, readjusting the scarf about my head to protect it. The road wound along the crest of the cliff to the convent beyond—the cottage closer to the edge that dropped dramatically down to the waves. I approached the wall that

1

enclosed the convent and saw a cemetery stretching from the lane that led to the cottage to the edge of the cliff that guarded the sea.

My gaze rested on the graveyard, so silent in the night, and even though the weather warned me, I couldn't help seeing whose souls it might contain. I knew I could linger but a moment more. The graves were marked with white crosses, some askew, pummeled by the wind. I looked at the first and read the name: Sister Eloise Barbette. The next read Sister Lorraine de Fay. And a larger cross bore the name of The Reverend Mother Fae Le Vanier. I then saw a marble headstone that sat facing the sea, so unlike those around it, and I couldn't resist discovering who its owner might be. I stopped and stood before it, the etched letters weathered to shallow relief by the passage of so many years. An arched recess in the top of the stone held an aged chalice, protected from the wind and rain and hidden from the prying eyes of man, a prized possession from the past that now seemed like a trinket used only to garnish a grave. I looked at the epitaph, aged by time: Lady Gabrielle, the woman who loved two men.

The rain fell harder. I hurried back to the lane and approached the convent wall. An iron gate hung on one hinge, broken beyond repair, and, as I glanced into the courtyard, I saw a man, stout with but a fringe of hair remaining on his head, standing at an open door. A wooden sign hung above him: The Boars Head Inn.

"Who goes there?" the man asked.

I realized the convent no longer existed, and an inn now stood in its place.

"Jean Antoine," I said. "Troubadour and son of a miller. Have you lodging for the night?"

"My prayers have been answered," the man said as he waved me toward the door. "Please come in, I beg of you."

I hesitated. His desperation was a mystery. I suspected an imminent robbery, with me as its victim. Or maybe the English, an enemy always, were hidden somewhere within, holding all who approached as captives, hoping to earn a worthy reward. But as the rain continued, and the temperature kept dropping, I had few options remaining and decided to step inside.

2

"I'm Graves, the innkeeper," the man said. "And a troubadour is what I now need most."

I felt more at ease and made a demand. "If I perform, my lodging is free."

"Agreed," Graves said with hardly a whimper. "I've an unruly crowd, men best suited for battle."

I wasn't sure I could serve as requested. "I know not what I can do," I said. "But if a song assists in calming the crowd, I'm happy to oblige."

"More than a song is needed," he continued. "They argue as they eat their meal and a brawl is about to break. And now the grog flows freely, so I suspect it will only get worse."

I assessed the situation, the innkeeper's plight, and knew I could leverage for more. "If I'm to perform throughout the night, then serve my meals for free."

"I'll gladly pay if you calm the crowd," he said. "Both meals and coins if you do as desired. But music and song may not be enough. I think a tale would best be told—the longest you've come to know."

I could hear the clamor as we approached the door, men shouting and cursing and calling out names. Warily, I walked into a spacious room, suspicious of what I might find there. But the fire that crackled within an open hearth, and a kettle of stew on the fire, welcomed me more than the host ever could. Grizzled men with mugs of grog before them hunched over about a dozen plank tables spread throughout the hall. Most were soldiers, recruited to fight the English, but scattered among them were seaman, their faces like leather from the rays of the sun and the sting from salt of the sea. Still more were merchants who came to barter their wares on the floor beside them. A handful of women were spread through the crowd, their intent not mine to ascertain.

"Come over here," Graves grumbled, guiding me to a stool beside the fire.

I placed my bags on the floor, warmed my hands for a moment, and removed my lute from the satchel. As I sat on the stool and began to strum one chord, then another, the noise began to subside.

"We're about to be entertained," Graves announced to the crowd. "Be quiet and listen."

"Music from a master," a soldier shouted in jest, and the room filled with laughter.

"They don't know what talent you bring," Graves said. "But as I say, it's more than a jingle that's likely needed to keep them from one another's throats. Tell a story that lasts 'til they find their beds, better than any you've heard before."

"It had better be good," a voice called out from a face in the back of the room.

My mind reeled as I rummaged through the ballads I'd collected and songs I had sung in the years past, but no words came to my lips.

Graves turned to me and whispered, "Best to begin now while the noise has died down."

I looked into the eyes of those hardened men who might slit the throats of folk like me for nary a reason or only a glance, and I knew I had to begin. Like a beacon, the gravestone of Gabrielle, the woman who loved two men, flashed before my eyes. I cleared my throat, strummed two chords, looked anxiously at the crowd, and commenced my tale.

"Our story begins at this very spot, a hundred years ago…"

Dramatis Personae

The Lady Gabrielle

A French noblewoman betrothed to Montague and held captive by Sir Michael Marston

The Combatants

Those who Defend

Sir Michael Marston: captor of Lady Gabrielle, the English commander

Captain Carney: assistant to Sir Michael Marston

Gideon: alchemist, inventor, advisor to Sir Michael Marston

Minerva: the witch of Marston Castle more powerful than any before

Those who Attack

The French:

Montague: Gabrielle's fiancé, the French commander

Piers: Montague's assistant

Alaric: French wizard at the sunset of his powers

Jamet: advisor to the French king; liaison to the English who rebel

The English who rebel:

James the Bold: commander of those who revolt

Blaise: an English warlock, immersed in evil

The Baron and the Holy Grail:

Sir Richard Tweed: initiator of the rebellion, holder of the Holy Grail

Paul the Pure: a druid who plots to kill Michael Marston

Trinity: a weak witch who steals the Grail

Chapter 1

Normandy, France in the year 1216

A convent sat on a cliff by the sea, witness to waves that rolled to the shore. Isolated and alone, battered by winds that came off the water, it was built of beige stone with veins of vermilion, its courtyard accessed by an iron gate, the cross at its center wrapped in roses, stems thick with thorns. The convent had stood for hundreds of years, avoided and unmolested, bypassed by armies that came and went, trampling the terrain to seek and destroy.

The English came that spring, refusing to let go of a land they had conquered and surrendered many times over as the years passed. As they captured the coast and turned north, sunlight reflecting from their metal helmets, their footsteps pounded meadows and glens, echoed through forest and field, like the even cadence of a drum that had no beginning and promised no end.

The nuns watched warily as the enemy advanced, the French forces retreating, scattered and defeated. But they knew the tide of battle tugged to and fro, and today's defeat often held within it the seeds of tomorrow's victory. Innocent but wise, pure but proud, the nuns were devout in their worship and known for their kindness. They cared for the sick and downtrodden, expecting and accepting nothing in return. Reclusive except in times of need, they kept a watchful eye on the farms and villages scattered along the Normandy coast.

It was just after dawn when the French arrived, thirty men on horseback fleeing the English invaders. They sheltered a woman close to their leader, the Lady Gabrielle. Her hair, the color of an autumn sun that melts mist from the dawn, caressed her head and framed her face, lightly kissing her shoulders. Her eyes were green, like a tranquil sea when the waves have waned, and her skin was like porcelain. Willowy and graceful but generously proportioned, she was known for both her beauty and intellect, said to rival even the most learned of those that graced King Philip's court.

The French stopped short of the convent, pausing to peek within. Their leader, Montague of Rouen, advanced and dismounted, approaching the gate. A respected soldier in times of war, he was famous for victories against all engaged. In times of peace, he was known for his love of Normandy and all it contained, a man who built cathedrals, blending a love of beauty with the worship of God. His brown hair fell almost to his shoulders and was accented by a short beard. His eyes, dark and inquisitive, showed strength and compassion that many had seen and never forgotten. Dressed in black leggings and a pale blue tunic emblazoned with the image of a roaring lion, a sword dangling from his belt, he studied the convent a moment more and then came forward, banging on the gate.

"A request from the king," he called.

The Reverend Mother, a stout woman with a round face, heard the noise and hurried to the entrance. Five nuns followed, for little happened in the convent that wasn't shared among them. She looked at the knight, confused and afraid. "What do you want, sire?"

"King Philip seeks your assistance," Montague said humbly.

The Reverend Mother looked to her companions, surprised the king even knew they existed. She hesitated, wondering whether he could be trusted, but opened the gate and approached. "What can those in the convent hope to do?"

"The English are coming," he said simply.

"They've come before," she said. "And neither defeat nor victory impacted our worship."

"But they advance quickly, driving a wedge between Paris and the sea."

"A problem most suited for you to solve."

He nodded with respect. "It's a fight we cannot win," he admitted, turning to point at his meager force. "At least not now."

"We give you our prayers but cannot offer more."

"But you can," Montague said. "There is a delicate issue only you can solve."

"And what might that be?" she asked. "We are only nuns, serving the villages that live in the convent's shadow."

"We need safe harbor for one among us."

The Reverend Mother seemed wary. "We have no means to shelter a soldier."

"It's not a soldier who seeks your assistance."

She looked at the men behind him, tired and dirty, fleeing an enemy they couldn't defeat. "Who might it be that seeks our aid?"

"A woman from the court of King Philip."

"And why come here?" she asked. "When refuge can be found in so many locations?"

"It was her request," he said simply.

The Reverend Mother paused, knowing there must be a reason. "Is she known only to the Lord?"

"She's also known to you," he said. "The Lady Gabrielle."

The Reverend Mother did not react. Her aged face showed neither emotion nor recognition. She turned to study a stone cottage tucked in a cleft and hidden from the road that led to the convent. It was lower on the bluff that overlooked the sea, its small but sturdy frame braving the winds that swept in upon the waves. A crooked path wound down from the cottage to the shore below.

"She's in danger." Montague's voice sounded urgent. "A plight I must correct."

The Reverend Mother hesitated, reflecting on days that had long since passed. "We welcome the Lady Gabrielle," she sighed, "and will ensure we meet any need she might have."

Montague bowed low. "I can offer my thanks each day that I wake, Reverend Mother, and still it would not be enough."

"No words are needed," she said humbly and softly. "It's a deed that most would gladly do."

As he motioned to the men behind him, a white horse moved forward, the Lady Gabrielle upon it. The cavalry parted to let her pass, watching her approach with awe and respect, as if time stood still and no English threatened to conquer their country.

Chapter 2

The Lady Gabrielle came forward, wearing a green dress that flowed to her buckled shoes, a ring of flowers in her hair—Shephard's Purse and daisies. Poised and graceful, she exuded beauty and serenity, a woman like most had never before seen. As she guided her horse to a halt, a soldier helped her dismount, carried the leather satchels that contained her belongings to the nuns at the convent gate, and then led her horse away.

Montague met her as she approached. "My lady," he said, nodding with respect.

She forced a smile and blinked back a tear. "I don't want to leave you," she whispered, her words meant for his ears alone.

He glanced at the men behind him, as if wary of their watching, but unable to resist. He raised his hand, gently caressing her auburn hair. His eyes showed a love few understood and most never know, even if they lived for decades. For a brief moment, their eyes said more than their hearts could reveal.

"You'll be safe," he said. "And now that's what is most needed."

"Promise you'll return," Lady Gabrielle whispered brokenly, realizing death was a fate he might not avoid. She knew the ways of war, how days became months and months became years. Her life with Montague had only begun and she had no desire to see it end. Although she tried to be brave, tears trailed down her beautiful, porcelain-like cheeks.

He moved his hand from her hair to wipe the tears away, clenching his jaw to avoid showing his own deep emotion. "I live for you, my lady," he assured her. "Nothing could ever prevent my return."

She, too, tried to maintain her composure, but couldn't. Regardless of who watched, not caring who judged, ignoring those who saw what shouldn't be seen, she rushed into his arms, hugging him tightly, safe in his embrace.

"Don't leave me," she whispered.

"Dearest one, I do what's best for you," he said. "Not what's best for me."

"I would rather stay with you," she said. "No matter what the danger."

He pulled her away from him gently and looked deeply into her eyes while his own sent a pleading message. "And I only wish you could. But this is a decision my heart cannot make."

She clung to him a moment more, absorbing his strength, his calmness. As the moments passed in silence, she seemed to draw within herself as if she were reconciled to her fate, realizing he did only what had to be.

"I will wait," she promised. "Forever, if I must."

He tried to give her a reassuring smile. "It won't take a minute more than needed."

She hid her face in his chest, knowing the dangers that might await. "Parting is so much harder than I ever thought it would be," she said. "And an hour won't pass that I won't worry for your welfare."

"I only do what must be done. Both for you, my love, and life itself."

She nodded, knowing he was right. Much was at stake-- the end to a world they had just come to embrace. "I'll greet each dawn like it's the day you return," she said tenderly, "after a night dreaming of the man I love."

"That day won't be far in the future," he said as he gently released her. "I would have it no other way."

She stepped back, her eyes trained on his, studying the man who loved her, the heart that held hers, the soul that completed her very existence and promised a future that any would envy. "Return as soon as you are able," she said softly.

"Nothing could ever keep me away."

She leaned forward and kissed him lightly on the lips. "I am yours," she said. "Today, tomorrow, and forever."

"A promise to sustain me, no matter what I face," he said.

She turned, hiding the sadness that captured her heart, and approached the Reverend Mother and the nuns who stood behind her. She waited, not watching, only listening to the sounds of men on the march—murmurs of conversation and horses' hooves.

"You are welcome to the convent's sanctity, Lady Gabrielle," the Reverend Mother said.

She closed her eyes, unable to bear what the future might hold. "I thank you for your kindness, Reverend Mother."

The elderly nun wrapped an arm around her. "Welcome home," she whispered so no one could hear, guiding her into the courtyard as the nuns closed the gates.

She heard only Montague galloping away.

Chapter 3

"Sisters, prepare the cottage for Lady Gabrielle," the Reverend Mother said after the soldiers had gone. "Her journey has been fraught with danger, and rest is among her greatest needs."

Two of the nuns left for the cottage, while the remainder waited, standing in their black robes and cowls, white scarves across their shoulders and wrapped around their heads. They looked at Gabrielle with fascination, admiring her beauty, but stepped away, knowing the conversation about to occur was not one they were expected to hear.

"You've come back, my child," the Reverend Mother said softly.

"I have," Gabrielle said. "To the only home I've ever known."

The Reverend Mother looked as if she still saw a child and not the woman who replaced her. "I see love in your eyes," she whispered, "where it did not exist before."

Gabrielle smiled. "I cannot deny it," she said softly. "Nor would I try."

"He adores you. As even a fool can see."

Gabrielle gazed at the courtyard, a garden against the wall where the nuns now stood, the convent and a chapel built of the same beige stone. Somehow it seemed smaller, but many years had gone by. "It seems like lifetimes ago," she said, reliving the years as they once had been.

"Who then knew that the blood of royal lineage flowed through your veins?"

Gabrielle leaned closer. "I had been mistaken for another," she whispered. "As you well know."

The Reverend Mother smiled. "Who are we to question the deeds that God performs?"

"My life changed forever on that day," Gabrielle said, still studying the courtyard. "I had hoped to serve the Lord."

"But you do serve God," the Reverend Mother said. "You have the gift to heal as so few others do. Many lives have been touched by yours."

A nun called from the edge of the courtyard. "The cottage has been prepared."

The Reverend Mother waved in acknowledgment. "Quarters not befitting a titled lady," she said, "but comfortable just the same."

Gabrielle smiled. "It's more than I deserve—just as are you. I know not how to thank you."

The Reverend Mother hugged her. "No words are needed, and they never were."

Gabrielle left the courtyard and walked the path to the cottage. A graveyard lay to the left, small white crosses and marble headstones poking from the soil, the inhabitants missing a generous view of the sea. And the humble cottage sat on the right, hidden by a rising knoll, sheltered from the storms. She paused to study the structure, the stone so randomly placed, the mortar strong and the thatched roof protective. And even though it had been vacant and a bit in disrepair, it still provided a sanctuary that most didn't know existed.

She opened the door and crossed the threshold, finding the rooms clean, with broad oak planks across the floor. A stone fireplace sat in the center of the main room, its gaping hearth intended for both cooking and heat. She noticed a bed nestled in the far corner, and a table set against the back wall flanked by shelves filled with wooden bowls and mugs. Fruit nestled in a bowl on the table—apples, grapes and pears—with a loaf of bread and a decanter of wine beside it.

As she looked about the simple room that would now be her home, Gabrielle wondered how long she would be there. She feared the dangers Montague faced. Each passing minute could be his last, each morning he woke promising a battle that few wanted to fight. Wrapped in the cocoon his love provided, gentle and caring and kind, she couldn't bear to lose him. Each moment they shared had been built in bliss. Now her heart seemed empty, her smile a frown, her soul missing the half that made it whole, and she counted the hours until he returned.

14

In late afternoon, she walked to the edge of the cliff and sat on a bench made of yew, the grain turning to tell the tale of the tree, as well as the life those who used it might lead. Roses that had once surrounded the cottage had long since withered away, the moss that crowned the cliff creeping ever forward to claim the beds. She stared far below at the foaming sea and the rock formations that rose from the sand, some weathered by wind and waves, others standing defiant, nary a chip or crease in their faces of stone. The water stretched before her, indigo blue with streaks of white, the caps from the waves as they rushed to the shore. She watched as the sun sank into the horizon, splashing rainbows across the sky, dipping clouds in lavender, pink, and orange, and casting shadows on the waves as they tickled the sand. Nothing was as majestic as the Normandy coast, and Gabrielle would not trade it for anywhere in the world.

"Beauty displayed in all its forms," she said to the gulls that flew over head, swooping down to see if she had food to share.

As she turned to watch the birds fly past, headed toward the south, she saw smoke in the distance, drifting lazily upward to mix with clouds that crawled across the sky. She knew it was the English, burning a village, just as they had done so many times in years gone by. They took what they wanted and destroyed what was left, just so no one could have it.

And she realized the convent might soon be next.

Chapter 4

Montague's men rode along the cliff, the shore below faint and far away. The water was calm, a mirror of the sky, the day so clear that they could almost make out the English coast in the distance. His men galloped forward, an anxious enemy not far behind, a sea of cavalry in pale blue tunics, a lion's image across their chests. Carrying shields that matched their tunics, some with crossbows hung over their shoulders, they knew the faster they found the French army, the safer they would be. When they were twenty miles northeast of the convent, a rider galloped toward them, racing across a rolling terrain painted by nature a dozen different shades of green.

"It's one of our scouts, sire," a soldier said.

"He rides in haste," Montague remarked, watching warily. "The enemy could be near."

Minutes later, the rider reached them. "Remnants of our army are just ahead led by Piers," he shouted.

"How many men?" Montague asked with relief. Piers was his most trusted advisor.

"At least a hundred, maybe more," the scout said. "They hide in the forest, a place you know well. And he urges you to join them."

"Ride ahead," Montague commanded, "and tell him we will soon be there."

Montague led his army inland. Fifteen minutes later they entered the forest, taking a dirt trail wide enough for a wagon, grass worn bare where others had passed. It twisted between trees that were strong and tall—oak and chestnut and beech—standing guard over moss-covered boulders sprinkled across the forest floor. Montague led his men to a pond that spread from the road, lily pads resting on the water, lavender sprouting from the shore. On the far edge, they found Piers and his men.

"Montague," greeted Piers, an older man with a short gray beard, and well versed in military matters, "a face I'm pleased to see."

"As I am yours," Montague replied, smiling.

"I feared the enemy had found you."

"A narrow escape, meant to be," Montague said, "but a battle I've no wish to fight again."

"And the Lady Gabrielle?"

Montague looked at his friend sadly. "Taken to the convent that lies on the coast."

"Not an easy decision, but the best one to make," said Piers, a man who knew his secrets. "Who knows what dangers the enemy brings?"

A sentry approached, interrupting them. "Jamet has just arrived with a message from the king."

Montague gave Piers a wary glance. "If Jamet has found us here, something is soon to develop."

A few minutes later, Jamet appeared. Young and brash, well-known in the French court and close advisor to the king, he was a brilliant man who lived his life in books rather than battles. However, a streak of arrogance might often lead him to count more as enemy than as friend.

"Montague," Jamet said. "May the heavens be thanked that you survived."

"A fate not given to all," Montague said, his thoughts on the dead and wounded he had left behind. "But I live and breathe, and so does Piers."

Nodding briefly to Piers, Jamet handed Montague an envelope. "I have word from the king." Breaking King Philip's wax seal, Montague read the terse message inside.

Jamet will convey my orders to you. Find my power in him, and obey his direction as if the words came straight from my lips. King Philip II.

Hiding an uneasy frown Montague put the note into his pocket. "The king's commands will come through you."

Jamet tossed his head and clipped, "An action made urgent by what is to come."

Piers glanced at Montague. "A secret you may be willing to share?"

Jamet answered, leaning toward them and lowering his voice, "An effort to overthrow King John has begun."

Montague was shocked. "And who performs this noble deed?"

"Two dozen English barons," Jamet said. "And France will soon stand beside them."

Piers looked at Jamet, confused. "But the English fight in Normandy."

"Only small bands of men remain," Jamet said. "As soon as the command is given, they, too, will take their leave."

"Truly the dawn will be brighter when King John is deposed," Piers said, "but what price will be paid for the blood that France gives?"

"No risk is taken without reward," Jamet assured them. "Louis the Dauphin, King Philip's eldest son, will soon be King of England."

Montague's eyes widened. This was a worthy prize, beyond any request he'd thought might be made. Soon, after centuries of war, peace would come to both England and France. But still, he felt wary.

Jamet watched his reaction. "Your thoughts, Montague?"

"I only warn of deception."

Jamet looked at him curiously. "Why would we be played for fools?"

"Because England and France have always fought," Montague said. "And I suspect they always will."

"A world that now is part of the past," Jamet said. "The barons can be trusted. I assure you."

Montague still wasn't convinced. "But why would an enemy now become friend?"

"Because it's a bargain that benefits all involved," Jamet retorted.

Piers, also suspicious, heaved a heavy sigh. "The passing days will show the truth."

"And time will soon erase your doubts," Jamet said with an assured arrogance.

Montague knew Jamet had more to share, and he suspected he and Piers were somehow involved in this plot to make Louis an English king. "What role will we play?" he asked. "And when do we play it?"

Jamet eyed Montague carefully. "The battle begins in two days' time," he said. "You will attack an English castle on the other side of the channel."

"But we've scarcely two hundred men," Piers retorted strongly..

"I will send more," Jamet said.

"We need many to avert defeat," Piers insisted.

"You'll also fight with the barons' men," Jamet said. "And I will be the liaison."

Montague thought of Gabrielle, hidden within the walls of the convent while he crossed the channel to attack a castle. A siege would likely follow. He had to warn her of what was to come. "I would rather remain in Normandy," he said, "than fight a war that never ends."

Jamet looked at him sternly. "But it isn't a decision that you will make," he said. "As the king has made perfectly clear."

The more Jamet pressed him, the greater Montague's doubts. He now suspected the king saw something in him that might not exist. "My father served as the king's commander," he said quietly. "Footprints I can make, but without the same impression."

"The king sees traits of the father living in the son," Jamet assured him.

Montague knew he could never be his father. And he wouldn't try. They were different men with different passions. "The king commissions me to build cathedrals," he said softly. "I fight only when France is attacked."

Jamet's gaze was fixed on Montague. "What could it be that you don't understand?"

Montague shrugged. "I do as the king commands," he said. "Although my preference lies in a different direction."

"A protest you've already voiced," Jamet said. "And which was once denied. I speak for the king, as you well know, so I've no need to remind you again."

Montague was silent, knowing he had no choice but to support his king and country.

"One last word," Jamet said, his eyes still trained on Montague.

"And what might that be?" Montague asked, just a bit too tartly.

"The king's apologies for Lady Gabrielle's betrothal," Jamet said slyly. "But his consent is now conditioned upon your success on English soil."

Chapter 5

The English came to the convent just as the sun began to set. Several hundred strong, they made camp by the bluff, settling in the grass that spread past the cliff. They had just left battle, weary and wounded, a white unicorn rearing defiantly on their red tunics. The breeze coming in from the sea swept away the cries of the wounded—voices begging for water, groaning in agony, pleading for someone to help ease their pain. As they prepared for the night, their small campfires dotted the cliff, looking like fireflies to any ships that might be sailing upon the sea.

The nuns could hear the soldiers from where they'd camped just beyond the convent wall. These nuns had known danger for most of their lives, but they also felt God protected them. Their calling demanded they help those in need, but they weren't sure it was prudent to aid an enemy who wreaked havoc up and down the Normandy coast, destroying the lives of so many who had sought only to live in peace.

Just after dawn, Reverend Mother knocked on the cottage door, a bundle of clothing under her arm. "Gabrielle," she called, "are you awake?"

The door opened a moment later. "I am, Reverend Mother."

"The English camp on the edge of the cliff," she said as she entered. "And now they stand at the gate."

"I heard them when they arrived," Gabrielle said. "Will their wounded need my care?"

"I'm sure a request will soon come," the Reverend Mother replied, handing her the clothing. "But first you must don a cowl and veil."

Perplexed, Gabrielle questioned, "Why would I dress as a nun?"

"A disguise so the English don't recognize the Court that you call home," the Reverend Mother answered. "If there are any among them who think they may know you…"

Gabrielle quickly changed into the nun's habit, and the two women walked the path and into the courtyard. The other nuns waited at the gate. Two Englishmen watched them on the other side.

"Good morning," the aged nun said solemnly. "I'm the Reverend Mother."

"I'm Captain Carney," the leader said, haggard and pale from battles fought that might not have been won. "From the army of Sir Michael Marston."

"Captain Carney," the Reverend Mother said softly, glancing at the blood that stained his tunic. "Do you need assistance?"

"Food and water, if we may," he said, bowing slightly.

She pointed to a well in the courtyard. "Send two of your men to collect what you need. And we have bread, freshly baked, and some fruit. It's not much. But it's all we have to give."

"You're most kind," Carney said. "A gift we will not soon forget."

A moment later, three of the nuns appeared from the refectory with loaves of bread and three baskets of fruit. The Reverend Mother opened the gate, and they handed the food to the Englishmen.

"Our thanks," Carney said. "Men may now live who thought they would die."

"Captain," the Reverend Mother said as he turned to go. "We will care for your wounded, if you desire."

He looked at her with surprise. "But Reverend Mother," he said. "We are your enemy."

She passed no judgement. "You're God's children," she said. "Just as we are."

"We offer our thanks, in word and deed," he said, humbled. "We have almost twenty that the enemy felled."

"We can treat but two at a time," she said firmly. "No more."

The English left to retrieve their wounded, and the Reverend Mother turned to the nuns. "Gabrielle will direct your labors," she said, "and I will control the soldiers."

"Is this wise, Reverend Mother?" one of the nuns asked.

"We don't choose what work we do," the Reverend Mother said. "The Lord chooses for us. Gabrielle knows what to do."

Carney and four soldiers arrived a few moments later, carrying two men on stretchers fashioned from tree branches. The wounded were pale, their injuries severe. Glancing at them, the nuns wondered if they might be beyond help.

"Put the stretchers against the wall," the Reverend Mother said. "I will summon you when we are done."

"We can wait, if you wish," Carney said.

"No need exists," the Reverend Mother replied. "And you'll only be in the way."

Carney obeyed, directing his men to lay down the wounded. They left, nodding to the Reverend Mother.

A section of the convent garden was set aside for herbs that possessed medicinal properties—ginger, skullcap, and lungwort. They also had a store of licorice, used for coughs and chest conditions, sage, willow, horehound, and several vials of worms' blood in glass containers kept partially buried to ensure the correct temperature was always maintained.

Lady Gabrielle surveyed the garden, impressed with the assortment she found. Reverend Mother assured her that many a wounded man could be helped, and a few might even be saved.

"Four of the nuns will act as assistants, harvesting herbs as you direct, creating elixirs as needed."

When they were ready to treat the wounded, Reverend Mother checked each of the men, assessing how severe their wounds might be. Another nun stood by her, reciting prayers, using the Lord's energy to help them heal.

"The first was struck in the chest with an arrow," the Reverend Mother said to Gabrielle. "He's lost much blood, but the arrow has been removed, and the bleeding has stopped."

Gabrielle turned to one of her assistants. "Prepare a mixture of licorice, lungwort, and worms' blood. Give the patient half of it to drink. Pour the remainder on the wound. Then give him willow to ease the pain."

The nun administered the medication just as Gabrielle directed. When she finished, she returned to the garden to make more of the tonic she had rendered.

Gabrielle bent over the injured man, observed the effect of the medication upon the wound, and touched his forehead. She felt the clammy warmth of a man who fought for his life.

"Thank you, sister," he muttered.

"Save your strength," she said, lightly brushing her hand across his cheek, "and try to rest."

The Reverend Mother stood by the second soldier. "He's been stabbed in the stomach with a lance," she said. "It's a horrible wound, jagged and inflamed, still bleeding badly."

Gabrielle approached the soldier and saw his red tunic soaked with blood that now dripped to the soil and turned it crimson. With only a glance, she knew he would die. But even though his fate was known to her, she directed the nuns to create a soothing elixir to ease his pain while he lingered, waiting for God to carry him home.

The Reverend Mother called for Captain Carney, who ordered the men removed and laid in the just on the other side of the wall. Within minutes, two more had taken their place, and the process began again.

As the minutes passed, pairs of wounded came and went, some more likely to live than others. Gabrielle and the nuns did all they could to ease their pain but knew the fate of most lay with the Lord, not with the simple treatments they did their best to provide.

During the rotation of the sixth set of soldiers, as Gabrielle bent over a man to staunch the bleeding of a deep gash, her veil slipped from her head. Before she could grab it, piles of auburn hair spilled to her shoulders.

Captain Carney stood by the front gate, watching. He stared, a look of vague recognition etched in his face.

"The Lady Gabrielle!" he called.

Chapter 6

Gabrielle's heart raced, her breath coming in labored gasps. She shoved her hair back under the veil, knowing the damage was already done. She had been exposed for only a moment, but any time at all was longer than need be. The enemy had glimpsed a secret kept since the battle had begun.

Carney studied Gabrielle closely, ensuring his eyes still served him, and walked slowly towards her. "It is you," he said. "Hardly the place where I thought you would hide."

The Reverend Mother intervened, forcing herself between them. "She's been promised the sanctuary of the convent, a protection the Lord will always provide."

Carney turned to an underling. "Guard the gates. No one enters, no one leaves."

"What do you think you're doing?" the Reverend Mother asked, her voice quivering.

"I haven't decided," Carney said, his gaze trained on Gabrielle.

"She's a guest," the Reverend Mother insisted. "Best leave as if you never saw her."

Carney paused. "My eyes can't unsee what they've beheld."

"The Lord made this convent a place of worship."

"And so it shall remain," Carney said. "But it shall give up a faithful daughter."

"I have no knowledge of armies, their methods of attack, or any defense they may have prepared," Gabrielle said.

"But you have beauty and intellect," Carney said, "as reputation heralds."

Gabrielle glared at him. "Neither of which causes harm to you or any that might be with you."

He turned to his soldiers. "Summon six men."

25

"Is this how you repay a kindness?" the Reverend Mother implored.

Carney held out his hand, beckoning Gabrielle. "Come with me."

"I will not," Gabrielle replied.

"You have no choice," the captain said firmly.

He took a step toward Gabrielle just as a soldier sprinted through the convent gates. He was winded, having come from a distance. "I've word for you, sire."

Carney turned to face him, knowing the message was important. "What is it?"

"The ships have landed," the messenger said. "We must go back to England."

Carney's gaze shifted to Gabrielle. "It's an omen," he said. "The ships arrive when least expected and make you more valuable than ever before."

Gabrielle was frightened, but she tried to be brave. Standing strong and defiant, she returned the gaze fixed upon her. She realized Carney was a dangerous man, but she didn't know what he plotted.

"Leave her here to do God's work," the Reverend Mother demanded.

"I cannot," Carney said. "Not now. She's no nun, though it may be what she pretends." He grabbed Gabrielle's wrist, but she twisted free.

"Tell me your intentions, for death might be preferred," she exclaimed boldly.

Carney was taken aback, surprised by her courage. "You'll be a gift for Sir Michael Marston," he said. "Master of Marston Castle."

"Don't you dare," the Reverend Mother fumed, coming forward as if to strike him.

"Stop," a soldier commanded. He withdrew his sword, aiming the point at the Reverend Mother's breast.

The Reverend Mother stopped, eyes wide, unable to believe the enemy would harm her.

"The Lady Gabrielle is royalty and as striking as she is clever," Carney continued. "A perfect match for my master."

Gabrielle's heart sank. She couldn't imagine a future more foul, taken captive to serve someone she would always despise. She glanced at the sword levelled at the Reverend Mother's breast. If she lunged forward, she could take it, pull it from the soldier's grasp, and drive it into Carney's heart or impale herself upon it.

"I won't let you take her," the Reverend Mother said, trying to step forward.

Carney moved the blade aside and blocked her path. "With a word, I could have you and every one of these sisters run through."

"And you'll burn in Hell for eternity," the Reverend Mother said. "And many years beyond."

Carney laughed. "My destiny already as many can confirm."

They stood at an impasse, facing each other. The nuns were aghast, Gabrielle defiant, the Reverend Mother afraid but determined to defend her charge.

Carney turned to his men. "Begin boarding the ships."

"Yes, sire," his underling said.

Gabrielle felt a twinge of hope. Maybe the enemy was hurried, their forces needed elsewhere, and their time for pillaging had expired. Why violate holy ground when they had no reason to do so?

"You'll be coming with us," Carney said to Gabrielle.

She studied the man before her, the sword a foot away. "I will not," she said.

"It's not a decision for you to make," Carney said. "You now belong to Michael Marston."

"What does he want with me?" Gabrielle asked. "If he's the man you claim him to be, any woman who walks would stand by his side."

"That's a decision that he shall make," Carney said. "He may discard you if he chooses."

27

"After he's had his way, I'm sure," said the soldier who held his sword at the ready. He turned to Carney and laughed.

Gabrielle lunged forward, ripping the sword from his grasp and pushing him aside. He stumbled backward, fighting to regain his balance, and fell to the ground. She held the sword firmly, resting the gleaming tip on his throat.

The soldiers rushed toward her, swords drawn. Carney held his arms out, and they froze. He knew Gabrielle couldn't be underestimated, and he didn't want to force a fight.

"If you harm him, you will die," Carney said softly.

"A fate I prefer to what you have planned," she replied.

The nuns stood by in silence. "Don't, Gabrielle," the Reverend Mother said softly.

"He's a good man," Carney continued, "with a fine family."

"Many a good man has breathed his last," Gabrielle said. "Mainly at the hands of the English."

"If you kill him, I'll be forced to kill your sisters," Carney warned.

Gabrielle knew she couldn't let that happen. Ever so slowly, she withdrew the sword.

"Give it to me," Carney said, reaching out his hand.

She gripped the sword all the more tightly and turned, pointing the blade at Carney. "No harm comes to the nuns," she said. "And no one touches me."

Carney studied her closely, a look of newfound respect in his countenance. "No one will touch you," he said. "You have my word."

"And the convent?" Gabrielle asked.

"If you come peaceably, I'll leave the convent and its inhabitants alone."

"And if I don't?"

He looked at the Reverend Mother. "I'll kill everyone in it and burn it to the ground," he said. "After my men are done with them, of course."

"It would give me great pleasure me to kill you," Gabrielle said with disgust. "Regardless of my fate."

Carney shrugged. "Such are the ways of war," he said. "Fate is yours to choose."

"Gabrielle, you don't have to do it," the Reverend Mother pleaded, standing in front of the frightened nuns.

Gabrielle looked from one trembling sister to another and then turned to Carney. "Have we reached an agreement?"

"We have," Carney said. "On my honor."

"And you ransom me back to France," she said, adding another demand

Carney looked at her, a flicker of compassion in his eyes. "I'll try," he said softly. "But I cannot commit to this final request. I don't control the dawn or anything it brings."

Chapter 7

Montague had much to tell Gabrielle, and he intended to go to the convent just after dawn, regardless of the risk. He was destined for England, not for days but for months, their engagement linked to his loyalty to the king. And with the English invaders leaving France, she could stay at the convent on the coast or return to Paris—whatever she most desired.

His night was restless, sleep elusive, so anxious was he to see her. But when he finally found slumber, he dreamed not of her, but a man with powers no other possessed—the wizard Alaric. When he woke, the dream still fresh, he realized he had been summoned, and his visit to the convent would be delayed.

"Are you leaving, sire?" Piers asked just after the sun showed its face.

"Briefly," Montague replied as a soldier brought Destiny, his horse, to his tent. "There is a friend I must go and see."

"You can't go alone," Piers said. "The English still ravage the countryside whether they plan to leave or not."

"But I must," Montague said as he leaped onto the horse. "It's a task that only I can do."

"Be cautious, sire," Piers warned. "We cannot afford to lose you."

Montague urged his steed forward, guiding him through the forest and onto the road beyond. He headed toward Rouen, rode for half an hour, then led Destiny into the trees. He slowed the stallion to a walk along a little-used path until he reached an ancient oak struck by lightning in the recent past, its limbs disfigured, broken and burnt. Then he turned north and went deeper into the forest, dismounting when the brush grew dense. He lightly tugged his horse's reins, looking for landmarks: a crooked stone that poked through the soil, a stream that vanished before his eyes, a tree that leaned far to the north, and a carpet of moss, forty feet wide. When the trees grew so thick their branches hid even the sun, he found the wizard, Alaric.

The wizard stood beside a giant oak, its trunk gnarled and spotted, twisted and stout. Its branches sprawled in all directions, creating a canopy over a clearing that bordered a brook. As Montague studied the tree and the vines that crawled upon it, he saw steps cut into the trunk, leading to the limbs above. A hut was anchored to the branches, its crooked sides made of wooden slabs, the roof thatched straw. A four-paned window winked at him from the south-facing wall, one panel badly cracked.

The wizard's hair, long and white, draped across his shoulders. A loose black robe flowed to his feet, secured by a gray rope around his waist. He stood before a series of shrubs, hewed waist-high with flattened tops, a slab of wood upon them. A brass cauldron, tarnished and pitted and ancient, sat on the shelf beside crystals of different sizes and shapes, pouches and vials of spices and herbs, pebbles of many colors and shapes, and the innards of spiders, snakes, bats, and frogs.

"I was wondering when you would come," Alaric said without turning from his work.

Montague was startled. "How did you know it was me?"

"How could I not?"

"I seek advice and know you always have it."

Alaric turned to face him, a beard that matched his silver hair spilling onto his chest. It seemed he had lived a millennium, even though it couldn't be true. His eyes were red, like rubies, his gaze, like a magnet, pulling those that met it into a nether world beyond the reach of most mortal men. Although he often smiled, his demeanor evoked power, courage, and strength. His very posture seemed to suggest he knew every secret the world had ever whispered.

Montague hesitated, intimidated by such a mighty force, but then took a step forward, his boots soft on the carpet of moss. Gazing at the cauldron and all around it, he suspected he witnessed the Devil at work, but he would never ask if this were true.

Alaric watched as he approached. "Do you want to know your fate?" he asked. "And that of Gabrielle?"

"I do," Montague replied, drawing closer. "Much has happened that remains hidden from me."

31

"Rest assured, my friend, that wherever fate takes you, I won't be far."

Montague was relieved. "I need your advice now more than ever, for difficult days arrive with the dawn."

"You travel to the enemy's home, I see," Alaric said, his gaze trained on Montague.

"By order of the king," Montague said, wondering how the wizard could know such a thing. "Although I wanted to walk a different path."

"If England is your destiny, I will be there, too," Alaric said. "But in spirit only."

Montague was confused. "And if I seek your counsel?"

Alaric handed him a small leather pouch. "Always keep this with you."

Montague didn't understand, and he wasn't sure he wanted to. "How might it be used?"

"The pouch contains my magic," the old man said. "It brings my image to you."

Montague looked at the tiny sack and started to untie the string.

"No need to look inside," Alaric said, stopping him. "It's filled with herbs and spices, a wasp's wings, a toad's eye, and slivers from two stones."

Montague left the pouch tied. "And why do I carry it wherever I go?"

"Because as long as you have it near, I can see you, and you can see me."

"And what must be done to make that occur?"

"Find a brook surrounded by trees. Stare at the water while holding the pouch. Call my name, and I will come in minutes at the most."

Montague put the pouch inside his tunic. "I shall do as you request whether or not I know the reason."

"'Tis the only way for us to share one another's thoughts," Alaric said. He paused for a moment and glanced at his cauldron, the liquid it contained simmering from the heat of a

32

crystal that had been set beneath it. "And now we'll see what can't be seen."

The wizard turned, searching through vials and pouches, spices and herbs. He began with shavings from a lavender stone taken from the highest hill in the land. Next, he added a pinch of cinnamon. Damiana, mugwort, and horehound followed, then eyebright powder, beige and fluffy, and red sandalwood to create an unstable stew. He shook a vial of green liquid and poured in the fizzy brew, then added the legs of a spider, a dash of black sand, and the feather of an owl.

Alaric studied the mix with a sorcerer's eye and signaled his satisfaction. It sizzled and burped then spewed a haze that hovered three feet high. When he was certain the mist was just as he desired, the wizard began to chant.

> "The past is gone
>
> And buried dead,
>
> No longer see
>
> What lies ahead.
>
> The moon moves quick
>
> And dawn arrives,
>
> Lives are lived
>
> And darkness dies.
>
> Rain falls fast
>
> But skies soon clear,
>
> As rainbows spawn
>
> Then disappear."

The shimmering image of Gabrielle and Montague appeared, a tree behind them. Alaric moved his hand in the air, as if turning the pages of a book, and the leaves on the tree changed color and fell, then sprouted anew, repeating the cycle of the passing seasons. As the images unfolded one into the next, Montague and Gabrielle aged, their hair turning an ashen gray, wrinkles creasing their faces.

Alaric looked up and peered through the trees, trying to see the sky. "It's the Lady Gabrielle," he said. He waved his hand in front of his face, as if cobwebs blocked the way.

"What's wrong?" Montague asked, fearing sickness, injury, or worse.

"The English took her," Alaric said. "I can see past the cliffs to the water where four ships move away from the shore."

Montague was shocked by the wizard's words. He had tried to protect Gabrielle but had tempted fate, and now she was in danger. "Where do they take her?" he asked, fear and worry joined as one. "Tell me wizard, so I can be there before the dawn."

"Marston Castle," Alaric said. "The home of Sir Michael Marston."

Chapter 8

Marston Castle
on the southeast coast of England

The morning mist hung heavy as the ship sailed north toward the shore, veiling the sea and the treacherous rocks that bathed the coast in an eerie cloak. But as the sun peeked over the horizon and began to melt the morning's dew, the steep cliffs of England began to reveal themselves, massive and imposing. They thrust upward from a rocky shore—white limestone laced with streaks where the face of the cliff had been darkened by the rain, capped with fields of green that sprawled inland as far as the eye could see. Waves battered the cliff base, and the beach was littered with stones, the force of the water tugging them to and fro, wearing them to rubble. Stretches of white sand ran up the beach in between, marred by the refuse of advancing and retreating tides.

As the outline of the distant landscape grew more defined in the early light, the silhouette of an isolated castle pierced the mist. It sat upon the tallest ridge high above the sea. The fortress fascinated friend and foe, offering refuge to the ally and an obstacle to the enemy. Stretching into the distance on all four points of the compass, its walls and towers stole the horizon from the clouds that drifted lazily behind them. Built of rough sandstone blocks, the castle rose to a lofty height, spearing the clouds that hid the sun to cast somber shades of gray across the land. Sprawling across an open field, its corners anchored by towers, the castle stood guard over land and sea, threatening those who were bold enough to trespass on English soil.

"Marston Castle," Carney announced to Gabrielle. "Sometimes known as Marston Manor."

"Am I to be impressed?" she asked, tired from a journey she'd no desire to take.

"It's your new home," Carney said. "You'll learn to love it. Just as I did."

"Your dream and my nightmare," she said.

"I promise you'll be treated well. Michael Marston is a man of honor."

"What weight does your promise carry," she asked, "when we know not what these heathens plan?"

"No harm has come to you yet, my lady."

"Yet tomorrow rarely echoes today," she said.

They peered through the mist as the coast loomed ever closer. She studied the landscape, the castle sprawling from the cliff's edge far into the fields beyond and imagined what it had taken to build—how many stones, how much mortar, how many men—and just how many nooks and crannies, tunnels or secret passages, existed within its walls and the rock base below. She was determined, once she arrived, to find a way to escape. When the English came to trust her, she planned to slip away, returning to Normandy and into the waiting arms of Montague, the man she loved more than life itself.

A rare hour passed when she didn't think of him, each minute pushing them farther apart, stealing strength from every inch of her body, dashing any dreams she may have had. Was she to ever again feel his arms around her, his lips on hers? She longed for his laugh, his smile which lit even the darkest of days, his tender caress that both calmed and excited her. Even though she'd tried to ignore what she knew might occur, she realized the day would soon arrive when he had no choice but to live his life without her.

"Michael Marston has no family," Carney said quietly as the castle came closer, the ship moving toward the shore. "The sickness took them."

Gabrielle felt as if her heart had been torn, and her own muted pain surfaced once more. "Nothing in life can be worse than the death of one's family," she said softly. "I, too, lost mine to the sickness."

Carney nodded, showing his respect. "We all grieve," he said. "Some more than others. But life goes on. It must."

"A feat readily spoken of but not easily achieved," she muttered.

"It has not been easy for Michael Marston," Carney continued. "He has never been the same. The spark that once lived in his eyes was snuffed out, never to light again."

Gabrielle wondered what type of man awaited her in the castle. Even though she hadn't stopped thinking of Montague from the second she'd left the convent, she realized difficult days were soon to arrive, days in which he wouldn't share. She was alone, more so than at any other time in her life, even when every member of her family had been taken by an inexplicable act of God.

"I first saw you two years ago during an English raid near Rouen," Carney said, interrupting Gabrielle's thoughts. "The peasants told me how learned you were. And I never forgot your beauty and grace."

"Your source may not be worthy," Gabrielle said humbly. She had been surprised, throughout their journey, by Carney's warmth, expecting a barbarian, but finding a man. Perhaps war turned all men into heathens, and they once more became human when the fighting came to an end.

"When I saw you at the convent, I thought you might be what he needed most."

"But you destroyed my life in an attempt to save his," she said quietly.

"You'll have another to live."

"Which I did not ask for and will not accept."

Carney fell silent, watching as the ship maneuvered to shore. "If you're unhappy, I will try to ransom you. Just as I promised."

"Please."

"I keep my word."

Gabrielle hesitated. "I must admit you speak the truth. You promised my protection, and every word you've spoken has been born out to be true."

"You were not harmed," he said, "and were given the utmost respect by all who came near."

"Treated more like a queen than a consort, I admit," she said. But now she knew she faced new threats in a world she had no desire to live in.

"No one touches what belongs to the master. They respect the man as much as I do."

"My heart does break, knowing his will never mend," she said. "Enemy or not, we do share a bond."

Carney nodded. "If a beautiful woman who knows books can make his life worth living, then so be it. He is a good and honest man who deserves another chance."

The pilot steered the ship toward a wharf below the cliff, the sails shifting so it was swept to shore. Jutting into the water like a stony limb, the wharf was built with the same material as the castle and would last through the ages, defying the onslaught of waves that tried to whittle it away with the passage of time. As the ship came along beside the pier, four men jumped ashore, pulled the creaking hull toward the dock, and tied it to the pilings. Three ships of the same design, each with a single mast, their hulls broad and low in the water, waited in the harbor until those in the first ship had disembarked and made their way to the castle.

Once the vessel had been secured, Carney climbed over the side and leaned forward, taking Gabrielle's hand and helping her to shore. He paused, studying a path worn through the rocks on the edge of the cliff that wound upward toward the castle.

"It's safe," he said as he pointed to a man atop the tower, beckoning to the crew. "A sentry who watches the waves. They have been awaiting our arrival."

Carney led Gabrielle and his men along the pathway. As they gradually climbed the cliff, rising higher and higher into the mist, the ship that hugged the dock became ever smaller. When they reached the top, they saw a large field that extended a great distance from the southern wall of the castle, groves of trees at its distant verge, a forest so thick Gabrielle wondered if the sun's rays ever reached its floor. They continued past the stone walls and the men who stood atop them until they reached the western wall of the fortress. Before them lay the grand entrance to a still grander castle. Carney resolutely made his way toward it.

The salient entrance, imposing in both scale and construction, spanned a steep ravine by way of a drawbridge. Waiting at the opposite end was a tall man who watched them curiously. He wore black leggings and a red tunic, a white unicorn across the chest. His shoulders were broad, his face firm.

38

His black hair was sprinkled with gray, and his beard was cropped short and close to the skin. His carriage hinted of royalty, someone trained from birth to lead men and, perhaps, a nation, someone who never doubts he has been selected by Providence to rule the masses. But the sadness etched in his face and the consuming ache that had lodged in his heart kept him anchored to a world that no longer existed. He couldn't see the future, for he was blinded by the past.

Chapter 9

Sir Michael Marston watched as Carney approached, a mysterious woman standing beside him. He looked at her closely, willowy with auburn hair and an air of sophistication, wondering who she might be. She had come to his castle aboard a ship manned by one hundred soldiers, and so he assumed she was a captive.

"I'm relieved by your safe return," Marston said as Carney drew closer. "Your courage is needed now more than ever."

Carney looked concerned. "What changed while I was away?" he asked. "Does the castle face a threat?"

"It does," Marston said. "Rumors claim that the barons revolt."

"Then may our arrival help crush the rebellion."

Marston's gaze shifted to the woman. He didn't know who she was or why she had come, and he hesitated to ask for fear of offending her—a curious trait for such a great leader. He saw sadness in her eyes almost masked by fear but not quite. He wondered what story she had to tell, and what had brought her to Marston Manor.

"Do you know if an attack will ever come?" Carney asked.

"An army is just forming," Marston said. "Scouts have been dispatched to keep watch of their arrival."

"Then we've much work to do to prepare."

Marston nodded, still gazing at the woman as he spoke to Carney. "I trust you are well, and your journey was a good one?"

"Yes, sire, it was. We did all that we'd planned but lost some good men."

Marston nodded but could contain his curiosity no longer. "And who might this be?" he asked.

Carney turned to Gabrielle. "Sir Michael Marston, may I present the Lady Gabrielle."

Marston bowed his head respectfully, wondering why a woman of the French court now stood on his doorstep. "And why are we so fortunate as to be graced with her presence?"

"She's a prize from a convent on the Normandy coast," Carney said. "And I offer her to you," he added humbly.

Marston was surprised but tried not to show it. "I'm honored," he said. "I truly am. But a woman hasn't been counted among my greatest needs."

Carney nodded. "With respect, sometimes the richest treasures are found when they're not sought."

Marston glanced at Carney, opened his mouth to speak, but hesitated. "She came willingly?" he asked at last.

"I did not," Gabrielle said, speaking for the first time.

Marston looked to the beautiful woman who stood before him. "Were you harmed?"

She paused for a moment but then replied. "No, sire, I was not."

"She insisted no harm come to her or the nuns in the convent from which she came," Carney said.

"Insisted?" Marston asked with some surprise. It was hardly a demand he would expect from a captive. But he admired courage, even when it was displayed by a foe.

"Yes, sire," Carney said softly. "She made her intentions known, both in word and deed."

Marston wondered what purpose she might serve, a supposed gift to him. He could refuse and cast her aside but would risk offending his captain. And he knew once discarded, her life would be destroyed if it hadn't been already. For her own safety, he had to accept her and try to provide a life that her title demanded.

"And why did the nuns forfeit such a prize?" he asked, suspecting he knew the answer.

41

"They had no choice," Carney said with a shrug. "Such are the ways of war."

Marston cringed but made no remark. Lady Gabrielle's presence offered more problems than he even cared to count, and although he could see where Carney's action might lead, he suspected his captain could not.

"She's learned, raised in a convent, and has read many books," Carney said. "And I can assure you she has been treated with respect and was untouched throughout the journey."

The expression on Marston's face changed, interest replacing doubt. "You were educated at the convent?"

"Yes, sire," Gabrielle said. "From the time I was a child. After my family died of the..."

Both Carney and Marston watched as her voice trailed off, waiting for her to complete her thought though they knew what she intended to say. Carney winced, not wanting memories stirred in his master.

"They died of the sickness," Marston said, finishing the statement for her.

Gabrielle nodded, her eyes misty, perhaps more at the thought of his loss than hers which had occurred, it seemed, a lifetime ago. She tried to compose herself.

"I'm sorry," he said, lightly touching her arm. "The sickness had affected us all. Pray it never returns."

"A blessing if it doesn't, sire," she said.

Marston hesitated, pushing aside the gnawing thoughts he'd tried to ignore. He turned to Carney. "Welcome home, Captain," he said. "Your men must be anxious to find their own beds."

"They are, sire, I'm sure."

"My lady," Marston said, offering a slight nod of respect. "Please come with me. I'm sure we can find quarters that befit you."

Gabrielle started to follow Marston into the fortress but paused at the sight of a mosaic set in the stone floor. It was a deep red and formed the shape of a rectangular shield with small white crosses in the upper right and lower left corners. In the center was the head of a unicorn. She recognized the pattern, for it adorned the soldiers' shields.

"What is this?" she asked. "It's a beautiful design."

"It's the Marston coat of arms," he said. "You'll find it in almost every room of the castle and the flags that fly upon the towers."

Chapter 10

Gabrielle stepped off the drawbridge, passing black iron chains that were secured to massive beams and pulled taut by a winch. A corridor opened before them some thirty feet wide—ample room for wagons to pass. Known as the barbican, it was built like the castle but on a much smaller scale, designed to be defended. The mosaic that graced the exit marked the floor of the entrance as well. Gabrielle followed Marston and Carney down the hall and through an iron gate. Together they stepped into a courtyard, and the sounds of a waking town swept over them on the breeze: the neighs of horses, the shouts of children at play, the steady ping of a blacksmith's hammer.

Gabrielle blinked in disbelief at the vibrant village the castle contained—streets and structures of varying size, people, young and old, who made their way down cobblestone lanes. "More like a town than a fortress," she said. "I must say I'm surprised."

"In many ways it is," Marston replied. "Whatever we need can be found within. The farms and towns that lie to the west also rely on the castle for their livelihood and whatever else their daily needs might be."

Gabrielle paused, her gaze wandering from wall to wall as she looked down the streets and into an open expanse beyond.

"Would you like me to explain how all is laid out?" he asked.

"I would like to learn," she said, eyeing the castle and all it contained and wondering at the purpose of each of its parts.

"The buildings along the wall," he said, pointing, "are for storage and stables as well as the blacksmith's forge, a butcher's shop and smokehouse, the brewery, and several barracks for the men in arms. Along the cobblestone streets that wind through the courtyard, also called a bailey or ward, you'll find houses and shops that many call home. The keep, the large building in the center, is for receptions of all kinds and houses offices to maintain the realm and a Great Hall that seats a hundred or more. It is also the premier defensive position, common to all castles, and where the leader and his advisors dwell. The design of the castle holds the keep supreme—the last bastion of defense."

They continued on down the broadest lane, pausing to watch a falcon circle high above as it searched for a place to land. It flew lower with each revolution, the circumference of its track nearly the width of the castle.

"My apologies, sire," someone called.

Marston turned behind him to see a muscular, gray-haired man wearing brown leggings and a black tunic holding out his left arm with a falconer's cuff on his wrist.

"Jenks," Marston said, "our village blacksmith. The Lady Gabrielle from Normandy."

"My lady," Jenks said with a nod. "May I offer assistance for a more pleasing stay?"

Gabrielle smiled, apparently finding the man both curious and considerate. "Thank you," she said. "But not as yet."

"She arrived minutes ago," Marston said. "But thank you for welcoming her."

Jenks nodded, about to reply when the falcon let loose a piercing cry. Gazing upward, the man suddenly remarked, . "Excuse me, sire, but I've a task I must attend to." Moving a few steps away, he withdrew a mouse from his pocket, waving it in his hand. Within seconds, the handsome, temperamental falcon with a curved black beak, tawny feathers and sharp, focused eyes, dove from the clouds and landed on Jenks' cuff. After feeding him, Jenks handed him to a small boy who had scampered up beside him.

"My passion," Jenks said. "But there are worse vices, I suppose."

"I can count many, and that's only with respect to the captain," Marston said with a smile. "I had best show Lady Gabrielle her quarters. I'm sure she's wants nothing but some much needed rest."

He led Gabrielle into the keep through a vestibule into the grand hallway, and they climbed an ornate, spiral set of steps to the third floor, delving deeper into the heart of the castle. She said little, but he pretended not to notice. He knew how afraid she must be, wondering what was to come.

They arrived at a spacious room. Gabrielle noticed steps leading to a window with a recess which defined the thickness of the stone walls. "My lady," Marston said, "this is one of the largest the keep has to offer."

Gabrielle walked toward an opened door and saw another room lined with shelves along the walls. In the center sat a grand feather bed surrounded by crimson and gold silk curtains bordered with a lacy white trim. Three intricately carved and curved wooden steps strategically placed beside the bed would facilitate a comfortable ascent to the height of the bed

Polished cedar chests sat on each of three sides of the bed. Gabrielle's eyes widened as they roamed further to spot a rectangular table with curled lions' paw feet against the opposite wall, a beautiful porcelain washbasin at the center, a fireplace made of polished white stone, along the northern wall, the carved keystone forming the firebox, and corbels of cherubs supporting the mantel. Beside the fireplace, two cushioned chairs flanked an oval table upon which sat a pewter candlestick and a half-burned candle.

Apparently, the room had not yet been fully prepared, for a servant with brown hair tied back from her appeared with a broom, , a bucket and rags, blankets for the bed, and a smile that seemed to be fixed on her face.

Gabrielle did not have time to react before Marston bowed slightly toward her. "I'll leave you now, my lady. Your comfort is my greatest concern, so any need you have is mine to fulfill. I promise, no harm will come to you. Not for as long as I shall live."

Chapter 11

Gabrielle studied the room after Marston left, watching while the servant cleaned. Surprised that it was far from the cell she'd expected, she noticed the elaborate adornments which included hand-carved roses on the chests . Her eyes wandered to the tiny window meant to thwart an intruder but yet large enough for the passage of light and air. From the steps that led to the window, she could see the eastern wall of the fortress and ocean beyond, the channel that spread between England and France, a seemingly tranquil sea of blue.

The grandeur of Gabrielle's quarters sent a signal—how Michael Marston defined her captivity and how he intended to treat her. She marveled at how her life had changed in so many ways in so few years. From a plague-filled house with floors of dirt to the piety of the convent to the French court, she thought it peculiar how powerful men and women had affected such a change in her life. From the day they claimed the discovery that she was royalty, against her protests denying that fact, her life had changed drastically.

All of the dreams she'd dared have as a child or adult had been answered when she'd met Montague, but as their future was about to begin, the English invaded Normandy, turning her dream to an unending nightmare from which she might never escape. Montague had hidden her away in the convent, their life together paused for a time, where hers, it seemed, had just begun. And now she was being held captive in an English castle, and the contours of her fate might never be known. But it could be worse. She knew that, and she was thankful even though her life might never be what she had dreamt of.

"I've just a bit more to do, my lady," the servant said apologetically, "and then I'll be on my way."

Gabrielle watched as she fussed about the room, sweeping the floor and wiping the furniture, making sure everything was as it should be. She put Gabrielle's satchels in the alcove against the far wall and opened the window.

"Some air will do the place good," the servant said, smiling. "Is there anything else you need, my lady?"

Gabrielle thought of Montague. He was all she needed, all she could ever want, regardless of where she was, and she felt her eyes moisten and tears slide down her cheeks.

"My lady?" the servant asked. "Is anything amiss?"

Gabrielle forced a smile and wiped away her tears. "No, there's nothing I need," she whispered. "I'm sure my comfort is assured."

The servant started for the door. "Call me if you should want for anything, my lady, and I'll come straightaway. My name is Anna."

Gabrielle gave her a tremulous smile. She liked the woman. "Thank you, I will."

Now alone, Gabrielle walked the room once more, examining the walls more closely, wondering if a passage existed or any other means of escape. Studying the mortar in every stone, she searched for signs of a hidden door, but after scouring the walls and floors, she was forced to admit no egress existed, at least not one visible to her untrained eye. She realized Michael Marston had put her in that room for a reason. She just didn't know what it was.

She considered their initial meeting and what she may have learned of her captor. He seemed a gentleman—polite, respectful, but with sorrow etched in every wrinkle upon his face. She understood the pain he endured, the agony of losing all one loved, and thought that if he continued to act as he did when first their gazes met, she could survive, she could endure, counting the hours until she found her beloved Montague again. Marston seemed a man she could trust, someone who honored his promises, made good on his word. He had assured her that no harm would come to her, and for the present, she wanted to believe him.

She looked through the window once more at the commanding view of the sea that stretched beyond the castle wall, the rolling hills that gave way to plains and forests to the north and south, the varying shades of green touching a pale blue sky. On another day such a view might be pleasing, offering a peace most would enjoy, but today the sight brought only pain.

Separation from Montague was no different than splitting her heart in half.

Would he ever find her? Or could she make her own escape and find the path to him? He fought in Normandy, thinking her safe, tucked away in a convent far from the prying eyes of men. How could either have known that the convent had been the worst of places she could have chosen to hide from the battle about to begin? The sanctuary it provided had offered no protection, for now she was a prisoner, held by the very enemy she had hoped to avoid.

She realized that this room, however spacious and beautifully appointed, was her cell, for how long she had no way now to learn. But she had to make do with what she was given, had to do whatever was necessary to survive. Sighing, she decided to unpack the few belongings the English had allowed her to bring.

Picking up the first satchel, she began to remove one by one the garments she had stuffed in haste and now neatly positioned them in the first chest beside the bed. When she opened the second, she removed two books, The Epistles of St. Peter and The Sequence of Saint Eulalia, a silver brush for her lustrous hair, vials of oils and perfumes, scented soaps from Paris, an assortment of coins, none of much value, two sketches from Montague, one of her, the other of his chateau, and a pewter pendent.

Her third satchel contained the tools of a healer: spices, herbs, and jars containing the viscera of various animals. It wasn't much, but she'd taken the few ingredients that had been stored in the cottage and a sampling from the garden. She ensured she had her favorite remedies and what she needed for a handful of rare tonics. She knew that the sick and wounded could be found anywhere in the world. Regardless of what a burden her medicines might be to carry, they would always prove useful to those in need.

She carefully placed her tinctures and herbs on shelves along the wall and stepped back to admire them, feeling more comfortable as if among friends. However, she suddenly had a thought that might be life-saving later. The vials of various animal parts—swallows' gizzards and bats' wings and skinned vipers' heads, so disturbing to the untrained eye, seemed to quaver in the firelight, and she realized how suspicious they might seem to anyone who saw them. Wary of the servants, she tucked them behind the pouches of dried herbs, hiding them from view.

Once she was settled and more comfortable, Gabrielle began to focus on a single thought.

How would she escape?

Chapter 12

Southeast England, twenty miles inland from Marston Castle

Baron Richard Tweed was an older man, mentally fit but in physical decline. A hero from the last Crusade, he had been wounded twice but had refused to leave the battle, so intent had he been upon winning the war. Now, still obsessed with capturing the Holy Land, intrigued by all it contained and determined to lead the next Crusade even at his advanced ag, he was currently distracted, determined that England should be properly ruled, which meant that everything was to be carried out as only he could offer. Given the rebellious times, the only result he could accept was to overthrow King John. Tweed sat in his study in his most comfortable chair and gazed at the two visitors who had just entered his sprawling manor home.

"I've known Michael Marston for many years," said the druid, Paul the Pure. He was older and stooped, forced to lean on a cane. A white beard hung to his chest, covering part of his robe. Only a fringe of hair remained upon his head.

"And I've met him also," added his daughter Trinity, "though I was only a child, and I doubt he would remember me." Her brown dress was tattered with wear, but those she met would likely not notice. They would notice her beauty and her blonde hair spilling onto her shoulders, but they would also notice that her eyes were unlike any other's, for one was blue, the other green.

"Michael Marston is the strongest supporter King John ever had," said Tweed, his gaze straying to Trinity. "At least in southeast England."

"His reputation is unblemished," said Paul the Pure. "Whether it deserves to be or not."

Tweed eyed them cautiously. "But he must be defeated, no matter the cost."

51

"Your plan ensures that he soon will be," said Trinity, flattering their host. She knew he held power that most only wished for, and if she could control both his thought and deed, a talent for which she'd never lacked, it would surely meet their needs.

"Do you think your plan will work?" Tweed asked as he stared at the pair.

"I do," said Paul the Pure, "though few would ever attempt it."

"It is a deed, if well-performed, that will reward you nicely," Tweed said.

Paul the Pure eyed his host as humbly as he could. "We're pleased we have your trust and promise to make good your request."

"You have done much to earn my respect and will do much more, I'm sure," Tweed replied, and then added, "If I'm to believe all that I've been told."

Trinity smiled coyly at Tweed, capturing his gaze. "We are your humble servants, sire. This is the first of many ventures I'm sure we'll come to share."

"And you're certain access to the castle can easily be gained?" Tweed asked, his gaze fixed on Trinity for more reasons than she suspected.

Paul the Pure chuckled and nodded to his host. "My dear baron, who would refuse an old druid, especially one who needs his daughter simply to help him stand?"

"Marston will be wary, for needful strangers are too often the downfall of good men," Tweed said. "No doubt he's been warned of the rebellion to come."

"I'll convince him he has nothing to fear," Trinity said and then smiled. "Even though he does."

Paul the Pure grew pensive, envisioning all that was about to take place. "Once the deed is done, how might we collect our fee? Do we return here?"

"No trail can be left for any to follow," Baron Tweed replied. "The warlord who will attack the castle also has your gold."

"James the Bold, a man known throughout England for every battle he fought," Paul the Pure exclaimed.

Trinity glanced at Tweed. "A vicious warrior, so I'm told."

"He is and always has been," Tweed said, "but you shall enjoy much of the credit for a victory well-deserved." His gaze wandered from her face to her lithe frame. He knew she led the two and was willing to do whatever was necessary to make sure she got what she wanted.

Paul the Pure nodded with respect. "We're honored, sire, to serve you."

Tweed eyed the pair and then chuckled. "A druid and his daughter. Who would dream you pose a threat?"

Paul the Pure grinned. "Sometimes the truth doesn't appear as most others tend to see it."

Tweed's gaze shifted from Trinity to the mantle that dressed the fireplace. "Your claim has been proven in many days past. Nothing is ever as it seems--a lesson I learned in the Holy Lands."

"Your bravery and exploits are known the world over," Trinity said, praising her host once again.

"It was a good and worthy cause," Tweed said. "And not to be forgotten."

"Perhaps only you can finish the fight," Trinity said. "And restore sacred ground to the Christians."

"I have the strength to do so," Tweet muttered. "And I will when King John is dethroned." He paused, still staring at the mantle, and then spoke reverently. "I'm guided by a higher power."

Paul the Pure eyed him with curiosity. "How so, sire?"

Tweed leaned toward them. "I'll share a secret," he said, "never to be repeated."

Trinity glanced at Paul the Pure to ensure he listened, too. "Please do," she urged. "There's nothing we would rather hear."

"Look at the chalice that rests on the mantle," Tweed said. "Old and tarnished like its best days have passed."

"So it seems, sire," Paul the Pure said, wondering where the discussion was leading.

"I recovered it during the Crusade," Tweed continued, "and brought it here from the Holy Lands."

Trinity looked at the chalice, worn and weathered, probably of no value at all. "But why, sire?" she asked. "It doesn't seem worth the bother."

Tweed leaned forward. "Because it's the Holy Grail," he said quietly.

Her eyes grew wide, and she gaped at her host before turning to Paul the Pure. "The cup that held the blood of Christ?"

"It is," Tweed said. "And in ten days' time, it will begin its journey back to its rightful home."

Trinity was cunning. She wanted to ensure he told the truth. "But it hardly looks like a relic."

"Nothing is ever as it seems," Tweed said. "Just as you have said."

"And where does it belong?" Paul the Pure asked.

"A ship will dock five miles south of Marston Manor," Tweed explained. "The captain acts on the behalf of a man who offers much gold to possess the Grail."

Trinity shot Paul the Pure a guarded glance. A knowing look passed between them. "And he'll return it to the Holy Lands?" she asked.

Tweed nodded. "Yes, to Jerusalem, where it belongs."

"I'm honored to be in its presence," said Paul the Pure. As he got to his feet, his cane fell to the floor.

"I'll get it, father," Trinity said.

She leaned over and picked up the cane, but as she stood her smile twisted into an evil grin. She swung the cane in a mighty arc, striking Tweed in the head with the handle.

Blood gushed from a gash on his forehead, and his eyes rolled back in his head. "Stop!" he cried out, holding up his hands. "What are you trying to do?"

Trinity swung the cane again, this time hitting the baron's temple. He fell from his chair and sprawled on the floor,

54

his leg quivering against the stone. She lifted the cane once more and brought it down hard on the back of his head.

"Hurry," Paul the Pure exclaimed as he hobbled to the mantle and grabbed the Grail. "We must get as far as we possibly can before anyone should come looking for him."

Chapter 13

Paul the Pure and Trinity hurried toward the coast. Their journey had few interruptions, only short stops when they required rest. No one knew from whence they came, and fewer knew where they might go, for they had traveled through many an English village, but none had ever been a place they'd called home. Their identities were as mysterious as the path they had taken, their history a long line of make-believe. They survived through deception and other false arts, doing whatever they could to put coins in their pockets and food on their plates. Each bend in the road offered new roles to play, an audience innocent of what they had planned.

Paul the Pure walked slowly, stooped and balding, his right hand gripping a crooked cane, his left carrying a gnarled stick, a green crystal affixed to the top. A symbol of an elite group of priests known as druids, the staff signified their belief that nature is the supreme manifestation of divinity, forming a bridge from the spirit to the physical, but for Paul the Pure it was but one more prop he would need for the role he intended to play.

He leaned on Trinity when the road was rough, relying upon her shrewd judgment as they made their way through the countryside. She kept a watchful eye on the road far ahead, wary of wagons that occasionally passed. Some said her mismatched eyes proved she was birthed by the Devil, while others claimed they were a gift from God. Trinity thought it all superstition, but she did have a talent that few could mimic, the power to see what the dawn delivers. And she leveraged her gift to trick the unknowing, taking what they couldn't afford to lose—even though she hadn't earned it.

They carried three knapsacks, one on each of their backs while she held the third. They moved as quickly as the druid's aged legs would allow, an eye to the rear should they somehow be followed. They avoided roads that were well traveled, using little-known paths to make good their escape, the treasure that had been sought through the ages tucked in a satchel Trinity carried under her arm. They knew the chalice could be sold to the highest bidder, and they could live off the gold that it brought. But first, there was one task they had to perform, one more crime they had to commit.

"Are you sure Tweed is dead?" Paul the Pure asked.

"You saw how he fell to the floor," Trinity said. He had asked the question a dozen times like an old fool, and she had offered the same reply. "As long as he does not follow, it should be no concern of ours."

Paul the Pure paused and gazed at the sun as it traveled across the heavens. "We shall reach the castle by nightfall," he said.

"Do you need to rehearse what words we will say?" she asked. She worried, as each year passed, that his memory was weakening and might thwart their success.

"I think not," he said. "It's no different from any other part I have played."

"One last time might mean perfection," she prodded. She knew the more he rehearsed the more he was likely to remember.

He adopted the role of the character they had created. "I am your father, a druid, a high priest from Glastonbury."

"And I am your daughter."

"Gifted by God with the ability to see what tomorrow will bring."

"Do you know Sir Michael Marston well?" she asked, repeating what they'd already practiced.

The druid laughed. "We need to make him think so."

"Now is not the time for jest," she said, scolding him. "What will you say?"

"I'll say we met many years ago. Briefly."

"And you're sure he'll remember?" she asked. "Even though there is no memory for him to recall?"

"Trinity, my child, I'll make sure he remembers. And even if he doesn't, he'll still assist. I've heard he's a good and Godly man."

"Let's hope that he is."

"All that know him claim it is true."

"Are you sure he's been to Glastonbury?" she asked.

"If he hasn't, I'll name another location."

"It had better be one that he's sure to believe."

"It will be, child. Mark my word."

They trekked onward, their pace slow and deliberate. They passed one field after another, rolling pastures sprinkled with farms and split by forests, some dense with hardwoods, others sparse. Finally, after several more hours had passed, they saw the castle in the distance perched on the cliff, strong and majestic, faint wisps of cloud hiding the towers and drifting to sea.

"It won't be long, now," said Paul the Pure. "A few more miles at most."

She eyed the sweat on his forehead, the haggard look on his face. "Maybe you should rest," she said, her tone insistent.

The druid paused. "Just for a moment," he said, sinking down onto a boulder at the road's edge. "My legs grow weary the farther we go."

Trinity sat beside him. She took a bottle from a pouch around her waist and removed the cork. "Have some water," she said, handing the bottle. .

The elderly man took several swigs. He handed the bottle back and used a kerchief to wipe the sweat from his brow. After a few minutes had passed, he rose. "It's time to be on our way."

"We can rest longer," she said as she watched him struggle to his feet. "Darkness is still several hours away."

The old man sighed. "I'd rather have the journey done."

"We have work to do when we get there," she reminded him.

He nodded, knowing what they faced. "We have to kill Michael Marston."

Chapter 14

Michael Marston stood atop the castle wall and studied the coast, the cliff ending abruptly and ceding to the sea. He looked for something he could not see, a voice he could not hear. Sensing peril, he foresaw disaster, and knew the country he loved might soon be destroyed. Should it survive, it would never again be the same. Some fostered rebellion, whispering words of revolution. Rumors claimed the rebels sought assistance from the French. But he might never learn the truth, not before the threat was upon him. If he hoped to see what the days ahead might bring, he had only one option that remained.

With a sigh of reluctance, he climbed down the steps of the wall, cursing the ache that age brought to his knees. He crossed the courtyard, passing soldiers, nodding to families, their children playing games in the grass, and entered the base of the northeast tower. Stone stairs led to several rooms at varying elevations, weapons stored in some, narrow crosses called arrow loops cut in the stone to protect archers who fired upon their enemies.

He glanced over his shoulder to ensure no one watched as he approached the stairway. On the third step, he reached a black stone that was unlike the thousands of others used to construct the castle and set in the mortar. Leaning forward, he pressed it. A wall behind the stairway shifted, providing barely enough space for a man to pass. Entering the corridor, he touched an amber stone at shoulder height, and the wall slid back into place. The hallway led to a crooked set of slender steps that hugged the wall and descended into darkness, exposing a world that few could imagine and most would deny.

The steps, chiseled from rock that formed the cliff, were steeply sloped and continually curved. He descended forty feet, grasping the wall as the steps spiraled down. They ended at a crooked stone arch made by nature, not by man. A tunnel in the rock led to a corridor that continued for fifty feet more before another set of steps appeared, chiseled from the rock like the others.

At regular intervals along the route, perched upon head-high ledges, red crystals glowed to light the path. Each was the size of an apple, and the faint light cast ghoulish shadows against uneven walls, warning visitors that they entered a domain meant only for those who knew no fear.

The stairway came to an end in a cavern far below the surface, wrought by nature when the cliff was created, hidden from the light of both sun and moon, and overlooked by all but a chosen few. A slender black stream sliced through it, separating one side from the other, and a creeping mist drifted from the water into the voids above. To Michael Marston, the stream symbolized the River Styx that guarded the gate to hell, and, as he leaped upon the stepping stones placed in the water for passage, he felt as if he walked in Satan's footsteps. He shivered as the water trickled beneath him, its depths unknown. A toad blinked as he passed. Three rock columns, slanted and stout, marked the entrance to the cavern and served as support for the weight above.

"Minerva!" Marston called.

He received no reply.

The floor beyond had been polished smooth though he could not say who, besides Minerva, may have made the harrowing passage. The witch had painted a nine-foot circle at its center, a crystalline blue defined by black, and placed candles upon each cardinal point of the compass. To the south, a red candle signified fire and all that could burn bright. A white candle to the east represented air, the empty void that surrounds us all. To the west a blue candle denoted water—rivers, lakes, and the raging sea—and a green candle to the north depicted the earth from which everything comes and all returns. Marston didn't know why they were there or what they were supposed to mean, he did know that powerful sorcery had long been practiced within the confines of the circle around which the candles flickered.

An altar built from rock and yew was perched in the circle's center, a brass cauldron placed upon it, dull and pitted and impossibly old. Sprinkled along the altar's edge was quartz crystal that offered a path to wisdom, two purple candles which acted as a bridge through space and time, and a flat yellow stone that symbolized wisdom. Cluttered on the shelves that sat below the altar were pouches and vials of spices and herbs, slivers of stone and mysterious liquids. The innards and limbs of creatures, from spiders to men, hung unnervingly in amber fluid until the day they were tossed in bubbling potions, coupled with chants and spells both wicked and virtuous. As Michael Marston watched and waited, a shiver went up his spine.

Such were the ways of the witch.

Chapter 15

Marston paused, afraid to move, wondering where Minerva might be. He knew she had to be close—she always was. But he could see no one in the inky darkness beyond the circle. Suddenly a screeching tore through the stillness, and Marston gasped as a crow flew past. It violated the sacred circle, mocked him a moment more with its cackling, and winged off into the shadows that clung to the corridors and snaked throughout the cave.

"Minerva!" he called again, growing impatient.

The witch came quickly, formed from mist, moving furtively from the darkness that shrouded the rest of the cave. As she approached, Marston could see her eyes, black like the night when the moon is new, and for a moment he felt her pointed gaze piercing his body and probing his soul.

She was slender, wrapped in robes of black. A mass of tangled hair lay heaped upon her head as if she were unable to tame it no matter how hard she tried. Her dark eyes changed to gold when reflecting any light, twinkling as if she knew the answer to every question ever asked.

"Michael Marston," she croaked sweetly.

She seemed different each time he saw her, like the facets of a precious stone. In another place or time, she might make men marvel at her rare beauty, but now she made men shiver and quickly turn away.

She came closer, eyeing him with a crooked smile. "Do you look for love?" she asked as her right hand snaked forward and caressed his graying beard.

He jumped at her touch, repulsed by her suggestion. She was not a woman, at least not in his eyes. She was as much a beast as the she-wolf. "You know why I came," he said with an air of annoyance.

"Enlighten me."

He sighed, always perplexed by her behavior. "My spies tell me an enemy comes."

"Then why do you need me?" she asked with mock indifference. "The answer to your question is already known."

"I must prepare for an attack if what the scouts tell me is true."

She held up a slender finger, the nail at the tip both crooked and long, and went to the altar, motioning for him to follow. "Danger comes with many faces as we will surely see."

He approached the sacred circle but stopped when he reached its edge. He was afraid to proceed and hovered at its verge. He had never before crossed into her innermost realm and stood back, watching and waiting, eager to hear what she might have to say but hesitant to come too close.

Minerva cackled, amused by his behavior. It seemed she knew what he would do before he even tried it. Perhaps it was a game she played; he would never know.

"What are you doing?" Marston asked.

She glided to the cauldron at the center of her altar, moving her hands through the mist it made. "It's not the work of the Devil, though you probably think it is," she said, a crooked grin turning the corners of her mouth.

"I'll have no part in the Devil's work," he said.

The witch nodded. "Why did you come?"

He wanted to leave, but his feet were rooted to the stone floor. Michael Marston, a man who knew no fear, shivered as he watched the witch at work.

Minerva reached beneath the altar to her shelf of pouches and vials. "I will need the ingredients for an ancient potion, one that reveals what the coming hours will bring." She withdrew herbs, slivers of several rare minerals, the teeth of a boar, an owl's feather, and a pair of spiders. She scanned the items, rejecting two before adding others as the liquid spit and hissed. She watched the concoction carefully, and, when she was convinced the brew was as it should be, she began to mutter a chant.

63

"Tomorrow comes, tomorrow goes,

Whispered words that no one knows.

Tell the tales of ghosts and men,

Search the signals serpents send.

Share the secrets of man's soul,

Sacred thoughts that evil stole.

Use the vision, use the light,

Haunted creatures of the night."

She studied the mixture as she spoke, repeating the horrid verse over and over and over again. Suddenly she stopped and turned abruptly to face him.

"They come in force," she whispered. "And they come to conquer."

Chapter 16

Marston left Minerva's cave, shaken after their encounter. He walked through winding corridors and climbed crooked steps, eerie shadows dancing off the uneven walls. He exited the labyrinth at the base of the northeast tower and went out to the grounds, making his way into the village that sprawled within the walls of the castle.

He crossed the cobblestone streets and walked alongside the stone houses that stood in a row past the spicery, the tailor, and the brewery. Two boys were playing ball, a mother tended her fussing toddler, and Jenks the blacksmith was on his way back from the well with two wooden pails of water. Marston nodded politely to those that he passed, paying special attention to the children, knowing now that their lives were at risk and a battle was soon to begin. He could do nothing more than prepare, make every effort to defeat the enemy, and save as many lives as he could. Still he knew that war brought tragedy and usually to those who least deserved it.

He entered the keep, the chambers on the ground floor divided into a map room which he used to administer the fertile countryside he had come to control, a kitchen, and vestibule. The second floor contained the Great Hall which was reserved for entertaining, a chapel, and some private rooms for visitors. The top story was comprised of the master's private quarters, but it also housed a library and rooms for more privileged guests.

Marston passed several servants and entered a series of rooms where he and his advisors conducted official business, administrative affairs to manage his realm. They imposed and collected taxes, conducted trade, and settled land disputes all in the name of preserving the peace. He started toward the map room but paused at the threshold, absorbed in thought. Minerva always gave sage advice and had never led him astray. Her words foretold what the days would bring, and if the future should need to be altered, she would do what had to be done. But Marston had never asked her to use her powers to such an end and only called upon her when in absolute need. She was a force never to be employed unless mankind was in peril.

He wasn't sure from whence she came or for how long she had been alive. She spoke of days which had passed a hundred years before Marston's birth as if they had just occurred, and perhaps to her they had. She had first appeared when the castle had been built, emerging like a demon from deep below its foundation. But she had always been loyal and true, holding his interests above all else, and he no longer cared who or what she might be and was only glad she was there.

Marston stepped into the map room and sat behind a large table built of oak. Tapestries lined the walls, each one embroidered with the likeness of an English king. Silver sconces were affixed to the walls, their candles casting a warm glow on the pewter goblets that lined the handsome buffet adorned with hand-carved scenes of an unforgiving sea. It was a room filled, top to bottom, with finery, befitting the lord of the manor.

Marston eyed the map of his realm and the craggy shoreline of France beyond. After a few minutes had passed, his mind still on the witch, he chose to seek further counsel. He called to a servant, and, seconds later, a young man appeared. "Summon my advisor," the lord said.

"Yes, sire," the servant replied. "As you request."

Moments later, Marston was greeted by a man with a billowing beard and dark eyes that intimated both wisdom and mischief. A mass of black curly hair crowned his head. The remainder of his face, or that part of it which could be seen, was chiseled and lean. Marston's most trusted advisor, Gideon of Guildford, known for his intellect, was an alchemist who spent much of his time in an underground workshop trying to transform various base metals into silver and gold. Often, he claimed he'd had success, though Marston had never witnessed his craft at work.

"Join me, Gideon," Marston said.

Dressed in a long, flowing brown robe, the alchemist entered the room. "How can I be of service, sire?"

Marston waited for the servant to take his leave. "How many ounces of gold have you fashioned today?" he asked, a sly smile on his lips.

"I've taken a different approach," Gideon replied. "I am attempting to change peat into pewter."

"With success, I'm sure," Marston said. "Any other experiments?"

"An elixir that offers immortality."

Marston laughed. "May I be the first to try it?"

"Of course, sire," Gideon said. "Right after me." He glanced into the corridor, ensuring the servant had gone, and then leaned across the desk. "Is there another question you might like to ask?"

"Several," Marston said. He paused, thoughtful, not sure how to begin. "The French woman that Carney brought," he said haltingly. "I never requested, nor would I ask, for such a prize, especially with the threat of war looming."

"The Lady Gabrielle poses a problem," Gideon said. "Especially if the whispers I have heard ring true—that the French have ties to the barons."

Marston frowned. "She gives them far more incentive to fight."

"In the end, it may be revenge they seek," Gideon said. "And if we're ever defeated and even a hair on her head is harmed, every soul within the walls would pay the price. None would live to see another day."

Marston was quiet, pensive. "Carney had good intentions."

"As did many who rest for eternity."

Marston nodded grimly. "Her presence creates more concerns than can ever be counted."

"And most are not yet known," Gideon said. "Although we hear that the French fight with the barons, we won't know how far their influence extends until they are near, and we've seen their faces."

"They still may not know Gabrielle is here."

"More shall be revealed in days to come," Gideon said. "And, if nothing else, she does have value."

"As a hostage," Marston said, the thought distasteful.

Gideon watched the master, knowing his suggestion met with little support. "As a last resort, sire. And that is all."

Marston nodded. As much as he abhorred the thought of leveraging the Lady Gabrielle, he knew it was an option that must be considered. "Who leads this rebellion? Tell me of the whispers you've heard."

"Many fit the role of culprit," Gideon said.

"James the Bold?" Marston asked. "Robin of Cantwell or Thomas of Thorne?"

Gideon paused and ran his hand through his beard. "James the Bold has the most to gain. And he has always wanted to depose the king."

"And rule in his place," Marston muttered.

"The most bloodthirsty, for sure," Gideon said. "But for us, it does not matter. The battle will come no matter who brings it."

"We had best be prepared and avoid surprise," Marston said.

"We'll stockpile food, water, wood, and weapons."

Marston nodded, images of death spinning through his mind. "I suspect a siege will likely result."

"And many attacks we can surely expect," Gideon said. "Some skirmishes meant to probe our defenses, others full onslaughts wherein many will die."

Marston considered the many battles he had fought and what he had learned from each of them. "They'll dig a tunnel, maybe more than one."

"We should assume they'll employ every tactic that's known," Gideon said.

"We'll need a strong catapult to thwart their attacks," Marston said.

"I'll have one built," Gideon said. "I've already prepared the drawings."

Marston chuckled. "The range of your talents will never surprise me."

"Thank you, sire," Gideon said, nodding with respect. "I shall always do whatever I can as long as you find it useful."

"I'll assign tasks to each of my captains to ensure we're ready when the battle begins."

Gideon hesitated, considering measures they might take to prepare for the coming siege. "We can also dig a tunnel, connecting the castle with earthwork beyond."

"There's a natural passage cut through the rock," Marston said. "It extends past the north wall. We need only complete it."

"Then that's a task we should be swift to begin. We can use the passage to dispatch our men and attack them from behind."

"Or use it to affect our escape. If it should come to that."

Gideon paused, thoughtful. "Is there anything more we can possibly do?"

"I could send a messenger," Marston said. "Perhaps more men could be rallied from different parts of the realm."

"And if none can be found?"

"I at least could warn the others," Marston said. "The attack will come to more than those who reside along the coast. All of England, it seems, is about to face war."

"But who can we trust with such a message?" Gideon asked. "We don't know friend from foe."

Chapter 17

"I've no desire for company and prefer to dine alone," Gabrielle said to Anna, the maidservant, as she stood at the door to her room.

"But the master insists," Anna replied.

Gabrielle looked at the girl, hoping she had found a friend in whom she could confide. She leaned closer. "I don't want to be alone with him," she whispered.

"He's a good man, my lady," Anna assured her. "You've nothing to fear. And even so, you won't be alone."

"Who joins us?" Gabrielle asked, wondering if it might be Captain Carney.

"Gideon, the alchemist," she said. "He's a good man, too."

Gabrielle hesitated but a moment more, and then shrugged. "I suppose I have no choice."

"Come, my lady," the young woman said. "I'll take you to the Great Hall."

Anna led her down the spiral staircase and then through a corridor into the Great Hall. The large reception room, which comprised much of the keep's second floor, was the seat of Lord Marston's public life. Therein, he presided over celebrations, state affairs, and banquets. The rectangular hall, adorned with finely woven tapestries depicting scenes of historical battles sported high ceilings almost twenty feet in height and supported by slender columns and marble arches. On the south-facing wall, narrow, evenly spaced windows allowed the sun's rays to filter into the cavernous space while still ensuring the keep was readily defended. A long table ran the length of the west wall facing the windows, the view of the sea and horizon beyond dizzying. It could easily accommodate sixty people, the center seat reserved for the master. Twenty other tables of varying sizes filled the remainder of the room. But as Gabrielle entered, she found the room empty save for one table set for three. Michael Marston and Gideon rose as she approached.

"My lady," they said, almost in unison, and bowed in respect.

"Good evening," Gabrielle said as Marston helped to seat her.

"The Lady Gabrielle," Marston said. "This is Gideon, my most trusted advisor and closest friend."

Gideon bowed once more. "I'm honored, my lady."

"We're pleased by your presence," Marston said. "I was concerned you might not join us."

"I was so inclined," she replied. "I've no desire to befriend."

"We're harmless," Gideon said, his smile largely hidden by his bushy beard. "And will treat you with the utmost respect."

"A promise I hope you intend to keep," Gabrielle said.

Marston nodded. "You have my word."

An elderly servant appeared and filled their goblets with rich red wine. A maidservant soon followed, a young woman in a plain green dress. She placed plates of bread and fruit on the table, followed by bowls filled with nuts and berries.

"The venison will soon be prepared, sire," the maidservant said as they took their leave.

Gabrielle sipped her wine, eyeing the two men with whom she dined. She didn't trust them and knew she never could regardless of how well they treated her. And that was something she could never forget.

"You were raised in the convent?" Marston asked, taking a slice of bread and placing it on his plate.

"I was, sire," she replied.

"You lost your family as a child?" Gideon asked politely.

"I did," she answered tersely.

"The sickness ravaged the world," Marston said.

"I realized, at a very young age, that life is precious," Gabrielle replied.

"But the pain of loss never dies," Marston said softly, his eyes glassy. "I lost my wife and four children, two sons and two daughters, as well as two sisters."

She could see the anguish etched in his face, a pain that mirrored hers. "I'm so sorry," she said. "That must have been more difficult than words can express."

Marston nodded, quiet for a moment. He took a sip of wine and then spoke. "The children died within hours of each other. My sisters lasted a bit longer. Some say my wife died of grief more than illness. But we'll never know."

"A loss none should have to bear and few could hope to survive," she said softly. She felt as if her heart had been ripped from her body so pointed was his pain. She couldn't imagine the suffering, even though it was plain to see. Tears misted his eyes, sorrow darkening a smile that would never be as bright as it once had been, and his heart, which seemed to Gabrielle to be good, had been forever scarred.

"Your loss is also beyond what can be measured, I'm sure," said Gideon, watching her closely.

She knew he hoped that she might share in Marston's misery, and a bond between them could be built. But she didn't want to speak. The anguish she had endured was private, the world in which she had lost her family only revisited in memories, and then with hesitation, since the pain was so great to bear. But somehow, she could not refrain, could no longer keep it secret, and she found herself recounting the horrors of a life once lived to men who had, only hours before, been strangers.

"It was spring when they died," she said softly, "the mornings crisp with just a touch of winter's chill in the air. Winter was dying," she sighed, "along with my heart."

"Sometimes words can purge the soul," Gideon said softly, urging her on.

Gabrielle nodded, her gaze passing between the two men who now showed her so much compassion. "It seems as if it just occurred," she said, "so sharp is the pain."

"Even muted, it is ever reappearing as if it never truly faded," Marston began as if he told his story with hers. "It only hides itself away until a memory once again forces it before your eyes."

She nodded and then continued. "Spring became summer, the sun a bit stronger, the wind a bit weaker. I was so lost in my own heartache I didn't know to mark the day I was brought to the convent as a new beginning, or that when the sun rose that morning, I would awaken to a day that would so drastically change my life."

Marston watched the veil of sadness cover her face. "Perhaps that is a tragedy best left in the past," he said.

"A farmer brought me to the convent," she continued, her stare vacant, her face pale. "I was called little Gabrielle then, just seven years old. And I stood at the iron gate, sad and afraid."

"So young to endure so much," Gideon said. "Often a stain the soul can't remove."

"Tears rolled down my cheeks, so many I thought they would never end," Gabrielle continued. "My world had ended, and I had no reason to remain within it."

"But, still, you prevailed and overcame what would devastate most," Marston said tenderly. "A testament to your strength."

"I had already seen the worst life could offer. And it seemed as if nothing could make that change."

"Was the farmer a family friend?" Gideon asked.

Gabrielle nodded. "He lived nearby, stooped from working the fields, his face weathered but etched with honesty, his hands calloused and strong. He held my hand gently, I remember. But I wish I could forget all before it."

"He must have done what was best for you," Marston said.

Gabrielle smiled faintly, having heard those same words when Montague left her at the convent. "He was a good man," she said. "And I wanted to stay with him, the only person I really knew. I begged him, but he would not listen."

"Were the nuns afraid you had the sickness, too?" Marston asked.

Gabrielle smiled. "The Reverend Mother acted like I was an animal she intended to purchase. She checked me for fever, searched for blotches and boils. It was only when she was convinced I bore no sign of the sickness that she nodded to the farmer discreetly and took me within the convent walls."

73

"It was good of the nuns to take you in," Gideon said. "A child left alone in the world."

"They saved my life even if it no longer seemed worth living. I had lost my parents and three sisters. Their faces, ravaged by the illness, pleading for release, I shall never forget. I see them still even though many years have gone by. And I could do nothing to help them."

"The swiftness of the sickness was its only mercy," Gideon said quietly, eyeing Marston, "its victims submitting in three or four days."

Gabrielle nodded. "I was the only survivor. The Reverend Mother said that if a whole family dies of the sickness, yet one child survives, it truly must be a miracle. And that's why the farmer brought me to the convent. He thought I should do God's work."

"I can feel your pain," Marston said softly. "The anguish that consumes you, the loneliness that holds your heart. And never being able to forgive yourself, no matter the time that passes."

Gabrielle fought this unexpected show of intimacy, the bond they had through their muted pain from a sorrow few others would know. She feigned indifference to protect herself, if nothing else, and to keep a distance between captor and captive. "I suffered more than most can imagine," she said softly.

"You lost the love of a mother," Marston said, "and the adoring gaze a father casts upon his daughter. You never knew your sisters' children, and they will never know yours."

Gabrielle looked at the two men, listening so closely, appearing so concerned. "Indeed," she replied stiffly. "But Montague filled that void with a love that never dies, and you have taken me away from him. And for that, I can never forgive you."

Chapter 18

Marston was about to speak a word of apology when the servants reappeared, laying silver platters of venison and bowls of sweet peas, carrots, and cabbage before them. They refilled their goblets and meted out portions of steaming food onto silver plates. Marston glanced at Gabrielle who stared absently at her dinner.

"I am sorry, my lady," he said, quite sincere. "But the decision to bring you to England was made by Captain Carney alone. I never requested, nor did I suggest, that he take the actions he took."

"And yet here I sit," Gabrielle said flatly. "An improper deed that is left uncorrected, offers no excuse for any involved."

"Are you not comfortable, my lady?" Gideon interjected. "For every effort has been made to ensure that you are."

"Quite comfortable but a captive all the same."

Marston locked eyes with Gabrielle. "It is a trying time in England and Normandy alike," he began. "Surely you understand the position in which we've been placed."

"I understand that you hold me here as a pawn to enhance your position, a chip with which to bargain. And an honorable man would not use a woman to try to win his wars."

"But I do no such thing," Marston exclaimed. "I only try to make a move with the powers I have been granted."

"No matter," she said curtly. "Montague shall come for me. And that day is one you will surely regret, should you ever live to recall it."

Gideon looked uneasily from Marston to Gabrielle. "I think you'll enjoy dinner," he said, trying to ease the tension. "Especially the sauces." He leaned toward Gabrielle as if sharing a secret. "We have our own spicery here at the castle."

Gabrielle smiled, but it was clear to both men that she was merely playing a role. "I'm sure I shall," she said, sampling the venison. She chewed thoughtfully for a moment and then spoke. "It's quite good."

"I thought you would find it to your liking," Marston said, watching her closely so as not to offend. "Most who dine here do."

Gideon took a sip of his wine. "Who then is Montague?" he asked.

Gabrielle's lifeless smile transformed, at once, into a look that was radiant with love. "He's a man like no other. An artist with talent not many have known, sensitive but strong, with a mind unlike any other. He builds cathedrals for the king."

"I have heard men speak of the houses of worship that adorn Normandy and beyond," Marston said. "It's even been said that the voice of God is writ in the very walls. Your beloved must be quite gifted, a man any king would covet."

"He is that and more," said Gabrielle. "His stained glass is known the world over, and produces awe in any who see it. His work exceeds the reach of most, if not all, and shall surely survive for millenniums."

"Is he your husband?" Marston asked.

"No," she said, unable to hide her disappointment. "Although it is my greatest wish."

"And what, might I ask, prevents your eternal bliss?" Gideon asked in jest.

Gabrielle frowned. "Only time, it seems. And a war that never ends. But someday we will wed, and I'll thank the Lord till my dying breath."

Gideon glanced at Marston and then turned to Gabrielle. "I can prepare a potion to hasten the arrival of that long sought-after day."

She laughed. "I only wish you could."

"Why would such a man visit the convent?" Marston asked. "If it's there, that you first met."

Gabrielle smiled. "He didn't. The convent was visited by few while I was in the nuns' care."

"You and the fair sisters took a pilgrimage to one of Montague's cathedrals," Gideon exclaimed, "and that is where you met."

Gabrielle sipped her wine. "No, fate took me to Paris as a member of the king's court. And that is where we met. And each day since has been brighter, each evening not as long. And I now count the hours until I behold him once more."

"It was a journey that can't be measured in miles," Marston said. "But you leave out the most important part of the tale you're trying to tell."

"I have indeed," Gabrielle said. "As you know, I was raised in the convent. The Reverend Mother provided love and direction, and I always assumed I'd become a nun. But the chance arrival of a soldier is what came to dictate my fate."

"The soldier brought you to Paris?" Gideon asked.

"He insisted I was a relative of the queen, and though I denied it," Gabrielle said, "I was soon summoned to the palace. The queen took one look at me and swore I was a cousin who had been lost several years before."

"But you weren't?" Marston asked.

Gabrielle shook her head. "I was born on a small farm, my family the poorest of those in the parish. There's no royal lineage in my blood. But the more I denied the queen's claim, the more she and the rest of court insisted that it was true."

"And your life was forever changed," Marston said. "A remarkable story for any to hear."

"I became a lady of the queen's court and was taught the ways of royalty," Gabrielle said and then smiled, reminiscing. "My tutors and maidservants endured trying days, erasing all hints of my former life. But what did not come naturally in the way of manners, I made up for with an unquenchable thirst for books. I read every one in the palace library and begged each of my tutors to bring me more."

"The knowledge of books that Carney referred to," Marston said.

She nodded. "I was eventually known for my intellect."

As well as your beauty, I'm sure," Marston said.

Gabrielle blushed in spite of herself. "It was in the library that I met Montague, the man I love more than life itself."

"And who now builds cathedrals for the king," Marston added.

Gabrielle paused, not sure whether or not to continue. "He builds cathedrals when France is at peace," she said softly. "But during times of war, he serves as the king's most valued commander."

Chapter 19

Five miles south of Marston Castle

Montague stood at the bow of the ship, watching the English coast as they approached. Towering cliffs loomed ahead, rising hundreds of feet from a rocky shore. They mirrored the cliffs of Normandy but were not as dramatic, the rock formations God had wrought in this land not nearly as bold. Still the two land masses did seem much the same, serving as book ends of the English Channel that flowed in between.

Atop the cliffs was an immense castle, the walls and towers posing a threat to any foe that attempted to reach its innermost sanctum. Montague studied the structure, a quavering and fragmented picture masked in the dispersing fog. The fortress hugged the coast and sprawled inward, perched on a plain and flanked by forests, the trees almost as high as the castle walls. The fog shifted, and the castle faded from view, cloaked in mystery as much as the morning mist.

With over a thousand men in the ships that trailed behind him, Montague commanded a formidable force, one that could best most any rival, even one shielded by such impressive walls. He suspected that, when his men were joined with his English partners, victory would be theirs for the taking regardless of the strength of the castle or those prepared to defend it.

Montague made a mental note of two well-guarded towers and told his men to make ready for landfall. He didn't like war, although most assumed that he did. His father had been the general, the commander once called upon by the king when the most difficult tasks appeared, the man who had lived to fight battles few would forget. It was his father who had been born with the gift of legends, the ability to see what an enemy would do and know what must be done to prevent it. He had saved France on many an occasion and, if he'd still been alive, would lead her to a glory greater than that she'd ever known. His father had been revered by soldier and civilian, peasant and king, and now that he was gone, Montague knew many hoped he had been born to step into his father's place. Such faith was as much a curse as a blessing, for even though Montague absorbed every lesson his father had taught him, fought with commitment, valor, and might, he could never compete with his father, not the memory or the man. All he could do was his very best and hope that it was enough.

When he'd lived in his father's shadow, war had seemed like a grand adventure, a passage to both glory and fame. But the first time he'd run his sword through a man and watched as the life left his body, he was sickened beyond what any human could understand. As the blood gushed from his wound, Montague wondered if there was, somewhere, a woman who was now a widow, children who had their father no more. The thought of the grief they were now forced to face stayed with him always.

Montague hated war and all it stood for. He was a contradiction—one of the world's greatest warriors who would do anything he could to avoid a fight. If it had been in his power, he would have put an end to war forever so he might return to his heart's greatest passion, bridging earthly beauty to the splendor of God by creating stained glass windows that seemed as divine as the message they conveyed.

As the ship drew nearer to shore, Montague cursed himself for having left Gabrielle in a sanctuary that protected her only from the Devil himself. He'd never imagined she would be taken by the English as a means to punish the French and had listened in horror when Alaric the wizard had told him the tale he had not wanted to hear. His beloved was gone, taken by a man named Michael Marston to the castle that bore his name. He knew if he found either, he would find Gabrielle—the light to his darkness, sea to his shore. He'd vowed to search every inch of the globe if need be, determined to whisk her away her away from a battlefield where victory had been his.

Montague scanned the clifftop. He could see the castle clearly now, its imposing hulk close to the chalky cliffs, the image crisp as the fog that hung upon the water began to drift away. He wondered if the Lady Gabrielle could be held within. It was the most logical location to house a captive, the closest fortification to the convent from which she'd been taken. Montague studied the task before him as the ship veered farther south and approached a wharf that jutted out from the shore. It was a fight he wouldn't have chosen, offering no advantage to the attacker, save time. He could surround the fortress and wait patiently while those inside starved. Such a siege would take months, each day keeping him from his beloved Gabrielle.

He had to somehow breach the walls to save her, and he prayed to a benevolent God that he could. If his prayers were answered, he promised to never harm another human being no matter how just the cause. He would live his life in peace alongside Gabrielle, hidden in his country chateau or a cottage along the coast, designing structures of unparalleled beauty and grandeur for his patron, the king. He would greet each day thankful that she stood beside him, for nothing could be more rewarding than to live a life reflected in her eyes.

Montague turned to the captain of the ship as it neared the wharf. "What is the name of the fortress?"

"Marston Castle," the captain said. "Commanded by one of the most gallant knights in all the land."

"Marston Castle," Montague repeated softly. Alaric had told him where to look for the Lady Gabrielle, and that's where fate had brought him. He would now fight for more than his love of France. He would fight to find his beloved.

Chapter 20

Four miles north of Marston Castle

The barons' forces began to assemble in preparation for battle, their camp hidden from the enemy by a forest that lay to the north. As their army grew and stockpiled more and more supplies, Marston's scouts warily kept watch of their position, but they could do little but wait for the barons' advance. Days would define the dawn of the conflict, but months would describe the siege it would likely become.

A cliff rose sharply along the coast, the highest elevation for some distance, and from its peak the castle towers and its colossal walls could be seen over top of the trees that sheltered the barons' army. As the sun bathed the landscape in golden rays of light, a giant of a man led his horse to the base of the peak. He studied the castle in the distance—a legend few would challenge but a marvel made by man and so, in some ways, vulnerable.

James the Bold was a ferocious warrior who had never tasted defeat, a warlord who did what was needed to win, no matter the cost. Feared throughout England, Normandy, Scotland, and Wales, his words alone terrified those less brave while his deeds convinced the remainder. For many reasons known to only a few, he'd been chosen to defeat Michael Marston, a staunch defender of England's King John. Many thought he should lead the rebellion, his talents wasted on a single battle, and that fate would choose him to lead the country, if not the entire world.

He looked as fierce as the tales men told about him implied. His blue eyes were icy and cruel, his right cheek horribly scarred, slit to the bone by an enemy sword. A scruffy beard hid much of his face and the angry scowl he constantly wore, but much of the scar extended beyond it, his lip and right eye connected by a jagged purple line. He wore a green tunic, the image of a charging boar on his chest, bearskin boots, a massive broadsword hanging from his belt, and a conical metal helmet on his head with two tusks jutting out from either side from the boar he had slain with the knife he kept in his boot. Carrying a shield covered in fur he was followed by a handful of men, loyal lieutenants, who waited a few yards away, ready to act should James the Bold make a request.

He turned to one of his advisors. "Blaise," he called. "I seek your counsel."

A mysterious figure, royally perched on a cloud-white stallion, stood apart from the rest. He exuded both power and a knowing serenity/ Those who were near stole furtive glances at his awesome presence as he nudged his white horse forward.

Blaise, wrapped in robes of gray with a black sash knotted about his waist and a pentacle dangling on his chest from a golden chain also wore a hood on his head, revealing only a shadow where his face should be. As he came forward, he shook his head, and the hood fell to his shoulders.

His straight blond hair, practically white, hung down to his shoulders. His skin was light, but his eyes were black, and they delivered a gaze that could pierce an opponent and set his blood to boiling. He reined his horse alongside his commander and looked into the distance, awaiting the question he knew James the Bold would pose.

"Can the castle be taken?" the warrior asked.

The warlock slid from his horse's back and bent to the ground, grabbing a handful of English soil. He held the earth to his nose, and smelled its dampness, while consumed by visions of all who had walked upon it in the many centuries past. He walked to the edge of the cliff and flung the dirt skyward, watching it spread through the air and drift to the rolling sea two hundred feet below. He studied the dust as if it told him the direction the days would take and which dawn would carry more weight than most. In the instant it took for the soil to scatter upon the wind, an image of the castle formed, visible only to Blaise. Seconds later he frowned as if confronted by a premonition, an unexpected omen that could never be ignored.

"Its soldiers are determined, its location a deterrent," Blaise said cautiously, trying to impress upon his leader that a difficult task lay ahead. He paused dramatically before continuing. "All who have faced them were defeated."

James the Bold was quiet. "But you forget one thing," he said coldly. "None were as treacherous as I."

Blaise grabbed another handful of dirt and threw it to the winds, watching as it was taken up by the breeze before falling to the shore below to mix with the waves that washed the shore. A vision appeared before him, an image the warlock knew would enrage his master should he be asked to describe it.

"What is it that you see?" James the Bold asked.

Blaise hesitated but then spoke. "Michael Marston hides behind the walls."

"Impossible," said James the Bold with disgust as a flicker of fear crossed his face. "He is in Normandy."

Blaise shrugged. "I can't explain his presence, but I can confirm his courage."

James the Bold frowned. "Is there a weakness to exploit?"

"Not in the man."

"It doesn't matter whom we face," James the Bold scoffed. "Victory will still be ours."

"I see another threat," Blaise said. "A potent force lurks within the walls, a power I feel but cannot see. We should be wary. It's a force that's difficult to define."

"More powerful than Marston?"

Blaise considered the question as if he didn't know the answer. "Power comes in many forms which can rarely be compared."

James the Bold sighed. He'd grown tired of Blaise's riddles. "Define the difference."

Blaise looked at the clouds as they drifted on the horizon, searching for an answer in the cotton that covered the blue. "Michael Marston is a man."

"And the force is not?"

"It's a spirit, I suspect," Blaise said. "Who knows the magic of the masters."

"Magic more powerful than yours?"

Blaise laughed, a hideous cackle that made animals run when it met their ears. "Such magic does not exist."

"Can this force be defeated?"

"The future has not been defined."

"Why not?"

"Because we shall define it."

James the Bold studied the warlock, wondering if he was man or myth, demon or the very face of death itself. He shivered and turned away.

"You're not convinced?" Blaise asked.

"I cannot fear what I cannot see."

"You know not fear of any kind," Blaise said. "Which is why you're a leader of men."

James the Bold stood quietly, looking beyond the horizon. Blaise, too, studied the water but made no mention of the men who crossed it. Instead he waited for his master to speak.

James the Bold turned and looked at the fortress. "The French should arrive shortly," he said. "Can I trust them?"

"It depends on the prize."

"The Dauphin becomes king," James the Bold grumbled, "which is far too much to give."

"Then you take the throne."

"It is not mine for the taking."

"A problem that's easily solved," Blaise said.

"It took many to decide what must be done," James the Bold replied. "How, then, is the problem easily solved?"

"The barons use the French to defeat King John," Blaise said. "But have the French ever been an ally to the English?"

James the Bold paused, pensive. "No. They have always been our rivals."

"The desired result is clear to me," Blaise said. "Once the barons have ousted King John, a new enemy will emerge."

James the Bold rubbed his scarred cheek. "What a devious plan," he said. "I like it."

"And when the fighting has ended, England will need a new king."

James the Bold considered the future and the ways he might shape an England reborn. "There are many who desire that role."

"But they can't have it," Blaise said.

"Why not?"

"Because it belongs to you."

A smile curled the lips of James the Bold, future king of England.

Chapter 21

Several passages led from Minerva's altar into the bowels of the cave the witch called home. She walked down a corridor that skewed to the east through a torturous path that twisted and turned. A muted glow cast by crystals perched on rock ledges spread ghoulish shadows on the uneven walls, their light piercing the darkness.

At the end of the passage was an irregular hole cut into the cliff by nature that provided a view to the sea. Two hundred feet above the waves that battered the rocks below, it provided a perch from which Minerva could watch the water and whatever lay beyond. The witch walked toward the gap and studied the rolling waves. Her tangled hair blew about her face in the stiff breeze as she looked out at a world she knew would soon change.

From the folds of her robe, she withdrew a crystal that fitted precisely into the palm of her hand. She held it close to her heart, the strength it provided a bridge to the chakras, the energy centers spaced throughout her body. She threw her head back, basking in sunlight as she gripped the crystal and closed her eyes, absorbing the strength that nature provided. She knew Michael Marston faced more threats than most could ever endure —the barons and those sent to do their bidding, the rebel English, the French, and mysterious forces only she could combat. She was determined to provide him with the courage he needed to conquer and overcome.

Thirty minutes passed before she opened her eyes. She took a breath, inhaling the salt air of the sea, tasting the minerals it contained. She peered across the water, knowing the coast of Normandy lay fifty miles away. As she focused on the horizon, images danced before her eyes, lasting seconds and appearing in no particular order. She studied them closely, knowing she might have to change the direction that fate was forced to take. The scenes were crisp, day rolling to night, child changing to man and turning to dust, as minute became millennium and eons sped by in seconds. She watched and absorbed, accepted what she could not change, but determined to alter what she could. Finally, when the images had ceased, she again closed her eyes, letting the energy she'd absorbed from sun and earth, sea and sky drain from her body like lava spewed from an angry volcano. At last, she slumped forward, exhausted, and breathed slowly until she had the strength to open her eyes.

Once she could stand without trembling, she made her way back down the corridor, at times touching the damp walls for support. The crystals cast their eerie glow as she followed the path through the ancient cliff. As each minute passed, Minerva grew stronger, her movements quicker, as she reentered her cavern sanctuary, her altar just beyond.

She sat down before the altar and conjured the visions she had pulled from the ether. They told a tale she hadn't expected. Her master, Sir Michael Marston, faced a challenge greater than any he had met before. The odds were against him. His courage and bravery, skill and intellect might not be enough, and defeat, the witch knew all too well, could appear when least expected. Even the power she possessed, a sorcery few on this earth could surpass, could prove weaker than the barrage of enemies that sought to bring Marston down. She might not be able to provide him with the victory he so richly deserved.

It was true, his greatest days had passed. The gray in his beard suggested a statesman, not the warlord he had become. But the world and the men who sought to turn it had no mercy for an aging man. The foes Marston faced were formidable, united in their efforts to destroy him, and she, loyal to her master, must stand by his side, prop him up, and do all within her power to ensure that he prevailed.

Determined in her cause, the witch examined the scores of pouches stored among the corridors of her cave, sorting through them to find a polished bloodstone, a twig figure wrapped in boar skin, and a white candle made from the wax of a bee. Then she returned to her altar.

She placed the figure in the center, a symbol of strength, and placed the candle and bloodstone beside it. A ghostly blue flame flickered atop the altar, its mysterious source never waning. Minerva used it to light the candle. Then she began to chant.

"Courage, strength, valor, might,

Darkness dies in days of light.

Fright, flight, doubt no more

Dream of what you're fighting for.

Stand among forgotten men.

Show the world you don't pretend.

Scream for justice, fight for right.

Live to be the bravest knight."

Once Minerva was satisfied the bloodstone had absorbed enough energy, she put it in a pocket of her robe and extinguished the candle. She stepped from the corridor, crossed the stream that bubbled through her domain, and walked into the shadows where stairs descended from the tower above. But instead of taking the steps she moved around them, past a flat stone that sat just off the rock face.

A narrow opening lay just past the boulder, and Minerva stepped through it. A series of corridors, carved in the rock by both nature and man, led to different parts of the castle and the buildings contained within its walls. Known to her alone, the network of tunnels let her roam about the castle at will, unseen and unheard by those without the powers she alone possessed.

Five minutes later, she stood at what seemed to be an end to the corridor, but she pushed a crooked rock that protruded from the wall, and a portion of the stone in front of her moved slightly, creating an opening two feet wide.

She stepped through the narrow door and emerged in Marston's quarters just beside a fireplace, stone carvings of winged serpents supporting the mantle. Ensuring the room was vacant, she walked around a bench toward the bed which was housed in a rich wooden frame and draped with green linen. She took the bloodstone from her pocket and inserted it into the mattress on which the great Michael Marston slept.

She stepped back and studied her efforts, moving her hands back and forth above the bed, her eyes closed. After thirty seconds, she stopped.

"This deed is done," she whispered.

Chapter 22

"The master wants to see you," said Anna, the servant.

"Do you know why?" Gabrielle asked as they walked through the keep.

"No, my lady, I don't," Anna said. "He only asked that I bring you to him." She led the Lady Gabrielle to the entrance where Michael Marston and Gideon were waiting.

"I thought a walk through the grounds might interest you," Marston said as she approached.

"You'll meet some of the villagers," Gideon added. Then he laughed. "And then maybe wish you had not come."

Gabrielle looked at the two men and checked her impulse to smile. They were still her captors regardless of how polite they might be. "I was quite comfortable in my quarters."

Marston nodded with respect. "Of course, my lady," he said. "But you're free to wander the grounds and do whatever else you please—within the confines of the castle walls."

She realized they were only trying to make her feel welcome, which, given the circumstances, was a difficult task to perform. She had no intention of befriending them, but she did want her stay at Marston Castle, regardless of how undesirable it was, to be as pleasant as possible.

"Thank you," she said. "It will be nice to leave my quarters, especially when most convenient for me."

"I'll even show you my laboratory," Gideon said. "Perhaps you can help me with some of my experiments."

She was forced to smile, so likeable did the alchemist try to be. "I can think of nothing more I'd rather do, for I've a strong desire to learn your art."

"Then let's walk to the east side of the baily," Gideon said. "There you'll see the catapult under construction. I designed it myself. It can even swivel to fire in any direction."

At the mere mention of design, she thought of Montague, poring over his drawings for an ornate stained-glass window or a flying buttress to support a cathedral nave. He loved to create, to make each building better than the last. He greeted each day as a means to prove tomorrow is ever brighter than yesterday. She shuddered at the thought they might never be reunited, but tried to keep her mind focused strong, determined they would happen if only given time.

Marston and Gideon led Gabrielle east through parts of the village where shops and rowhouses mostly of stone with thatched roofs stretched side by side along narrow cobblestone streets curving through the baily. To her, the place seemed more like a countryside than the heart of a fortress. Marston stopped when they'd reached a cottage at the end of the lane where a woman and a young girl sat outside, churning butter.

"This is Mrs. Carney, the captain's wife, and her daughter Maud," Marston said. "May I present the Lady Gabrielle?" He paused, as if uncertain how to proceed, and then continued. "A guest from France."

"My lady," Mrs. Carney said with a slight bow. "Welcome to Marston Castle."

"You have pretty hair," the tiny child said, shielding her eyes from the sun.

Drawn to the child, who resembled her long-passed sister, Gabrielle smiled and kneeled to address her. "Thank you very much," she said. "Aren't you a big girl, helping your mother?"

"I always do," Maud boasted.

"Good for you. I'm sure your mother is most grateful for all the help you give."

Continuing their stroll, s they reached an open expanse where Marston pointed to a man wearing a falconer's cuff. "You've already met our blacksmith, Mr. Jenks."

"How are you today, my lady?" Jenks asked.

"I'm well, thank you," she said with a nod.

"See, my lady," Gideon said. "The English are good people."

Gabrielle frowned, confronted with images of burning villages, homeless children, widows and orphans.

Marston stared at her with an impassive look. "You don't agree."

She stared back, unemotionally. "The English take what isn't theirs and destroy what's left.".

"Normandy has been a battleground for centuries," Marston replied. "Trod upon by not only the English but also the Danes."

"Which doesn't excuse what has occurred," she retorted..

"Don't let the past flavor the present," Gideon said. 'Or you'll never rise to greet the new day."

Gabrielle stopped and looked at both men incredulously. "How can it not?" she asked. "I was a child when the English first came to Normandy."

"Did they harm you in any way?" Marson asked, his face expressing genuine concern.

"A memory can harm a child as severely as an act or deed."

"If I could erase it, I would," Marston said softly.

She felt the compassion he offered but chose to ignore it. "I was wrapped in the cocoon the convent provided," she said. "I knew no enemies. I was free of want or worry, free of fear. But my life was forever changed the day the English rode up to the gates."

"We don't have to speak of it," Marston said "Why open wounds that are now only scars?"

Bur Gabrielle, reliving the horror, continued speaking. "They came right in. Two of them. On horseback."

"The ways of war," Gideon muttered. "Even a convent can be violated."

"Their trespass proved that the only shield God can offer waits for us in heaven," Gabrielle said, remembering the fear she'd confronted all those years ago.

"We know not why He chooses the methods He does," Marston said gently. "We've both endured unspeakable suffering."

"Suffering loss from an unknown disease, which is truly an act of God, is quite different from suffering at the hands of men whose cruelty knows no bounds," she threw back. "Children are innocent for good reason. They know no enemies. But the English taught me differently."

"If I could restore your innocence, I would not hesitate to do so," Marston said. "And any other child the world may have wronged."

"But you can't," she said, "however good your intentions may be."

"Let's continue our walk," Gideon suggested uneasily, "and leave the wrongs where they belong, buried in the past."

"Those wrongs continue to this day," Gabrielle exclaimed, "or I would not be here."

"Please do not place blame where it truly doesn't belong," Marston said.

"How can I not?" she asked. "I was but a child when your countrymen came. Their leader drew his sword and pointed it at me. He had much to fear from a seven-year old girl, coward that he was."

"Such behavior is not encouraged or condoned, I assure you," Marston said.

"He filled my heart with a fear I can never forget," Gabrielle countered, her throat flushed with emotion. "Nor can I erase the sight of villages burning, of innocent people screaming in terror. And now I face captivity. All at the hands of the English." Her eyes filled with tears, though she tried hard to look stoic.

Chapter 23

Pensive after his strained outing with the Lady Gabrielle and an unnerving message he'd received from Minerva, Michael Marston picked at his evening meal in the Great Hall as he considered the witch's warnings. They were now confirmed by his scouts' reports of the barons' men to the north and a French army to the south. His greatest difficultly, as Gideon had so deftly pointed out, was knowing whom to trust while the rebellion raged. Life-long friends will became enemies, and families may take different sides. Even when the battles have ended, when the dead had been buried and the living cease to mourn, what once existed will never exist again.

"Excuse me, sire," a servant said, shaking Marston from his private thoughts. "Two travelers just arrived. One, an old druid, claims to know you from days long since passed."

Marston was suspicious. With a battle on the horizon, two strangers harkening at his door presented a risk he shouldn't take. Nevertheless, he would try to be compassionate. They could be fleeing from fighting that has already begun.

"What is his name?" Marston asked.

"The druid is Paul the Pure," the servant replied. "His daughter accompanies him. Her name is Trinity."

Marston thought for a moment. Neither were names he remembered. Paul the Pure might be an old acquaintance, but he couldn't be sure.

"They came from the west," the servant said. "But how far I cannot say."

Marston's suspicions grew stronger. "I have no recollection of father or daughter."

"You would remember her, sire," the servant said. "Her eyes are different colors, one blue, the other green."

"Why are they here?" Marston asked, trying to imagine such a trait.

"They won't say, sire. They will speak only to you."

Marston frowned. "I'll meet them in the Reception Hall."

A few minutes later, the servant led Paul the Pure and Trinity through oak double-doors etched with scenes of ships sailing through the seas. They entered the spacious room that seemed enveloped with walls of tapestries of red and gold and lavender. A large chair with legs adorned by hand-carved roses was perched in the center of the room with a heavy cushion of rich gold on its seat. Two smaller chairs sat before it.

Marston settled into his chair while the servant led the strangers across the room. Paul the Pure leaned on his cane, Trinity helping him, as they strode to where Marston sat. Their heads bowed in respect.

"We are your humble servants, sire," Paul the Pure said as he knelt, his cane serving to steady his body. His left hand held his druid's wand, tightly grasping the gnarled tip.

"Forgive our appearance, sire," said Trinity as she knelt beside him. "Our garments are torn and tattered from a journey we didn't expect."

"Sit and rest," Marston said, casting a careful gaze upon them.

"Thank you, sire," the druid said. "I am Paul the Pure, and this is my daughter Trinity."

Marston smiled faintly. "I'm told we met some years ago, but I'm afraid I don't recollect our encounter. Neither your names nor your faces are familiar, at least not as of yet."

"I'm not surprised, sire," said Paul the Pure. "It was but a brief meeting, but one I never forgot."

Marston was not convinced. "Where, may I ask, did this meeting occur?"

"At Glastonbury," said Paul the Pure. "Near the abbey, I believe."

"You have been to Glastonbury, haven't you, sire?" Trinity asked.

Marston noticed how quickly she intervened as if to lend credence to her father's claim. "I've traveled the country north to south, east to west, on many missions for the king," he said, evading the question and keeping watch of what they said and did.

"Then it easily could have been elsewhere," said Paul the Pure. "My memory is not what it once was, though I was sure it was Glastonbury or somewhere nearby."

"It's of no consequence, sire," Trinity said quickly. "A meeting you scarcely remember could have occurred at any place."

Marston noticed she controlled the conversation as if she feared Paul the Pure would say something wrong. "What made you journey so far east?" he asked, wondering why they were here now.

"Danger," Paul the Pure said softly. "Beyond what you would ever believe."

"The barons," Trinity added. "And the battle they soon will bring."

"Do they fight in Glastonbury?" Marston asked. "I received no word that fighting occurs, although I think such a battle imminent."

"They may have attempted to take Glastonbury, but we can't say for sure," Trinity said. "We fled before the barons arrived."

"And you saw no unrest while you traveled?" Marston asked, assessing the threat, the battlefield drawn on a map in his mind.

"No, sire, but that doesn't mean it didn't occur," said Paul the Pure. "If not today, the battle will begin tomorrow."

Marston hesitated, still suspicious. "Why travel here to the distant coast? Surely you could have sought refuge somewhere closer to where you came from."

"We considered boarding a ship on the western coast," Trinity replied. "But time was not our ally."

Marston was confused. "But if you'd traveled west instead of east, you would have reached the coast in hours, sparing you a journey that I'm sure took you days."

"Which is just what the barons expected," Trinity said. "And now we are at your mercy, sire."

"But I'm not sure why," Marston said cagily. "The words you speak present a puzzle, yet you offer no pieces to solve it."

"We speak the truth, sire, I assure you," Paul the Pure exclaimed.

"Tell me then why the barons wish so feverishly to find you," Marston demanded.

The pair shared a secretive glance, and then Paul the Pure spoke. "It's because we have something the barons hold dear."

Marston paused, studying the druid and his daughter who now sat so meekly before him. He sensed deception but wasn't sure what they might be hiding. "And what might that be?" he asked softly.

Trinity reached into her satchel and withdrew a golden goblet. Its gleam had long ago turned dull, discolored by untold years. She held it high, letting the light reflect off the once-lustrous metal.

"That is what the barons want?" Marston asked. "An old chalice that has lost its shine?"

"It's more than that, sire," Paul the Pure whispered with awe. "Much more."

Marston eyed the druid, perplexed by his behavior. "What is it?"

"It's the Holy Grail," Trinity said reverently as if God alone had granted her so precious a gift.

Marston stared at the chalice for a moment more. Then he shifted his gaze to the druid and his daughter. "The cup used by Christ at the Last Supper?"

"Aye, sire," Paul the Pure said, his eyes twinkling. "And the cup used to collect His holy blood when the crucifixion was over and done with."

Marston again studied the chalice. "You are certain it's the Holy Grail?" he asked. "It possesses none of the splendor that might relate the glory of God."

"We are sure, sire," Paul the Pure said solemnly. "There is no doubt."

"Why do you have the Grail?" Marston asked. "It seems it should be kept in a place of worship, somewhere close to the Lord."

"It was, sire," Trinity said. "At the abbey in Glastonbury where it's been closely guarded for three hundred years."

"But the barons sought to take it," Paul the Pure said.

"We acted more swiftly than they to keep such a treasure from them," Trinity said.

Marston didn't believe them. "If it was housed at the abbey for all to admire, why do the barons want it?"

"To sell to the highest bidder. To help fund their war," Trinity said.

Marston nodded. Such a motive seemed likely. "Do they know you've come here?"

Paul the Pure cringed, not wanting to displease his host. "They may, sire. If they followed the path we took."

Marston hesitated. "I have no desire to incur their wrath any more than I might already," he said. "Especially when I stand to reap no reward."

"But you will be rewarded, sire," Paul the Pure insisted. "I shall bid you access to my daughter's greatest gift."

Marston wasn't sure he understood. He narrowed his eyes at the old man who seemed to be offering his daughter in such a shameful manner. "But there is no service I seek."

"You misunderstand, sire," Paul the Pure said.

Trinity nodded, her eyes averting the master's. "I can see the future and all that it contains."

Chapter 24

Marston considered their proposal, a gift for which he had no need. He didn't trust the pair, but he wasn't sure why. "You must be weary from your journey," he said. "We can discuss your talent once you've known the comfort of a bed."

"Thank you, sire," Paul the Pure said humbly. "Rest has eluded us for much longer than a day."

Marston turned to the servant. "Give them quarters near the kitchen," he said, referring to rooms of lower standing used for travelers and minor dignitaries. The location of the rooms was a symbol, not so much of what the druid and his daughter were, but what they weren't.

Once they were gone, Marston considered the tale they had laid before him. The story of the Holy Grail was more myth than truth, given what most in the world now knew. It was thought to exist but believed to have been lost, hidden in the sands of the Middle East or taken to parts unknown. Tied to the legends of King Arthur, many thought Tintagel, the king's home, or Glastonbury were likely locations for where it might be kept. Others thought the chalice still lay hidden in the Holy Lands, waiting to be found.

Marston walked through the keep and out the door into the spacious courtyard between the castle's massive walls. He saw Gideon near the front gate, supervising the construction of a hoist, and he walked over to the sage to seek his counsel.

"Gideon, may we speak," he called as he approached.

"Of course, sire," Gideon said as he made his way to his master's side. He looked back at the men toiling around the contraption rather than using it to lessen their load. "Men don't understand," he said. "The purpose of a machine is to have it do the work."

Marston chuckled. "It seems strong men insist on proving their strength."

"They shall learn," Gideon said.

Marston studied the hoist. "Is that your design?"

"It is, sire."

"Your skills know no limit and are much appreciated."

"Thank you, sire," Gideon said with a nod. "How may I be of service?"

"A delicate situation has made its way to our door—at least if all that has been said is true."

Gideon studied Marston, knowing he was about to reveal something important. He leaned forward. "And what might that be?"

"We have two guests who claim to have fled from the barons."

"Who are they?"

"A druid and his daughter. They call themselves Paul the Pure and Trinity."

Gideon paused, trying to picture the pair. "What have they done that caused them to flee?"

"They claim to have the Holy Grail," Marston said.

Gideon's eyes widened. "In their possession?"

Marston nodded. "Yes, they showed it to me," he said, "although I would not have guessed from sight that it's the relic from which myths were made."

"Where did they get it?" Gideon asked.

"Glastonbury, or so they say," Marston exclaimed. "just before barons came to claim it."

Gideon seemed confused. "And why do the barons want it?"

"To help fund their effort to fight this war."

Gideon paused, pensive, his thoughts sifting through all that was known of the sacred cup. "Legend claims it may have been there."

"How would they know what the barons intended?" Marston asked. "And how were they able to take it?"

"Questions that beg a reply," Gideon agreed.

"Something is missing from the tale they tell," Marston said.

Gideon paused, considering the dilemma. "Maybe one of the barons fought in the Holy Land, found the Grail and brought it back to England."

"An explanation I also considered," Marston said.

"It could be true. Many barons fought in the Crusades."

"And Paul the Pure stole it."

"I presume," Gideon said. "Why else would they be in danger?"

"But why tell me their tale?"

"The strangest question of all," Gideon said. "I suspect to gain your trust. But why?"

"Your thoughts mirror mine," Marston said. "We have to discover the truth."

Gideon frowned. "Not an easy task, as war also knocks upon our door."

"The only truth we've discussed, given what we know," Marston said. "As mysterious as the barons' intent in bringing battle to the land, there's still more mystery wrapped around our guests."

"And what else could there possibly be?"

"The daughter claims she has the power to see the future."

Gideon chuckled. "A claim made by many but accomplished by few. I suspect her past would interest us more."

Marston laughed. "So it would seem, at least to me."

"I'm more concerned with the barons and all they may do."

"We know they're a threat," Marston said. "But revenge and revolt combined may be more than we can bear."

"The druid's story is suspect," Gideon said, considering all aspects of what they might face. "And we know nothing of the daughter."

"I can grant them sanctuary, but since an attack may come in days or less, they would be wise to flee."

101

"Which makes me think they have reason not to."

Marston considered the words of his advisor, always wise, always intuitive. "What could it be?"

"I know not their purpose, but they undoubtedly have one," Gideon said, "Holy Grail or not."

"Maybe we should test her," Marston said. "To see how strong her powers are."

"Assuming she has any."

"I can easily determine if she is a fraud," Marston said, thinking of Minerva. "I need only ask."

"Perhaps," Gideon said. "But you may not have to. I don't believe they speak the truth."

"It would be quite a risk to lie," Marston exclaimed, "when frauds are so easily exposed."

"Let me see what I can find," Gideon said. "We have scouts just returned from the west. They may know more of what these strangers have claimed."

"And what of the Holy Grail?"

Gideon smiled. "What better home could it have than Marston Castle?"

Chapter 25

"Set your doll down in the grass," Gabrielle said to Maud, Captain Carney's daughter. They stood in an open expanse beyond the clamor of the bailey, tossing a ball back and forth between them. "Then you can catch the ball."

Maud put her clay doll down on the ground. "She can watch us play."

Gabrielle tossed the ball, jute fabric stuffed with grain, and Maud struggled to catch it. She wrapped her hands around it but didn't close them quickly enough, and the ball fell to the ground.

"Throw it to me," Gabrielle said.

Maud took the ball in her right hand and threw it harder than need be and slightly askew.

Gabrielle moved quickly to her left and caught it. "What's your doll's name?"

"Rose," Maud said. "Like the flower."

"That's a pretty name," Gabrielle said, "for such a pretty doll." She tossed the ball gently in an arc.

Maud caught the ball, using both hands. "I did it!"

"I knew you could do it with barely a try," Gabrielle said, her heart warming at the sight of the little girl's smile, again reminded of her sister.

"Maybe Rose can catch one, too," Maud said.

"Are you enjoying the morning?" Michael Marston asked as he approached.

Gabrielle turned to face him. "I am," she said. "Good morning, sire. Maud was teaching me how to play catch." She tossed the ball once more to the little girl.

"Maud, time for your chores," Mrs. Carney called from the front door of their home.

"I have to go," Maud said as she picked up her doll. "But we can play later."

"There is nothing else I'd rather do," Gabrielle said.

"Are you finding your stay comfortable?" Marston asked as Maud scurried away.

"As well as it can be," Gabrielle said.

"If there's anything you may need, you have only to ask."

"Thank you," Gabrielle said. "I do appreciate all that you do. Especially for someone who would rather be anywhere else in the world."

Marston nodded. "I understand," he said. "Your capture is a wrong that will be righted as soon as it can be done."

"I should hope so," she said, having heard Marston make such a promise before.

He hesitated, reluctant to proceed. After a moment, he spoke. "May I ask a question? It concerns a number of books you might have read."

She looked at him curiously, wondering what he might what to know. "Yes, of course," she replied. "Books are my greatest passion. And there's little I would not discuss."

"Do you have any knowledge of the Holy Grail?"

"I do," she said with a smile. "More than you might be willing to hear."

"Enlighten me, please, with all that you know."

She paused, collecting her thoughts. "The tale was told by word of mouth, passed through generations," she said. "But thirty years ago, it was captured in verse in "The Story of the Grail." A second work followed, Joseph d'Arimathie."

"Do you believe it exists?"

"I do," she said. "For many reasons."

"It's the cup that held the blood of Christ?"

"It is," she said. "Confirmed by more than one account."

"Or perhaps a legend described in two tales."

"It's much more," she said. "It's a tale that's been told through the ages and confirmed by Crusaders."

"You've read both of these books?"

"I have, sire," she said. "And I've spoken to nuns from southwest France who stayed for a time at our convent. The Grail was taken there first before its journey could again resume."

Marston found the story compelling. "Where is the Grail now?"

"It was supposedly brought to Glastonbury and buried upon the hill. The rain runs red upon the soil because it carries the blood of Christ."

Marston studied Gabrielle for a moment, gauging her conviction. "A traveler who came to the castle claims to have the Grail."

"From where did he come?"

"Glastonbury."

"His tale could very well be true."

He was quiet for a moment, digesting all she had said. "We'll speak more of this later," he said, turning to go.

"It would please me to discuss it further," she said. Rarely was she recognized for her knowledge. Her beauty seemed always to supersede it.

Marston paused and turned to face her. "Where would you put the Grail if you had it?"

"At my convent in Normandy," she said with no hesitation. "No better home exists."

Chapter 26

Michael Marston journeyed through the crooked corridor that descended into the bowels of the castle. When he reached the stream that trickled through the cavern, he paused, looking for the witch whose realm he was about to breach.

"Minerva," he called.

All was quiet save for the riffling of the water meandering through the cave. A toad croaked from some unseen corner, and a black snake slithered through the rocks, narrowly missing the toe of his boot. He looked at the altar cloaked in darkness, enshrined in mist, a dim light coming from the faint glow cast by the crystals that adorned it. He peered into the darkness, down the corridors that cut through the rock and traveled, but saw nothing, no shapes or shadows to hint the witch might be somewhere nearby.

"Minerva!"

Still there was no reply. Marston waited a moment more, his eyes almost accustomed to the darkness. He scanned the cave in all directions but saw nothing still and assumed the witch was gone, lost in one of the many corridors that led to the gates of Hell.

He turned to go, and there was Minerva, just behind him, a twinkle in her eye.

"Minerva!" he said, startled. "When did you come in?"

"I've been here all the while."

"Why didn't I see you?" he asked, angry at the tricks she played.

"You see only what you want to see. And nothing more it seems."

"That may be true, or it might not," he said, annoyed he let her bother him.

The witch looked at Marston closely, cast a crooked smile, raised her hand, and gently wiped it across his brow. "You seek advice, sire?"

"I have many questions," he said, pulling away, wondering why she always managed to lay her hands upon him. Did she collect fragments of his person—sweat, hair, threads from his clothes—that then found a home in her bubbling brews? He dismissed the thought. Whatever the answer, he didn't want to know it.

"Then come with me," she said. "And we'll see what the future holds."

She led him across the stream to the circle around her altar. He stopped at the edge of the circumference, as he always did, not wanting to know what lay beyond.

Watching him intently, she smiled. "So brave yet so fearful."

"Tell me about the Holy Grail," he said. He had no interest in anything else.

"Shouldn't you be telling me?" she asked.

Marston bristled, annoyed that the answer to each of his questions would be posed before he'd asked it. But that's the power a witch possessed. "A druid arrived with his daughter," he said. "They seek sanctuary at the castle."

"From whom do they flee?"

"The barons."

Minerva moved to her cauldron, waving a hand across the top, muttering as she did so. Seconds later a mist began to form, drifting lazily into the voids above.

"The barons are many," she said. "Two dozen or more."

"The druid claims the barons come because they have the Holy Grail."

"Do they?" she asked, prompting him to solve the problem he had posed.

"They have an old chalice, hardly remarkable."

"The Holy Grail is remarkable for what it held, not for what it looks like."

He paused. It wasn't the answer he'd expected. "Do they have the Holy Grail?"

"They claim to," she said. "Why should that claim be false?"

"And they took it from the barons?" he asked.

"They came from a place much closer than then one they claim to hail from."

Marston was confused. "Did they take the Grail from the barons in Glastonbury?"

"The barons know nothing of the Holy Grail," she said. "All except for one, that is."

"Where, then, did it come from?" he asked, perplexed.

Scattered about the altar lay the vials and pouches containing the makings of her potions, predictions, and spells. From these mysterious mixtures, t she weaved her webs, finding answers to unanswerable questions, defeating all her foes.

Into the hissing cauldron, she dropped a pinch of powder and a dash of herbs, added drops of purple fluid and slivers from a stone. She spit into the brew at least three times, and a steamy fog issued from the pot, drifting to the top of the cave. Then she dropped three butterfly wings into the mix and watched while it burped and bubbled. Closing her eyes, she began to chant.

"Lost, controlled,

Tricked, confused,

Twisted thoughts,

And deeds abused.

Troubled mind

And broken heart,

Shattered dreams

That drift apart."

After repeating the chant thirteen times as she stared into the cauldron's contents, Minerva stopped abruptly, muttered no more, and quickly turned to face Marston. "The Holy Grail came to this land in the hands of an ancient knight. It was taken during the last Crusade."

"Is the true Grail within the confines of this castle?" he asked, unable to believe what he heard.

"It is," she said. "And meant to be. For what better place is there for it?"

"The druid speaks the truth?" he muttered, truly amazed.

"The man is not a druid, and the woman is not his daughter."

"Does she have powers?" he asked. "Or does she only pretend to see what can't be seen?"

"She's not a witch, but she does possess the second sight. For now, that is all that you need to know."

He paused, Minerva's words weighing heavily upon him. "Do they pose a threat to the castle?"

She left the confines of the sacred circle, advancing toward him as if she floated across the floor. "They pose a threat to England," she said. "And they pose a threat to you."

"Tell me more," he demanded, knowing he faced danger.

The witch came close and leaned toward her master. "You face many threats, sire—the druid and his companion, the barons and their army, the French and the rewards they hope to reap. But none could ever match you. Except," she whispered in his ear, "the one with auburn hair."

Chapter 27

The French made camp on the southern edge of the forest, a few miles from the castle and north of the wharf on which they had landed. The rolling plain, elevated a hundred feet above the shore, offered a generous view of the sea spilling beyond to the coast of Normandy, the sunlight twinkling on the waves as they washed ashore. The beach below the cliff was barren, the sand laced with pebbles and stones, once mighty boulders that nature had whittled away at as years had gone by.

Montague, Piers, Jamet and a handful of soldiers made their way through the forest and stood at its edge. Still sheltered by trees and shrubs, they took stock of the fortress sprawled beyond. The majestic castle, spreading along the rolling landscape between two groves of trees, its entrance to the west, faced the English countryside from its position on a cliff two hundred feet above the swirling sea. The towers seemed to touch the clouds.

"An impressive sight," Piers muttered with the full scale of the fortress now in view.

"Far larger than expected," Jamet admitted.

Montague studied the construction, the extensive length of the curtain walls reinforced by central towers and pilasters, and compared the design to the cathedrals he had built, searching for a weakness his men could exploit. "It's finely built," he said. "A deterrent to any attacker."

"We've barely enough men to stage a siege if we were to surround the entire castle," Pierre predicted.

"The barons' men are to the north," Jamet reminded them. "An army larger than ours."

"Who commands them?" Montague asked.

"James the Bold," Jamet replied. "No stranger to Normandy."

Montague knew the name, but not the face. "A man I may have faced in battle."

"Whom now you fight beside," Jamet said.

Montague nodded, bewildered by the ways of war. Enemies one year became allies the next. Wars were waged, won or lost at the expense of the dead and defeated, but forgotten, it seemed, as the seasons went by. The price paid in human suffering meant nothing to those in power, the privileged few who controlled the world, moving men on the battlefield like pawns on a chessboard. A sustainable peace seemed out of reach, but if Montague won all the battles, he could then end all the wars. It was a dream he knew could never come true, but it gave him hope to dream it.

"The fight will be bitter," Jamet said, "but that shall make victory all the sweeter."

Montague was not impressed by his comment. He wondered if Jamet had ever killed a man. If he had, he might not speak so confidently about the horrors incurred in winning war.

"When are you to meet this James the Bold?" Piers asked Jamet.

"As soon as his message is received. He knows we've arrived, I'm sure."

"As do those within the castle walls," Montague muttered.

"We'll likely attack from the south," Jamet said, "while the barons' army attacks from the north."

Montague continued his assessment of the fortress, his gaze shifting from tower to each of the curtain walls and then back to the towers. "Many men will die," he said.

"That will depend upon how the battle is waged," Jamet offered.

"For me, there is only one tactic," Montague said, "and that is one that ensures the least lives are lost."

"The method you use is yours to define as long as you succeed." Jamet eyed the commander sternly. "Just as King Philip expects."

Montague didn't like being reminded of the condition the king had placed upon his engagement to Gabrielle. But he didn't reply. He paused for a moment as he considered how best to stage an attack as he observed Jamet gazing smugly across the plain. "What do you think would be most effective?" Montague asked him.

"Catapults, siege towers—the typical workhorses of war," Jamet said.

Montague imagined catapults flinging boulders at the walls, masonry cracking and stones beginning to fall, bundles of burning brush arcing through the sky, the village within the castle catching fire, innocent people darting about, trying to save their homes. The siege towers would have to be rolled into position against the walls so his men could scale them, climbing over the battlements to attack the castle's defenders. It would be complete chaos and pandemonium, as in all wars.

"What about digging tunnels to destroy the foundation?" Piers asked.

"It takes too much time," Jamet said.

"So does a siege, but we may have no choice," Montague said. "Many a life will be lost if we choose an open offensive over starvation."

"A siege is one of many options," Jamet said.

Montague grew more and more pensive as he surveyed the castle. "The fortress boasts an excellent design, avoiding errors I've often seen made like square towers instead of round. If I commanded the castle, I would fear no enemy."

"But you are not its commander," Jamet said.

"And we don't know how many souls defend the fortress," Montague continued. "Their number could be many, or it could be very few."

"The first wave of attacks will tell," Jamet said.

In his mind's eye, Montague surveyed another battle he didn't want to fight. "How large is the force the barons' men command?"

Jamet thought for a moment. "I'm told it's larger than ours, perhaps twice the size."

Montague turned to Piers. "How many men are we?"

"A thousand, twelve hundred at most."

Despite his misgivings, Montague knew it was time to prepare. "Have the men construct two catapults," he said. "At least for the initial attacks."

"And we'll stage boulders to fling at the fortress," Piers said.

"We should save animal carcasses, too," Jamet said.

"For what purpose?" Montague asked though he feared the answer.

"To toss them over the castle walls," Jamet replied.

"Why would we do that?" Montague asked.

"To spread disease," Jamet said as if his answer were obvious.

Montague hesitated, visions of sickened children who didn't deserve to die flooding his thoughts. "Not the most honorable way to wage war."

"The victors decide what is honor," Jamet said coldly, "while those defeated simply die."

Chapter 28

James the Bold watched as one of his captains led the Frenchman into his camp, his pale blue tunic so different from the green worn by the barons' men. He wondered if he had faced him during the Normandy campaigns or if the man had fought his battles from the comfort of King Philip's court.

"James the Bold," the messenger said, "this is Jamet, our French liaison."

"I've heard much about you," Jamet said, nodding in greeting.

"Not all words spoken turn out to be true," remarked James the Bold.

"Be that as it may, you're respected by friend and foe alike."

James the Bold nodded, still assessing the Frenchman, a young, intelligent man who had, no doubt, studied military tactics. I wonder if Jamet has ever led men in battle, borne the brunt of a sword, or taken an arrow in his flesh. It doesn't seem as if he has.

"Our forces have made camp on the other edge of the forest, south of the castle walls," Jamet said.

"Have you looked at the fortress closely, or have you only surveyed it from afar?"

"We have studied it from the forest's boundary and all its southern approaches."

"And what is your assessment?" asked James the Bold.

Jamet paused, perhaps reflecting on his discussion with Montague. "The castle is better built than expected."

"Sometimes the house isn't important," James the Bold said. "What matters is who lives in it."

"I'm told Michael Marston is a formidable foe."

James the Bold shrugged. "He once was," he said. "But many years have passed. I suspect there's now a shadow where the great man once stood."

Jamet hesitated, afraid to offend the warlord. "Sometimes the mind makes the man, not the muscle," he offered cautiously.

James the Bold considered his statement but then discounted it. "No matter the makings of his reputation, a powerful name only frightens those who seek reasons to be afraid," he said. He studied Jamet for a moment, his face chiseled and scarred. "I fear nothing. Michael Marston is no match for me."

"I suspect few are," Jamet said with just a hint of disdain.

"I should command the entire force the barons field," James the Bold continued. "And after I take this castle, I suspect I will control every man of arms in every corner of England."

Jamet hesitated, but then said, "And we'll all be better for it, I'm sure."

"How many are the French?"

"A thousand, maybe more."

James the Bold considered the size of the French forces, just over half that of his own. He didn't know how many stood behind the castle walls, but he knew his force was comprised of strong, disciplined soldiers who hungered for the plunder victory would bring. The attack would be successful. He was sure of it.

Jamet studied the man who continued to study him. "What is our strategy?"

"We'll surround the castle for three days' time to allow the extent of our forces to be seen."

"Surely Marston's scouts know our number," Jamet said. "Why would we wait?"

"I have more reasons than one," James the Bold replied flatly. "Don't assume a delay is a sign we're not intent on waging war."

"We should strike before they're fully prepared."

"You'll know when the time is right, and I'll make sure you do."

"As you wish," Jamet said with a gracious nod. "But we shall pay a substantial price when we finally do attack, as I'm sure you understand."

"Battles are fought in different ways," said James the Bold. "And for now, that is all you need to know."

Jamet paused, considering the risk. "A siege would be most practical."

"Such a tactic might take months to prove worthwhile."

"We could bypass the castle," Jamet suggested. "Conquer England while the fortress withers like a grape on a vine."

James the Bold turned to look at his companion, a scowl on his face. "Or we could destroy them--quickly and savagely."

"How do you propose to meet that end?"

"First I will rain burning arrows down upon them.".

"To set fire to the village within?"

"We will kill as many women and children as we possibly can before the battle begins. And the men will lose their will to fight."

Chapter 29

Soldiers loyal to the barons' cause continued to pour in from the farthest reaches of the country, assembling at the far edge of the forest some distance from the plain that led to the castle. Most were eager to serve James the Bold, a warrior known never to have tasted defeat, destroying every enemy he'd faced and showing no mercy. Some had served with him before in battles on the Normandy coast. Others knew him by reputation and came to fight for "a man with no equal." The newly arrived masses joined the others, making camp on the field that marked the forest's edge, their tents and supplies spread across the plain that stretched to the edge of the cliff.

Blaise, the warlock, eyed the encampment, watching as the number of men in his master's command exceeded two thousand, all of them ready for war, determined to overthrow the king. Moving away from the main camp and into the forest where a moss carpet crept skyward upon the rocks that littered the forest floor, he could hear the ocean at the base of the cliff, waves battering the beach and then fading away. It was tranquil, with only the sounds of the forest—birds and owls and scampering squirrels—and the growing camp in the distance, groups of men swapping tales around the fires they'd built to cook their meals.

Blaise preferred to keep his distance from others, and most men avoided him, frightened by the very sight of him, believing he was not a mere mortal, though they didn't know what he was. He looked different, his black eyes unnerving, and acted in ways they could not understand, a combination which led them to believe he probably spoke to the Devil. At least that's what Blaise overheard when their voices whispered on the wind.

The warlock set up his own camp on the moss, a stream nearby for water. He knew that on the other side of the forest, on the far side of an open plain, stood the castle walls, and he sat for a moment, thinking of the battle about to begin. He waited, making sure none of the others ventured too close, and sat quietly, enjoying nature's gifts.

Away from prying eyes, Blaise grabbed a leather satchel he had laid upon the moss. Rooting through his store of powerful herbs, his vials and stones, he withdrew a long, narrow pouch and emptied its contents—dozens of slender sticks, each about eight inches long—onto the moss. He took up the sticks, which numbered near fifty, and filtered them through his fingers, gently clenching them. Closing his eyes, he let his head fall back, absorbing the energy sent from the sun. Then he rolled the sticks through his fingers and tossed them into the air. They fell to the ground in a scattered heap, overlapping and eluding each other, a few stray sticks landing apart from the rest.

He studied the way the sticks arranged themselves, the compass direction each now faced, and the angles they formed. Moving his hand over them, slowly slicing through empty air, He closed his eyes and muttered a chant known throughout the ages in a tongue that hadn't been spoken in hundreds of years. The warlock opened his eyes and reached for his knapsack, searching through its contents. He removed a pouch and untied the string that held it closed, withdrawing just a pinch of green powder, and sprinkled it over the sticks. Next, he withdrew a vial from a pocket within his robe and sprinkled drops of a yellow liquid upon the sticks. Seconds later, a blue mist formed and hung hazily above them.

Blaise's face transformed into a mask of concentration as he waved his hands about the fog, continuing to chant in the same ancient tongue. Ever so slowly the haze faded, drifting away with the wind that blew in from the sea.

Silent and brooding, he studied the heap in the greatest detail, observing each stick's position as well as the pattern they collectively formed. From the scattered stack he'd enhanced with powder and liquid and the blue mist that swirled upon the wind came an image of the castle. It rolled back and forth, left to right, revealing each of the fortress's sides and what lay within. Blaise noted the position of Marston's men and a catapult they had built in the bailey. He saw the strength of the keep, the thickness of the walls, the structure of the towers. The vision also revealed the people who lived within the castle, including the men who commanded the army—Gideon, Captain Carney, Sir Michael Marston. Blaise also saw soldiers and livestock, weapons and supplies.

And deep within the bowels of the fortress, he could see Minerva.

Chapter 30

Dinner was always served in the Great Hall. On occasion the room was full, barely an empty seat at any table, as Michael Marston was fond of inviting many of the people who resided within the confines of the castle to dine with him. At other times, Marston ate alone or with Gideon or Captain Carney. Gabrielle had dined with Marston and Gideon begrudgingly at first, and she had only been at the castle a few days when summoned once more to dinner. But when she entered the Great Hall, she found a table set only for two.

She was always overcome by the vastness of the room, its rich, dark paneled beams accenting the stone walls, graceful arches supporting the ceiling, and only a series of narrow windows providing air and light. The long table that dominated the center of the room, capable of seating sixty guests, was built of the finest English oak. Strong and steadfast, it was a symbol of the master and the nation he served.

When Marston entered the hall, Gabrielle was waiting awkwardly at the fireside, a tiny figure swallowed by the room. She stood beside the open hearth large enough to cook a hog on a spit as was the custom when the master held large celebrations.

She turned to greet him, nodding respectfully and offering a slight curtsey. "Sire."

"I trust you enjoyed your first few days at the castle," he said. "I thought it best to give you privacy and let you wander around at will."

"Thank you, sire," Gabrielle said warily. She was still uncomfortable in his presence, all too aware the controlled her destiny whether she wanted to admit it or not.

"You've made a friend in little Maud," he said.

Gabrielle smiled. "She's a delightful child. I make a point to see her every day."

"I'm sure she appreciates having a playmate."

"No more than I am, I'm sure."

Marston paused, studying his guest as if seeing her through different eyes. "I'm grateful for the information you gave me on the Grail."

Gabrielle felt herself blush, but she wasn't sure why. "It was nothing."

"But it was," he said. "And I'm sure there is much more I could learn from you."

"Likewise," she said without thinking. She chastised herself for having encouraged him, offering a friendship she didn't want or need, or suggesting something more.

"I think you'll enjoy England even if your stay is brief," he said when he noticed she was anxious. "For I promise to return you to both the man and land you love."

"A day which can't come soon enough."

"I understand," he said, not willing to argue. "But England is a beautiful country with dramatic scenery."

"As is France," she replied, wanting him to know that, no matter how beautiful England might be, it would never compare to her home.

"The sea gets angry at times," he said, ignoring her comment, "with powerful waves that wash all sorts of treasures onto the shore from remnants of once-proud ships to dead fish."

Gabrielle smiled but offered no reply. Even though his politeness was endearing, and she suspected he would treat her well, she didn't want to be at Marston Castle. The sooner he understood that, the better it would be for both of them.

"I seem to find more dead fish than long lost treasures," he added, trying to make a joke.

Gabrielle considered her captor. What was it that he wanted with her if he wanted her at all? Did he find the situation as awkward as she did? Would he let her go back to Normandy as he'd promised? Or was she now his property? He knew her heart belonged to another, and, surely, he would not violate the scared bond that tied her to Montague—at least for now.

"Forgive me if I ramble," he said. "I'm not accustomed to guests who are ladies."

She smiled. "You're not rambling, my lord."

"It's just been many years since a woman as beautiful as you has dined alone with me."

Gabrielle looked askance into the flames. "Thank you, sire," she said. "That's very kind." She was impressed by his sincerity, touched by his sadness. He must have loved his wife deeply. The pain he felt echoed in every word he spoke.

"Let's prepare for dinner," he said, his eyes coming alive, a smile forming on his face.

He led her to the table, pulled back her chair, and, after she was seated, helped edge her forward. He sat down across from her as a servant, a staid older man who wore a gray tunic and white moustache, appeared with a decanter of wine and filled their goblets.

"I've wanted to share some of the realm's bounty with you," he said, raising his glass. "The castle and the community it serves are self-sufficient. In the fields beyond the walls, we grow all of our grain, the nearby farms provide cattle and pigs. The sea offers a variety of fish. There are probably thirty servants, dozens of farmers, and, as you've seen, a blacksmith, tanner, fishmonger, barber, potters, bakers, and a seamstress, all of whom provide the basic necessities of life as well as many of its luxuries."

Gabrielle thought about Montague and the life she'd left behind. "Montague's chateau is much the same," she said, "But smaller in scale and purpose. I love it more than any castle, and if your eyes could see it, you would, too."

"More even than the chambers in Paris, used by all who grace the court?" he asked, appearing somewhat amused.

She smiled, knowing he teased. "I may be biased because I shared the chateau with the man I love. And I only hope to see it again."

"And in time, I'm sure you will," he said tersely.

Noticing his jaw had clenched, she didn't want to offend him. "But your castle is very beautiful, too," she said. "How many soldiers are housed here?"

"About a thousand," he said. "And their families. Their quarters are in the towers and the buildings that flank the castle walls."

The servant brought their meal, roast lamb and turnips served with a dense brown bread. Marston, who likely dined alone more often than not, seemed to enjoy her company.

"Normandy and England are very much alike—the windswept coastline, the bountiful countryside, the majestic cliffs that crown the shore," he continued. "Especially Cornwall, which has some of the most dramatic scenery, and is much like some of the Normandy coast."

"I haven't seen much of the country, sire. I was taken here directly from the ship."

"It was for your own safety, I'm sure," he said. "Perhaps someday you'll see more."

"Perhaps," she said, lifting her goblet to her lips.

He watched her for a moment. "I know you miss your home," he said almost apologetically

She nodded, smiled weakly, and again thought of Montague. She wondered where he might be. Hidden in a Norman forest, preparing to fight the English, perhaps? If he only knew where she was, he would come to save her. But it might be years before the king released him from his duties, and longer still before he found her. There was no telling where she might be by then.

"You're learned and well read," Marston exclaimed, jarring Gabrielle from her innermost thoughts. "A fact you've already proven."

"Books are my closest friend," she said and then added, "excepting Montague."

"Knowledge fascinates me," Marston went on as if he hadn't heard her lover's name. "Its power, the freedom it affords. Knowledge gives the mind the ability to go where the body might never travel."

"We may have much in common, sire," Gabrielle replied, impressed by the man and his thoughts.

"I think we do," he said. "And in time you'll feel more comfortable here. With me."

"Yes, I'm sure I will," she said tentatively but she felt nauseated at the thought of Marston Castle becoming anything more than a memory. She considered mentioning an exchange—

he could trade her for an English prisoner in France—but she thought it not the time or place. Perhaps someday soon.

"I want you to have every comfort you enjoyed in France," Marston said. "So I've arranged for the seamstress to visit you in the morning."

"Thank you, sire. I have little clothing with me."

"I've instructed her to create five different ensembles and all the accessories," he said, "as well as one gown, strictly for entertaining."

"Whatever will I do with five sets of clothes?" Gabrielle asked even though she had many more in France. Marston's offer made her stay seem permanent—a future she could not bear.

"Enjoy them," he said. "Only a small token of our friendship."

Gabrielle nodded cautiously. Marston was polite and attentive, in every way a gentleman, but was it a charade? Was he laying a trap to earn her trust only to change like day to night? She held his gaze, searching for any sign of deception. Was the man before her the man he would always be?

When dinner ended, Marston stood and helped Gabrielle to her feet. "I enjoyed our time together," he said softly.

"As have I," she responded, regretting it the moment the words left her mouth.

She bowed and left the Great Hall, climbing the spiral staircase that led to her quarters on the upper floor. She was no longer afraid to move about the castle on her own. No harm would come to her--she didn't think Marston would permit it. But she was terribly lonely, loving a man she couldn't see and might never see again.

She paused on the stairs. All was quiet. She could slip out the servants' entrance to the kitchen and into the bailey, find a way beyond the castle walls, but she didn't know whether or not to try to escape. No one guarded her, but what would she do if she succeeded? She would have to find someone to take her back to France, and that seemed unlikely. If Marston continued to treat her as he would a distinguished guest, there might be no reason to flee, and Montague would surely find the trail that led to the castle. Maybe it was more prudent to wait until she was rescued or ransomed. Slipping into her bedchamber, she settled

124

onto the settee before the fire, no longer as anxious nor as afraid. Marston seemed to hold her with the highest respect and esteem.

But she didn't understand why.

Chapter 31

In the darkness before dawn, those eerie hours meant for neither the living nor the dead, soldiers paced the curtain walls, manned the towers, and scanned the plains surrounding the castle, searching for signs of an imminent attack. The remainder of souls within the walls slept more or less soundly, though some tossed and turned, the upcoming battle weighing heavily upon them.

Minerva crept through the crooked corridors hidden in the walls. Carved by nature and enhanced by man, the corridors crawled through the keep, three of the four towers, and throughout the rocky cliff upon which the castle had been built. Most of the passages were known to her alone, some to the master, but none of the other people who walked above and around them knew of their existence. Minerva used these secret corridors as personal roads to not only travel throughout the castle, but also to avoid the gaze of a people who would tremble at the sight of her.

Branching off the corridor that led to Michael Marston's room was another narrow hallway dimly lit by an occasional crystal. It was barely wide enough to accommodate Minerva's slim frame, and she had to stoop to pass from one side to the other, her hand on the wall to steady herself. When she came to the end of the corridor, she reached for a metal lever just above her knee and unlatched it. On the opposite side of the wall, a narrow slab of stone, barely twenty inches wide and adjacent to a fireplace, slid out into a room. Minerva stepped through the void it created cloaked in darkness, only a faint glow of moonlight passing through the window beyond.

The witch paused, searching the room with eyes that somehow saw what others could not, studying all it contained. Across from the fireplace sat the bed which was ensconced in crimson curtains on three sides and open to the heat from the flames on the fourth. Three steps led to the mattress where the Lady Gabrielle lay sleeping.

Minerva slid across the room, pausing when Gabrielle shifted and turned onto her side. The witch glanced in all directions, ensuring no one and nothing watched her as she studied the lady lying in bed. She took a step closer then froze, turning her head abruptly toward the hearth, the slightest motion attracting her attention. She crouched at the fireside, studying what seemed to be but a stone, her bony fingers darting forward and grabbing a spider before it could scurry away. She picked it up, holding it close to her face to examine the legs that sprawled from its body and the tiny fangs that foamed, eagerly searching for prey. When she was satisfied it was a creature she could use for a spell, she stuck it in the folds of her robe. It would stay there until she got back to her cave and put it in one of her vials, safe and secure until she needed it for one of her many potions.

Slowly, Minerva got to her feet, her attention focused once more on the Lady Gabrielle. She waited, watching her curiously, and then moved stealthily toward her. She climbed up the steps and stood at the foot of the bed, hovering over the sleeping body, eyeing her closely—auburn hair, flawless skin, a few freckles that would have marred any but her perfect face. She extended a crooked finger to gently caress the beauty's cheek.

The Lady Gabrielle moved not at all. She sighed, still lying on her side, facing the curtain that enveloped the bedstead so securely. Perhaps she dreamed, her loyal Montague by her side, the pair walking the rooms of his chateau in Rouen. Or perhaps she battled a nightmare, stuck in an English castle she had no desire to visit, let alone remain within, kept a prisoner for days ahead that, it seemed, would never end. But as Minerva lightly caressed her cheek, she made no further sound, nor did she stir, so deep was the dream she chased, the nightmare she eluded.

After a few seconds, the witch turned away and crept across the room to the alcove where Gabrielle's satchels sat upon the row of shelves. She moved those that hid the ingredients Gabrielle used for healing, eyeing every pouch and vial, running her hands across and around them to feel the power their contents contained.

Once she'd examined all the stores the Lady Gabrielle possessed, Minerva turned to the chests that sat beside the bed. She ran her hands over them, her eyes now tightly closed, visualizing the garments within. The clothing was practical, nothing more, the frocks far from the splendor of the gowns she had known. Minerva imagined the life Gabrielle had lived, a stark contrast to the days she currently kept as a captive.

The witch moved to the table against the wall and took up a hairbrush. She held it high, capturing a faint glow from the moon that trickled through the window, and picked auburn hairs from the bristles. She rubbed them between her forefinger and thumb, moved them to her nose, breathing in their sweet musk, before placing them in the folds of her robes, far away from the spider. Then she returned the brush to the table top and crept from the room, leaving the way she had come.

Chapter 32

Trinity and Paul the Pure had been given humble quarters, adjoining rooms close to the keep's kitchen with tiny windows, cramped though each contained only a bed and a table. Early on the morning of their second day, after they had unpacked and stowed their belongings, Paul the Pure came into Trinity's room.

"Do—" he said.

She grabbed his arm, a finger to her lips.

"What?" he asked, confused.

She pointed to the door. "Someone could be listening from just the other side," she whispered.

Paul the Pure looked at her with surprise and put an ear to the door. He listened for a moment and then turned to her and shrugged.

She tugged at his arm, leading him to the far side of the room.

"Be quiet," she whispered. "At least until we know we are well and truly alone."

He nodded. Spies were a threat he hadn't considered.

She glanced about the room, searching for any sign someone might be watching—a small hole in the wall or floor, anything an eye or ear could employ to learn what happened within the confines of their quarters.

Paul the Pure returned to the door. Paul placed his ear against it once more, listening for footsteps or any other sound that might prove someone was there. After a moment, he was convinced no threat existed and beckoned to Trinity.

"I think it's safe," he said.

"Speak softly," she said. "We know not where their ears might be."

"Do you think we fooled him?" he asked.

"I'm not sure," she said. "He didn't seem a man who's easily fooled."

"He thought we'd met before."

"We don't know that he did," she warned. "It would be a mistake to think we knew any of his thoughts."

Paul the Pure frowned. He didn't understand why she was being so cautious. "He gave no indication he thought it a lie."

"Which doesn't mean he didn't. I'm sure he has spies throughout the land. No doubt he's dispatched them to verify where we've been. Or where we said we've been."

"They won't find anything," he said. "We left no clues behind."

"They may find another trail—the one that leads to the Grail," Trinity exclaimed. "They might discover how it truly came into our hands."

"How could they?" he asked. "We stole it from Tweed who had long been a foe of Marston's. With him gone and his house in disarray, there's no one to tell the truth."

"Assuming Tweed is dead," she said. "We didn't take time to check. We simply fled."

"But that was days ago," he said. "We would have been pursued if he still lived."

"Who's to say we weren't? Our only hope is that all our enemies are too consumed with the coming battle to take the time to bother with us."

"I'm sure they are," he said. "The whole of the country is torn by civil war."

Trinity paused, taking stock of all that had taken place. "We still need to fear Marston," she said. "At least until it is done."

Paul the Pure shrugged. He saw no reason to worry. "I'm sure he has doubts. But he doesn't know where they lead."

"He will still try to prove we speak the truth," she said. "He'll fashion a test for me."

The druid seemed confused. "What sort of test?"

"To see if I can truly glimpse what the dawn might bring."

He scoffed. "You have the gift, and it's easy to prove."

Trinity considered the path that lay before them. "We have time to humor him," she said. "We'll refuse him nothing until it no longer matters."

"But how long can we play at this," he asked, tugging at his druid's tunic, "before we risk our reward?"

She shrugged. "A few days. A week at most."

Paul the Pure hesitated, counting the days before them. "We must be ready to meet the ship when the time arrives," he said, "or we'll never sell the Grail."

"We had best hope that Tweed isn't waiting where the ship comes to the shore."

"Tweed is not our concern," he said. "Still we must leave the castle before the barons attack."

Trinity paused, studying the face of Paul the Pure. "Only after we carry out the deed we agreed to perform."

"Yes, yes. We'll collect our money and then depart before any of these fools is the wiser."

"We must learn Marston's routine—what he does during the day, where he goes, and whom he sees. Then we'll be ready to act," Trinity exclaimed decisively.

"A new day will then dawn for England, and a tidy sum will be ours."

Chapter 33

Michael Marston eyed the entry to the Reception Hall later that morning. "They should appear shortly."

"We'll bait the hook," Gideon said, "and see if the fish is caught."

A moment later, a sentry opened the carved wooden doors, revealing two visitors awaiting entry. Paul the Pure, dressed in white robes, leaned on his cane. Trinity wore a plain gray dress, her eyes striking—one green, the other blue.

"Join us," Marston said. "Paul the Pure, druid of the west, and his daughter, Trinity, meet Gideon, my trusted advisor."

Gideon rose and bowed, eyeing the pair carefully. "We're honored by your presence."

"And we are honored by your reception," Trinity said, her gaze fixed upon the alchemist. She understood her audience. To convince Marston, she had to convince Gideon.

"We've considered your words of warning," Marston said, "and the barons' forces concern us. Our scouts claim they gather to the north to threaten our defenses."

"We, too, are troubled at such a danger when we thought it circumvented," Trinity exclaimed. "Especially after a journey that, in itself, was such a risk."

"Why come so far," Gideon asked, "when other paths were open to you?"

"Because we knew by reputation where safety could be found," Trinity said.

Marston eyed the pair warily, convinced the arresting woman who stood before him was the leader and Paul the Pure the prop. "You have my protection," he said, "and access to all the amenities the castle can offer."

Trinity breathed an audible sigh. "Our thanks to you, sire. You know not the burden we've been forced to carry."

Marston acknowledged her solemnly, although it was difficult not to smile, so dramatic was their performance. "Just be forewarned," he said. "The barons' threat is real—and they have an ally in the French."

"Who are, as we speak, establishing their camp to the south," said Gideon.

Marston paused, acting as if he thought the druid and his daughter possessed knowledge he could use. "Since you know more of their intent than we, can you tell us if they plan to attack? Or is their show of force merely a threat until the king concedes?"

Paul the Pure shrugged meekly. "I could not say, sire."

Gideon looked at them with confusion in his eyes. "But we thought you would know," he said, "having faced them in a similar fashion."

"I cannot read their thoughts," Paul the Pure said, "nor predict their deeds."

"But Trinity can," Marston said coyly, laying the trap.

Paul the Pure turned to Trinity. "Will you tell us, daughter?"

She looked at Marston warily. "I will answer the question if it's in my power to do so."

"Please," Marston said, "show us now what lies ahead, so we may know what must be done."

"Of course, sire," she said halfheartedly. "I just need a moment to prepare."

She removed a satchel from her shoulder and knelt upon the floor. From the bag she took a narrow pouch and emptied its contents—a few dozen runes, rectangular stones roughly three inches long with characters carved upon their faces—onto the floor.

Marston watched closely. He had never seen the black arts practiced in so strange a manner. He wondered how powerful her magic was if it was magic at all.

Trinity took the runes and tossed them lightly in the air. They fell to the floor in a scattered heap, a few stray runes at the edge of the pile. She withdrew a vial from the pocket of her robe and sprinkled drops of a lavender liquid onto the stack of stones. A green mist formed and hung in an eerie haze above the pile.

She waved her hands about the fog, her face drawn with concentration as she mumbled in a tongue that sounded Gaelic, but Marston couldn't say for sure. When the haze began to fade away, she focused on the runes. She stared at the stones for several minutes, deciphering their haphazard message by examining the heap in great detail, noting the position that each stone took and the patterns they formed. All the while, she never spoke. At last, she took a deep breath, rose abruptly, and turned to Marston.

"The attack will come," she said, "in forms that are hard to fathom by most."

Gideon glanced at Marston with alarm. "We had best prepare, sire."

Marston looked at the pair before him. "Thank you for your wisdom," he said, acting as if he were impressed with their powers. "I'll summon you when our plans are known."

The sentry guided Paul the Pure and Trinity back to their quarters.

Once they had gone, Gideon leaned toward Marston. "Does she have the gift?"

Marston smiled. "I think not."

Gideon nodded. "Indeed with enemy forces all around us, second sight is hardly needed to foretell what's about to occur. What have you learned from your scouts?"

"They don't speak the truth," Marston replied. "Neither the druid nor his daughter."

"What are they trying to hide?" Gideon asked.

"They flee someone who once held the Grail, but who that is we never may know."

"What do they intend to do with it?"

Marston grew pensive, considering different possibilities. "I think the treasure will soon be sold, no doubt to the highest bidder."

"We should watch them closely," Gideon said. "With the barons' forces prepared to attack, they won't be leaving the fortress, not if they hope to survive."

"We still don't know what brought them here or what it is they seek."

"Would it be prudent to learn their intentions?" Gideon asked. "Or at least make a determined attempt?"

"It is time we got answers," Marston said. "Tomorrow I'll summon Paul the Pure and speak to him alone. Let us hear what he has to say without his daughter beside him to form his thoughts and direct his tongue. And then the truth will be known."

Chapter 34

Montague sat at the edge of the forest, his back against an English oak. With a parchment and piece of charcoal, he sketched the lady he loved. He captured the hair, flowing to her shoulders, the face so flawlessly formed, but the charcoal couldn't catch the twinkle that her eyes contained. He hesitated, his drawing near completion, and reflected on all that had passed. He couldn't forgive himself for bringing her to the convent, no matter how hard he tried. What had seemed to be so safe, what had always been secure, had been nothing but a façade. And she had been whisked away to the castle that now loomed just ahead.

An hour barely passed without Gabrielle's image consuming his thoughts. The simplest pleasures they once shared seemed worth the greatest treasure: their first kiss, the sunsets they'd watched hand in hand, the first time they'd made love, the home they'd hoped to make in Rouen. Even her attentive gaze as he sketched his cathedrals, creating beauty that couldn't compare to what God had made in her, was etched in every thought and deed he needed to perform.

He knew their dilemma could be far worse, and, if nothing else, she was now held near, within a mass of mortar and stone. Half the battle had already been fought-- had found where she had been taken. But the war soon to be waged would hold her life in the balance. And no victory would ever taste sweeter than when he once again held her and felt her embrace.

Montague's thoughts were interrupted when Piers approached with Jamet. He hurriedly put his sketch in a satchel, not wanting it to be seen.

"I have word from James the Bold," Jamet informed them. "When he gives the command, we'll surround the castle, showing our full force."

Montague rose and stood beside them, the French camp on the edge of the forest, the soldiers dispersed throughout the trees. They studied the castle they were about to confront, each knowing the risks of the task before them.

"The barons' men will engage from both the north and west," Jamet continued. "The French will come from the south. With just a sliver of land between the east wall and the cliff's edge, it can support no forces."

"And then the siege begins?" Piers asked. "Or do we soon attack?"

"Future plans are yet unknown," Jamet said.

"But why would we ever wait?" Piers asked.

"James the Bold expects a signal of some sort," Jamet said. "Its source is a secret he has yet to share with me."

Montague watched the castle, the men pacing the walls. "The English know we're here. And how many we are. I wonder what plans they make."

"I suspect their commander has more plans than one," Jamet said.

Montague tried to imagine the sort of man Marston might be. Was he young or old, good or evil, selfish or kind? Was he a ferocious warrior, known throughout England for his many victories, or was he a statesman, fighting wars with words, winning battles with talk, not tactics? But, most important, what were his intentions for Gabrielle?

"What else has been said of this man we face?" Piers asked.

"I'm told he's cautious," Jamet replied, "and never seems to fail."

"He knows the castle is difficult to breach," Montague said. "He has the advantage, at least at the start."

"But the longer the battle, the less likely he'll prevail," Piers said.

Montague stared at the keep, its bulk rising above the walls, a castle within a castle, and the place where Gabrielle was most likely housed, if she was there at all. He feared for her safety but was, at that moment, powerless to help her, a plight he had never envisioned.

"What preparations have been made?" Jamet asked. "Have we determined where our catapults will be staged?"

"The curtain walls are the weakest," Montague said, "even though a buttress was built to support them."

"Should they be the focus of our assault?" Piers asked.

Montague eyed the imposing fortress that commanded the countryside. Shrouded in fog from a recent rain, it conjured a magical image that brought myths to mind. "It's the only flaw in its entire construction," he said softly.

"Then I suspect an assault will hold the most promise," Jamet said. "After the wall has been pummeled."

Montague looked at the vast open space his men must cross, each step making them easier targets for enemy archers.

"The men are anxious for battle," Piers said, "and loyal to their commander."

"Just as their commander is loyal to them," Montague said. "I only hope they realize that the man who leads is the son of the man they so revered."

"They do," Piers assured him, "and their feelings are unchanged."

Montague nodded, not sure if the claim was true. "I fear their talents are about to be tested, their courage about to be tried, for they face a foe who is also highly regarded, if legend speaks the truth."

"They welcome the challenge," Piers said. "As do I."

"But if Marston is the warlord they claim him to be," Jamet said, "I suspect they are more than prepared."

"And we best be, too," Montague warned. "Or we'll pay with the blood of our men."

Chapter 35

Once Jamet had gone, returning to the camp of James the Bold, Montague knew he needed counsel of a kind that Piers could not provide. He had to know where Gabrielle was, had to see inside the castle, and that would require a skill only Alaric possessed.

He reached into the pocket of his tunic and withdrew the pouch the wizard had given him. The leather twine that bound it shut was as taut as the day he'd received it. He assumed it housed a mysterious powder and had no desire to know what it was, for whatever the wizard used to bridge the sea or glimpse what a fortnight would bring should remain known to him alone.

Montague began to make his way through the woods, and sentries tried to follow, but he convinced them he wasn't going far and would alert them if he faced danger. Reluctantly they retreated, but still they remained nearby. Montague moved through the underbrush, the trees flanking him both straight and tall, their branches forming a dense canopy that hid the ground from the sun. He found a narrow stream, cold water trickling over the stones, and he sat in the moss beside it. He could see his guards in the distance, ensuring he was safe but staying away to give him the privacy he'd requested. Recalling Alaric's direction, he stared at the water, the pouch in his palm.

"Alaric," he whispered, as he studied the course of the stream.

The morning was quiet, marred only by the faint chatter of birds and squirrels that darted about the forest and the soft shifting of branches in the wind. In the distance he heard an owl hoot, as if it asked his identity. He could see the bird's outline in a far-off birch, his eyes trained on Montague. It was almost as if he knew the commander was about to practice witchcraft, and he would bear witness to ensure it was done as required.

"Alaric," Montague said louder.

The wizard's image appeared. His white hair spilled onto his shoulders and robe as his image shimmered in the water.. "I'm here, sire," Alaric said, his voice hoarse and distant.

"I need your help."

"Anything you wish shall be granted."

Montague turned, ensuring the sentries were still a safe distance away. "Is Gabrielle in Marston Castle?" he asked. "I need to know for certain."

Alaric looked into Montague's eyes. He could see, for the very first time, the shadow of fear in his image. "She is," he replied.

Montague sighed with relief. "At least I've found her. And as soon as the time is right, I must attempt a rescue."

"No. Such an effort is the least of your concerns, based on what is now before you."

Montague studied the hazy image, wondering what the wizard knew that he did not. "An attack will come ... I know not when. And the battle could put her in danger."

"Even if you remain where you are, the barons' men will attack. And the havoc they shall wreak may turn many to few, day to night."

Montague wasn't sure what it was that the wizard implied, but he knew the battle could be horrendous by the time it ended. Still, his only concern was Gabrielle. "How can I prevent the battle from ever reaching her?"

Alaric paused. The wrinkles in his face seemed deeper in the tumbling water, an ancient man who seemed even older when viewed through this magical lens. "Some deeds are meant to never be performed."

Montague frowned, not expecting the reply. "Then she must be rescued. Is there a way that I might find?"

"Through the door that cannot be seen," Alaric said.

Montague was growing weary of the wizard's riddles. "The castle is strong. I know as much with only a glance."

"And so are the men within it."

"Where might Gabrielle now be?"

"She's in the keep near Michael Marston, master of the manor."

"Has she been harmed?"

"No," Alaric said. "Not a hair on her head has ever been touched."

"Are you sure?" Montague asked, ready to kill whoever violated his beloved, even if he died while trying to avenge her.

"She's treated with kindness and respect. Marston is an honorable man."

Montague sighed with relief. One of his greatest fears had vanished, but just as it disappeared, another replaced it. "Except for the battle, I have nothing to fear in regard to her welfare?" he asked.

"Words that never escaped my lips."

Montague was confused. The reply was ply not direct. "I don't understand."

"They share the same pain."

Montague had no idea as to what the wizard referred to, his cryptic replies causing only frustration. "Who shares the same pain?"

"Marston and the Lady Gabrielle."

"You must explain." Montague's voice reflected his impatience..

"The sickness took his family, as it took hers. Their pasts have been marked by the same tragedies, misfortunes best left forgotten.

"So, they share a common bond," Montague said, "as do many others. Is there more?"

"The deepest love grows where broken hearts are healed."

Overwhelmed with despair, Montague closed his eyes, his hand to his head. He couldn't lose the love of his life, the soul that formed the mirror image of his own. He knew he had to act quickly. "Tell me about Marston," he said, ready to assess the facets of his foe that he hadn't before thought crucial.

"He's a formidable warrior, closer to sunset than the dawn."

"Older?"

"In body and spirit."

"Can I defeat him?"

"Physically."

Montague thought it a strange answer. War was physical, a fight to the death. "What other ways exist?"

"Emotionally and spiritually, you may have met your match."

"Then I need your help," Montague said, almost pleading. "I have to overcome him."

"I will do all I can to ensure you find success. But there is an obstacle that must be faced."

"What is it?" Montague asked. "I am prepared for any foe."

The wizard closed his eyes as if he were trying to see with his mind what couldn't be seen with his eyes. "Montague has Alaric," he intoned.

"A trusted advisor I could not do without."

"And Marston has his own guide, a powerful force."

"Can we defeat them?" Montague asked, fearful of the Devil's work.

"The question cannot be answered," Alaric replied. "Not until the battle has begun. The attack and all that will precede it can be seen through your eyes only."

Chapter 36

Gabrielle walked along the eastern wall of the castle, watching the sea far below, white waves leaving imprints in the sand as they advanced and then retreated. Driftwood, once the mighty limbs of trees, was strewn along a sandbar. A wooden beam lay beside them, hewn by men to serve as the rib of a massive ship, destroyed by nature and then reclaimed. She knew Normandy lay just beyond the horizon, across the dark sea, and she counted the hours until she returned to the only home she'd ever known.

How many more mornings, she wondered, will I gaze at the horizon. How many nights will I dream of my homeland, praying Montague will find where I am and brave the castle to spirit me away? Though she was at ease amongst her captors, she grew ever more restless for the man she loved, and while she waited for him to appear, anxiously watching the sun as it rose, she searched for a means of escape.

"This is where you spend your mornings," Michael Marston said.

Gabrielle flinched, startled to see him. So immersed had she been in her dreams of what might be, she hadn't heard him approach. "Sire," she said, nodding in respect. "Just a morning walk."

"This is my favorite time of day," he said, watching the sun creep higher into the heavens.

"It is mine as well," she said softly, trying to hide her discomfort. He was stealing her private moments.

"I don't want to intrude," he said as if reading her thoughts. "I only study the terrain to assess the pieces of a terrible game that will soon be moved into position."

"Are we in danger?" she asked, rescue foremost in her mind.

"Our enemies surround us," he said. "But we're prepared." He pointed to the soldiers who manned the walls.

Others carried quivers of arrows up into the towers and pushed a catapult in the bailey, the mechanism almost completed under Gideon's watchful eye.

She felt a surge of optimism. "Is it the French?" she asked anxiously.

"Allied with English barons who plot to oust the king."

Gabrielle feared for her safety, knowing how vicious an attack could be whether she was protected by the fortress or not. But she also knew if Marston was forced to surrender she would most likely be freed.

Marston watched her closely. "The attack will likely fail," he said softly. "I don't want you to hope for something that probably won't come."

Gabrielle averted her eyes, unnerved that he had divined her thoughts once more. "Has the castle been attacked before?" she asked coolly.

"The past can't always predict the present," he said, evading the question.

"How do you know it's the French who have joined forces with the barons?"

"We have sources, all of whom I trust," he said. "Word of the first skirmishes has already reached us."

"Am I in danger?"

"Not as long as I live," he said softly.

Gabrielle paused, considering Marston who held her gaze unwaveringly. He'd spoken tenderly, protectively, with words she hadn't expected to hear. She nodded with respect and appreciation. "Thank you, sire."

"The battle might not be waged," he added, trying to quell her fears.

She was curious, not seeing a solution that would satisfy what went on beyond the castle walls. "How can that be," she asked, "if rebellion is the outcome that most desire?"

"They may only launch probing attacks in an attempt to judge our strength."

"And then depart if they find a full-scale attack would end in their defeat?" she asked, a hint of disappointment in her voice.

"Perhaps," Marston said with a sigh. "But I would expect a siege."

"I don't see how they could win," she said. "Surely we won't surrender."

"The will to go on will wane," he said. "As will the stores of food."

"How long might it last?"

"We have provisions for months," he said.

Both Marston and Gabrielle fell silent. Together, they stared at the sea. The future, like the waves, could not be controlled, no matter how hard they tried.

"We're so close to Normandy," Gabrielle said. "not far from the convent where I was taken."

"Just across the water, I'm told."

"This castle would be a desirable objective in times of war."

"It is, one of the first the enemy seeks to conquer."

"Is that why the king wanted his finest knight to guard it?" she asked.

"Perhaps," he said and then smiled. "Or perhaps not. My family has been here for generations. I think my station here stems from loyalty and birthright more so than courage or ability. But I do appreciate the compliment."

Gabrielle studied his face, his eyes such a bright blue, his short beard speckled with gray, and his smile, warm and genuine. Still a sadness consumed his eyes.

"I suspect your station has more to do with the latter," she said.

He bowed slightly, surprised by her further commendation. "Even so, the battle will not be easily won."

"What battle is? My whole life has been tainted by war, and I can't tell if either side was the better for it."

"My days have been likewise stained," he said, "by war and sickness."

She touched his arm lightly, more from compassion than affection. "I'm so sorry for your loss. What a horrible cross to bear."

"And I yours," he said. "What a brave and courageous woman you are to endure all the pain you've suffered."

"It has never been easy," she said, each memory like a knife that pierced her heart.

There was an awkward silence, the topic too painful for either to discuss, the past better left forgotten. Finally, Marston spoke. "Your heart belongs to Normandy," he said softly.

"And it always will."

"I want to assure you no harm will come to you here, no matter what comes to pass."

"Thank you. I can rest assured."

Marston's brow furrowed as he scanned the horizon. "The castle is yours to enjoy as you wish," he said, "but it still isn't Normandy. I know that as well as you."

"Yes, sire."

"You should know I see the truth," he said, a somber cast to his voice.

"And your compassion is appreciated."

"I promise you when the battle is done, I'll take you home, back to the man you love."

146

Chapter 37

Gabrielle had been at the castle for little more than a week when she realized that no one, not the servants nor Gideon nor any or Marston's men in arms, kept watch of anything she did. The master did not request her presence, save for a dinner here and there, and she could come and go as she pleased, wander through any part of the fortress, speak to whomever she liked, and eat when and where she chose. She could have walked straight out of the gate if only it was open. But it wasn't.

The castle was immense, much larger than those she had visited in France. The walls were thicker, towers higher. The grounds were extensive, encompassing a wide expanse of open space threaded by narrow roads and studded with a collection of houses and shops. She wasn't sure how many people lived within the castle walls, but she guessed it was several hundred, a number which she then tripled to account for all of the soldiers.

Having little to do, she walked the grounds several times each day, all the while searching about keenly for a means of escape—a little-used exit that had been overlooked when securing the fortress for battle or the entrance to a tunnel that might take her to the forest that spread past the fields beyond. She observed everything—when guards changed stations, which section of wall was manned by the fewest soldiers, which gates seemed least protected. And she wandered the keep, studying its corridors and dark hallways, searching for the secret passage she suspected was hidden there, used by noblemen and women to escape should the castle face defeat.

Each day she watched while Marston's soldiers prepped for war, staging bows and arrows, swords and lances and stockpiling food and water, chickens, cows, and pigs. In an empty expanse of the bailey, men scrambled about the catapult. Its stout arm could hurl boulders over a distance most could not begin to fathom. It sat on rollers, and the soldiers could spin it when needed to fire in any direction, while wooden chocks held it in place. It was a fearsome weapon, hidden from those beyond the walls, and she suspected many a man would lose his life when the battle began.

No matter where she wandered or what she beheld, Montague was always in her thoughts. She wondered where he might be and what he had done since their lips last met, hoping he'd avoided danger and was no longer bound to fight wars for the king, but she knew his reputation and assumed the king had insisted he fight in yet another battle. Perhaps he's with the French outside the walls, or maybe far away in Normandy or another part of England, fighting forces to the north. No matter. She tried to give herself courage. Whatever obstacles we're forced to face, someday we will be together.

She stopped just beyond the catapult to watch Jenks and his falcon. On his signal, the bird alighted from the blacksmith's leather cuff and flew into the heavens, vanishing into the clouds just north of the castle. Several minutes passed before he reappeared, drifting lower when Jenks enticed him by waving a sardine in the air. The bird landed on his wrist, tearing into his reward.

"Are you enjoying your stroll, my lady?" a voice behind her asked.

Gabrielle turned to find Gideon. "I am," she answered. She wondered if he'd followed her and noted her curiosity at how the castle was constructed. Maybe she was being watched after all. She just hadn't realized it.

He smiled, or at least appeared to, behind his bushy beard, and pointed to the catapult. "Our preparations are almost complete."

"I've watched you oversee construction," she said, "and I'm told it's your design."

"It is," he replied. "As are many devices throughout the castle." He pointed to the sling on the massive catapult. "I think the range will surprise even the most formidable foes."

For an instant a horrifying image of boulders crushing the advancing Frenchmen flashed behind her eyes. She was not afraid; she had faced the English before, but the army outside was more vulnerable than they could ever know. For a fleeting instant, she felt she had to warn them. But then she realized they had undoubtedly seen battle before and knew the hazards of war.

Gideon saw the way her eyes lingered on the catapult. "We're well defended," he said. "No harm will come to you."

She nodded, glancing around the bailey at the houses, soldiers' quarters, and the many shops that supported those within the walls. "It's a large space to defend."

"One that we've defended before."

"Against an enemy as formidable as those we face?"

He paused as if he didn't know the answer. "I've never fought the French," he admitted, "but I suspect they're a gallant foe. The barons' men, to our north, are supposedly led by James the Bold."

"I've never heard the name," she said.

"He is an infamous warrior known for his ferocity and love for battle. Victory has been his constant reward for every effort he's made. But he's vicious when necessary to achieve that end and kills whoever stands in his path—soldiers, women, children."

Gabrielle's eyes widened with fear, as she made a show of seeking refuge nearer the alchemist. She knew if she played her part well, he might reveal what should have been kept secret. "What are we going to do?" she asked, her voice quaking ever so slightly. "Is there any way to escape?"

"There could be," he said guardedly, watching her closely.

His reply, whether he realized it or not, had provided the answer she'd sought. There must be a corridor or tunnel, known to a privileged few, that leads to safety. She had only to find it. "Perhaps a means for all to escape should promptly be made ready," she said, "given the savageness of the enemy it seems we're about to face."

"Rest assured, my lady," Gideon replied. "Fate has given us the finest warlord in England to command the castle."

"Michael Marston," she breathed. Although she assumed the king had chosen Marston on the merit of his former feats, she wondered how such a gentle man might best a barbarian like James the Bold.

"You seem surprised," he said.

"He is older than most."

"And wiser."

"Can he confront an enemy as vicious as James the Bold?"

"I've never had a doubt."

"Perhaps his finest days have passed," she continued, probing.

"And he would be the first to admit it."

Gabrielle thought his reply curious, but it reflected her own discussion with Marston. "Should someone else command?"

"No one else is better fit," Gideon said.

"From the ramparts, but what of the battlefield?" she asked, testing him.

Gideon looked at her, his eyes betraying a shade of doubt. "I suppose that remains to be seen," he said, "but no one is shrewder than Michael Marston, as the enemy soon will learn."

Chapter 38

Minerva crept through the shadows, making her way through the corridors that twisted through her cave. She moved stealthily, like a cat about to pounce upon its prey, ready to set in motion the workings of a spell that would join two hearts as one, a love neither of her targets expected or would be able to deny. She did it for her master to both mend his breaking heart and temper the attack, for the enemy would not continue if victory meant her death. Her life was worth more than a castle filled with gold. French royalty had never been held in the castle, and Minerva knew they would pay any price for Gabrielle's freedom if it came to that. And should the day arrive when these reasons no longer mattered, she alone could break the spell.

Her hands, the fingers long and slender, nails crooked and sharp, clutched the ingredients she'd carefully selected, some born of nature, others of man, as she moved to the altar. Her cauldron sat simmering from the heat of a powerful crystal, a ring of red candles flickering beside the aged pot. Minerva laid the parts of her potion before the mystical fire, so they were evenly spaced and not touching. She surveyed her collection carefully, pleased with what she saw: three herbs, three stones, and three symbolic charms, all needed to intensify the potency of her magic. Eager to begin, she poked at a pouch and shook a vial to make sure the contents were properly mixed. She had waited for a waxing moon, the best time to make her magic.

"What a fine spell we'll cast with this brew," she said slyly to a toad that sat on a rock beside the stream. "Aaah, I'll begin with the herbs: cinnamon to ignite the flame of an undeniable love, jasmine to extend its reach to the spiritual realm, so the energy of the universe will forever keep it growing, and white willow bark to foster a future, ensuring the lovers stay intertwined for all the tomorrows yet to come." She sprinkled each into the pot, and a pleasing aroma drifted up and into the crooked corridors of her cave.

Next, she added slivers of three stones: a green emerald to attract new love, a red garnet to conceive passion, and pink magnesium to heal the heart of prior wounds, restoring it as if

151

the damage had never been wrought and barring the pain from returning. She mixed the shavings in her hand and dropped them into the cauldron, watching as the liquid boiled and bubbles broke the surface.

Running her hand across the red candles' flames, she looked toward the ceiling, and whispered a string of powerful words in an ancient tongue. When she was satisfied with all her preparations, she was ready to continue and join two hearts as one.

Minerva closed her eyes and focused her energy, moving her hands about the mist that snaked its way upward from the belly of the cauldron, watching while the mixture burped, bubbled, and hissed. When the murky mixture pulsed at the rhythm she desired, she reached for the three charms she'd chosen: hemp twine tied in love knots, an apple slice, rosy and red, and three rose petals, picked at midnight from a bush laden with many thorns. Then she took up the most important element of all, a charm she used only when needed to create the strongest link—the heart from a pregnant dove.

To reinforce the efficacy in the hearts of those who would receive her spell, she took the strands of Gabrielle's auburn hair she'd collected from her brush and dropped them in the cauldron. Even though Montague was the man Gabrielle would always love, Minerva worked to alter fate, a feat not easily done. The last component she needed to link two souls as one was a lock of Michael Marston's hair. She had swiped it one of the many times she'd managed to draw near to him, though it caused discomfort. Her master had a grieving heart, deserted by love, his future as dark as his past, and Minerva would now change his path so Gabrielle walked through life beside him.

At last, the ghostly brew was done, and Minerva stepped up to the altar. Shimmering in the vapor that settled just above the cauldron was the image of Lady Gabrielle, Michael Marston at her side. Minerva began to chant.

> "One to seek him,
> One to find him,
> One to bring him,
> One to bind him.

Heart to heart,

Blood be mixed,

So say I,

This spell is fixed.

So shall it be."

The witch repeated the spell nine times. Then she returned to the cauldron and studied its contents. A broad smile spread across her face.

"Now love will bloom where it was once denied."

Chapter 39

"Now could be the time to strike," Trinity said as she sat in her room with Paul the Pure.

The druid didn't seem convinced. "Why would Marston wish to see me alone?" he asked. "Something must be wrong."

"Don't let doubts defeat you."

Paul the Pure looked pensive. "I think it's a trap."

"A trap for what?" she asked. "He knows nothing."

"He suspects something. I'm sure of it," he said. "Why else would he not summon you, too?"

Trinity's frustration with the old man was mounting, but she didn't show it. Where she saw an opportunity, he saw a risk. "Perhaps he wants to discuss your meeting," she said as she tried to calm him.

"Or he may have found some truth to counter what we told him," said Paul the Pure.

"There's nothing for him to find," she insisted,"especially while the country is mired in rebellion."

"He can still seek the truth," he said, "and may have asked others where we came from."

"Whom shall he ask when he knows not whom to trust?"

"He does not trust us, of that I am certain," he mumbled.

"Does it matter?"

The druid gnawed at a fingernail. "I suppose not," he said. "We came with a mission. And now it's time to fulfill it."

Trinity studied him closely, wondering if courage could be counted among his traits. Somehow, she had to make sure it was. She considered the task before them, a plot they'd spent weeks planning, which would be employed in hours. "When the time comes, do you think you can kill him?" she asked.

Paul the Pure sighed as if the truth were hard to admit. Murder couldn't be counted as a deed he had performed, and completing such a treacherous act would be more difficult than it seemed. "Not by force," he said. "I'm an old man. He's a warlord."

"No, not by force," Trinity said. "By trickery."

He studied her closely, wondering if she saw what couldn't be seen. "How will I do that?"

"Are you sure he'll be alone?" she asked.

"I'm not," he replied. "I only know he's requested I come alone."

Trinity thought for a moment, the details forming and beginning to firm. "I know what can be done."

"It must be clever and cunning," he said. "Anything else will likely fail."

"Of course," she said as she went to the shelves lining the back wall of the room. She grabbed up her leather satchel and sorted through vials and pouches, muttering in an unknown tongue.

"What are you doing?" he asked.

"Let's assume he will have a chalice beside him," she said, "and that he's drinking wine."

Paul the Pure shrugged, not knowing what she was about to suggest. "He very well could," he said, "since we're to meet in the Great Hall."

She took an empty vial and sprinkled a greyish powder into it. Then she added drops of a yellow liquid, placed a cork in the top of the vial, and gently shook it. "Pour this into his drink. It's a powerful poison."

"But that won't work," he balked, surprised by the path she'd chosen. "If he falls to the floor with me blinking beside him, they'll know it was me who killed him. I'll be hung within the hour, if not sooner."

"But he won't fall to the floor," she assured him. "Not then and not a day later."

Paul the Pure looked at her closely "You said it was a potent poison."

"It is," she said.

"Then he'll die," he said in exasperation. "And I'll be blamed."

"He will die," she said, "but not for days."

The druid fell silent, considering all his partner had proposed. "Are you absolutely certain?" he asked. "If not, it's a risk I cannot take."

"I'm certain," Trinity replied. "It's a toxin I've used before."

"How long before he dies?"

"Two days will pass before signs of sickness make themselves known."

"And then?"

"He'll die an agonizing death."

Paul the Pure chuckled. "Just as he deserves."

"And it gives us all the time we need," she said. "We can birth his death, and then we can flee."

"And collect what's owed us from James the Bold so long as the battle doesn't break out."

Trinity considered the timeline—what was supposed to occur and what would likely happen. "James the Bold may be waiting for signs of Marston's death. The attack may not begin until he sees it."

A look of doubt crossed Paul the Pure's face. "But if he tires of waiting and attacks too soon, we'll never get away."

Trinity rolled her eyes, tiring of the old man. "You kill Marston," she said. "I'll plan the escape."

Chapter 40

Paul the Pure entered the Great Hall, awed once more by the grand expanse of room, its graceful arches, and the tapestries that hung upon its walls. Hobbling on his cane, clutching his druid's wand, his robe hanging loosely upon his fragile frame, and his beard drooping to his chest, he looked weary as he walked toward Marston who sat at the head of the table. He paused often, as if he barely had the strength to continue. Once he reached the master of the manor, he nodded respectfully.

"Welcome," Marston said, motioning to the chair beside him. "Please sit."

The priest sank into an oak chair just to Marston's right and leaned his cane against the table.

"Two goblets of wine," Marston called out to an unseen servant.

Paul the Pure shifted in his seat. He wasn't sure why he'd been summoned, but he knew he had to be careful. He couldn't allow himself to be tricked into saying what was best left unsaid.

An older servant, lean and haggard, appeared with two goblets. He poured a glass of red wine for his master and a second for the druid. "Is that all, sire?" he asked.

"For now," Marston said, nodding in appreciation.

Paul the Pure waited until the servant had gone. "How can I be of service, sire?"

"Are you and Trinity comfortable?" Marston asked.

It wasn't the question the druid was expecting. "We are, sire," he said. "And we appreciate your hospitality."

"Have you considered your final destination?"

"It's unknown as of yet," he replied. "The journey has tired us greatly as did the trauma of fleeing the barons."

Marston held up a finger, signaling silence. He watched the shadows that fell across a doorway as if searching for his servant. "It's not easy to know who serves the barons and who may still serve me," he whispered, "so quickly was the war thrust upon us."

"A difficult task for one of your stature, I'm sure," said Paul the Pure.

Marston got to his feet and strode toward the hallway.

Paul the Pure leaned forward furtively, emptying the vial of poison into Marston's goblet.

Seconds later, Marston returned. "My apologies, but I needed to ensure we were alone," he said. "Who knows whose ears might be trained upon us."

"I'm flattered your time is devoted to me."

"Hardly an imposition for such an old friend," Marston said, taking one last glance at the entryway. "I suppose you prefer to remain at the castle if you've no desire to travel."

"I am weary," said Paul the Pure. "A long rest might be best."

"Your journey would tax a young man. How arduous it must have been for someone who's seen so many seasons pass."

Paul the Pure nodded. "The thought of the castle and the protection it provided was the only thing that kept us moving."

"From what direction did you come?"

Paul the Pure hesitated, for Marston surely recalled the answer. He wondered if he was being lured into a trap. "From the west," he replied.

"Which barons pursued you?"

"I know not their names, sire, only that they dispatched soldiers to follow, and our fate, if we'd been captured, might never have been known."

"I'm thankful they didn't find you," Marston said.

"As am I," said Paul the Pure. "I've borne witness to their acts of war, and I need see no more."

Marston picked up his goblet, leaned toward the druid, and bumped the old man's cane. He tried to grab it but failed, and it fell to the floor with a clatter. "My apologies," he said. "I'm not as quick as I once was."

"No need, sire," Paul the Pure said. "I should have set it elsewhere." He bent over and picked up the cane, struggling as he did so, then leaned it against the table beyond Marston's reach.

"To your continued safety," Marston said, raising his goblet.

Paul the Pure drank from his goblet just as Marston drank from his.

"If I could be of service, sire, there's little I won't do," Paul the Pure said, watching as Marston drank the wine. His skin prickled at the thought of the poison that would soon flow throughout Marston's body.

"That's a welcoming thought, old friend," Marston said, a worried look upon his face. "Especially in times like these."

Paul the Pure eyed him curiously. "What is it, sire?"

"There is something that continues to trouble me, though I really don't know why."

"And what might that be?"

Marston remained quiet as if the question plagued him. Finally, he spoke. "What of the Holy Grail?" he asked. "Does it have a final haven?"

"For now, it shall stay here. But it should rest in the abbey at Glastonbury. That is its rightful home."

"I am honored to house it," Marston said. "Even for so short a time."

Paul the Pure nodded respectfully. "It's a wondrous thing you do, sire. And I could not be more grateful."

"You are welcome here until the rebellion has been quelled," Marston said decisively. "And as soon as the danger which faces us passes, your journey can again begin."

"What danger is that, sire?" Paul the Pure asked guardedly.

"The castle will soon be surrounded," Marston said. "The battle is about to begin."

"So soon?" asked Paul the Pure. "I had hoped the barons and the king would somehow come to terms."

"It seems not," Marston said and drank more of his wine.

"I wouldn't want war to wage such a war if it could be avoided."

"It seems the conflict comes whether we want it or not," Marston sighed.

"And the castle will be attacked?"

"A siege seems much more likely," Marston said. "You could be here for many months."

The news of an impending siege made the druid anxious. It wasn't at all what he'd expected to hear. He had to get out before it was too late, or he wouldn't be able to get out at all. A buyer for the Grail was waiting. "Perhaps we should leave promptly, sire. Before the battle begins."

Marston cast him a look of concern. "You shall have to hurry," he said. "As we speak, they tighten the noose that lies around our necks."

Chapter 41

Deep below the castle courtyard, nestled in her cave, Minerva stood at her altar and sorted through the pouches and vials she'd removed from the nooks and crannies where she hid them. The cauldron was before her, its contents belching a mist that hung in the air. The fog formed an image—a man with white hair, black eyes, and a face that knew the wisdom of the ages and all the evil it contained.

She made her way to the nearby stream and scooped up a goblet full of water. Then she let it drip slowly into the pot, measuring the size of each drop. As the contents began to hiss and bubble, she opened the first vial, which was filled with the slime of a frog, and poured it in. The cauldron belched, the mist grew thick, and a stench saturated the air.

Minerva took up another pouch and untied the string. She emptied the contents— dirt from a freshly dug grave—and watched as the liquid consumed it. She then added ashes from a corpse's rib, burned one minute after midnight on the last day of a waning moon. Next, she took out the spider she'd taken from Gabrielle's room and dropped it in the stew. As the creature struggled to escape, she opened a vial of elder tree sap and added it to the potion. Then she stirred in a pouchful of dirt laced with the urine of a diseased cow. The brew roiled in protest and then settled down.

The last vial contained the most potent element of all, phlegm from the lungs of a dying man. Minerva poured it into the pot and passed her hand above the burbling potion, the sloshing gruel matching her every motion and fusing into a thick syrup. An otherworldly stink drifted throughout the cave, strong enough to gag a man, but Minerva hardly noticed it.

When she was satisfied the potion had reached the perfect consistency, she made it all the more powerful by adding the eye of an owl. Then she chanted nine times:

"Face familiar, foe for friend

Bonds broken, bait, bend.

Trust taken, timeless toils,

Pus, pimple, pain and boils."

A strange sheen appeared like a skin atop the brew, and Minerva removed the crystal to let the contents of the cauldron cool. She fetched a fistful of sea salt and poured it into the pot. The mixture hardened slowly, emitting a hideous scream so chilling it could wake the dead, and then turned to powder. Carefully, the witch placed the powder into an empty pouch, slipped into a particularly dark corner of the cave, and hid it in a cleft in the wall. Then she returned to the altar and wiped the cauldron clean, using a rag drenched with water from an angry sea. Seconds later, the rag burst into flames. She let it fall and burn until only ashes remained.

Her mysterious deed complete, Minerva threw her head back, the sound of her laughter echoing off the walls. "My gift to you, warlock!" she shouted.

Just as she shouted her threat, far across the rolling terrain on the north side of the fortress, the first hint of a boil appeared on Blaise's pale face.

Chapter 42

The sore appeared on Blaise's right cheek. Not an hour later the second formed over his left eye, a pocket of pus that stretched the entire length of his brow. By the end of the day, boils and lesions, some dripping yellow liquid, others swollen crimson pimples, had spread all over his body. He even had biting sores between his toes.

It didn't take long for him to realize what had happened. He knew a powerful force lived within the walls of the castle, a female who'd been born to the ways of the witch. Her power fated them as foes in the battle that soon would begin, a truth the warlock had known since he'd sensed her presence. But he hadn't known how strong she actually was, not until now. She knew he was with James the Bold, plotting an attack. The boils were a test to see if he could counter the strength that she possessed. It was also a warning that he come no closer, a sign that someone powerful could see all that he did.

Blaise tried to conjure an image of his rival from his secluded camp at the end of the forest, overlooking the cliff. It was quiet, the sloshing of a cold stream the only sound his ears could hear, and that's exactly what he wanted—no one near to interrupt his thoughts or deeds. He lived alone, worked his magic alone, and intended to remain alone just as he always had. And now, while he attempted to counteract whatever spell had been placed upon him, he needed to avoid James the Bold, Jamet, or any other human being.

Slowly, for the boils ached all the more when he moved, Blaise removed a small brass cauldron from his satchel, old and pitted, a dent on one side, and sat it in the moss beside a lofty oak. Scooping some water from the stream, just enough to wet the bottom, he set the cauldron back down, stood up and standing directly above it, urinated into the pot, his bodily fluid providing the strength to overcome the spell. When he'd finished, he rummaged through his satchels, withdrew a vial of cider vinegar, and added seven drops to the cauldron. Then he removed a single black candle from a large sack, stuck it into a brass holder, and set it in the cauldron. He added more water from the stream until the liquid was just below the candle's wick. Then he stuck a twig in his campfire and used it to light the candle.

He closed his eyes, visualizing his body without the hateful boils, the way it had been only days before, and kept repeating a chant in Gaelic:

"Pus, pain, pimple, boil,

Spell broken, fail, foil.

Pimple shrink, pus dry.

Spells broken; spells die.

Sickness go and don't return,

Spell broken, twisted turn.

Witch will try but do no harm

Spell broken, failed charm."

Keeping his eyes closed, he repeated the chant until the candle burned down to the water, extinguishing the flame. Then he opened his eyes and studied what remained. The liquid had solidified and turned to yellow mush. Not to be fooled, he knew the remains were potent and had to be handled in just the right way.

Blaise moved a few feet away, downhill from where he camped, and dug a hole in the soil, battling the roots of trees and shrubs. He cleaned the candle holder in the stream and placed the contents of the cauldron and the candle into the hole. He poured four more drops of vinegar into the sluggish mix and filled the hole with the soil he had just removed.

An hour later the boils began to shrunk, and the pus no longer wept from their hideous cracks. By the end of the day, it was as if they had never existed.

And now it was time for revenge.

164

Chapter 43

James the Bold sat on his horse, hidden by trees and shrubs at the edge of the forest. Across the plain lay Marston Castle, mocking those who tried to invade, challenging any attacker to a battle they most likely wouldn't win. He studied the men that lined the walls and then eyed the lofty towers, massive round fortifications stretching into the sky, where archers could rain arrows upon an invading army, destroying those who tried to advance. On the northwest tower, a flag flew atop a pole, a red rectangular shield with small white crosses in the upper right and lower left corners. In the center was the head of a unicorn—the Marston coat of arms.

As James the Bold scanned the walls, he looked at each tower in turn and saw the same flag, visible to any approaching, even from a ship that sailed the sea below. Even though the towers reached high into the heavens, the flags bearing the Marston coat of arms stretched still higher, a signal to friend and foe alike that the castle housed one of the greatest warlords in history.

"You shouldn't be alone, sire," Jamet said as he came up behind him. "It's too dangerous."

James the Bold waved him off dismissively, the image of the wild boar on his green tunic a testament to his strength. "The cowards hide behind the walls," he said.

"They may intend to stay there," Jamet said. "Many castles withstand sieges, especially if well stocked."

"And many castles surrender. After all the rats have been eaten."

Jamet looked at the warlord, wondering what motivated him. "The castle could be lightly defended. A probing attack would tell, if true."

James the Bold still studied the fortress. "I don't yet know which road we'll take, but it ends with Marston's head on a pike. Even if I have to kill him with my bare hands."

Jamet shuddered, the image too graphic for him to envision. "A strategy succeeds more often than not," he said tentatively.

James the Bold turned to face him, the scarred face showing the vicious mind behind it. "I see every step that we shall take," he said, "and I always do. That's why I've never lost a battle."

Jamet studied the warlord. He, too, could envision the battle that was about to begin, but foresaw a different outcome. "Can you share your intentions?" he asked. "We fight side by side."

James the Bold scrutinized him closely, searching for a sign that loyalty did indeed exist. Enemies just weeks before, it was difficult to treat him as an ally, let alone a trusted advisor. He pointed to a pile of rocks at the edge of the forest just across the plain from the northwest tower, deposited by nature when the cliff had been formed. A line of men milled about them. "Do you see those men?"

"Yes, they've been camped there since we arrived."

"They're miners," James the Bold said. "Digging a tunnel to the curtain wall. But they need more time. Several days. Maybe a week"

Jamet watched the miners, envisioning victory by way of their actions, but the vision was short lived. "And what if they fail?"

James the Bold smirked. "I have a secret weapon, perhaps two."

"And what might they be?"

James the Bold fell silent, his gaze trained on the fortress. He liked keeping the Frenchman in constant suspense. "Watch the flags—the Marston coat of arms."

"I know not why," Jamet muttered.

"You don't need to know why," James the Bold said. "You need only watch them."

Jamet stared at each of the flags in turn but was puzzled. "Is there a tale they tell?"

James the Bold shrugged, not interested if Jamet understood or not. "The flags reveal who rules the manor."

"We know that's Michael Marston."

"It is today," James the Bold said.

"And tomorrow as well."

"Even a great leader's reign does not last forever," James the Bold exclaimed.

Jamet glanced at the warlord and offered a guarded suggestion. "If we wait, we give them more time to prepare. We don't know what lurks within the walls."

"But we know what we have outside the walls."

Once more, Jamet studied the leader, fearful that he was overconfident. "Have you chosen locations to stage the catapults?"

"I have," James the Bold said, pointing to landmarks. "Just in front of that grove of trees on the west side of the fortress, and here on the northern side by the rocky ledge that winds to the cliff. Just past where the miners dig."

"The men, they are prepared?" Jamet asked.

James the Bold glared at his French advisor, the scar running down his face made all the more fearsome by the cast of the midday sun. "We're ready to fight as we always have been. But is Marston ready to die?"

Chapter 44

Alaric's words weighed heavily upon Montague, and he could not help but dwell upon them. He knew the Lady Gabrielle was safe from harm, confined to the keep by a gentleman captor, but the revelation that Michael Marston posed a threat not only to the armies that stood at his gate but also to his beloved, cut his soul to its very core. And then there was the secret passage, which he had only to find, and he could enter the castle unseen, find Gabrielle, and take her home. But with a battle about to begin, or at the very least a siege, he knew his chance to free her from the castle was fleeting and might never occur.

Piers approached him as he stood, studying the southern wall. "Your thoughts, sire?"

"The wizard confirmed that it is true," Montague said. "Gabrielle waits within the castle walls."

Piers eyed his leader, knowing the agony consuming his soul. "I pray no one harms her."

"She's treated well, at least for now, so her safety isn't an utmost concern. But it does impact the battle and how we'll come to fight it."

"In what building do they house her?" Piers asked. "And is it one we can avoid?"

Montague's countenance stiffened. "She's in the keep," he said tersely.

"The safest place in the fortress," Piers said guardedly, for it was also the objective of the attacking forces.

"I must affect a rescue," Montague said softly. "Before the battle begins."

"But we have no means to access the castle and no prisoner captured to request an exchange."

"I suspect a tunnel leads to the keep, and that is how I will find her," Montague said. He turned to his loyal lieutenant. "If you were to construct a passage so the master could escape, where would you place the exit?"

168

Piers paused, trying to think like a builder. "Definitely not to the west," he said. "An escape that leads to the castle entrance is most certain to fail."

"And if the west cannot be considered a viable escape route, and the east leads to the cliff, an exit from the south would cross the plain before us and empty into the brush that skirts its border. And the north would do the same."

"Our men are camped along the fringe where the trees begin to thin out," Piers said. "Any passageway would have to be hidden or emerge farther within the forest."

"The terrain supports the former theory," Montague said, turning to look behind him. "And the underbrush is littered with boulders."

"We can search for such an entrance," Piers said, "if you think it will bear fruit."

"Perhaps," Montague muttered as he weighed the likelihood of their success. "But I suspect the cliff would be the most likely way out. The passage would wind its way beneath the walls and emerge at an exit that is somehow hidden."

"Difficult to find in the best of times," Piers said, "and impossible with guards patrolling the walls."

"I don't dispute that fact," Montague said. "Which is why the cliff seems the most likely location."

"Even if that is true, what can be done?" Piers asked. "It's hardly a path for an army."

"No, it isn't," Montague said. "The men would meet their deaths as they stood upon the beach. But it might be a path one man could take."

"Enter the castle and open a gate, so the army could stream in," Piers said, seeing merit in the plan.

Montague turned to face the man he trusted most. "Or rescue the Lady Gabrielle."

Piers studied his old friend, the pain in his face all too apparent. He knew a successful rescue would be impossible to achieve with a battle looming. "A daunting task for one man," he said. "Unless he is aided by an army."

Montague realized that logic, not emotion, should dictate his actions, and though his proposal had merit, it was motivated by all the wrong reasons. "A plan that must be much better prepared," he muttered.

"But it still provides alternatives to what we now will do," Piers said. "And hidden access, no matter how it's used, will only aid in our victory."

"It's a path I can't abandon," he said softly. "No matter what is found."

"And still a good one," Piers assured him. "Even if we use it to capture someone we can later ransom."

"Gabrielle commands too high a price," Montague said. "Marston is no fool. He knows that as well as we do."

"It remains an option we can try."

Montague nodded, his thoughts on Gabrielle. He had to undo the wrong forced upon her by what he had done—leaving her at the convent. And if he lost his life to save hers, it was a trade well worth the price.

Chapter 45

Michael Marston crossed the bailey, on his way to the northwest tower. He wanted to view any enemy actions, using his own eyes to access their plans. He was an active commander, heavily engaged, and would wage the war from atop the wall for both his men and the enemy to easily see. As he started to ascend the steps, he saw Gideon hurrying toward the eastern wall, no doubt to check on his catapult.

"Gideon," he called. "A word, please."

"Of course, sire," the alchemist said.

"I've information to share," Marston said. "If you have a moment."

"I was drafting an updated sketch of the catapult's trajectory. I think the enemy will soon find themselves in the way of a forbidding surprise."

Marston smiled. "May we continue to meet them with such surprises."

"I'll ensure that we do," Gideon said. "What mischief does the enemy make?"

"More than we care to consider, I'm sure," Marston said, "but it's Paul the Pure I reference. None of his words ring true."

"The portrait he painted on the day that he arrived has been easily exposed."

"He is an accomplished liar," Marston agreed. "If I didn't know the truth, I would think he spoke it."

"What fate awaits him and his daughter?"

"I haven't yet determined," Marston said. He didn't trust Paul the Pure or Trinity, and he knew he never would, but they might, nonetheless, serve a purpose. Perhaps they would provide a piece to the puzzle that might serve the king. He just didn't know what secrets their true identities would reveal, at least not yet.

Gideon watched his master, sensing something was amiss. "What troubles you most, sire?"

Marston paused, trying to solve the riddle of the mission and the man. "Why would Paul the Pure tell us he had the Grail?"

"A sinister motive, I'm sure."

"He could have said nothing, hid here until those who pursue him departed for other realms, and then made his escape."

"I believe he aspires to be seen as someone he is not."

"But why is he so desperate to gain my trust?"

"You graced him with your presence," said Gideon. "The question that begs an answer is did he get what it was he wanted?"

Marston looked at his trusted advisor, a glint of awareness in his eyes. "In a day or two, we'll have an answer, but I suspect he did."

Marston left Gideon and climbed the stairs to the northwest tower. When he reached the top, he could see signs of the enemy to the north, beginning to emerge from the fringe of the forest. To the west, a winding road sliced through farm fields, the chimneys and thatched roofs of a small village visible in the distance. Rows of wagons were coming down the crooked lane, laden with wheat and other supplies, destined for the army who hid within the trees. As he studied the surroundings, Captain Carney approached.

"Our scouts have confirmed that the barons' forces are gathering to the north," Captain Carney said. "Their numbers still grow but not by much. Stragglers arrive each day."

"Does James the Bold lead them?"

"He was seen in the enemy camp with a Frenchman whose name we do not know."

"James the Bold is a formidable foe," Marston said. "And one I prefer not to face."

"But still no match for you," Carney said to the man he had served for so many years.

"Not in days past," Marston said, "but he is more than my match today."

172

"You don't face the man, sire. You face his army."

Marston hesitated and again turned to the north to reassess the situation. The growing army concerned him, as did its leader. He knew if he was to win, he would have to rely upon his wits and remain always ahead of the enemy he faced. "How many strong?"

"Two thousand, maybe less."

"Do they prepare to attack or only lay siege?"

"Perhaps both," Carney replied. "But it's unclear when they'll make an advance."

Marston's brow furrowed at his reply. If he faced the barons' men alone, attacking from the north, he might be confident of victory. But he had more than one threat to consider. "And what of the French?"

"They're to the south, hidden in the forest," Carney said. "They are a thousand men, maybe more."

Marston considered the strategies he might employ, tactics tried and proven over the course of human history. "Who leads them?" he asked.

"One of their better knights," Carney said. "Maybe the best."

"Did you face him in France?"

"Aye, sire," Carney replied. "His father, too, though he died on the battlefield a few years ago. The son tries to replace him in name if not in stature."

Marston contemplated the commanders he would face, one ferocious and familiar, the other respected, his skills as yet unknown. "And what might the name of this good knight be?"

"Montague of Rouen."

Chapter 46

Gabrielle had always loved books, and she'd discovered that although manuscripts were hard to find, the well-stocked English oak shelves in the library contained books on different topics: religion, politics, history, medical treatises, and several farming guides. For Gabrielle's unquenchable thirst for the unknown, the library was not long in becoming her favorite place, making a difficult stay much easier to bear. She spent afternoons immersed in knowledge, poring over page after page. Sometimes Michael Marston joined her, but he respected her privacy, reluctant to use the room while she was there reading, though at times this became unavoidable.

"I'm so sorry," he said as he entered the library late one afternoon. "I don't want to intrude, but there is something I must see."

Gabrielle smiled. He was always polite, always mindful of her feelings, never attempting to violate her and always treating her with respect. Grateful that, having found herself forced upon a strange man, he had turned out to be someone as good as Marston, she nevertheless continued to watch him warily, never certain the peace between them would continue into the upcoming days.

"You are not intruding," she said. "This is your home."

He smiled faintly and nodded. "It is," he said. "But I won't be more than a minute."

She watched as he crossed the room. Something seemed to trouble him, for his movements were both distracted and rushed. He went straight to a shelf against the far wall, having long since memorized where each volume sat, and removed a book from the second row.

"Is everything all right?" she asked.

"Here it is," he said to himself and began to thumb through the pages.

Captain Carney crossed the threshold, an anxious expression he couldn't control pasted upon his face. "Can you help her, sire?"

Marston looked up at him with compassion. "If it can be done, the answer will lie in this treatise," he said.

"Will it tell us what to do?" Carney asked.

"It offers cures for such ailments and more," Marston said.

"Is someone ill?" Gabrielle asked.

Marston turned to face her. "Captain Carney's daughter, Maud."

"What's wrong with her?" Gabrielle asked, alarmed that her little friend was sick.

"She has a terrible fever," Marston replied.

"She's even begun to see things that aren't there," Carney added.

"We have to break the fever," Marston said. "If we don't…"

Gabrielle rose from her chair, gently took the book from Marston's hand, and returned it to the shelf. "You don't need that," she said softly. "I will take care of her."

Marston looked at her with surprise. "You've shown no ability to heal the sick."

"No one has asked, or I would have complied," Gabrielle replied.

"She treated our wounded in Normandy," Carney said, his tone edged with skepticism, "but two of them later died. I'm not sure she should be let anywhere near a child as precious as Maud."

"I can help her," Gabrielle insisted.

"Are you sure?" Marston asked, glancing at the book she'd returned to the shelf.

"Do not pretend to be what you are not," Carney warned. "Not when my daughter's life is at stake."

"I possess the skills of a healer," Gabrielle said. "The men you brought to the convent gates were beyond the help of any, save God. Let me see the child. I'm sure I can cure her ills."

Marston glanced at Gabrielle and then at Carney. "Should we let her try?"

"I can't let anything happen to Maud," Carney said, fighting for control.

"Something already has," Marston interjected.

"Just let me see her," Gabrielle pleaded.

Carney nodded weakly.

"Come with us," Marston said, leading Gabrielle from the room.

She followed them from the keep to a house in the village beyond the baker. Built of stone, it sat at the end of a row of houses, all of them humble, their roofs of thatched straw.

Carney's wife waited at the girl's bedside. She looked at them anxiously as they entered a cramped room off the kitchen. "Can you make her better, sire?" she asked Marston.

"We're going to try," he replied.

Maud stared up at them from her straw bed, swallowed by blankets, her face flushed.

Gabrielle sat on the edge of the cot and took the child's hand. "I'm going to try to help you," she said. "Is that all right?"

Maud nodded. "I just want to be better."

Gabrielle examined her quickly, touching and probing her gently for any sign of pain, checking for any symptoms she might show. Maud lay quietly, too sick to protest, her breathing labored. In a matter of minutes she'd finished assessing her condition.

Marston and the Carneys watched intently. "Can you help her?" Mrs. Carney asked, the desperation shown in every wrinkle on her face.

"I think so," Gabrielle said. "I have medicine. I'll go and get it."

She hurried to the keep. When she got to her room, she went to the alcove and studied the stores contained upon her

176

shelves. After careful consideration, she selected a handful of herbs: sage, St. John's wort, white willow bark, and cinnamon powder. She placed them within her mortar and ground a portion of each into powder. Then she returned to her shelves to retrieve more ingredients—flax, eucalyptus, and ginseng—and added a generous pinch of each to the powder. A vial of red liquid followed into which she poured the powder, shaking the contents vigorously until they were well combined. Finally, she took a couple pinches of lavender and added them to the elixir she'd made, satisfied it would work.

"It's almost ready," a voice behind her exclaimed.

Gabrielle turned with a start to find a slender woman dressed in black, her untamed hair sprawling in all directions from her head. Something about the stranger made her shudder. She had no idea how or when she'd appeared. Or why.

Chapter 47

Gabrielle glared at the woman who'd seemed to materialize from the ether, unsure if she were even human. "Who are you?" she demanded.

"Minerva," the stranger purred as she reached out to stroke Gabrielle's hair. "The witch of Marston Manor."

Gabrielle shivered and moved away. "Don't come near me."

"You need not be afraid."

Gabrielle stared at the witch, mesmerized by her gaze. Piercing and deep, it was as if she were peering into Gabrielle's heart and soul.

"I won't hurt you," Minerva said. "I'm friend, not foe."

In spite of her fear, Gabrielle was drawn to the witch, connected to her by some invisible thread, unable to disengage. There was something compelling about her, not mere attraction but a magnetism of subtle control, as if she could master the human will with only a wave of her hand.

"Rest assured," Minerva urged Gabrielle, her voice both soft and soothing.

Gabrielle felt her body relax, the witch's words hypnotic. "What do you want?"

"It must be perfect. There is no margin for even the slightest mistake."

"What must be perfect?" Gabrielle asked, confused.

"The remedy you now prepare."

Gabrielle's mind moved to Maud. She knew all too well that time was precious. The little girl's life was at stake. "But I can't delay, regardless of the reason."

"Haste sometimes has its place. But not now."

"I must tend a sick child," Gabrielle said.

"That's why I'm here. To offer guidance."

"I've been a healer for many years."

"I know, my lady," Minerva said. "I see all and know even more."

"And I've used this treatment many times."

"But it needs to be stronger," the witch insisted. "Maud deserves another day."

Gabrielle shook her head, reaching for her medicine. "I trust in my art and in this particular tonic. It's always worked before."

"Always?"

Gabrielle hesitated. "Usually," she muttered.

"Now is not the time to fail."

"How do you propose to make it better?"

An eerie smile crept across Minerva's lips. "A ribbon or bow is all that is required."

Gabrielle shivered when the witch swept past her, a chill breeze draping her body. She wanted to protest or try to resist, but, somehow, she couldn't do it.

"It's all right, child," Minerva said as she approached the table where Gabrielle had measured out each of the herbs. She studied the vial with a practiced eye.

Gabrielle surrendered. "Show me what it is that I should do."

Minerva moved her long bony fingers, waving them over the vial. Then she began to chant.

> "Blood, bone, bile, brain,
>
> Plague, palsy, pox, pain.
>
> Scurvy, septic, scratches, sprue,
>
> Ascites, abscess, aches, ague.
>
> Grippe, gleet, gravel, gored,
>
> Cough, croup, colic, cured."

As Gabrielle watched, a mist drifted above the mixture, rising to the ceiling and smelling faintly of roses. She wasn't sure what the witch had done or how she had created something so wonderous, but she wasn't about to protest.

"It's ready now," Minerva whispered.

Gabrielle grabbed up the vial. "I thank you for your efforts," she said, "but I must hurry. The child awaits."

But Minerva had vanished.

Chapter 48

Gabrielle looked about the room, aghast. She ran into the hallway, but no one was there. Minerva's mysterious appearance, her enthralling energy and bizarre chant, had her rattled, and she was not sure what she should do. Was the spell meant to make her medicine fail? Or had it made the tonic much stronger as the witch had claimed that it would? There was no time left to hesitate over what Minerva's intentions might be. Gabrielle could only hope and pray that the cure they'd prepared would work as they both intended.

She hurried across the courtyard, passing soldiers, their tunics emblazoned with the Marston coat of arms, swords dangling from their belts. The men had grown more vigilant, preparing for the attack. She hastened down the village's cobblestone streets until she reached the Carney's door, knocked, and hurried in.

"Her fever has gotten worse," Mrs. Carney said in dismay.

"This will help her," Gabrielle said, holding up the glass vial.

She entered the child's room and settled upon a stool beside the bed. She uncorked the vial that held the precious tonic, lifted the child's head, and helped her drink it.

"How are we to know this will cure her?" Captain Carney asked anxiously, his wife at his side. "We tried a tonic the tanner made, but it didn't help at all."

"And the seamstress gave her a powder to take, but her fever never waned," Mrs. Carney added.

"The failure of other methods does not mean Lady Gabrielle's attempt will fail," Marston said, standing to the side.

"I've brought others safely back from death," Gabrielle said simply, "and I shall do the same for your sweet Maud."

"We just want our daughter well, sire," Mrs. Carney cried.

"And she will be," Marston replied, and he turned to Gabriele. "Is there anything else you need or something that we should do?"

Gabrielle brushed the hair from Maud's face. "A moist cloth would now help her most."

Mrs. Carney shifted the fussing toddler on her hip and stepped into the kitchen. She came back a moment later with a cloth she'd dipped into a bucket of water.

Gabrielle laid it on Maud's forehead. "It'll be all right, child," she whispered. "You'll be running through the bailey in a day or two, playing catch with me."

"I must go," Marston said, eyeing the child with concern. "But I would like you all to join me for breakfast in the morning. Maud, too."

The Carneys nodded respectfully, as did Gabrielle. They took to heart his confidence in the lady's cure, praying that he saw what they could not, but every one of them was afraid the child might not live to see another day.

As the evening wore on, Maud's fever heightened and then lessened, took hold once again, and then gradually subsided. Many hours later, in the darkness just before dawn, Maud opened her eyes.

"Momma," she said hoarsely.

"I'm here, darling," her mother said, holding her hand.

"Can I go play with Gabrielle?" the child asked.

Gabrielle smiled down on the little girl, sighing with relief, as Mrs. Carney and her husband broke into tears.

"You put quite a scare into us, child," Mrs. Carney said.

Maud was weak, her skin pale, but her forehead was cool. "I feel better, momma. But I'm thirsty."

"I'll get you some water, darling," Mrs. Carney said as she hurried into the kitchen.

Captain Carney turned to Gabrielle, wiping a tear from his cheek. "I cannot say what my heart now feels."

She smiled and gently touched his arm. "You don't have to."

182

Two hours later, when the sun had climbed the eastern sky to deliver another day, Maud was sitting up on the edge of her bed, her eyes clear, her face bright.

"How are you doing, child?" Mrs. Carney asked.

"I'm all better, momma."

"Can I get you anything?"

"I'm hungry," Maud said.

"Let us go and eat," Captain Carney said cheerily. "The master invited us to the Great Hall to dine with him."

They gathered up their children, wrapping Maud in a blanket as a precaution, and made their way to the Great Hall. Michael Marston was waiting for them at the head of the table. He smiled when he saw Maud.

"I knew I would see you today," he said. "Are you feeling better?"

Maud pouted "Yes, but I'm terribly hungry, sire."

"There's plenty to eat," Marston said. "And we're so grateful you're here to share it."

"Lady Gabrielle made me better," Maud said.

"And we couldn't be more thankful," Mrs. Carney added, nodding at Gabrielle. "We don't know what we might do in return."

"You needn't do anything," Gabrielle said. "I assure you."

"But you saved her life," Mrs. Carney said.

Gabrielle could only smile humbly, but she was as grateful as Mrs. Carney that the cure had worked. She thought of the witch and wondered what role she had played. "She's a strong girl," she said, "and I'm sure she would have recovered. I just sped it along."

"I will never forget that you made me better," Maud sang out. "And I will always be your friend."

Mrs. Carney smiled, gazing proudly at her daughter. "As will I."

"We're all grateful," Marston said. "We're privileged to have someone with your gift grace the halls of Marston Castle."

"Thank you, sire," Gabrielle said, nodding respectfully.

Marston studied her for a moment. The rest of the party fell silent. "Unfortunately, I must impose upon you," he continued.

"In what way?" Gabrielle asked, perplexed.

"I know you're here against your will, and though I have tried to treat you with the respect you deserve, it's time I took another step."

"Thank you, sire," she said, wondering where the discussion would lead. Her heart beat a little faster in the hope that the time for her release was suddenly drawing near. Marston was a good man, kind and compassionate. She was sure he would let her go, maybe even go so far as to take her back to Normandy himself.

"Someday, we'll right this wrong," he said, "and your life will once more be what it was."

Gabrielle did not reply. She remained silent, daring to hope he would set her free.

"But with a battle about to begin and many wounded expected, I must insist that you direct their treatment."

Gabrielle nodded, her heart sinking. "As you wish, sire."

Chapter 49

Minerva paused at the bend in a narrow corridor to study a spider as it crawled up the cave wall. Amused for only a moment, she reached out and pushed a ragged rock that protruded above the creature's legs. The wall slid aside, and she stepped through the crack and into a fireplace beyond. The flames flickered before her, the heat enough to scorch human flesh, but she barely noticed it was even there. She heard the logs crackle and watched the shadows cast by the flickering flames. From her vantage point amid the blaze, she was able to peer into Trinity's room and study the occupant who would soon know she was there.

Trinity rose from the mattress. The room had grown warm, and she stood before a narrow window that afforded her a meager view of the bailey and the buildings perched beyond. She sighed, returned to the bed, and sat back down to await any news from Paul the Pure, but her attention was diverted. She studied the flames as they tongued the logs. Her gaze found a hazy outline amidst the blaze, and she leaned closer, eyes wide, but she knew not what it was.

Minerva smiled as she forced her image to become more and more defined, then let it fade. She seemed to grow smaller and then taller, here ghostly form ever changing before Trinity's watchful gaze. The witch's smile broadened, so amused was she with all the tricks she could play.

Trinity peered into the flames, wondering whether sanity was soon about to leave her. She stared at the unnerving image, trying to understand it. Although very little scared her, her skin pricked at the potent power she sensed was in the room, for even now her soul could see she was attended by an entity far mightier than she could ever be.

Minerva tired of her game and stepped straight through the flames. The fire flared but had no impact—not on her robe, her skin, or the hair about her head. Once clear of the fireplace, she positioned herself in the center of the room, a grin upon her face.

Trinity bolted upright in the bed and backed against the wall. She pulled the blanket about her, hoping it could somehow shield her from the witch, her eyes gaping and her breathing rapid. She froze, not sure what it was that she was supposed to do.

"A pleasant evening," Minerva crooned, "isn't it?"

"What do you want?" Trinity asked with a quivering voice.

"I won't hurt you," Minerva said, trying to reassure her.

Trinity shuddered. "What are you doing here?" she demanded.

Minerva took another step forward and stood before the bed. "I came to see who casts the spells that are but shadows of my own."

Trinity could only stare, wary of a witch with power so much greater than her own.

"Don't be afraid," Minerva said, her soothing voice a strange complement to her frightening image.

"Who are you?" Trinity asked, her whole body pressed against the wall.

"Minerva," she replied. "Witch of Marston Manor and all of its domains. And who are you?"

Trinity's expression changed, in a heartbeat, from fear to defiance. "You seem to know the answer," she said, "so the question need not be asked."

"I may know the name you give yourself, but I know not the woman," Minerva said. "Or perhaps I do."

"If your power is truly what you claim, you must know both."

Minerva cackled softly, enjoying the withering effect she had on a woman who tried to be so brave. "Maybe I do, maybe I don't."

"Leave me," Trinity demanded, trying to sound strong.

Minerva laughed. "I determine who comes and goes. I always have and always will." The elder witch took a step closer, looming, now, over Trinity. "Who taught you the arts?"

She hesitated. "Why should I tell you?"

"Because I'll learn the truth if I don't already know it."

Trinity narrowed her eyes at the witch, still unsure of who or what she was. "A wizard in Glastonbury."

"Lie after lie does not spell truth."

"Speak plainly."

Minerva's face grew taut. "You've never been to Glastonbury."

The shadow of fear reappeared in her mismatched eyes. "What do you want?"

"The Holy Grail."

"It's a fake," Trinity said. "An old chalice I only pretend is the Grail."

"You may be a fool, but I am not," Minerva said. "Where do you take it?"

Trinity paused, realizing that Minerva did already know the answers to the questions she posed. "To the highest bidder."

"Why did you journey to Marston Castle when there were other fortresses nearer at hand?"

"Sanctuary," Trinity said. "The barons come for me."

The witch scrutinized her face, which had paled with dread. "Why do I not believe you?"

"It's the one truth I have told."

"One baron may chase you but no more."

"Does it matter?"

"Thief, murderer, and charlatan all in the same skin."

Trinity glanced nervously about the room as if looking for a means of escape.

"He's committed more crimes than most can count," Minerva said. "How close is he?"

Trinity shrugged. "I cannot say for sure, but my powers tell me he's near."

"Your powers are weak. He doesn't come at all though you stole the Grail."

187

"It doesn't matter how I came by it," Trinity said. "It belongs to me."

"It belongs to Michael Marston. Its home is now his castle."

"When I go, I take the Grail with me."

"A threat you should not make if you manage to escape at all."

Trinity paused, her gaze hardening into a scowl, projecting every ounce of strength she could summon. "Leave me, witch."

Minerva ignored her. "Who's the old fool who pretends to be your father?"

"No one of consequence, but he's useful," Trinity said. "At least for now."

"What becomes of him when you carry out the deed you came here to undertake?"

Trinity's eyes widened. "That depends on what the future holds."

"But you have the gift, my dear. Surely you already know what shape tomorrow takes," Minerva said.

Then she stepped into the flames and vanished.

Chapter 50

"I was terrified when I saw her," Trinity said, describing her encounter with the witch to her accomplice.

"Are you sure it wasn't a nightmare?" asked Paul the Pure.

"I'm certain," she said. "I was as awake as I am now."

"Where did she come from?"

"She appeared from nowhere and stepped through the flames that raged in the fireplace."

"Maybe it was a trick, a bit of magic, instead of the sorcery you think you saw."

"If that is true, such a trick would take years to master, for I never doubted its reality."

Paul the Pure shook his head, trying to see what Trinity had described. "She must possess powers we cannot begin to imagine."

"She does," she replied. "Her presence alone was overwhelming."

"Do her powers exceed your own?"

Trinity hesitated. "She seemed to know my words before I spoke them. And she knows of our past. I fear the arts with which she works may indeed overshadow my own."

He was confused. "How can that be? You know the darkness better than you know the dawn. I can't imagine anyone could ever know more."

"I know tricks," she said. "I play with trinkets. I predict a future that may never come. I can fool a fool but no one with a thought in their head. This Minerva is different—much different. She's a real witch."

Paul the Pure nodded, seeming to understand the danger they faced in being exposed. "Do you think she knows why we're here?" he asked quietly.

"Does the rain fall to bathe the earth?" Trinity asked. "When someone appears from within a smoldering fire, their powers over the physical world are only the beginning—whether your eyes believe it or not."

"Then she must know I'm not your father."

"She does," Trinity said. "And that you've never been a druid."

His eyes widened. "She knows we stole the Grail."

"Only a fool would not," Trinity said. "But she didn't seem to know from whom."

"We've heard nothing from Baron Tweed. Marston never mentioned his name."

"That doesn't mean he breathes no more, and if he does, he's still a threat."

"We've only a day or two more to wait before the poison takes effect," he said. "Then we escape."

Trinity thought of the insidious liquid worming its way through Marston's veins. "How will we know when he is dead?"

"The flags will be lowered."

"What flags?" she asked.

"The coat of arms," he said. "They fly atop each tower. They lowered only when the master of the castle has met his end."

"It won't be long," she said. "Tonight or tomorrow."

"Does the witch know what we've set in motion?"

"It seemed she did," she said. "But she speaks in riddles and might know less than what she pretends."

Paul the Pure frowned, worried his plot would fail. "Do you think she's told him?"

Trinity heaved a sigh of distress. She was accustomed to being in control, not being controlled, and she felt as if Minerva dangled her on a string like a puppet. "I'm sure she has."

"But we can't assume she did," he said, "just because she lives within the walls."

"Who knows where she lives if she lives at all," Trinity said.

"But the castle is her domain, no matter where she walks."

Trinity glanced at her partner, still undecided about the role he would ultimately play. "I think trouble is about to find us," she said. "And the witch will lead the way."

"What should we do?" he asked. "We have few paths to take."

"We must leave as soon as we are able."

"We can't go far," he said. "We have yet to sell the Grail."

"We can hide in the woods if we must," she said. "At least until we meet the ship."

Paul the Pure fell silent, considering their options. "Marston said the barons' men and the French are about to attack."

"Then we must go before they do."

"But we have no way of knowing when the battle will begin. It could be days. It could be hours."

"Who knows we have the Grail?" she asked.

"Only Marston," he said.

"The man poses no threat," she said. "He'll be dead within a day."

"Then we best make our escape. Before the witch—or anyone else—sees our faces behind these masks."

Chapter 51

Gabrielle spent much of the day converting the Great Hall into a hospital as Michael Marston had directed. Five women volunteered to assist, Mrs. Carney among them, and they gathered all the medicine and bandages they could find and requested more from the captains who commanded the soldiers. They also collected dried herbs, vinegar, and lye soap from those within the walls. They then asked soldiers to bring fifty mattresses and place them on the floor in the hall to make ready for the wounded when they arrived.

After they'd finished, Gabrielle walked the castle grounds, pretending to watch the soldiers prepare for the impending battle while searching for a means to escape. She was hardly a stone's throw away from the keep when Maud came running up to her.

"I'm all better now," she sang out, breathlessly. "All because of you."

Gabrielle knelt beside her. "Yes, you are," she said as she hugged the child. "And I am so glad. I had no one to play with while you were sick."

"I can play after I do my chores."

"I would like that," Gabrielle said. "I'll be back when you're done."

As the child scampered off to help her mother, Gabrielle made her way toward the castle gates. She saw stockpiles of weapons, rocks, and timber, as well as food. Livestock were crammed into stables and chickens stuffed into coops. The villagers milled about, doing what they could to assist the soldiers, while the shopkeepers did a brisk business, selling their wares to a throng of people wary of the battle that was about to begin. Again she saw Jenks, his falcon flying high above and then beyond the fortress and returning several minutes later.

"Hello, Mr. Jenks," she said as she stopped to watch him.

"Good day, my lady," he replied.

As the falcon came to rest on his wrist, he turned away, fumbling about the bird's talons and retrieving something from its grasp.

"Is everything all right, Mr. Jenks?"

He looked over his shoulder. "It is, my lady."

She nodded politely. "Good day to you, then," she said as she walked away.

She completed her circuit of the grounds, having found no apparent means of escape, and returned to the keep. She entered the library where she found Marston scanning the shelves as if unable to find a specific volume. He seemed annoyed at himself for not being able to do so.

"Can I help you find something?" she asked as she entered.

He turned and smiled at her faintly. "No, it's not here. I'd procured an excellent collection of sketches of catapult construction. Perhaps Gideon has them."

She came closer, eyeing the shelves. She ran her fingers along the volumes, saw the manuscript he'd referenced on a lower shelf, withdrew it, and handed it to him.

"Is this it?" she asked.

"It is," he said, surprised. "How did you find it?"

She shrugged, hiding a grin. "I looked."

"Thank you," he said with a slight bow.

"I've spent the morning readying the hospital," she said, "with help from some of the soldiers and women in the village. And I saw Maud. She's doing well."

She watched as he nodded, thumbing through the manuscript in one of the chairs that sat before the fire. It was hard not to like the man. He was kind and compassionate, though she knew he must have darker facets, corners of his soul left unpolished which allowed him to slay men in battle.

"Do you have everything you need?" he asked.

"Not yet. The soldiers will add more beds, and they're gathering the ingredients we'll need to fashion cures."

193

"I am still hopeful our preparations will be for naught in the end."

Gabrielle eyed Marston, confused. "Aren't your enemy's forces massed outside the walls?"

"They are, but the barons and king might yet reach a truce."

"I thought negotiations had stalled," she said, a spring of hope rising within.

"They did indeed," he said, "but no matter the terms, peace is always preferable to war. It might not be too late."

Gabrielle studied her captor closely. An aging warrior, his best battles were surely behind him. She hoped he was right. A war not waged is surely won, defeat not found by any.

He noticed her watching him and smiled faintly.

"You look troubled," she said.

"No, not troubled."

"Deep in thought, perhaps?"

He studied her for a moment more. Then he spoke. "There's something I want to show you," he said softly. "It's for your own protection."

"What is it?" she asked.

"Life in a castle is dangerous," he continued.

"Especially when the enemy surrounds you."

"Our defenses are strong and our soldiers skilled, but the outcome of any battle can never be foretold."

"I understand," she said, wondering if the conversation had a double meaning, perhaps applying as much to them as to the battle at hand.

"There are those who want to conquer, enslave, or entomb."

She thought of her life in Normandy and the happiness that had been stolen from her. "Yes, I know," she said softly. "More than most."

He rose from his chair. "Come with me," he said. "There's an escape route. I want to show it to you."

"Do I need to escape?" she asked, shocked that he'd entrusted her with such a secret. He must know that, given the chance, she would flee at once and attempt to find her way to Montague.

"Yes," he said, his eyes trained on hers, the pain behind them apparent, the sorrow so sincere. "If there is any reason you no longer wish to be here, I give you my leave. You can go anywhere you want."

It was impossible not to share in the anguish of such a compassionate man, gentle and kind and always aware of what she seemed to need the most. "I know a love you never expected, has suddenly appeared," she said softly.

He smiled weakly, almost apologetically. "Although it was not intended, it can no longer be denied."

"You're a good man," she said. "More than most deserve."

He nodded with respect. "But I will never be Montague."

"No, you will never be Montague," she affirmed. "A man who loves me more with every breath he takes. But you've no need to be Montague. Not when Michael Marston can compare."

He laughed lightly. "No, I could not, nor would I try. I see your eyes when you speak his name, hear your words like a melody when you talk of times you shared. It's a love that can't be challenged, not by any man on earth."

She appreciated his insight, wisdom most would never know, and she saw a man who, until this day, she had never seen before. Her gaze was fixed on his, his eyes saying more than any word he spoke.

"If you do choose to stay," he continued, "even though you likely won't, I will treat you like the princess you have every right to be, give the love you do deserve, share each day the dawn shall bring as if it were my last. I will love you like no other as you would surely see."

She reached out her hand, lightly brushing the beard that dressed his cheek. "Yes, you would," she said. "And every word you've spoken is a promise you would keep. You possess every trait a man could have that I would ever seek."

195

"My lady," he said, bowing with respect, but knowing there was more to come.

"But so does Montague," she whispered.

"So he does," he said, his eyes a little sadder. "And fully deserving of such a prize that you offer any man."

She smiled and hugged him lightly. "Show me this secret passage that my eyes now ache to see."

He made his way to a bookshelf beside the fireplace. Where each shelf met its vertical support, a carved unicorn's head, identical to that emblazoned on the Marston coat of arms, hid the joinery. Marston eyed the right-hand support and grasped the unicorn's head on the middle shelf.

"Only a handful of my most trusted confidants know that this exists," he said.

The unicorn's head moved in his hand. He then pushed it inward, and the shelf began to rotate. It spun ninety degrees, revealing a stone passage beyond, large enough for a person to walk through.

"Come," he said, stepping into the corridor. It was dimly lit, a crystal casting a weak glow.

A cool breeze met them as they entered the tunnel. Built from the same stone as the castle, the passageway was narrow, hidden within the walls of the keep. It led them lower, down many slender steps, and then underneath the structure before it opened into a corridor that had been cut through the bowels of the cliff. Winding down and to the east, it extended a half mile more. The crystals that were spaced at varied lengths cast a dim light on the uneven walls, and Gabrielle shuddered at the sight of the scores of insects crawling along the rock.

"We're almost there," he said.

When they'd gone another fifty feet, the passage ended abruptly, a large stone blocking the path, a man-made wall abutting it with crisp lines of mortar. Marston crouched along the right-hand side and showed Gabrielle a cavity large enough for a hand.

"Look," he said, leaning forward. "Can you see this lever?"

He pointed to a sliver of stone, eight inches in length and as wide as a man's hand. "You just push it forward."

As he did so, the stone which blocked the passage that was six feet high and three feet wide turned on an invisible hinge, rotating ninety degrees just as the book shelf had done. As the rock spun, first the sky and then the sea beyond became visible, spilling golden light into the passage. They could hear the faint sound of water, the ocean rushing up to meet the shore.

Together, Marston and Gabrielle emerged from the passage and stood in the sunlight. They were perched on a ledge in the cliff's face thirty feet above the sandy shore, the base of the castle high above them.

"The sea," Gabrielle said, inhaling the salt air as she squinted toward the French coast.

"There's a path to your left that leads to the beach. You'll have to climb in some places."

"I could manage," she said. "If I had to."

"From here, you could escape by sea or journey beyond the castle's wharf to where the cliff is shallow and easily scaled." He pointed upwind. "Or you might stay in the forest, seeking safety in the shadows cast by the trees."

Gabrielle looked to where he'd pointed. "The trees are to the south?"

"Yes," he said, his eyes saying more than words ever could. "Where the French army now hides."

Gabrielle put a hand to her forehead and squinted up the coastline at the trees beyond.

"Montague leads them," Marston said softly.

"Montague!" she said, her voice alight with an excitement she could never try to contain. "He lives!"

"And he's only a mile away," Marston said, watching her closely.

"Now I know he's safe," she breathed. "At least for today, perhaps tomorrow."

"If you should need to flee," Marston continued, "the forest extends for several miles and wraps around the castle to the south. There is a road at its southernmost end. It leads to a

197

dock that is frequented by scores of ships—traders who carry goods to foreign lands. From there, you can reach any destination in the world," he sighed. "Even Normandy."

Chapter 52

Later that evening, Gabrielle stood on the wall, watching the waves in the silver light cast by the moon. The castle had been surrounded just before dusk, the barons' men to the north and west, the French to the south, sprawled along the forest's edge and strung across the castle entrance. But they never attacked. They remained visible to all, but not close enough to be reached by an archer's bow. They made a show of their strength, marching onto the field for a battle that had not yet been fought as if victory was theirs. They had only to take it. The vivid display of such a formidable force accomplished just what James the Bold intended it would, instilling fear in all who peered over the ramparts. The battle would begin if and when he and the barons chose, lasting minutes or months, sparing all or none.

Gabrielle looked down at the stone beneath her feet and realized that the secret passage lay just below her, hidden to all but a few. It had been well-built, a precious life-line that may never have been used, and she would tread its corridors that very night before the battle began. Or she could leave after it started. It was her decision to make.

After she'd soaked in the serenity the night provided and carefully considered the paths that lay before her, she decided it was worth the risk to flee. She had only to access the corridor, follow it to its end, and climb down the cliff to the shore. Then she could avoid the sentries who stood on the walls and the archers who might use her as a target and make her way to the south to find Montague, waiting with undying love.

She watched the sentries who were stationed in the towers and patrolling the castle walls, surveying the terrain. They were vigilant, knowing an enemy attack was near, and warily watched the camps that sprawled along the forest's edge. She walked back along the wall, following the same path from which she had come. She kept looking over her shoulder, ensuring she wasn't being followed, as she passed a patrolling sentry and slipped into the keep.

Gabrielle hurried through the halls and went straight to the library. She knew Marston's quarters were in the adjacent room, and she listened closely for any sound that might reveal he was there, but all was quiet. He was probably atop one of the towers, watching the enemy just as she'd been doing. Or he might be within the library bent over a codex of military tactics. She stood at the doorway, listening for footsteps or voices.

After several moments of silence, Gabrielle pushed the door open and strode over to the bookshelf beside the fireplace. She opened the bookcase, just as Marston had shown her, and quickly stepped inside. It was dark and damp, moisture clinging to each of the walls of the narrow corridor. She stood tentatively at the entrance as her eyes adjusted to the dim light of the crystals that lit the way to the stairs. She gently closed the door behind her and advanced slowly, reaching her hand out into the gloom to ensure that nothing was there. Her heart raced as she moved forward cautiously one step at a time.

Gabrielle had faced many horrors, and yet the close darkness of the secret passage, the scores of spiders climbing the walls, made her blood run cold. She descended the narrow staircase, making her way ever nearer freedom with each careful step she took. As she continued forward, her courage mounted, and she began to move more quickly, hurrying through the halls until her hands skimmed across rock, and she knew she was below the keep. She was about to cross under the bailey and make her way to the cliff. She spurred herself on, gasping, not knowing what to expect. When she reached the end of the corridor, she found the lever Marston had showed her and shifted the stone. It yawned open before her.

She was enveloped by a warm breeze and the faint taste of salt from the sea. She peered across the waves towards Normandy and stared down the cliff face, envisioning the climb she would make from the ledge to the sand. Then she turned to look to the south, hoping that Montague awaited her somewhere in the trees that sprawled along the coast. Knowing he was so close made her miss him more than she could have imagined only a few short weeks before.

She summoned all of her courage and moved to step over the threshold of the corridor and into the moonlight, but she couldn't. She tried again, and once more her feet remained rooted, not moving even an inch. She was helpless, stranded on the ledge, but she didn't know why. Again and again, she tried to force herself into the open, and each time she was met with failure. Tears trickled down her cheeks as she struggled to go on, not knowing what was right or what was wrong. She wanted to leave. She wanted to escape.

Or did she?

Chapter 53

Deep in a Norman forest, on a bed of moss beside the tree that served as his home, Alaric watched the moon as it glowed in the clear night sky. His cauldron hung beside him from a branch above a fire, the mixture coughing mist into the air. He waved his hands through it, back and forth, muttering softly in Norman French. Gradually an image formed in the fog, the shimmering figure of Gabrielle, standing atop a ledge on a cliff thirty feet above the waves.

"Go, child," he urged, once the image became clear. "Montague awaits."

He watched as she waited, moving not an inch. She stared at the deserted shore, studying the sand that sprawled beneath her from north to south, and looked across the sea as if she could see the Norman coast. Her eyes were glassy with fear. She trembled before the unknown and tried to take a tentative step but failed with each attempt.

"Come to me, Gabrielle," the wizard said, trying to persuade her. "You have the strength."

She studied the cliff face, glancing left and right, and then, after several seconds passed, and it seemed as if she found her courage, she tried to take a step. Her body pitched forward, but her feet were frozen, rooted to the earth.

Alaric held out his hand to her image and beckoned her to move. "Come, child," he coaxed. "Come." Still she stood transfixed, held captive by an energy the wizard didn't know was there. His red eyes flashed with anger. "You can do it. You must," he said, no longer coaxing but demanding.

Gabrielle gave it one more try, her body language and the set of her jaw showing that she wanted nothing more than to climb down the cliff to the shore below. But she couldn't, no matter how hard she tried, and tears dripped down her face with every failed attempt.

Alaric moved his hand forward, urging her to take her freedom before it disappeared, the future that she dreamed of now within her grasp. When his effort met with failure, he tried to plunge his hand into the mist, so he might grab her image and force it down the cliff. But he couldn't. His hand would move no farther. He tried to push forward, using all his strength, but he was met by a wall he could not see, unable to pierce the fog that held her image captive, to change the direction she had taken and the decision she had made. It was as if he were faced with a mountain that would never move, a tide too strong to turn.

"Come, Gabrielle," he demanded, his anger flaring as she glanced backward over her shoulder.

He raised both hands, pulling as hard as he could, but he couldn't persuade her, his words unheard or ignored. Incensed by his weakness against this unknown force, the wizard again tried to pull Gabrielle away from the grip of her captors. He focused all of his mystical energy and stared at her image as it floated in the fog, training his powers on her feet, willing them to descend the rocky ledge to the beach below.

Seconds passed, and still he failed. Gabrielle's image began to fade. It shimmered in the mist, growing fainter and then brightening, but a moment later it was gone, and only the steamy vapor remained.

Then the faint flicker of another image took her place. It was difficult to see, so Alaric dropped his hands and leaned forward, staring in the mist. At first, he didn't believe what he was seeing, but the longer he stared, the crisper the image became until it betrayed the likeness of a figure few could ever miss. It was a woman's shape, first a tiny fleck no bigger than a bug, but gradually it grew bigger, revealing a slender woman dressed in black, her eyes dark but twinkling gold, a tangled mass of hair heaped upon her head. The image swelled until its vividness rivalled his own and then grew even more luminous as if to threaten all that was. The woman towered over Alaric, now twice his size. She glared at him angrily, pointing a finger tipped with a long, crooked nail.

"Beware, wizard," she hissed. "Stay away!"

Chapter 54

As Gabrielle struggled to move, fighting to take those first few steps to recapture the dreams she once thought would be hers, Minerva cackled, knowing that no matter how hard she tried, Gabrielle was now bound to Marston. The spell the witch had cast had finally taken hold, and like a tree whose powerful roots spread invisibly underground, her magic was forging a clasping love, joining the hearts of Michael Marston and the Lady Gabrielle—whether they realized it or not. It had been a challenge, muting the love between Montague and Gabrielle, their affection so strong and true. But Minerva had gradually driven a wedge between them, splitting their intertwined souls in two. The witch continued to cast spell upon spell, wrapping Marston and Gabrielle ever tighter in a web from which they never could escape. Their bond would be unbreakable to all except her.

As she watched Gabrielle struggle against the pull of her magic, Minerva also sensed another force opposing her own, urging Gabrielle forward, tugging her in a direction the witch didn't want her to go. The efforts of this unknown entity were weak and distant, coming, as they did, from someone whose days were numbered. Her rival sorcerer was scores of decades old, perhaps even centuries, and he had long ago left summer and autumn behind to enter the winter of his life. His power was a shadow of what it once was, dissipating like the mist that carried with it the morning's dew.

For Minerva, he was a toy to be played with, a child among adults. She used her crooked finger to poke a circle in the mist and surrounded him. Then she drew a pentagram and pinned his image in it. She smiled, knowing he was powerless to do a thing while she held his image fast, trapped in her realm of potions and spells. With tears dripping down her cheeks, Gabrielle turned and retreated down the corridor. She didn't understand why it was that she couldn't move. The one chance she'd been given might never come again. But what she could not know was that her love for Montague wasn't strong enough to overcome Minerva's spell. And though she could not name what drove her back from where she came, she noticed she felt different, overcome by a strange new sensation, her love for Marston starting to bloom.

Minerva fumbled with the ingredients on her altar, rooting through her pouches and vials, making ready to enhance the spell she'd already cast. When the Lady Gabrielle reentered the library and closed the secret door behind her, the witch waved her hand through the vapor that hung above her cauldron, and the images that swam before her quickly disappeared.

She hurriedly sorted the ingredients she needed and tossed them into the brew: the feathers of a swan, the petals of a rose, a fistful of lace, the eyelashes of a maiden, lavender, and blood which would act as glue. The liquid burped and bubbled, spewing steam into the voids above. Once the mixture settled to a simmer, Minerva put aside all her things, took up two lustrous auburn hairs, and dropped them in the cauldron. Then, with slender fingers, she gathered up several hairs that had come from Michael Marston's head and dropped them in, too.

She began to chant.

"One to seek him,

One to find him,

One to bring him,

One to bind him.

Heart to heart,

Blood be mixed,

So say I,

This spell is fixed.

So shall it be."

Chapter 55

Montague rode his steed along the edge of the French camp and studied the plain that led to the castle. An open expanse of green, quiet and unmolested by nothing save the occasional rabbit, it would soon be littered with the dying and the dead. The castle stood, proud and defiant, daring the invaders to come, ready for any assault the enemy might thrust upon it. Sentries marched back and forth along the curtain wall, archers stood poised in towers, bows on their shoulders but too far from the French to do anything but wait and watch. All of the soldiers wore a red tunic bearing the Marston coat of arms. Some had donned metal helmets, others with coats of mail. Montague wondered how many men would lose their lives in the battle about to begin.

The battle would be vicious and in years might not matter. But for Montague it was so much more than a fight on foreign soil, because the Lady Gabrielle, his very reason for greeting the dawn, was hidden behind the castle walls. Somehow, he had to defeat an enemy, had to foist upon the English all the murderous weapons of war, without harming her. And although it was a feat not easily achieved, it was one he resolved to accomplish.

"The men have moved forward as far as they dare," Piers said, bringing his horse alongside Montague.

Scores of cavalry and hundreds of infantrymen were camped along the southern side of the castle, a sea of men in pale blue tunics hugging the forest, just as the barons' men did to the north and west. Together they surrounded the fortress on three sides, keeping out of range of the archers and the catapult arm they could just make out behind the fortress walls.

"Let's patrol the line," Montague said. "It's good for the men to see me and know I share the risks that they've been asked to take."

They rode parallel to the line, and Montague eyed his men, greeting soldiers and commanders, most of whom he knew by name. Horses were tethered to trees in the forest, and wagonloads of supplies were arranged in a row, easy for all to access.

"Gathered before me is the best army in all of England," Montague called out to his men.

"And we've the best commander on earth," one of his men shouted as others cheered.

Montague nodded, the compliment appreciated. "And who might you be?" he asked the grizzled knight, a man who was older, slender, and lithe.

"Luc from Lisieux," said the elderly soldier. "I fought for your father, and I now fight for you."

"It's by efforts like yours that wars may be won," Montague said. "And your courage is a model for all men to follow."

Luc bowed majestically, his respect apparent. "My thanks, my lord, for what you have done, for without you Normandy would no longer exist."

"A compliment shared by all who are here and not meant for any one man alone," Montague said. "Luc of Lisieux, it's an honor to know you. Come to my tent when supper is served, and you shall dine with Piers and I."

"My thanks, my lord," Luc said with surprise. "It's a dinner I shall never forget,"

Montague and Piers galloped away. "It's my only wish that men like Luc live to see the Normandy they love once again."

Piers hesitated, glancing at his commander. "Victory sometimes takes those who don't deserve to be taken."

"Then may victory be ours but with very little cost."

"It seems we prepare for a siege more so than a battle," Piers said, referring to the ring of men that surrounded the castle. "Perhaps the show of force is meant to steal their courage."

Montague nodded. "It is my hope we win without a fight. It seems that, by design, we fight with the mind as well as the body."

"I think the attack will come," Piers said, "whether we want it or not."

Montague was quiet, watching the fortress as they moved down the line. "One way or another, I must find her," he said softly.

"You are sure she is there?" Piers asked. "The wizard no longer sees as he once did."

Montague studied the castle, focusing on the keep. "You speak the truth," he said. "But he offers the only thread to which I cling. And I will do what must be done."

"Are you suggesting, sire, that you sneak in, alone, and rescue the Lady Gabrielle?"

"I am."

"Should I not be by your side?"

"Not this time, my friend. If I don't return, you must lead the men."

Piers stared fixedly at the castle. "It would be difficult to get in and even harder to get out."

"There's still the secret corridor."

"But how will you find it?" Piers asked.

"If I can't, I must scale the wall, perhaps in the cover darkness just before dawn."

"A difficult task in a castle left unguarded, suicide in one manned such as this."

"I will get in," Montague said, "no matter the odds."

"No path is obvious," Piers said.

Montague turned to face his loyal lieutenant. "Unless the wizard can find one," he said. "And if he can't, my task is only harder. But it will never be avoided."

Chapter 56

As Montague's men took their positions along the southern face of the castle, James the Bold eyed his own forces sprawled across the plain in the north and west. He sat astride his horse, ready for battle should it come, the wild boar on his green tunic embodying the courage of its owner. The two tusks which sprouted from his metal helmet seemed to pierce the very air, and his broadsword dangled from his belt beside a spiked club. A single iron thorn was missing, likely left in one of his victim's skulls. Jamet was beside him. In his pale blue tunic, the emblem of a roaring lion affixed to his chest, he seemed not to belong amid the forest of green tunics worn by the barons' men.

Blaise fell in beside Jamet and James the Bold as they patrolled the line, his face hidden in a hooded cloak. His white stallion kept pace with little effort and exhibited such a gallant gait that many of the men wondered why their leader wasn't mounted on the horse instead. Blaise's imposing figure, which brought to mind the fearsome reaper, caused some of the soldiers to shudder at the sight of him, knowing he possessed a gift that few on earth could mimic.

James the Bold snickered. "We must be a frightening sight to behold from within the castle walls," he said.

"They've likely never faced such a foe," Jamet said.

"And never will again," said James the Bold, "for this will be their final fight."

"When do we attack?" Jamet asked.

"We don't," James the Bold replied. "At least not now."

Jamet looked at the warlord, his gaze briefly falling on his scarred cheek, before he turned to the castle, its walls lined with defenders. "Merely a show of force? Or the beginning of a siege?"

"Let them see our faces," said James the Bold, "and in a few days' time, we'll know."

"They could be lured from the castle walls if pushed to desperation," Jamet said.

"Marston is too cautious to be trapped," said James the Bold. "Or he would already be dead."

"But he can be tricked," Blaise said. "Deceit is a valued ally when properly employed."

Jamet turned to the warlock. "What do you propose?"

Blaise looked at the two men, one a warlord, the other versed in wartime tactics he may never have witnessed in the flesh. "When we're certain they've assessed our strength, we hide half of our forces."

"In hope that Marston leaves the fortress to attack?" Jamet asked.

"He may assume our men have left to fight another battle," Blaise said.

Jamet glanced at the warlock, seeing merit in his plan. "Or we can vary the number of fires throughout the encampments continuously along with the French," he suggested. "More fires than men on one side of the castle, far less on another, yet the forces will number the same. Marston won't know which wall to defend."

James the Bold listened to the advice of his lieutenants, not swayed to change what he had planned. "Just one more tactic we might use," he said. "It's a clever ploy under cover of darkness, but it will likely fail in the light of day. Marston is no fool. He'll recognize the trap."

"True, but if a trap is properly set, it will catch even those who know it exists," Blaise replied.

Jamet narrowed his eyes at the warlock who tended to speak in riddles. "But why would he let himself be snared if he knows what we intend?"

Blaise studied both the Frenchman and James the Bold. "If he is faced with a force far smaller than his, why would he suffer a siege?"

James the Bold eyed the wizard, finally understanding. "He wouldn't," he said. "He would attack. Just as I would."

"And then he can be defeated," Blaise said. "Caught in a spider's web."

"Is this to be our strategy?" Jamet asked with disbelief. "Try to trick a master into a move no one would make?"

The cold grin of a killer spread across James the Bold's face as he glared at the flags flying on the castle towers, the Marston coat of arms in full display. "We need no strategy as of now. We simply wait 'till the flags no longer fly."

Chapter 57

Lady Gabrielle sat in the library until late in the evening, wrestling with emotions she couldn't control. She loved a man from Normandy, his image always with her—his warm smile, the look of love housed in his eyes. But each day he seemed to grow more distant, though he was only a mile away. The ache she felt since she'd left his side had never subsided, but it was slowly starting to fade, a shadow of what it once had been. She had been given the chance to escape, to find her way to his waiting arms, but, somehow, she hadn't been able to flee. It didn't seem to matter how badly she'd wanted to go, or how hard she'd tried. An invisible anchor confined her to the castle, and she didn't know why.

She had been taken against her will, made a captive at the very time in her life that happiness had found her, drying those childhood tears that had never quite subsided after losing her parents and sisters. She had yearned for release, thought of nothing but her reunion with her beloved Montague, yet, somehow, she was powerless to leave. What kept her tied to a country in which she didn't belong, bound to a man she didn't know, unable to live the life she'd dreamed of? She wanted Montague of Rouen. Or did she? She had to find out.

She left the library, ascended the stairs that led to the top of the castle wall, and watched the waves in the distance. The night sounds had changed. No longer was the stillness broken only by the crashing waves and the hoots of owls asking who it was that trespassed up and down the plain. Murmurs from far-away conversations drifted upon the gentle breeze, their talk accented by outbursts of laughter and curses. She glanced north and south where the enemy camped along the fringe of the forest, myriad campfires reflecting in the sky like stars on a cloudless night.

"What is it that has grown between us?" a solemn voice asked from behind her.

She turned to find Michael Marston, the look in his eyes searching and lovelorn, saying more than words ever could.

"It seems we are bound to one another," he said. "Whether it was planned or not."

"You knew?" she asked, her mind reliving images of her failed escape.

"I could feel it."

He knew she'd tried to flee but could never feel her struggling at the threshold of her freedom. He spoke in metaphors and probably wondered, as she did, why she had chosen not to go. Aside from her fear of the unknown, which had paled beside her desire for Montague, only Michael Marston could have kept her at the castle.

"I offered the passage to give you the choice, but I must confess I had hoped you would not leave," he said. "My heart was pulled, with every step you took, as was yours."

Gabrielle blinked at Marston, her thoughts beginning to reel. "Something drew me back. But what it was I do not know."

He moved closer, his body almost touching hers, his face close. But he didn't speak. He merely looked into her eyes.

"Or perhaps I don't want to admit what it was that held me," Gabrielle breathed.

"You may have been afraid, wary of the dangers that might befall you in an unknown land."

She hesitated. "I've been in strange lands before."

"The battle then, fear of the attack."

"I've lived through the darkest days of war," she said quietly.

"Perhaps the journey, knowing how difficult it might be, made you reconsider."

"I have traveled," she said. "Both near and far."

He paused, looking at her flawless face, her eyes so vivid and green. "Could it be that someone has caused you to return?"

"Perhaps," she said softly. "Whether I choose to confess it or not."

Marston reached for her, his hand lightly brushing the auburn hair that cascaded down her back. "And what are we now to do?"

"What would you like to do, sire?" she asked, incapable of pushing him away. She wanted to scream that it was Montague she loved, to declare it so loudly it woke the dead, yet, somehow, she couldn't.

"On my honor, I will never hurt you," he promised.

"I know," she whispered. She realized he had expected her to leave, had imagined that one day he would find the passage door ajar and his captive gone.

"You are always welcome here, for as long as you choose to stay. I shall keep you safe."

She looked at him, such a sincere and compassionate man. "Maybe you've shown me what a man can be but rarely is."

He stared into eyes reflecting the soft light of the moon. "I can make you happy," he whispered. The Englishman leaned toward her, his lips lightly brushing hers.

With a tantalizing shudder, she realized she could not resist. She now didn't want to.

He kissed her again, harder, and pulled her closer, then broke away, looking deep into her eyes, seeking acceptance or denial.

She did not pull away. Instead, trembling as he held her hands in his, she said softly, "May we go inside? My bones are chilled."

"Whatever you wish," he said, feeling that once they took a drastic step of acceptance of each other, there would be no turning back.

"I'll be in my chambers," she whispered as she slipped away.

214

Chapter 58

Michael Marston waited on the curtain wall a moment more, watching the stars spread across the sky, mirroring the campfires surrounding the castle. He realized a new day was about to dawn. The tragedies of yesterday were muted, if only for a few minutes. He had been blessed with a reprieve from the pain that forever shrouded his heart. Though he couldn't explain what was happening and dared not question why it was so, he felt he was fated to be with Gabrielle, and nothing, not even Montague, could break the bond that had mysteriously grown between them.

He turned toward the keep and walked slowly along the wall. He passed a sentry, nodding, giving him words of encouragement as he stood guard watching an enemy assembled just beyond the range of an archer's bow. When he went inside, the corridors were empty, servants in their quarters, enjoying the few hours each day that belonged only to them. Others, including Gideon, had retired to their rooms and were either asleep or preparing for the battle the dawn would surely bring.

Marston made his way to Gabrielle's room and knocked lightly on the door, almost timidly. He waited anxiously in the corridor, wondering if she would indeed allow him to enter or if their conversation on the curtain wall been only a dream. If it had, he would live forever within a renewed nightmare, suffering the mental torment that losing loved ones engraves upon the heart.

A few seconds later, he heard a voice, tentative but determined, urging him to enter. He opened the door to find Gabrielle sitting on a wooden bench by a small fire, the glow on her face as warm as the embers.

"I've been waiting, sire," she whispered, her voice husky.

He sat beside her, not sure what would happen, uncertain if the feelings that had joined their hearts would ever be acted upon, or if it was a step too great to be taken. They sat side by side for a few awkward moments, neither speaking. Finally,

Marston could not resist touching her auburn hair. His calloused fingers grazed the soft skin of her neck.

She smiled shyly and leaned towards him, her body radiating an intoxicating warmth as she laid her head on his shoulder. He kissed her lightly on the forehead, pulling her closer, and held her hand. She raised her head, her eyes slowly closing, and their lips met. The kiss was long, sensual and satisfying, and when they pulled apart, he lightly kissed her neck.

She looked at him as if questioning what was about to occur and how it had come to be, and he pulled her toward him, and they embraced, his lips on hers, his hands trailing the length of her torso, cupping her breasts, and moving to her hips.

When she began to shudder, he cupper her face with his hands and whispered softly,

"Yesterday is a memory, and tomorrow is a dream."

She seemed to mutter, "Then may today erase all yesterdays and usher in tomorrow."

Their lips met again, tentatively at first and then more urgently, pressing and probing, their bodies entwined. Gabrielle felt their hearts beat as one, the blood pounding through their veins, surging to their loins. And then, abruptly, she broke free of Marston's kiss, panting and breathless, her head spinning, her heart racing.

"Only an angel could rival your beauty," he said softly.

He traced the curves of her body with his fingers, aroused by her moans, and eased her onto the bed, lying down beside her. He gently lifted her skirt above her waist, his hands pulling at her undergarments as she fumbled with his leggings. He teased her, kissing the yet hidden wonders of her body with his fingertips, while she felt every fiber of her being responding, yielding, as he tasted and teased, prolonging what was to come.

He took what he desired, his need at once forceful and tender, practiced and attentive where a younger man might blunder ahead, seeking only his own satisfaction. She was undone by both his vulnerability and insistent longing, and soon they joined as one, clinging together in a passionate embrace, their lips sensuously searching, their passion a testament to their newfound love.

When their bodies were spent, they lay breathless in each other's arms, caressing one another with tenderness, neither having ever experienced such passion. Their faces glowed with the overpowering warmth of a love neither knew existed.

Chapter 59

Deep beneath the castle, buried in the bowels of the earth, Minerva watched Gabrielle and Michael Marston, the image of their clandestine embrace perfectly captured in the mist that rose from the murky brew in her cauldron. As they drifted off to sleep, Minerva smiled slyly. Her spell had been among her strongest and had succeeded in taking two hearts and making them one.

But the witch hadn't time to relish her triumph. Blaise, the warlock who accompanied the barons' men, would be a constant battle. She also fought Alaric, the wizard allied with the French, and kept a wary eye on Trinity, the insipid witch who posed as a seer, and her partner, Paul the Pure.

Blaise would be difficult to keep at bay. His power was strong, almost rivaling her own, his commitment firm. He had countered one of her more insidious spells, casting his own to banish the pus-covered boils that had spread across his body. Her action had served more as a warning than an attempt to render him powerless. Still, she had been impressed by how quickly he had countered her magic. He was evil, his soul as black as a booming thunderhead, and she knew she could never rest while he threatened the castle and all who lived in its domain.

Alaric, on the other hand, was a gentle being whose powers waned with every passing day. The aged wizard could peer into the night, see through to its end and into the morrow, but he couldn't change what was about to come nor alter anything that had already occurred, at least not drastically. And he had weak defenses. His will could easily be overcome. Minerva viewed him as more of a nuisance than an enemy. Nevertheless, she would keep a watchful eye on where he was and what he was doing.

Her third adversary, Trinity, was trouble. Though she was a witch with little power, she was cunning and could somehow shield prying eyes from peering into her soul, whether that was her intention or not. Minerva knew she schemed and plotted, fooling even those not easily fooled, and foresaw a future in which she left only disaster in her wake. Sometimes Minerva could see her thoughts, but often her visions were clouded, and she wasn't sure why. Trinity had not the strength to thwart her, and Paul the Pure had no gift at all. Or did he? Could the powers of the spirit realm live in the old fool while only a shadow of the gift resided in his supposed daughter? It was a question that begged to be answered, but Minerva was not terribly concerned. She would overcome. She always did.

She returned her attention to the image that quavered above her cauldron. Gabrielle lazed in Marston's arms. He stroked her hair, his eyes closed and his body completely relaxed. Such an embrace was what her master needed most. He might now forget the sorrow that had become his past and instead dream of tomorrow. What's more, Gabrielle could give him the confidence he needed to wage a war meant for younger men, to fight a battle destined for those in the summer of their lives. Now she had only to give him the strength to win, the courage to recognize he had it, and the intellect to see what was best for those who served him and looked to him to lead. Gabrielle would take the pieces that Michael Marston had become and mold them into the man his people needed him to be. She would be the glue that held him together for as long as he needed her.

She fiddled with her cauldron, adding a handful of potent black sage, and the image of Michael Marston and the Lady Gabrielle slowly disappeared. She turned to her altar and searched through dozens of bottles, vials, and pouches containing powders, herbs, and crystals. Still others contained the body parts of an unfortunate assortment of creatures. Minerva began her new spell by selecting slivers of a gray stone streaked with black that came from a distant island in the Mediterranean Sea and placing them into the cauldron. Four leaves followed, mixed and mashed: dandelion, damiana, mugwort, and horehound. A pinch of cinnamon, eyebright powder, and red sandalwood were next. A turquoise liquid followed, blended from the ingredients of other vials she possessed. The murky potion hissed a plume of vapor followed by a puff of purple smoke. The witch dropped in a hapless spider next before finally adding clay from the northern coast and a tiny orange crystal.

She leaned back, studying the product with the eye of a practiced sorceress. Then, with a dab of her finger and a sniff of the vapor that hung in the air, she nodded with satisfaction. She spat into the brew three times to augment the force of its enchantment.

The concoction sizzled with a flash of cobalt smoke as the granules of herbs caught fire. The flame spread a few inches from the cauldron and cast a gray haze three feet into the air and spread over an area several feet wide. The liquid continued to boil and bubble, and the smoke revealed an image of the sun rising over the sea. Minerva watched the concoction carefully, and when she was convinced she had produced the desired effect, she began to mutter a chant.

"Tomorrow comes, tomorrow goes,

Whispered words that no one knows.

Tell the tales of ghosts and men,

Search the signals serpents send.

Share the secrets of man's soul,

Sacred thoughts that evil stole.

Use the vision, use the light,

Haunted creatures of the night."

She kept stirring the murky brew, studying the mixture as she did so, repeating the verses of the chant in a whisper.

Seconds later, a dusky image of the future appeared, rising over the cauldron, shimmering in the dim light her crystals cast. It wasn't an image she wanted to see.

But it didn't really matter. She could change it.

Chapter 60

"The barons' men surround the fortress," Trinity said. "Escape may not be an option."

"I have to ensure that Marston dies," said Paul the Pure. "Regardless of our fate."

"The flags still fly," Trinity said, pointing out the window.

Paul the Pure looked up at the closest tower, the Marston coat of arms perched on a pole above the stone. "Only for an hour or two at most," he muttered.

Trinity knew they'd delayed too long. "We're trapped," she said. "Unless we can find a way to pass, unmolested, through the armies' ranks. We haven't much time."

"The ship won't arrive for two more days."

"If we don't leave now and the battle breaks out, we'll never make our escape."

"They won't deny passage to an old man who leans on a cane," said Paul the Pure.

"Marston will not let us leave," she said, rolling her eyes, "and the enemy would take us captive."

"For what purpose?" he asked.

"To ask questions about the castle's defenses," she said. "They will surely torture us, too, if they don't like our replies."

Paul the Pure was quiet, realizing their dilemma was far more serious than he had imagined. "At least we're safe here," he said, "no matter what direction the battle takes."

"Our only hope is that Marston dies," Trinity said, "and the captain surrenders the castle quickly."

"We have a friend in James the Bold no matter how the days unfold."

"In the meantime, we cannot ignore what's most important."

"The Grail?" he asked.

"Yes," she replied, tiring of the doddering fool. "It's worth much more than Marston's head."

Paul the Pure grew pensive. "What should we do?"

"Sell the Grail as planned," Trinity said. "Which is why we have to somehow leave this accursed castle."

"Can't we sell it to someone else?"

"It only has value to the buyer who knows it."

"Everyone knows the Holy Grail."

"They know the legend, not the chalice," she said, growing more and more irritated by his clumsy questions. "No one knows how it truly appears."

"Baron Tweed did."

"And Marston didn't. Not until we told him."

"The least of our problems, it seems to me," he said.

"And the witch can still stand in our way," Trinity said, afraid of her power. "We can't foretell what she will do."

Paul the Pure sighed, overwhelmed by the obstacles they faced. "Can you consult the stones?"

Trinity shook her head, doubtful. Her powers were genuine and always had been, but she couldn't compete with the witch. "I'll try," she said. "But the witch is clever. She may prevent it."

Paul the Pure seemed surprised. "She sees your thoughts?"

"No, but she sees the future."

Trinity grabbed up her satchel and withdrew the runes. She sat on the floor, focused her thoughts, and tossed them in the air. They landed in a scattered heap, each symbol bearing a different meaning. She waved her hands above them, and an image which she alone could see gradually began to form.

It was the barons' army preparing for battle, aided by the French. They stood at the edge of the plain, their forces surrounding the castle. Then a second image appeared—Michael Marston, a look of concern upon his face, consulting with

Gideon. She was confused, not knowing if she witnessed the future or the past.

She waved her hands in the opposite direction. The image of Marston faded but soon was replaced by the entrance to the keep and the steps that led to highest reaches of the castle. Intrigued, Trinity kept swirling her hands above the runes, urging the image forward, all of her attention focused upon where the steps might lead. She marked the passage of each step as if she trod upon them and emerged in the Great Hall. She crossed the cavernous room, climbed a spiral staircase, and entered a corridor that led to a library. Shelves of books lined the walls, and a fireplace built of stone yawned at the far end of the room. She focused on the bookcase beside it, saw the unicorn that dressed the middle shelf, and watched as an invisible hand twisted it to the right. The shelf slid along the wall, exposing a corridor lit by crystals.

Trinity held her breath, waving her hands as the image continued slowly changing as the seconds passed. She was led through the corridor, winding down through the castle walls to a corridor far below. It stretched a good distance before it came to an end, a large rock blocking the path. The witch watched, not daring to blink, as the invisible hand pushed a stone lever, and the rock began to rotate.

Suddenly, she was standing on a ledge thirty feet above the sea.

Chapter 61

After Paul the Pure had gone, Trinity made her way to the highest floor of the keep, peeking around corners to make sure each corridor was clear. When she reached the library, she glanced inside and found the room empty. She waited at the threshold, listening, and when she was met with nothing but silence, she hurried to the bookshelf beside the fireplace. She studied the unicorn carvings that matched those the runes had revealed and searched for one that would open the secret door.

When she was sure she'd found the right one, she paused and again listened closely, ensuring she was alone. Then she twisted the unicorn bust on the top shelf, but nothing happened. She furrowed her brow and tried another and then another, moving about the bookshelf, but finding no success. But when she got to the middle shelf and touched the unicorn on the right side, pulling and then pushing, the shelf moved away from the wall just as it had in her vision. She peered inside, saw a rocky corridor dimly lit by crystals, and knew the images she'd seen weren't a dream, that the runes had not failed her. Perhaps she did possess the gift, more so than she'd ever believed.

She closed the doorway and hurried back to her room, moving stealthily down each hallway to ensure she wasn't seen. She now knew she could escape, and she would do so, but only when the time was right. She debated whether or not to tell Paul the Pure. He was a good partner—together they had plotted many a profitable deception—but he was obsessed with killing Marston and collecting his fee from James the Bold. It seemed to her that the real reward was bound to the Holy Grail and whatever riches it might bring. For all she knew, James the Bold had no intentions of paying them anything. He might kill them both so the crime they'd committed would never be revealed. She didn't think that risk justified the meager reward that might await them—if any did at all.

Not long after she'd returned from the library, Paul the Pure knocked on her door. She let him in.

"I discovered a route that we can take," he said as he sat on a bench across from her bed. "A small door, a sally port, that's near the southeast tower. It's not well sealed."

Trinity considered the path he'd found and all who might see them take it. "Can we avoid the archers? Those that guard the wall?" she asked.

"If we leave tonight, just before dawn," he said. "Both archer and enemy may not be at their best."

Trinity knew she could escape whenever she chose. She only had to decide if she wanted Paul the Pure to come with her. "Should we wait one more day to be certain of Marston's demise?"

"Surely the poison has started to act."

"If he doesn't die today, tomorrow will be his last," she replied.

"And surrender may come and still provide time for us to sell the Grail."

She hesitated, wondering what course of action would be best. "Our escape should be timed to sell the Grail," she said. "Whether Marston lives or not."

"What of our payment from James the Bold once Marston has breathed his last?"

"If time allows, we shall attempt to meet," she said. "But I hesitate to proceed. James the Bold is a man we scarcely know."

"He can be vicious, I've been told," Paul the Pure nodded. "And if he knows we have the Grail, he might simply try to take it."

"It may be best to take two paths," she said slyly. "You collect from James the Bold while I go sell the Grail."

Paul the Pure paused, and, for an instant, a flicker of mistrust flashed across his face. "And meet when our tasks are completed?"

"An option to consider," she said, sensing his hesitation.

He frowned, glanced toward the door, ensuring all was quiet, and leaned toward her. "I still worry about the witch," he whispered.

"As do I," she said. Minerva possessed a power Trinity hoped to avoid. "I shall consult the runes to be sure she makes no effort to bring about our failure."

"We need only take the path through the sally port before she tries to expose us."

Trinity gathered her runes and she sat on the floor. "We can't risk the riches we deserve."

Paul the Pure paused, struck with an answer to a question he had not thought to ask. "What if we were to kill the witch, too?"

Trinity shook her head. "That is a task fit for talk, not for deed," she said, her mind beginning to wander.

"Yes. Better to try to use her," said Paul the Pure. "Together we may be able to fool her."

Trinity knew she could never outsmart the witch, and neither could her feeble partner. "We should make good our escape instead."

She tossed the runes in the air. Again, they landed in a scattered heap. She studied them very carefully, slowly waving her hands back and forth. Gradually, an image appeared, visible to Trinity alone.

It was a blond woman, one eye blue, one eye green, boarding a foreign ship in the night. She was alone.

Chapter 62

Michael Marston stood in the courtyard, studying the lofty walls, the towers that seemed to touch the clouds, and the soldiers manning their posts. The morning air was cold, laced with salt from the sea, and he breathed deeply and began the long climb upward, battling the narrow stone steps that led to the top of the wall. His ascent was fraught with concern, for he knew, as any tested general does, that no amount of preparation is ever enough. A premonition of death and disaster hung before his eyes, and his scouts had confirmed his fears. The enemy far outnumbered those he could count to defend the castle. As he fought his way up the steps, he was almost hesitant to continue, for he feared that the Devil himself might await him at the summit.

He was gasping when he reached the top. His hair and beard were streaked with gray, and the weathered lines life had etched upon his face were as deep as the tragedy that had torn his heart. Since losing his family to the sickness, he had never been the same—not as strong nor as quick. His eyes often dimmed from memories too painful to relive, but the Lady Gabrielle brought light where darkness had, for so long, enshrouded his every thought. And now his longing for life no longer waned but grew more fervent with each coming sunrise.

Gideon stood at the top of the northwest tower, watching the barons' men who had mustered, once more, into a fighting formation. "The attack is about to begin, sire," he said as he eyed the enemy. "Or they feign a move to battle."

Marston looked at the imminent advance, a formidable wave of infantry enhanced by a few dozen cavalrymen. "Yet they stay far beyond the archer's range."

"Our men are ready," Gideon said. "As the enemy will learn."

"Captain Carney mans the south wall, facing the French," Marston announced.

"Then defeat awaits them, I'm sure."

227

"Be my eyes to the north," he said, "while I inspect the rest of our defenses."

Marston strode along the narrow walkway that ran along the castle walls. As he approached a string of men waiting with their bows and arrows poised, he paused to offer words of encouragement.

"They remain too far to act as targets," Marston said to his men. "They know that death awaits them."

"We're ready for them, sire," a soldier said, "should they ever find the courage to advance."

"Our enemy knows that no better men than you have ever fought in battle," Marston said, offering a compliment. "Should a need arise, come find me."

"And where would we look, sire, once the battle begins?" asked another soldier.

"I'll be on the wall amongst you," Marston assured them. "Never far away."

He continued his inspection, walking the wall and surveying the enemy. When he reached a neglected length of wall, he paused to ponder his defenses.

"You're troubled, my love?" asked the Lady Gabrielle as she crept up behind him.

He was surprised, so focused had he been on evaluating the enemy, that he hadn't heard her approach.

She smiled. "I didn't mean to startle you."

"A warlord is never taken by surprise," he said, pleased to see her.

She stood beside him and scanned the shore, then turned and squinted at the landscape beyond. "Will the enemy attack?"

He hesitated, studying their tepid advance. "I suspect it's only games they play, but I really don't know why."

"In a few short hours, the truth may come," she said. She looked at the men who stood ready to fight, the archers waiting for the enemy to move within range.

He smiled as he watched her, her beauty arresting, her bearing gentle, and her mind beyond all others—all a man could want. "Do you regret being taken to England?" he asked. "Now that the battle begins."

"Most would envy the life I live," she said, "and the love I have for the man who stands beside me. But I must admit, and I'm sure you must, too, that its source is sometimes a mystery."

He wrapped an arm around her. "It is a love that came swiftly," he said, also wondering how it began. "Like a massive wave that overtook us, leaving us too weak to fight it."

"I stopped trying to understand it," she said softly. "And only welcome that it came."

They were quiet for a moment, standing together, studying the plains, the forest, the sea beyond.

"What were you thinking when I first came upon you?" she asked.

"I had a dream," he muttered. "Or perhaps a nightmare."

"You are troubled?"

"Who would not be with a battle about to begin?"

"Something more plagues you," she said. "I can feel it as if the dream were mine."

"I sense disaster. Even though every precaution has been taken."

"A premonition?"

"A suspicion," he said.

"And what might your suspicion be?"

"I sense treason, a treachery that cannot be seen."

Gabrielle tenderly caressed his cheek. "Why let it torment you?"

"Because fate knows no favors."

She paused, growing pensive. "You know what path to take to find what your ears must hear."

He nodded but offered no reply, still studying the enemy as its seemingly endless ranks continued to assemble.

She watched him just as intently as if she knew him better than he knew himself. "You could see the future if you chose."

He shook his head solemnly. "I have not yet chosen to do so."

"Perhaps you should," she urged.

He sighed, knowing she was right. "Yes," he said but made no move to go. He needed every weapon at his disposal, including the witch. He rarely descended into her cavern and was reluctant to do so now, but there were times when he knew he must, and this was one of them.

Gabrielle smiled at his indecision. "I shall be inside. I need to ready the hospital," she said and squeezed his arm tenderly. "Go and see Minerva. Seek her advice."

"I have avoided her longer than I should have," Marston said quietly as his beloved turned to go.

"Tell me what her eyes behold," Lady Gabrielle called as she started down the steps.

"I shall," he replied. "As soon as my ears have heard it."

Chapter 63

After Gabrielle had left, Michael Marston turned his attention to the enemy once more. The rows of additional soldiers approached cautiously, staying beyond the archers' range. He was troubled by what he saw, not by the battle that was about to begin but the continued effort to delay it. He knew a reason must exist, especially given the enemy's numbers. Something sinister was at play, a threat that couldn't be seen. The display of force was a diversion, but for what he did not know.

He left the wall and crossed the courtyard, which had been stockpiled with supplies in preparation for a siege. The villagers had staged troughs of water throughout the bailey, knowing they would soon be met with flaming arrows, and they would have to move quickly to save their homes and shops. Marston paused to watch them.

"If the enemy could see what you've prepared, they would surely turn and flee," Marston called to a group that stood by a well.

"It's our homes we try to save, sire," said an older man who made candles.

"And I stand beside you to save them," Marston assured them. "Our foes know not what they'll soon face."

"We'll beat them back, sire," said a toothless woman who carried a bucket. "We've known war before."

"And pray we never know it again," Marson said, "once this victory is won."

Marston continued across the baily, entered the base of the northeast tower and made his way to the stairwell. Then he pushed the third stone on the side of the third step. A wall behind the stairway shifted, and he stepped through the opening and closed it behind him.

He approached Minerva's altar and peered into the darkness. A deathly stillness filled the cave.

"Minerva!" he called.

The witch appeared at once, materializing from a rock wall as if she'd passed through it, more mist than woman. She glided toward him, dressed, as always, in black robes, her eyes twinkling in the dim light.

"Yes, sire?" she asked.

"The enemy prepares to attack."

"As I warned when you last came."

"I need your eyes," he said, afraid to admit it. "To show me all I cannot see."

"Enlighten me, sire."

"Their force is larger than my own," he said. "Led by gallant men whose courage may be hard to face. How can I best defend the castle and those within my realm?"

"Your men are prepared. As are their leaders."

Marston paused, wondering what he could say to make her understand. "I have an uneasy feeling," he said. "I fear we shall fare poorly in battle, and victory may not be ours."

She studied him for a moment, a man who had once been the most formidable warlord in England. "Perhaps the man who you really fear is Michael Marston."

He blinked at her, perplexed by her riddles. "I don't understand."

"You dream of the man you used to be without seeing the man you are."

Marston frowned. "I'm not as strong as I once was. I'm older—much older."

"And your mind knew not what it does today. You believe you do not possess the strength to overcome your foe, yet both traits win battles."

He looked into her eyes, finally understanding, but doubting the outcome she predicted all the same. "I don't believe we can win."

"You doubt only what you can do, not the effort your men will make."

"Perhaps," he said, his voice trailing off.

"But that can easily be remedied."

She moved to the brass cauldron at the center of her altar while Marston hung back at the boundary of the circle as he always did. She ran her hands about the pot and then passed them through the flames that flickered atop the candles beside it.

He watched but did not speak. It seemed to him that every visit to the witch was like a visit to the Devil himself, or so his faith had taught him. Seconds later, Minerva disappeared before his eyes. He looked anxiously about the cavern, wondering where she could have gone, when she reappeared in a corridor to his left, carrying a handful of pouches, vials, sticks, and stones.

"How did you do that?" he asked in amazement.

"You see what you want to see," she said. "Not what really is."

She returned to the altar, stirring the contents of the cauldron, muttering in unknown tongues. She took a strip of orange cloth, a red ribbon, thyme, basil, and black peppercorns and dropped them into the brew. She then took a vial that contained a viscous red liquid and held it aloft, eyeing it closely.

"Boar's blood," she said and cast a meaningful look at Marston before she poured it in the pot.

He looked on warily as she mixed the ingredients, afraid to ask what the potion would become or what it was meant to do. He knew the witch's powers exceeded all others' but had no desire to know from whence they came. She slid noiselessly to the edge of the circle that defined her altar and placed an amber stone on the southern rim. Then she approached Marston, her body casting an inhuman chill, as she glided to a stop within his arms' reach.

He felt himself shiver as if bathed by a cold breeze. "What are you doing now?"

"Stand straight and true," she said softly. "And dare not move until I'm done."

She took six pieces of carnelian, a brownish-red stone, and set them around him in the form of a six-pointed star. Marston watched her apprehensively, wondering what manner of mischief she could possibly muster with the help of such a rite. He considered leaving, not taking part in whatever it was she planned, but the witch had never failed him before, and he doubted she would do so now.

She returned to her cauldron, eyed it carefully, and then added a few pinches of orange powder. The brew bubbled and hissed before her, and she closed her eyes and moved her hands back and forth across the mist that it belched into the air, muttering a chant.

"Bull, lion, bear, boar,

Michael Marston, doubt no more.

Courage taken, strength gained,

Never touched or bloodstained.

War waged and lives lost,

Bows drawn, swords crossed.

Larger now than once before,

Marston's name lives evermore."

Again and again, Minerva continued to chant in a throaty whisper, her eyes closed. When she'd repeated the phrase twenty times, she stopped, opened her eyes, and turned abruptly.

"Victory awaits," she whispered. "And it's yours alone to take."

Chapter 64

When Gabrielle entered the Great Hall, the five women assigned to assist her were already there, as was Mrs. Carney's daughter Maud, a most able helper. They were all making preparations to receive the wounded once the battle began. The soldiers brought more straw-filled mattresses and staged them along the walls. The former dining hall had been almost entirely cleared out with only a few tables remaining to stage the wounded for their initial treatments. Gabrielle looked over their store of salves and tinctures and advised the women as to which of the various medicines they should stockpile to be sure they'd have enough for when the battle was waged. Then Gabrielle hurried back to her room, knowing Marston would soon arrive to reveal secrets that only the witch would know.

She waited patiently, watching from her window as the villagers hurried about the bailey, preparing for the attack. She saw Marston emerge from the northeast tower. He began to make his way across the courtyard, paused to speak to one of his lieutenants, and pointed to the southern wall. They talked for a moment more, and then Marston hurried toward the keep. He was interrupted by a man who ran the stables, and they spoke briefly, no doubt about the impending battle. As soon as they had finished, Marston walked quickly to the keep, and Gabrielle's heart began to throb, knowing he was soon to arrive.

A few moments later, he knocked on her door. "Did the witch have words of wisdom?" she asked as she let him in.

"Doesn't she always?" he asked, answering her question with another.

He strode to the window, peering out to check the enemy's advance. The vantage point was a good one, for it faced east and afforded him a view of the enemy's preparations to the north and south.

She watched him, framed in the rays of the morning sun that streamed through the window, and realized what a great man he was, a leader like no other. He would face insurmountable odds and come through better and stronger than he ever had been before. She felt privileged to stand by his side, to help shoulder his pain, to share his joy.

"The witch had much to say," he said as he turned to face her.

"Will darkness mask light?" she asked tentatively.

He hesitated as if he wanted to protect her but then proceeded. "It will," he said. "But the witch claims that, in the end, we shall prevail."

It was the answer she had been waiting for, still she received it with a foreboding twinge, a pin prick that became the blade of a knife. "We defeat the French?" she asked, thinking of Montague who never left her heart even though Marston had taken it.

"We defeat the barons' men," he said. "The French are only their shadow."

Although his words seemed sincere, his expression betrayed a far different message. "What troubles you, my love?" she asked.

"I've fought many battles, seen more tragedy that I care to relate or remember, and I have never ceased wondering when such madness will end."

"Maybe it never will."

"My heart aches for peace as my body aches at the thought of yet another fight."

Gabrielle realized he doubted not his men nor the outcome of the war about to be waged but himself. "It's the price one pays for being the best."

"My most heartfelt desire is to be whatever is best for you, not what's best for any battle."

"Fate won't always let you choose," she said, caressing his rugged face.

"No," he said hesitantly. "I suppose not."

"The battle is soon to begin, sire. It needs only you to direct its outcome."

"A truth I know all too well."

"You must go, I'm sure, to where you're most needed."

Marston nodded, unable to speak for a moment. Then he cupped her face in his hands tenderly. "I wanted only to look upon your fair face once more."

She kissed him lightly on the lips. "I am the reward that fate has given you for the fight you're destined to win."

"If you were indeed my reward, I would fight each day I drew breath."

She smiled. "King John is blessed to have a knight like you."

"King John needs more than a blessing to defeat the barons."

Gabrielle sighed, knowing he was right, that the road ahead was a long one, marked by crooked curves and steep declines. "And their leader, James the Bold."

"Never has there been a man as evil as he," he said. "If he leads the attack, I'll launch the arrow myself that finds his breast."

Gabrielle's heart clenched with worry, knowing an arrow might find her beloved just as easily. "And where will you fight the battle, sire?"

"Wherever my men need me most but mainly on the wall."

She paused and gazed out of the window pensively. "Why would they attack this castle? Is it because you're the king's greatest knight?"

"It has nothing to do with me," he said. "They attack the castle because it exists, and as long as it does, it poses a threat."

She hugged him close, not wanting to let go, but after a moment had passed, she did. "I must make ready for the wounded," she said, her voice quavering ever so slightly.

"You've no need to worry," Marston assured her, tenderly stroking her auburn hair as if he might touch it for the last time. "I'll protect you until my dying breath."

She smiled, knowing he loved her and always would. "So long as you're near, I shall know no danger," she whispered.

Chapter 65

As the barons' men and their French allies surrounded the castle, Blaise retreated into the forest. He had otherworldly tasks to perform, different realms to explore, impossible questions to answer.

He made his way to his camp, which remained tucked away in the glen by the stream. Sheltered by trees, the warlock's domain lay roughly a hundred feet from the edge of the forest. The camp of James the Bold, his captains, and Jamet, his French advisor, were all within sight behind a screen of trees to the rear of the battle lines that had just been drawn.

Blaise ran his hand over his face, feeling the smooth skin that had, only days ago, been marred by a terrible pox. He had tried to see inside the castle to glimpse the force that had caused such pain, using spells that had served him well. But he had failed. Every one of his attempts had been blocked; the witch he'd tried so hard to see might possess powers stronger than his. Now he was forced to consider what other paths he might take, detours to plans he would otherwise have made, for he knew, if the entity within Marston Castle possessed such power, she could dictate the course of the battle and deliver defeat to the barons' men.

Blaise stood by the stream wrapped in his gray robe, the hood covering his head, leaving only a shadow of the face within. He considered what he had just witnessed—the terrain, the approach to the castle that the soldiers were taking—and he was haunted by a vision of men falling, pierced by arrows, crying out in pain.

He opened a black leather sack and removed the brass cauldron that had survived the ages and set it on the moss. He placed a handful of soil in the bottom, scooped water from the stream, and made a watery mud. Then he withdrew a knife from the satchel and stuck it in the ground on the east side of the cauldron. To the south he placed a yellow crystal that emitted a soft glow of light. In the west he placed a goblet, a chalice he often drank from, and to the north he laid a bone taken from a

238

rabbit that had once been his dinner. Lastly, he fished a dried lavender bulb out of the sack and mashed it in the mud. He spit in the bowl three times and began to chant.

> "Blinded, broken
>
> Walls that hide,
>
> Help me see what
>
> Lurks inside.
>
> Spells and magic,
>
> Witch's brew,
>
> Hidden horror,
>
> Passes through.
>
> Cast the image,
>
> Cast the light,
>
> Pierce the walls
>
> And grant me sight."

Blaise peered into the cauldron, the muddy water reflecting his image. He ran his right hand back and forth over it, and his face gradually faded, replaced by the image of a stone wall. He tried to peek over it, but the wall stretched skyward, growing ever higher. Changing tactics, he tried to see around it, but again he was thwarted as stone after stone was added by invisible hands, blocking his view. He stopped, gazed at the wall, and considered another approach. After a few seconds had passed, he swiftly extended a finger, poked one of the stones in the center of the image, and it broke free, falling to the ground. He peered through the opening before his rival sealed it and, once more, saw the image of a witch dressed in black. She was slender and stooped with golden eyes, a mass of untamed black hair heaped upon her head.

The witch turned, glared at the hole in the wall, and approached it slowly. She put her face close to the opening.

"Your days are done, warlock!" she cried.

Chapter 66

"Could Marston have a strategy we have yet to see?" Jamet asked.

James the Bold studied his French advisor. "Marston is a puppet on a string, doing as I command."

Jamet didn't seem convinced. "His reputation suggests otherwise, as would the man who earned it."

James the Bold narrowed his eyes at the Frenchman. "I underestimate no one. And never have."

"A tonic that comes in two doses," Jamet said. "Don't underestimate the enemy, and don't overestimate whatever gifts you might possess."

James the Bold looked away, tiring of the Frenchman who claimed to know so much. He hid an evil grin, his thoughts now on the future, a plan Jamet could never know, for if and when an English victory came, he would turn on Jamet quickly and slit his throat from ear to ear.

"The French came to fight," Jamet said. "They tire of pretending. If a siege is our strategy, then let it be known."

James the Bold was silent for a moment, wondering whether or not to trust his French advisor. "I'll share a secret," he said at last.

Jamet looked at him curiously, wondering what hidden thoughts the warlord had. "Please do," he uttered, "so I can see what your eyes do."

"We wait because the flags fly from the tower."

Jamet shot him a confused look. "The flags matter not to me."

"As long as the flags fly, Marston lives."

"But why would we ever think Marston is so near death?"

James the Bold laughed. Jamet was only a child who tried to be a man. "Because I am about to have him murdered."

Jamet showed no surprise and looked at the flags with defiance. "It seems he lives."

"Patience, Jamet," said James the Bold. "Sometimes a battle is won without need for a fight."

"Even if Marston dies, someone will stand in his place. Unless you have a traitor staged within."

James the Bold cast a cruel gaze. "Perhaps there's more than one."

"Deceit has been known to win a war, of that I cannot argue," Jamet said. "But more roads can be traveled than the one you take. Marston must be overwhelmed if we're to be successful."

"We attack tomorrow," James the Bold said, "whether or not the flags still fly."

"As the battle was intended," Jamet said. "And I'll ensure that we're prepared. Do you have more secret weapons?"

James the Bold pointed to a group of men, less than twenty, who appeared to study the terrain—the rise of hills, the distance to the castle. "We have the miners who are almost to the castle."

"And what is their intent?" Jamet asked.

"They will undermine the wall until it collapses, killing as many men as they can. And our army will enter through the breach."

Chapter 67

Montague sat astride his horse, staring at the castle, the keep foremost in his mind. It was where Alaric claimed the Lady Gabrielle was held, drawing ever closer to a man he now despised—Michael Marston. Somehow, he had to get into the castle. He had to find her before it was too late. Each day took her farther away than mere distance implied, and he had to recapture the love of yesterday when he lived life in her eyes. He could visualize her standing before him, tall and willowy, her auburn hair cascading to her shoulders, her green eyes gazing into his. Nothing would keep him from living his life with her, from relishing each day that dawned from now unto eternity. He knew the time had come when he had to right the wrong that the English had committed.

He rode to the eastern edge of the line, stopping when he reached the southeast tower to look at the curtain wall beyond, suspecting it was a weak link in the castle's defense where Marston and his men relied on the narrow wedge of land between the wall and the cliff to keep attackers at bay. It was also the best location to scale the wall, because it was so lightly defended. He would only have to reach its base unseen. But Montague knew there must be a far better option to gain access and reach Gabrielle—a secret passage. He only had to find it.

When he finished reviewing the eastern defenses, he returned to his usual location, centered among his men in the long line that ran along the southern wall of the castle. He dismounted, tethered his steed to an ash tree at the edge of the forest, and made his way through the trees. When he was sure he was alone, he turned abruptly south to the stream. He bent over the swift flowing water, holding the pouch Alaric had given him tightly in his hand.

"Alaric, come to me," he whispered. "Show yourself, wizard."

Minutes passed, and Montague repeated the request. At last, a mist appeared above the water, the wizard's face, his eyes red, his hair and beard long and white, hovering within it.

242

"Montague," Alaric said, his voice a whisper in the wind. "You are in need?"

"I am, great wizard," Montague said. "I wouldn't seek your wisdom unless I needed it to guide me through the day."

"What can I do to assist you?"

"The secret passage of Marston Castle. Tell me where it emerges."

Alaric paused, his eyes closed, his image shimmering in the fog above the stream. After a few minutes, he spoke. "In the cliff," he said.

"The passage can be accessed from the cliff?"

"There's a hidden door, a large stone, thirty feet above the waves."

"Where does it go?"

"Directly into the keep to a room beside the master's."

"Is Gabrielle nearby?"

Alaric looked at him, his face drawn with pain. He hesitated to tell the truth. "If you find Michael Marston, you'll find the Lady Gabrielle."

Chapter 68

Michael Marston lay in bed, eyes open, images of the upcoming battle drifting through his mind. He turned onto his right side, closed his eyes for a moment, but then rolled to his left.

"Are you awake?" asked the Lady Gabrielle.

"Sleep eludes me," he said. "For more reasons than I care to admit."

"Is it the battle?" she asked, turning toward him, her hand caressing his face.

"It's the absence of battle. Another day passes with no attack."

"And why does that worry you, my love?"

"I know not what games the enemy plays."

"Perhaps it is a trick to instill fear into the men who patrol the walls."

"If that is their intention, they will fail," he said. "My men have no fear. They have faced death on many days and lived to tell the tale."

"Why else would they hold off their advance? I see no other explanation."

"It's a trap," he said. "Deception is the weapon they've chosen."

"I don't understand."

"They're trying to force my hand—to make me attack."

"To lure you out from behind the walls?" she asked.

"Yes, it's the only explanation. They spend each morning assembling their ranks, but by afternoon it's clear that an offensive action will not be taken.

"Will you strike first?"

"Only a fool would make such an attempt."

Marston rose from bed and walked to the window, squinting down at the opposing army. Two catapults sat cocked at the forest's edge, and he knew two others lay in wait before the western wall.

"Come to bed," Gabrielle said, coaxing him with her sweet voice.

"I must keep watch. We face a cunning enemy."

"How different is their position from the last time you looked upon them?" she asked. "Are you not prepared?"

"We are."

"Then there's nothing left for you to do. Each day the attack does not come is a day more of your brave men shall live to describe."

He didn't reply and kept his gaze trained on the catapults and a half-built siege tower. He had all but memorized the stance his enemies had assumed, and though little changed in their daily movements, he knew something wasn't right.

"What do you have to fear?" Gabrielle asked as she slipped from bed and draped her arms about his waist. "Has a finer knight ever fought for the king?"

"I'm sure there have been many."

"The man who can best you in battle does not exist," she went on.

"I fear he may," the graying captain said softly.

"I cannot agree," Gabrielle scoffed. "Do not give power to a man who breathes only in your head."

"I grow old," Marston sighed as he led her back to bed. "Maybe my days of fighting have ended."

"You are older, true, but also wiser," she said. "Wisdom wins as many battles as do speed and strength."

"My bones creak as I climb into bed."

"Which doesn't mean you cannot fight. Or that your men can't, either."

He smiled and kissed her softly. "No matter what I say or do, you find it worthy."

Gabrielle laughed. "And for good reason."

He lay down beside her, wrapping his arms around her. "His army far exceeds our own in number."

"Does it matter?" she asked. "Have you not bested armies larger than your own?"

"I have," he said quietly. "But those victories have long since passed, the triumphs of a younger man—a stronger man."

"You have not lost your strength, nor have you lost your courage," Gabrielle replied, then paused and studied him for a moment. "Or have you?"

He shook his head. "No. I have not lost my courage. And I never will."

"Then what is it that troubles you?"

"A fear I cannot conquer, one I have not known before."

She propped herself up on her elbow, studying him in the darkness. "And what is this fear?"

He hesitated for a moment, but then spoke. "I've fought many battles, and I've lived to see them through."

"And you shall live to see this one to its end. Your fear merely shows you've become too accustomed to victory."

"I have no fear for myself," he said, trying to explain.

"Then what is it you fear?"

"I fear for my men," he said. "I fear I may be leading them to their deaths."

"No. You will lead them to victory," she countered.

Marston smiled in spite of his private anguish. "Sometimes I feel my life began the day you walked into it."

Gabrielle hugged him tightly. "Dream, my love. Dream of victory."

Chapter 69

The sun peeked over the eastern shore, a golden glow that arced across the castle. Michael Marston slipped from bed once more, careful not to awaken Lady Gabrielle, and strode to the window to gaze out onto the plain. The catapults facing the northern wall had not been moved, the boulders James the Bold's men would use as ammunition still staged beside them. With the practiced eye of a military genius, he judged their distance from the castle walls. They were still too far away to strike. The enemy would have to push them farther onto the plain, well within the range of both the archers on the castle wall and the catapult that sat like a tightly coiled snake, in the bailey. Marston squinted against the early morning light at the enemy ranks still camped along the edge of the forest. A few men had begun to stir with the coming of dawn while a handful lined the western edge of the castle, more to prevent escape than launch an attack.

He considered the enemy's actions over the last few days. They had bluffed, probed tentatively at the verge of their defenses, but had not launched a single arrow. Marston was befuddled by their behavior. If their intent was to lure him from the castle to do battle on open ground, they had failed. If they'd defined their territory in preparation for a lengthy siege, then their actions were warranted, but it seemed they delayed for a more tactical reason, one the seasoned warlord suspected they would soon share.

He turned his back on the window and walked to the oak table that sat against the far wall. A porcelain washbasin sat upon it, and he bent over the bowl to wash his face.

"Ah!" he cried, leaping back in surprise at the image that had appeared in the basin. Whether real or imagined, he could not be sure and feared he might have lost his mind. Taking a deep breath, he summoned the courage to look into the bowl once more. Rippling in the water was the image of Minerva. She beckoned him to come with a crooked finger.

He stared at her quavering form, wide-eyed with fear at the Devil's work and amazed by the witch's power. At first, he

247

thought that what he beheld was a dream, but the longer he stared the more certain he became that it was real. He placed his finger in the bowl, disturbing the surface, and the shimmering image disappeared. Marston closed his eyes and sighed. The witch had sent a signal. She wanted to see him, and he knew that he must go.

He glanced at Gabrielle as he dressed. "Are you awake?"

She smiled, barely visible in the soft light. "Yes, my love. I am awake."

"They will launch their attack today," he said softly. "I am sure of it."

She propped herself up on one elbow. "Are they preparing now?"

"No, they still sleep, but all will change in the next few hours."

"How do you know if they make no move?" she asked.

"Because the reason they've delayed has failed. I know it, and so do they."

"Then why attack?"

"They need to determine how well defended the castle is —how many men lie in wait within its walls, what type of weapons they might wield."

She rose from bed and reached for her clothes. "I must make sure the hospital is ready."

He paused, admiring her beauty. "Surely a gift from the heavens," he muttered.

She smacked him lightly on the arm and dressed. "The women who have chosen to help me see to the wounded have learned very quickly," she said. "They will do well."

"We shall need their skill and their heart today."

"I'll make sure all is prepared," she said.

"Are you afraid?"

Gabrielle smiled confidently. "No, my love, I'm not afraid. I know that you'll protect me."

He took her in his arms and kissed her. "To my dying breath, I will protect you," he said, smiling at her lovingly as he stroked her hair.

"I will never leave you," she whispered. "If that means dying beside you, then so be it."

Chapter 70

Minerva watched while Michael Marston stepped from the secret passage that led to her cave. He shivered as he made his way into the depths of the cavern, inching forward through the darkness. Seeing no sign of the witch, he continued to the circle that marked the boundary of her altar. He stopped, afraid to go any further.

"Minerva!" he called.

She waited in the shadows, watching what he did.

"Minerva!" he called again.

"Michael Marston," she creaked.

He jumped, startled to find her standing behind him. "You startled me," he said, shooting her a look of annoyance. "Again."

"I didn't mean to," she said mischievously. She reached forward and caressed his arm.

He moved away, repulsed by her touch. "Why did you summon me?"

She smiled, amused, as always, at how uncomfortable she could make him--history's greatest warlord unnerved by her touch. "Come and sit," she offered, motioning to a rock beside her altar.

Marston sat on the flat stone, Minerva beside him. Her black eyes, twinkling with gold, betrayed a magic no human could hope to replicate.

"Do you have something to tell me?" he asked.

"I do," the witch replied. "The eyes of the invading army were in the castle last night. They know where we are strong and where we are not."

"How did they get in?" he asked, alarmed, suspecting a weakness in the fortress. "The sentries saw no one pass."

"They came in secret," she said. "The work of a warlock."

Marston's eyes grew wide. "Is he as powerful as you?"

She shrugged, toying with him. "Maybe he is," she said, leaning close. "Maybe he isn't."

Marston rose from the stone bench and paced the floor. "Did you find this intruder?"

The witch said nothing.

"Did you find him?" Marston insisted, his tone more frantic.

"I know where he was," she said, "and where he wanted to go."

"Can the enemy enter the same way he did?"

"No, the path opens only to those who live in darkness."

Marston shivered, confused by her reply but wanting to know more. "Is this warlock allied with James the Bold?"

"He is," she said. "Standing by his side as I stand by yours."

Marston hesitated, evaluating his opponent. "Have the years tempered the man that James the Bold once was?"

"They have not," she said. "He's as vicious as the day he killed his first foe."

"Satan's sibling," he said with disgust. "The warlock stands in good company."

"The sum of their power does not equal ours," she said. "Worry should not be counted among the tasks that now await you."

He sighed, relieved. "How can we defend ourselves?"

"As you always have, sire," Minerva replied.

"But this battle is different," he said. "I fight more than a man."

"No one has ever defeated you in battle," she assured him.

"And no one has lived their entire life without having to taste defeat."

"Which doesn't mean it will now occur."

He nodded, willing himself to believe her. "I suppose the past does, at times, predict the future."

"Your courage will not be challenged," she said.

He studied the witch for a moment, his thoughts consumed by the different approaches the enemy might employ and how best to combat them.

"You have questions?" she asked.

"Tell me more of the enemy."

"They're well prepared," she said solemnly, "and they attack in hours."

He nodded and turned back toward the passageway. "I have much to do," he called.

No sooner had Marston left, Minerva returned to her altar, hunched over her cauldron, and filled it with ingredients for a different task at hand. She pored over the mixture, tossing in a pinch of powder, a dash of herbs, animal innards, and slivers of stone, before producing a clear vial filled with red liquid.

"The blood of a fox," she whispered to herself, "to counter the warlock and bring victory in battle."

She stirred the brew for a few moments more before waving her hands over the steam it spewed into the air. Then she started to chant.

> "Legend, god, myth, or man,
>
> Satan's son will understand.
>
> Grant the creature strength and might
>
> To overcome the dark of night.
>
> Fight the battle,
>
> Wage the war,
>
> James the Bold,
>
> Will be no more."

She repeated the spell nine times. Then, in the mist the murky mixture produced, a wavering image of the battle materialized. Throngs of men clashed along the castle's ramparts. The dead and dying littered the field. Boulders careened over the walls, blasting buildings and littering the ground with fragments of what had once been stone. Flaming arrows found thatched roofs, and villagers fought the growing blaze with water and pail. An ominous haze hung in the air, choking all who came near. Soldier and citizen ran through the bailey, carrying wounded to the Great Hall for treatment. And captains from each side of the wall watched the course of the battle tug to and fro--the victor one minute, defeated the next. But gradually all the smoke cleared, the cries of the wounded ceased, the arrows no longer littered the sky, and men on both sides slumped where they were, too weary to continue the battle.

And Michael Marston held his victorious sword high in the air.

Chapter 71

The Lady Gabrielle finished dressing and went to the window to assess the enemy's readiness herself. Many of the men began to stir, stoking fires and cooking meals, and she wondered if this was, indeed, the day the battle would begin. She left Michael Marston's room, hurrying through the keep's corridors, destined for the Great Hall that now served as a hospital. It was early, the air crisp and the plain illuminated by the faint glow of the moon.

She entered the hall, dimly lit by the dwindling torch perched in a sconce on the wall, and walked the length of the room, checking the beds, the shelves of ointment, cloth dressings, and medicines. Tables which she'd directed the soldiers to arrange in the center of the room would serve as makeshift beds to treat the wounded. The women who had been trained to assist her would arrive shortly as they did each day, ready to do their own part in fighting a battle that might never come.

Gabrielle had just completed her inspection, satisfied that all was in order, when Michael Marston marched into the room.

"Did you see the witch?" she asked.

"I did. Sometimes I fear her more than the enemy," he muttered, his voice fraught with frustration.

"Why did she summon you?"

"To warn me of the enemy's might," he said. "They are allied with a force I had not considered, one I can't ignore."

"Did she tell you how to combat it?"

"A task best suited to skills she possesses," he said.

Gabrielle was confused, but Marston didn't seem willing to discuss it further. She made one last attempt. "Did she speak of an attack?"

Marston nodded. "The battle soon begins. They intend only to probe our defenses. But each day forward will only get worse."

Gabrielle studied the man before her, knowing he sometimes doubted the strength he possessed. "I can bear any day, no matter what we face, if it's shared with you," she said quietly.

He took her in his arms and held her close. "Soon this will be over, and our lives will be our own."

"I shall await that day like no other," she said. She lifted her head and kissed him softly on the mouth.

Reluctantly, Marston pulled away and glanced around the room. "Do you have everything you need?"

"I do," she replied. "Or at least it seems, to my untrained eye, that all is as it should be."

"You know more than any within these walls."

"I am thankful for the women in the village who have agreed to assist me."

"Let's hope they're not all needed," he said. He gave the room one last look. "I must go, my love. To ensure the barons' attack is properly met."

"Play the part that destiny has planned," she said, her voice unwavering though she worried for his welfare. "You were born to make men do what they never thought they could."

He smiled, touched by the concern so apparent in her eyes. "I'll do as fate directs me."

"You hold my heart in your hands," she said softly.

He kissed her gently one last time. "As you hold mine."

She watched as he hurried off, the many details a defense requires weighing heavily upon him. She was fearful he might shoulder more than any man could carry to prove to both himself and the enemy that his name would live forever—even if he did not.

"He'll be fine, dearie," an eerie voice behind her said.

She turned to find Minerva, an unnerving smile upon her lips.

"Where did you come from?" Gabrielle asked.

"Not the depths of Hell as many would assume," Minerva said mysteriously.

Gabrielle studied the witch, her strange eyes and mane of unkempt hair. She seemed to enjoy the riddles she spoke, the fear she instilled, the confusion she created.

"I'll spend the battle by your side," Minerva said, "while you treat the wounded."

Gabrielle wasn't sure if it was wise for Minerva to assist her. Although she understood, as Marston did, that the witch had good intentions, those within the castle walls would see only a monster. They would be afraid of her. Some might even run away, preferring to face an enemy lance than confront a woman they thought had been birthed in Hell.

Minerva cackled, reading Gabrielle's mind. "Not here, my dear. I know all too well that only a sacred few are believers."

"Then how will you help?" Gabrielle asked, feeling she faced an insurmountable task. "For I shall gladly accept any assistance you can offer."

"You need know only that I will be watching from afar," the witch replied, "Just to be sure all goes well."

Gabrielle glanced about the vacant hospital at the rows of cots and the shelves of medicines, the tables that would soon be laden with the wounded. She suddenly felt overwhelmed at the thought of the many souls who would rely on her expertise, which, she had to admit, was middling at best.

"I feel so much better knowing you will guide my hands," she said, turning back to the witch.

But Minerva was gone.

Chapter 72

Just as dawn broke, Trinity heard a frenzied knock at her door. She opened it quickly, and Paul the Pure stumbled across the threshold, his face flushed, his breathing labored. Beads of sweat dripped from his forehead, and his chest violently rose and fell, his eyes wide with fright.

"Are you all right?" she asked, shocked at his disheveled appearance.

"I don't know," he gasped, grabbing her shoulder for support. "I can't breathe."

"Come lie on the bed," she said as she guided him in. "How long have you been like this?"

"About an hour, maybe more. At first, it seemed only a bother, and I thought for sure it would pass. But it keeps getting worse."

By the time he reached the bed, the druid was stumbling, his body quaking. "Help me, please," he pleaded.

Trinity eased him onto the bed and helped him lie down. She touched his forehead and cheeks with her hand. They were warm.

"Lie still," she said. "I'll get some water."

On the table across from the bed sat a pan filled with water, a cloth beside it. Trinity dipped the cloth into the water and wrung it out. When she returned to the bed, she found Paul the Pure's breathing all the more frantic, a caged expression on his face. She placed the cloth on his forehead. A few moments later, the redness in his cheeks began to fade.

"Where is the pain?" she asked.

"It's not a pain that words can define," he said. "Nothing aches. But I'm losing control of my body. I can't walk. I can't breathe. And I can't stop shaking."

She watched him closely, concerned for his welfare. "What could have caused it?"

He lay weakly on the cot, a pathetic portrait of a frail old man. "I don't know," he said, wheezing. "But please make it pass."

Trinity dabbed at his brow, unsure of the cause of his pain. Maybe it had sprung from too much excitement. Disposing of Baron Tweed and stealing the Grail, the imminent battle, their plot to kill Marston—any of these could have spurred an attack that was simply born by panic.

"Please help me," he urged. "I feel as if a horse sits upon my chest."

She took the cloth from his forehead and dabbed it on his face, fearing that the cause was far more than his nerves. "Perhaps you ate something that had spoiled."

"No," he said, shaking his head. But then his eyes widened, and his face contorted with rage. "Marston!" the old man howled. "He must have switched the goblets! I've been poisoned!"

Trinity gaped, knowing her accomplice's death was near. A younger man might recover, if given the proper treatment, but not a man as aged as Paul the Pure. "Are you in pain?" she asked, trying to determine what treatment to render.

"I can't breathe," he gasped.

She felt about his torso. "Is there a tightening in your chest?"

"No," he said nervously. "Only the feeling of a terrible force that pushes upon it."

"How long have you been feverish?" she asked, returning her hand to his forehead.

"I don't know. I'm cold, and then I'm hot, but it is unlike any fever I've suffered before," he complained. "Can you stop the poison from flowing through my veins?"

"Is the pressure constant?" she asked, ignoring his plea, focused on how best to help him. "Can you breathe now?"

"For the moment, but maybe not the next," he gasped, his breathing labored.

"I'll fetch some herbs," she said, recalling a potion that might offer a cure.

"You have to do something," he said as his gasping subsided. "Before it starts again."

"I'll make a medicine," she said. "Just lie still."

Trinity retreated to an alcove at the far end of her room and bent over her knapsack. Choosing two pouches and a vial filled with yellow liquid, she placed them on the table along with a clay plate.

"This will make you feel better," she said. "And it will only take a minute to make."

"Please hurry," he urged.

She sprinkled gray powder from the first pouch onto the plate and tiny green crystals from the second, then added four drops of the yellow liquid. The mixture smoked and then caught fire. A tiny flame, about three inches high, burned brightly in the center of the plate. She watched as the flame grew shorter and shorter and then suddenly disappeared.

She glanced at Paul the Pure. He was resting quietly, his eyes on the ceiling. She waited for her concoction to cure and a few moments later was left with a black, smooth, odorless paste. She hurried to the bedside.

"Let me rub this on your chest," she said as she opened his robe. "It should attract the poison, drawing it from your body."

"And then what happens?"

"We'll peel off the paste, and you should be well."

"I'm so fortunate to have your help," he said. "As many thanks as I could give would still not be enough."

Trinity smiled. "You deserve all the good that can be given."

She rubbed the paste over his chest, massaging his frail and fragile body gingerly. As soon as the ointment made contact with his flesh, it turned clear and invisible. In minutes, she had applied the entire concoction, rubbing it thoroughly into his skin.

"That should make you feel much better," she said. "Today's pain shall be tomorrow's memory."

"Thank you so much, child," he said, smiling up at her benignly.

259

"I'll get some fresh water," she said. "I'll only be a moment."

She hurried outside to a well near the keep, one of several scattered throughout the bailey. She cranked a lever, and water burbled forth from the mouth of a pipe. Hastily, she filled her pitcher with water and raced back to her room.

"A drink of water will do you good," she said as she closed the door behind her.

But Paul the Pure made no answer. He was dead.

Chapter 73

Trinity burst into the hallway just as Michael Marston exited the Great Hall. "Help me, sire, please," she cried. "My father has breathed his last."

Marston called for a servant and rushed into the room. He found Paul the Pure lying on the bed, his face drawn in death's mask.

"Oh, father," Trinity cried, tears streaming down her face. "I've no cause to continue, no reason left to live."

Marston moved his hands about the body, checking for a shallow breath or a heart that might yet beat, but he found nothing. "I'm so sorry," he said. "I wish there was more that I could do."

Tears streamed down Trinity's face. She collapsed at the bedside and clung to the corpse, screaming in agony as if she felt the pain Paul the Pure had endured just before he died.

Two servants entered, an older man and a boy, perhaps his son. "What will you have us do, sire?" the elder asked.

"We've lost a great man," Marston said solemnly. "Arrangements for his burial must be made at once."

The elder servant ducked into the hallway and called out for help, and a woman soon appeared, holding linens with which to wrap the body.

Marston gently touched Trinity's arm. "I'm sorry, but I must go," he said. "The enemy prepares to attack."

"Fight the battle you must," she said sadly. "I shall grieve alone."

Marston left, and Trinity bent her head over Paul the Pure's body, continuing her tears. The servants wrapped the druid in a sheet, continually expressing their condolences, and took the body away.

Finally, Trinity was alone, the silence deafening. She took a deep breath, and a sly smile crept across her face. She had given a most convincing performance, had thanked Marston profusely, attempting to leave him no doubt that her pain was real, but now that her show of tears was no longer needed, she began to plot her escape. She had to act quickly, knowing all within the castle walls were consumed by the battle that threatened to break out at any moment.

Quietly she collected her belongings, the Holy Grail among them, and opened the door to her quarters. She tiptoed down the warren of hallways, hiding in shadow when she heard footfalls or approaching voices. Finally, the tortuous path delivered her to the doors of the library. The runes had revealed a means of escape, and now she intended to take it. Pausing at the doorway, she listened for the slightest sign that someone was near. When she was satisfied she was alone, she crept into the empty room, made her way to the fireplace, and twisted the unicorn carving on the middle self. The passageway yawned open, and she hurried into the darkness, closed the bookcase, and descended the narrow staircase within the wall. She moved as fast as she dared, eluding the spiderwebs that stretched from ceiling to floor, squinting in the faint light. Twenty minutes later, she reached the large stone that marked the end of the passage and searched for the lever she'd seen in her vision. She fumbled about in the gloom and finally hit upon the mechanism. She pulled it firmly toward her, and the rock slid ajar, exposing the sea thirty feet below.

The sun had risen high into the cloudless sky, but it was still not midday. Trinity knew if she tried to make her escape now, she would be easy prey for the soldiers who patrolled the walls. Though Marston's men would be preoccupied with preparations for war, it would be wiser to wait until darkness draped the landscape to make her escape. Under cover of the early morning twilight, just before the sun started to rise, she would make her way along the shore, hiding behind rocks to ensure she remained unseen.

Hidden in the cleft dug into the cliff, she sat on a boulder, watching the sea,. The runes had guided her well. She had found a means of escape. Now she had only to make her way south to the dock where the foreign ship would be waiting, the captain eager to handsomely pay for the Grail. She'd have to concoct a story, some explanation of why she'd come in the place of Baron Tweed, assuming he was dead.

If he wasn't, she would kill him, and this time she would wait until he'd taken his last breath.

Chapter 74

Later that morning, Minerva tiptoed stealthily about her domain, preparing yet another potion that would alter space and time. In a remote corner of her cave, hidden in the shadows of the crooked corridors, lay her most valued treasures—a bizarre collection of herbs and plants, pebbles and crystals of various colors, vials filled with mysterious liquids and gases, and glass jars that housed the viscera of a multitude of creatures.

She selected four glass vials, two slivers from exotic stones, one lavender, the other crimson, and an assortment of herbs from the Mediterranean climes. She returned to her altar and poured the contents into her cauldron, watching curiously as an angry hiss issued from the pot. The rank stench of sulfur leached throughout the cave and hung in the damp air for several minutes before it began to fade. A hazy fog rose from the pot, lingered above the altar, and then shimmered in place, forming a canvas on which the witch would set about her work.

Pleased with her progress, Minerva swept her hand through the vapor, making three deliberate passes until it disappeared. A bubble formed in the pot, tiny at first but gradually swelling until the entire cauldron was filled to the rim by the translucent orb. Then it burst. A second took its place, grew even larger than the first, and also burst. A third was quick to follow. It slowly escaped the confines of the cauldron, gradually expanding until it consumed the area above the altar. But seconds later, it disappeared.

Minerva studied the viscous liquid in the cauldron. At first, she was met with her own reflection, but then another image gradually formed to take its place. It was hazy at first but then grew sharper, and soon she could see the library within the keep, shimmering in the cauldron.

The image in the cauldron shifted from the library threshold and through the open bookshelf into the dimly lit corridor beyond. Seconds later, the witch saw Trinity's ghostly figure as she tiptoed down the steps, descending ever lower, until she reached the corridor that ran beneath the castle.

"I see you've done just what I wanted," Minerva said, "and you never knew it was my hand pushing you down this path. Did you really think I would let a trifling man such as Paul the Pure kill a legend like Michael Marston? I made the old fool pay for the nasty deed he'd planned, and now you'll get your turn, too."

As Trinity settled in the shadows of the cliff, waiting for darkness to come, Minerva placed both hands, palms down, over the top of the cauldron and passed them back and forth, revealing what the hours to come would bring. She watched Trinity's image fade and reappear until it was enveloped in darkness, and she started climbing down the cliff. She crept along the beach, eluding the sentries that paced the wall many feet above her, passed the wharf that served the castle, and moved beyond the French line, all without being seen. She marched on, destined for her secret rendezvous.

Minerva peered intently at the vision, using all her powers of concentration, her mind seeing what was and what was soon to be. Then she chuckled, watching as Trinity's image receded into the darkness, every step carrying her farther and farther from Marston Castle.

Resting on the altar, just beside Minerva's cauldron, sat the Holy Grail.

Chapter 75

Michael Marston left the Great Hall and climbed the southwest tower to take stock of the enemy from a different vantage. He also intended to seek out Gideon to discuss the death of Paul the Pure, the Holy Grail, and the upcoming battle.

He greeted a dozen men atop the tower, all among the best archers in the whole of England. They stood at the ready, most wearing helmets, some wrapped in coats of mail, their tunics displaying the Marston coat of arms. Stockpiles of arrows lay beside them along with extra bows.

"Have you everything you need?" Marston asked as they gathered around him.

"All but targets," said one of his men.

"We wait for the enemy," said another.

"You're the finest archers in the land," Marston told them. "When the enemy comes, they'll wish they had not."

"Aye, sire," said an archer. "The plain will be littered with those who try to scale the walls of this castle."

Marston nodded and made his way along the west curtain wall, headed north. In the shadows cast by the midmorning sun, he spied Gideon a hundred feet away, studying parchments and eyeing the catapults and the enemy position beyond the castle walls. When he saw Marston, he hurried along the rampart to meet him.

"The attack will surely come today," he said.

"If it does not, they have no need for an army," Marston replied.

Gideon looked to the forest where the enemy was milling about, falling into the formations that would race across the plain. "They aren't moving the catapults."

"They may fire from where they stand."

Gideon slowly shook his head. "Then they'll litter the field with stone." He unrolled one of the parchments, which was covered with diagrams of different trajectories. "I've calculated the arc based on my estimate of the length of the catapults' arms, and they're far too short."

Marston examined the barons' machines and then his own. "Our catapult might reach them."

Gideon pointed to a different sketch. "It surely will if they move any closer."

"Our arrows will find them as well with only the slightest advance," Marston said. "Let us pray their attacks find no weaknesses in our defense."

"We shall know by day's end." Gideon gazed upon the plain for a while and then spoke. "A servant told me that the druid has breathed his last."

"It's true he is no more," Marston replied. "His death was sudden, its cause a mystery."

"He was a man of advanced years," Gideon said, "so stooped his cane could barely support him."

Marston smiled slyly. "I suspect he met a much more sinister end, one he intended for me."

Gideon was puzzled. "I know not what you mean, sire."

"It was poison that took his last breath, a potion he'd tried to drop into my goblet when we met alone."

"Yet you spoke not a word to me," Gideon frowned.

"I did not know for certain what his intentions were," Marston began and smiled wryly. "I swapped our goblets, just to be sure."

"Then the poison found the right stomach."

"If I am correct, he was only a puppet and Trinity the puppeteer."

"Which I've suspected since the day they arrived," Gideon said.

"Their treachery explains why the attack has been delayed," Marston said. "The enemy waited for me to die."

Gideon laughed. "If that is their intention, they will sit in their camp for years to come. May fate drive James the Bold to his own death instead."

Marston glanced over his shoulder at the keep, pensive. Trinity posed a host of problems, and with a major battle to confront, he had little time to address a traitorous witch who wanted to see him dead.

"Trinity doubts you know her purpose," Gideon said. "I suspect she'll make every effort to succeed where her partner failed."

Marston paused, a smile curling the corner of his lips. "She played a fine part—the bereaved daughter in a strange land." Marston paused. "If Paul the Pure did die from poison, then killing me was always their intent. Sanctuary played no part in their ploy."

"Let me give Trinity the reward she deserves," said Gideon. "As soon as the battle has ended."

"A task I will gladly impart should she ever open the door to her room," Marston said. "She'll accept no visitors while she grieves."

"And the Holy Grail?" Gideon asked.

"I've no doubt it's never leaving her side."

Chapter 76

James the Bold sat astride his horse, watching his men prepare for battle. Some carried ladders, others pikes—long poles with steel blades affixed to the end they would shove in the faces of defenders atop the castle walls. They formed a line parallel to the north face of the fortress and prepared to race across the open field, hoping to reach the castle wall before the archers could cast their deadly rain upon them.

Jamet, an advisor in the current conflict, but a potential enemy when it was ended, sat astride his own horse beside James the Bold. "I propose a probing attack," he said, "so the enemy's weakness might then be known."

"We'll feign an attack with a few dozen men just to see their response," said James the Bold.

Jamet eyed him curiously. "A few dozen men are sure to die. What could be your objective?"

"To see if Marston's men are diverted from any other wall," said James the Bold. "We'll know from where his forces come, how future attacks can best be staged, varied in time and location."

Jamet looked at him apprehensively. James the Bold was a ruthless warrior as any who knew him would say. But Jamet was sickened by a man who sacrificed men only to gauge the response of the enemy.

James the Bold motioned to one of his captains, and the man rode over to meet them.

"Captain Fletcher," said James the Bold, "we launch a probing attack where we think their defense is the weakest."

"Aye, sir," Fletcher replied. "And what will be our objective?"

James the Bold paused, eyeing the long stretch of stone that comprised the north side of the castle. "It's a focused attack on the north curtain wall to see how they combat it. Take three dozen men who've seen battles before, and we'll see how many defenders the castle might have."

269

"And the battle is fought by us alone?" the captain asked.

"If you reach the wall, the entire army will soon attack behind you," said James the Bold.

"And if we don't?" Fletcher asked.

"Retreat is a weapon you can use whenever you deem it needed," said James the Bold. "I need to see how they shift their men when faced with the threat that we will pose."

"Aye, sir," Captain Fletcher said. "My men will be ready in minutes."

Before he galloped away, he heard, "Captain."

"Yes, sire?"

James the Bold gazed coldly at the Frenchman. "Jamet will join you. Leading the charge"

Jamet's eyes grew wide. "But, sire, this isn't the attack that I should lead."

James the Bold smiled slyly. "It's as good as any other."

Fletcher and Jamet led a band of forty men, only a handful on horseback. They advanced slowly until within range of the enemy's arrows and then raced toward the castle.

As the English army crossed the field, Marston's men waited on the wall, watching while they approached. When the army had crossed half the distance to the castle, Marston's soldiers launched a hundred arrows, the dreaded iron rain arcing through the sky.

Jamet galloped forward, never before having been in the midst of a battle. As his men raced across the field, the arrows whistled through the clouds, descending at a rapid rate.

"Ah!" cried a man on foot beside him, an arrow finding his chest. He fell to the ground, clutching the shaft as more men sprinted past him toward the wall.

In seconds, Jamet realized his mission would meet with failure. He spurred his horse over to Fletcher, avoiding the arrows that sped through the sky. "Many are manning the walls," he screamed, fearing death would soon come to take him. "Far more than we'd ever thought."

Fletcher paused as the defenders released the next wave of arrows from their bows. He hollered above the cries of battle, the wounded screaming and arrows shrieking. "If we reach the wall, as James the Bold ordered, the rest of the men will come."

Jamet could only follow, Fletcher a braver man than he. The Frenchman was certain death would greet them before any of their number reached the wall. Still his compatriots pushed forward. But when the second wave of arrows fell and more men hit the ground, it was easy for any on the field to see that the wall would never be reached.

Fletcher pulled his steed up short, assessing their plan to continue. He looked at his men, many of whom littered the ground, and raised his hand up high. "Retreat!" he screamed so all would hear and motioned them toward the woods.

All of those still standing turned and fled for the forest beyond. Moments later, a breathless Jamet approached James the Bold as he calmly watched the disaster.

"None of the enemy left their positions," Jamet said, his heart racing as he fought to catch his breath. "Far more men are walking the walls than we ever thought existed."

"The battle has only just begun," said James the Bold calmly, accustomed to watching men die. "The victor's tale will be told when it ends."

Captain Fletcher approached a moment later. "Six men are dead, four more are dying, and we never reached the wall."

"It would seem the castle is heavily defended," Jamet said, doubting the genius of James the Bold. "May the French fare better with the attack they launch."

271

Chapter 77

Montague listened to the sounds of battle as the barons' forces launched their attack. He would lead his men forward when their battle ended, both armies intent upon a probing attack to gauge the defenders' response. He studied the castle, his gaze drifting to the keep where the Lady Gabrielle was held. Alaric had said that she hadn't been harmed, and he'd never spoken a word that wasn't true. But now, with the initial attack about to begin, he was eager to find a weakness in the castle's defense, a flaw that would lead to her rescue.

He looked at his men at the fringe of the forest, ready and waiting to receive his command. They wore pale blue tunics, the heraldic lion on their chests, conical metal helmets on their heads, and pikes and swords at their sides. Most of them carried bows, a sheaf of arrows in each of their quivers, as they buzzed with a nervous fear, about to face an age-old enemy whose strength they had not yet determined.

Piers approached, guiding his horse alongside Montague's. He greeted his commander. "The men are ready."

"We'll probe the southeast corner but with just a hundred men," Montague said.

Piers shifted his gaze to the plain beyond, which was soon to be littered with the dead and dying. "And if we reached the wall, a massive attack will follow?"

Montague nodded. "Just as Jamet directed."

"And where will the battle find you?" Piers asked, their roles as yet not defined.

"I will lead the attack from the right flank," Montague said. "As the battle begins, I will drift to the east with a handful of men but only to test their defense."

Piers' eyes widened. "Is it wise for you to engage, sire?"

"It may not be wise, but it is just," he said and then nodded to his men. "Give the command."

Piers ordered the troops to advance. Montague led the right flank with thirty of his cavalrymen. They moved across the open plain, knowing their attack would be answered and that death could come at any time.

As soon as they reached the range of the enemy's bowmen, arrows arched in the sky and then dropped at a frightening speed, whistling louder than the wind blowing across the cliff. The French raced forward, edging nearer to the wall, as men began to fall. A warrior collapsed, screaming as he lay on the ground, an arrow piercing his thigh. The rest ran past, arrows raining upon them in a terrible flurry of iron.

Montague galloped far ahead, exposed to the greatest danger. When he neared the tower on the southeast corner of the castle, he veered south, five of his men beside him. As he raced onward, he looked up and found scattered bows along the wall, all now trained on him. An arrow struck the dirt beside him, narrowly missing his horse's head. Another whizzed past his shoulder. He spurred his horse and bolted ahead, determined to ride the entire wall.

As he charged farther northward along the cliff's edge, the raging sea two hundred feet beneath him, he saw that the eastern wall was lightly defended. Only a dozen archers manned the eastern rampart, all aiming their arrows at him. He led his men boldly forward, all narrowly evading the arrows that rained from atop the wall, until a lightning-quick shot tore through the neck of the man riding beside him. The man fell from his horse, dead when he hit the ground, open eyes staring up at the Heaven he'd hopefully reached. The remainder of Montague's men charged on to the northeast corner, but when they saw the barons' men scattered across the plain, dozens of them dead and dying, they turned back toward camp, their raid to test the enemy completed.

The retreat along the eastern wall was no different from the advance. A dozen archers fired upon them, and even though a threat existed, none came to their aid. Montague noted the softness of the soil, the proximity to the cliff, and realized an attack on the eastern face would be difficult, but with the right men, it could be achieved. He also recognized that if he alone tried to scale the walls in search of the Lady Gabrielle, this was where he would do it.

Once he'd cleared the southeast tower, Montague saw his men strung out along the boundary of the forest in retreat, carrying the wounded with them. None with ladders had come close to the wall, the arrows far too many to risk moving forward with as little as one hundred men.

Montague ordered his cavalry to shield his retreat. They raced back and forth before the wall, taking the brunt of the enemy's arrows and providing cover for the infantry to withdraw. Twenty minutes after the battle had begun, the French returned to their original position having left no mark upon the defenders. Three men were dead. Five were wounded.

But Montague had found the weakness. It was the eastern wall.

Chapter 78

Michael Marston watched the attacks from the top of the wall, rallying his archers, encouraging his commanders. He knew with a glance that each assault was only a meager attempt to gauge the castle's defenses, and how well he led in time of need. After the enemy retreated, giving no indication of a second assault, he met with his chief advisors, Captain Carney—the most gifted warrior among all of his men as well as the most trusted—and Gideon, who was keenly observant, worldly, and well-versed in both political and military matters. None were their equals.

"We've spurned their advances with hardly an effort," Carney reported.

"But their intent was only to test our defenses," Marston reminded him.

Carney nodded. His eyes had seen the same. "The French were scouting the eastern wall. It might be wise to move more men along its ramparts."

"The next attack will be worse," Marston said, "with all their forces deployed."

Carney pointed to the enemy's catapults, two in the west and two to the north, all focused on the northwest tower. "They did move their catapults closer. As soon as the battle ended."

"But still outside the range of our archers," said Gideon.

Marston studied the machines, dwarfed by his own contraption within the bailey. Still, they could cause a great deal of damage. "I would expect they'll use them to pummel our walls. And likely at dawn."

"I suggest an aggressive defense when they next attack," said Gideon. "Drench those who approach with oil, and follow with flaming arrows."

"Screams of agony and burning corpses would strike fear in any man," Marston said. "Even the most seasoned of soldiers."

"And Gideon's catapult will destroy morale as well as the men who stand in its path," Carney said. "The next enemy effort is the opportune time to use it."

"It can fling a boulder a quarter mile." Gideon informed them. "As the enemy will soon realize."

"I suspect that the northern wall is their main objective," Carney said. "I've moved men from the west to increase our forces should it bear the brunt of their next assault."

Marston stared down the expanse of the castle's walls, the towers that guarded each of its corners, and the vulnerabilities he knew existed. He turned to Carney and Gideon. "Let's place ten more sentries on the walls tonight to keep watch of the enemy's movements."

Carney and Gideon nodded.

Marston eyed his lieutenants, confident in their assessments and abilities, but he wasn't convinced they knew the enemy as they thought they did. "There could be more to their strategy than our eyes can see or that past battles may have revealed."

Carney and Gideon shared an uneasy glance, perhaps confused by their master's comment. "We're well prepared, sire," Carney said. "As the enemy will soon discover."

"We're prepared for battles we've faced in days past," Marston said, "but they have much more planned for tomorrow, I'm sure. Something we have not considered—miners or weapons we've never before seen—and it's how we react that determines whether we live or die."

Chapter 79

"I don't want Rose to get sick," Maud said, pouting. She was following Gabrielle around the hospital, holding her doll like a baby.

"I'll make sure she doesn't," Gabrielle said. "If she were sick, we wouldn't have anyone to play with."

"She's a good girl," Maud said.

"I can tell," Gabrielle said. "She's always very well behaved. Just like her mommy."

"Maybe we can all go outside and play?" Maud asked.

"Maud, please leave Lady Gabrielle alone," Mrs. Carney said as she approached the two of them.

"She's no bother, really," Gabrielle said, smiling at the child. "I enjoy her so much."

Mrs. Carney laughed. She leaned closer to Gabrielle and whispered, "They're always a joy when you can give them back to their mothers. You'll find out soon enough."

Gabrielle smiled. Having her own child was such a precious thought. "If I ever do have a daughter, I hope she'll be just like Maud."

Mrs. Carney rolled her eyes. "You see the best of her. Only I see the worst."

One of the other women who'd volunteered to help Gabrielle burst into the Great Hall and interrupted them. "The attack is over," she said, "and not a single injured soul."

"Thank the Lord," Mrs. Carney said and turned to Maud. "Help us out, child, and put the linen strips on the tables back on the shelves. We've no need of them today."

Gabrielle thought of the battle that had been waged just beyond the walls. The barons' advance had failed, and no English had been injured, at least none that she knew of. She thought of Marston leading his men to victory. He was his own worst enemy, not seeing the gifts that God had given him, minimizing the talents that he had so long possessed. She would find him and remind him of the man he was, a man many sought to mimic.

As she left the keep, she thought of Montague, the other man who held her heart, and she wondered how he had fared in the fighting. Did he command his men from afar like many a great warlord, or did he lead the attack, riding boldly at the forefront of the battle? Was he safe at the enemy camp, or did he lie in the field between castle and forest dead or dying, screaming in pain?

When she reached the steps at the base of the northwest tower, Marston was descending. She ran to him. "Sire," she said. "I sought your face the second I knew the battle had ended,"

"And I came as soon as my duties permitted."

"I couldn't bear the thought you might have been harmed," she whispered.

"Your worry was for naught," he said as he hugged her close. "No harm will come to me."

"Please, do nothing rash."

"I won't," he promised. "It took my whole life to find you. I don't intend to leave you now."

"My sorrow could never be contained," she said as she kissed him deeply on the mouth.

"Nothing risks our happiness," he said as he led her away from the tower. "We've both suffered enough. The rest of our lives are ours to enjoy."

She leaned against him, a man who remained strong when others felt weak, who was calm when others were vexed with anxiety. "The enemy retreats?"

"For today," he replied. "But they'll return. Today's skirmish was only the beginning."

She wondered what had happened to Montague, the man whom she had once vowed to love forever. "None of our men were wounded," she said. "How did the enemy fare?"

He paused, recognizing the question that lay behind her concern. "At least a dozen dead or wounded," he said, "but only among the barons' men. I know not how the French have fared."

Gabrielle didn't reply. She dismissed the thought of Montague charging a wall of English arrows. He was her past. Marston was her present, and he would be her future.

But she couldn't understand why.

Chapter 80

"Marston still lives," James the Bold muttered, pointing to the coat of arms that flew atop each tower.

"Your spy within knows not what to do," Blaise said.

James the Bold studied the warlock, never sure of what to make of him. Was he man, myth, or maniac? The fearsome commander could not say. "He has not yet driven the dagger home."

"He's had days when hours would have been more than enough."

"Perhaps Marston lingers, a wraith knocking on death's door," James the Bold said.

"If so, why not finish what you have started?"

James the Bold eyed the flags that flew atop the towers. "Maybe Marston is dead," he said, "but those within still fly his flag."

"Do you think deception their only defense?" Blaise asked.

"No other account rings true."

"Are you sure the spy remains within the walls?"

"I know Baron Tweed," said James the Bold, "and I know the pair he chose for the task, an old druid named Paul the Pure and his daughter, Trinity."

"Do you know the deeds that shape their past?" Blaise asked. "Or is this a grisly road they've never before taken?"

"Tweed assured me he had arranged for Marston to be murdered. His word is all I need to hear."

The warlock didn't reply. He studied the castle and then his master. Finally, he spoke. "I can see within the walls," he said. "If that's a path you choose to take."

James the Bold's gaze met the warlock's, and, when he was convinced the sorcerer could accomplish what he'd said he could, he glanced around the encampment, making sure no eyes or ears were too close.

"Would you like me to try?" Blaise asked.

James the Bold was quiet for a moment, watching the warlock. He had no interest in the Devil and his works but thought, at times such as these, that the warlock did. Still he had little left to lose. "Tell me what your eyes can see."

Blaise reached into his satchel and withdrew a slender leather pouch. He opened it and emptied dozens of slender sticks onto the mossy ground.

"What are they?" James the Bold asked.

"Eyes that see tomorrow."

James the Bold looked at the warlock curiously but didn't reply. He felt a faint flutter of fear, which he immediately dismissed, took a step back, and watched.

Blaise scooped up the sticks and held them in his hand, making sure they were evenly stacked. He muttered something in an ancient Gaelic tongue understood by him alone. Seconds later, he tossed the sticks gently into the air, watching as they fell. They landed in a haphazard heap. Two stray sticks rolled away from the pile, the first coming to rest a hands' breadth from the heap, the second spinning to a stop and pointing at the rest of the pile.

Blaise examined the sticks, and when he had considered every nuance of the shape they'd formed, he began to chant.

Who lives?
Who dies?
Truth told,
No lies.
Breath stopped,
Cold feet,
Eyes closed,
Heartbeat.
Soul lost,

Curse said,

Body stiff,

Who's dead?

He repeated the chant nine times. When he had finished, he studied the pile closely once more—assessing the location of each stick, the two laggards and their position in relation to a setting sun.

"What do they tell you?" James the Bold asked.

Blaise looked up from the pile and into his master's eyes. "Michael Marston lives. But Paul the Pure is dead."

Chapter 81

Montague watched the sun fade as darkness draped the English coast, inching across the fields that stretched beyond the castle walls. He knew after the day's failures that a massive attack would follow. And Gabrielle would be most at risk if the castle defenses crumbled and the fight moved to the keep. He had little time to act if he hoped to get her out of the castle and only two methods he could employ to save her—scaling the wall or finding the passage.

He slept restlessly, dreaming of the past and the life he'd enjoyed before he'd been awakened and realized it was only a dream. He fell back to sleep but only briefly, consumed by a nightmare—the keep roiling with men engaged in a bloody battle, his own hand held high in victory, Gabrielle lying dead upon the floor.

He lay awake, thinking of the failed attack and those that were to follow. How many men would he send to their deaths? How many survivors would live the rest of their days maimed or wounded, never quite the men they had been when that fateful day had begun? Even after drifting off to sleep, he still tossed and turned, engaged in a fight that raged on in his mind for hours until he woke up and rubbed his tired eyes.

His tent of pale blue linen adorned with the image of a roaring lion was one of the few luxuries the battle afforded. Rectangular in shape, it contained a bed and small table and sat at the rear of his soldiers' camp, guarded by sentries devoted to him. Piers and their captains enjoyed similar quarters spaced among the soldiers.

Montague rose from his bed, exited his tent, and studied the moon pinned high above the castle. Under a cloudless sky, he walked through the trees to the front lines where his men camped along the fringe of the forest beyond the range of enemy arrows. Most slept-- some soundly, others not. Moving eastward along the line, he passed sentries who stood guard as he tried to slip back into the forest.

As he made his way toward the sea, Montague was suddenly challenged by a sentry with an arrow trained at his chest. "Who goes there?"

"Montague."

"Show yourself or take an arrow in your heart."

Montague stepped from the shadows and into a clearing.

"Sire, I knew not who it was," the sentry said pleadingly once he recognized his commander. He lowered his bow. "Is something wrong?"

"No, I was only restless," Montague replied.

"I could have killed you, sire," the sentry said, his eyes wide.

"And no man would deserve to die more than I," Montague said, putting him at ease. "You're a fine sentry, more hawk than human. Our men are safe with you standing guard."

"Thank you, sire," the sentry said, nodding humbly. "Is there anything that you need?"

"A walk."

"I'll be beside you, standing guard to ensure you are safe."

"I have my sword should I meet any danger."

"With respect, sire, such a defense may not be enough," the sentry said. "I will follow but remain at a distance."

"Do what you must," Montague said, grateful for the man's devotion. "I shall walk to the shore to study the cliff and east wall of the castle."

"I'll be just behind you, sire."

Montague continued toward the sea, listening to the waves as they crashed upon the shore. He emerged from the trees and stood atop a knoll that gradually rose to become the base of the cliff upon which the castle was built. He skirted the edge of the bluff, moving toward the fortress, studying the sentries upon the east wall, for if they were few, he might have a chance to breach the castle and find the Lady Gabrielle.

He pushed on toward the castle, which was still some distance away, and suddenly saw a woman emerge from the hillside. She appeared from nowhere some thirty feet above the waves as if she'd walked through solid rock. Montague watched as she made her way down the cliff, hiding behind boulders to avoid castle sentries, until she reached the shore. Furtively she moved forward, hugging the cliff, hiding in shadows, and keeping a close watch on those who patrolled the walls. The farther she travelled, the less careful she became, but she continued to cast a wary eye in all directions as she hurried along the shore.

Montague squinted after her as she continued south, her silhouette growing ever smaller until she finally disappeared. He turned back toward the castle and studied the cliff, fixing his gaze upon the spot where the mysterious woman had emerged. She had either been there, hiding at the edge of the outcropping until nightfall, or she'd come out of a secret passageway.

He had found the hidden entrance to the castle.

Chapter 82

The heavens were lit by a thousand stars, the coast a dreamlike silver beneath a cloudless sky, the balmy spring night about to yield to summer. Michael Marston stood upon the northern castle wall and stared at the hills and forests that rolled inland from the shore, the Lady Gabrielle beside him. They were alone, save for the sentries patrolling the perimeter of the fortress, and together they kept watch of the barons' forces moving restlessly about the northern plain.

"You're deep in thought, my love," the Lady Gabrielle whispered as she watched the warlord survey the landscape.

"I watch the campfires spread across the plain," he said. "It's hard to remember a darker day for the kingdom."

"They will attack tomorrow?" she asked.

"The witch says as much."

"Their last attack met with failure. Not an injured man among your ranks."

"It was a test," he said. "They measured our response, searched for our weakness, tried to destroy our resolve. But tomorrow will be different.

"You will prevail, sire, whether they send one man or a million."

He smiled, bolstered by her confidence, grateful for her loyalty, but his gaze remained on the forces sprawled along the edge of the forest.

"You look puzzled," she said as she studied his weathered face.

"I'm confused," he replied.

"By what?"

"The enemy campfires," he said. "I've watched them every night, growing in number, changing location. They were so many the last few nights that they lit the plain like rays of the sun. Now they're greatly diminished, and I need to know why."

"Perhaps some have deserted or gone to fight battles elsewhere."

"Which is what the enemy hopes to portray, but I suspect there's treachery before us."

They were silent for a moment, the warlord planning his defenses, the woman dreaming of a future that might never come to pass.

"No matter what occurs, I would not trade a minute in your arms nor a second in your heart for anything," she said softly, impacted by a magic spell as well as the man before her. "And I never will."

He hugged her, drinking in her scent, his hands caressing the curves of her body. "And if I were to breathe my final breath as I stand before you, my life could be called complete because I have lived it in your eyes."

She pulled him closer and kissed him. "I'll leave you to plot your defense," she said.

He held onto her a moment longer, afraid to let go.

She paused, sensing something amiss-- a shadow of doubt in his eyes, a darkness she had never before seen.

"You must remember," he began, "should anything happen to me, you must escape. Don't let these heathens anywhere near you."

"Nothing will happen to you," she said and kissed his cheek.

"Just because I've never lost a battle doesn't mean I never will."

"You're creating an enemy that doesn't exist."

"And what enemy is that?"

"The enemy that gnaws away inside you, trying to destroy a great and gifted man."

"Time wears away the rocks that line the coast, no matter how great," he said. "I suffer the same fate."

Gabrielle looked at him for a moment, wondering what to say, and then turned to study the landscape. In the distance, just past the catapults, was a massive English oak, its branches sprawling in all directions.

"See that tree," she said, pointing to the west. "That tree is you, strong and steady with arms reaching out to protect everyone who walks within your shadow."

"I don't deny that," he said softly. "Never forget, my love, that you are my roots, and you always will be."

Chapter 83

Michael Marston watched as the Lady Gabrielle slipped away toward the tower stairs, her long emerald dress brushing the stone walkway. As she approached a sentry she nodded, paused for a moment to share a few words of encouragement, and then started down the steps. Quivers of arrows were stacked at the base of the tower, waiting to be hoisted up to the archers when needed to fend off the coming attack. She crossed the bailey, her path lit by torches that flickered atop poles lining the empty streets, and disappeared into the keep. Marston knew she would be waiting when he returned. She always was.

He turned back to the enemy, a gnawing doubt wearing away at his resolve. The number of fires, less than yesterday and fewer still than the night before, remained a mystery. He wondered what James the Bold and his French allies had planned, what devious plot was about to unfold, for his adversary was known not for the fairness of his fight, but for the horrors he brought to the battlefield. Fear was his greatest ally, terror his universal tactic, no matter his objective. Would they rush one side of the castle after pummeling the walls with their catapults Marston wondered, or would they strike from all sides at once, trying to overwhelm the forces within?

"Don't be deceived, Michael Marston," a voice behind him creaked.

He turned to find Minerva standing in the shadows, her black robe and dark hair seeming to merge with the night. It was rare for her to venture from her subterranean lair, and he knew she only did so if there was something she needed to tell him at once. She didn't have stand on the wall to see what the enemy did. She could see the same scene Marston beheld reflected in her cauldron deep within the bowels of the earth.

"Whatever brings you to the top of the wall," he asked, "when your eyes can see all without leaving your altar?"

"I came to see the master in his most grievous time of need."

"Must you always sneak up on me?"

"It's never my intent," she said sweetly, reaching out to lightly caress his arm.

"I thought you preferred never to leave that forsaken cave."

"Only to see you, sire," she whispered.

He bristled at the strange game she played but held his tongue, knowing she had a reason for seeking him out, a purpose for leaving her cavern, and she would tell him when she was ready. Until then, he had to submit to her unnerving advances or act as if he didn't care. He turned and again studied the campfires.

"You're troubled," she said. "Not like a man who is master of many."

He pointed to the hills. "The light cast by the enemy's fires grows weaker by the night."

The witch scanned the landscape, studying the plains, the forest, and the edge of the cliff. She turned, focused on the ocean, as Michael Marston was, and watched the water rushing to the shore.

"What do you see?" he asked.

"Fewer fires do not mean fewer men," she said.

"But fewer men can be seen. At least from where I stand."

"If the others have gone, think where they might be."

"This is not the only battle occurring on this island," he said. "They may now fight elsewhere."

"Or perhaps they are hidden amongst the trees."

"Some who advise me are certain that part of the enemy army has gone to engage in battles far away," he said. "And we are forced to wither on the vine, waiting for an onslaught that never comes."

"And what do your confidants tell you to do?"

"They advise we launch an attack while the enemy forces are scattered."

"Are they scattered?" she asked. "Or do two stand where one is seen?"

He hesitated, conjuring the picture she tried to paint in his mind. "Some claim the enemy now plans a siege, an agonizing tactic that shall gradually choke us like a noose about our necks."

"Your men are not leaders," she reminded him. "You alone lead."

"Leaders can be wrong."

"But you are not."

Marston didn't reply. He studied the campfires and then the dense forest that stretched on and on into the darkness. He couldn't see through the black curtain of trees, couldn't be sure of what they might hide, but he trusted the witch.

"You know best," Minerva said, "and you always have. Do not act a fool for the first time in your life."

He turned to reply, but the witch was halfway to the tower stairs, her black hair and robe blending seamlessly with the night.

Chapter 84

"More than half the men have been hidden," said James the Bold. "Long enough to mask their presence and make Michael Marston think they've gone."

"Still he makes no effort to leave the confines of the castle," said Jamet, "and likely assumes we'll settle for a siege."

"We know that he lives," James the Bold said, glancing at the flags atop the tower. "The man who was to take his life has lost his own instead."

"If ever there was a time to launch a full-scale attack, it is now," Jamet said.

James the Bold nodded, marking the rare occasion when he agreed with his French advisor. "We'll focus our initial assault on the northern part of the western wall."

"Just a diversion to pin Marston's men?" Jamet asked

James the Bold nodded, his blood coursing with the thrill he always felt before a battle. "And we'll attack the northern wall with the men who now show their faces—roughly half of our actual force."

"And what of the French?" Jamet asked. "Do they have a part in this play?"

"I'll send an order to the French to pummel the southern face," said James the Bold, the course of the battle mapped in his head

"In hope that Marston moves men from the northern wall to confront them?" Jamet asked, guessing at the warlord's strategy.

James the Bold nodded, an evil grin curling his lips as he enjoyed his vision of what was to come. "We'll manage Marston like a pawn who's soon to be taken," he said.

"And what of the men we have hidden?"

"As soon as Marston moves men to meet the French assault, they will emerge from the forest and strike the northern wall with the full force of our army," said James the Bold. "And you will lead the attack."

"An honor I do not deserve," Jamet said, his heart starting to race. "But one I gladly accept."

Minutes later, the assault began. Two dozen men drove the catapults that'd been staged on the northern and western faces into position. Two dozen more dragged wagons laden with boulders they'd collected from the field.

As the barons' men edged the catapults into place, Marston's archers knocked their arrows, aimed their crossbows, and began to fire from atop the walls. Three of the barons' men fell, their chests spiked with arrows, but others were quick to take their places.

The barons' archers let their arrows fly, but few met their mark, the distance too great, although some struck the walls and fell to the ground. Marston's men replied, and in minutes the skies were littered with arrows soaring in both directions. A wave of the barons' men advanced, a swarm of green tunics and shields surging toward the castle.

The French launched their attack to the south as soon as they received their orders. James the Bold and Jamet watched from a shallow crest on the plain as the men atop the wall frantically darted about, but no one could tell where the castle's forces were focused.

James the Bold tried to guess what Marston was doing and how many men he had under command. The plain between the walls and trees was soon littered with wounded and dying. Arrows bristled in the ground, and two dead horses lay in the field, their riders slain beside them. The barons' catapults flung boulder after boulder at the walls, cracking the mortar with colossal blows before crashing to the ground.

James the Bold turned to Jamet. "Lead those who are hidden into battle!"

Chapter 85

Montague staged his men as he waited for word to attack, and as soon as it came, he and his army sprang into action, willing to fight to the death. They moved the two catapults into position, aiming them at the same location on the south wall. He gave the order to fire, and several soldiers pulled back the arms and piled boulders into the buckets. Seconds later, they released the ropes, and the stones hurtled toward the castle, arcing high into the sky. They landed far short of the wall.

"Move the catapults closer," Montague commanded.

It took a dozen men to drag the machines forward, but they did so without complaint. They knew that each step they took would bring them closer to the enemy's arrows, but they pressed on as their captain had commanded.

Once they'd moved the catapults another fifty feet, Montague raised his hand. "Ready the catapults to fire," he directed.

It took two men to lift each boulder, given their weight and size. They pulled the sling back into place so that it was cocked and ready to fire and loaded the rocks onto it.

Montague squinted at the castle wall, the defenders watching warily, and raised his arm high. "Fire!" he shouted, dropping his arm.

All eyes on the battlefield watched as the boulders careened toward the wall. Marston's men scattered from where they might land, but again they fell short, burrowing into the ground.

"Move forward thirty feet," Montague called.

His men complied. As they pushed the catapults forward, the archers standing atop the curtain wall cocked their bows, the tips of each of their arrows trained upon the hearts of Montague's men. They fired, the twang of a hundred bows snapping at once echoing across the plain. An avalanche of arrows bore down on the men who manned the machines. Some fell short while others struck the catapults and carts, their lethal tips imbedded into the wooden frames.

Three men were struck and fell to the ground, but six others hurried forward, replacing those who had fallen, a wary eye on the fortress. Still others loaded the wounded on stretchers and carried them away from the archers' range.

The soldiers loaded the catapults again. "Fire!" Montague commanded.

Boulders crashed into the southern wall just east of the central tower, careening off in showers of dust and splintered stone. With enough pummeling, the mighty walls of the fortress would crumble and eventually fall, and the French would race forward, using grappling hooks to rip down the remainder. And if the wall refused to come down, they would move the catapults forward and fling boulders into the bailey.

As the barrage continued, both infantry and cavalry prepared to attack. Montague looked up and down the line, a sea of pale blue tunics and metal helmets a hundred yards long that stretched the length of the southern face. He waited a moment to be sure his men were ready, then advanced before them, leading them on with a wave of his sword.

"Attack!" Montague bellowed.

The cavalry stretched along the line, shielding the infantrymen as they raced toward the wall. They carried grappling hooks, bows and arrows, lances and battleaxes, and crude wooden ladders—all of the weapons which had worked in the past. When his men were halfway to the wall, the English archers fired. A barrage of arrows bore down on them, wounding some and killing others. Still, they pressed on, and just as they reached the base of the wall, their cries echoing against the stone, the full force of the barons' men unleashed their attack from the north.

Chapter 86

Marston hurried along the castle wall, watching the enemy advance from the west.

They came slowly, marching tentatively into the archers' range. They eased two catapults into position, launching boulders that didn't quite reach the wall.

Twenty men manned the northwest tower, prepared for the battle unfolding beneath them. Marston approached and saw a man in the corner, young and slight and likely afraid.

"And who may you be, good soldier?" Marston asked.

He was barely a man and awed by the sight of Marston. "Scottie, sire."

"Are you ready, Scottie?" Marston asked. "Just as the men beside you?"

Those nearby turned to look, nodding to their commander.

"They're almost in range, sire, it won't be long," said one of the men.

Marston eyed the approaching army. "May I borrow your bow?" he asked the young lad.

"Of course, sire," Scottie said, handing it to him. "And here's an arrow to lend to one of the baron's men."

The group laughed as Marston knocked the arrow. He sighted a man leading the team that pushed the catapults forward. He closed an eye, drew the string, and let the arrow fly.

The men in the tower watched as the arrow sliced the heavens. It traveled farther than any Marston's men fired that day, a good thirty feet beyond them. Whistling down in a frightening plunge, the tip pierced the man it was meant for, and he fell to the ground, too far away to hear his anguished cries.

The men cheered as Marston returned the bow. "Fear not, Scottie," he said. "I'll be right beside you."

Marston nodded to his men and left, walking the walls of the castle. No more than a few minutes passed when James the Bold launched the enemy attack, first in the west and then in the north. They were shortly followed by the French in the south. Boulders from a half dozen catapults peppered the castle walls, arrows fired by the advancing army finding a few of Marston's men. But those who manned the walls held fast, trained to make each arrow count.

The enemy maneuvered their catapults ever closer, shattering sections of stone and mortar and forcing large chunks to fall to the ground. Other boulders bounced through the courtyard, burst through the roof of the stable, and broke the walls of the fishmonger's stall.

Marston watched the battle unfold. He looked to the southwest tower, eyeing the French as they prepared to attack, fumbling to position their catapult while arrows kept them at bay. One thousand Frenchmen streamed from the forest and charged toward the castle, some carrying makeshift ladders. Satisfied that his men could thwart the attack, Marston made his way down the western wall. He assessed the meager force bearing down on the barbican and saw they posed no threat. He moved on to the northwest tower so he could weigh the greatest risk to his men: the attack led by James the Bold, an army of two thousand in a concentrated assault on the castle wall.

Captain Carney commanded the forces defending the northern wall, and Gideon was stationed in the bailey, ensuring the defenders received whatever supplies they needed and that all the contraptions he'd designed to assist—levers, hoists, and pulleys—remained in working order. Marston watched as Carney directed the counterattack from atop the central tower.

"Prepare the oil," Carney yelled.

Small fires were spaced across the wall, and cauldrons filled with oil bubbled above them. The defenders grabbed small buckets and filled them with the oil. They waited until the attackers had their ladders propped against the wall, their men rapidly scaling the rungs, and then emptied the oil upon them. As the men tumbled from the ladder, screaming in agony, the defenders kicked it away from the wall and fired flaming arrows. The attackers who had been splattered burst into flames, dying quickly, but not soon enough, so horrendous was their pain.

In the castle courtyard, Marston's men readied their own massive catapult. Under Gideon's command, they maneuvered it into position and loaded boulders into its sling. They turned to Carney who stood atop the wall, his hand raised high as he surveyed the battlefield. When he was sure the enemy was within range, he dropped his arm.

The boulder hurtled forward, arcing in the air, and crashed to the ground upon two attackers. One was killed instantly, the second lay dazed on the ground as the boulder rolled on a few feet more before coming to rest at the base of one of the catapults, its intended target.

Marston's men moved the catapult forward and loaded another boulder. Carney eyed the enemy and gave the order to fire. The second boulder crashed into the enemy's catapult, snapping the log that served as its arm in two. The soldiers nearby scattered to avoid the flying debris, but one was not quick enough, and a large splinter from the catapult's frame impaled him, and he fell to the ground, screaming with pain, only to die a few minutes later.

For the men on the south side of the castle who were facing the French, the battle was much the same. The archers who lined the wall rained arrows upon them until they were forced to retreat. The soldiers in the bailey spun the catapult to face them and launched boulder after boulder, adjusting their aim with each blow they fired, and killing many men. They soon posed such a threat to the French catapults that they had to be withdrawn.

And so ended the day of the barons' attempt to take the castle. The invaders fared far worse than those who defended Marston's fortress and the many souls within its walls.

Chapter 87

The Lady Gabrielle paced the floor of the Great Hall, ensuring all was prepared. She watched the women who would assist her and the girls who would help them, checking supplies and arranging the shelves, nervously waiting for wounded. Linen for bandages, herbs, oils, and tonics for treatments, tables arranged as makeshift beds upon which they would treat the wounded, stood at the ready.

The sounds of battle reached their ears, shouts and cries and commands. The crash from boulders smashing the walls, flung by enemy catapults, echoed throughout the bailey and into the keep. The women shared anxious glances. This was the first of the fighting most had seen. Gabrielle, who had long lived on the edge of conflict, now knew the sound and taste and smell of what men could do to each other.

"And this is the beginning?" Mrs. Carney asked with an anxious look as boulders crashed into the castle walls and the sound of stony fragments falling and hitting the ground reached their ears.

"Pray it ends before it begins," said a woman who tended the chickens. "Perhaps a truce or plan for peace will appear when least expected."

Lady Gabrielle listened as the women spoke among the noises of war in the background. It was more than she could endure, waiting here in the keep while Marston fought atop the wall, her eyes blind to the carnage of what occurred beyond the walls. She hesitated, knowing the wounded would come quickly now that the battle had begun, but she had to know the ways of war and ensure that Marston was safe.

"I can resist no longer," she told the women who stood beside her. "I'll be gone but a moment."

"Where are you going?" Mrs. Carney asked, confused by her behavior.

"We will surely need you," said another woman, wife to the tanner.

"And the wounded will come in minutes, though I pray they don't come at all," said a woman who made jewelry.

"I must see with my own eyes what those in the battle are facing," Gabrielle said as she hurried for the door.

"Can I come with you?" little Maud asked, her eyes wide with wonder.

The Lady Gabrielle smiled and knelt to kiss the child's head. "Not this time, little lovely," she said. "It's a walk that I must take alone."

"I've got chores for you to do," Mrs. Carney called to her daughter.

Maud turned and went to her mother, and the Lady Gabrielle left the keep. As she descended the steps into the bailey, she walked into a world she had never before seen. Chaos reigned before her, soldiers and citizens running about, climbing the steps that led to the walls or fetching supplies for the battle. A dusty haze clung to the air, born by the walls that had been pummeled and punched, the stone crashing to the ground in fragments, but the cries of the men were louder. She paused and watched for a moment and then took the steps to the northwest tower.

She wasn't prepared for what she saw. Twenty men knocked arrows upon their bows and let them fly. The terrain beyond was cluttered with men, all racing toward the castle. She paused and watched, mesmerized, as enemy arrows coursed right past her. A soldier turned and saw her, a boy trying hard to be a man.

"Please, my lady, you must leave," he cried. "Before an arrow finds you."

"But I only wanted to see first-hand the fight you have before you," she said, pale at the battle that raged around her.

"It's just the beginning and will only get worse, so please let me take you to safety," the man said as he ushered Gabrielle into a safer position within the tower.

Gabrielle saw worry and fear on his face. "Have you seen Sir Michael Marston?"

The young man smiled. "I have, my lady. He fired my bow. Tell him you spoke with Scottie.'

"Do you know where he is or if he is safe?"

Scottie shrugged. "He's likely on another tower or patrolling the walls. He's a commander like no other, fighting beside his men."

Gabrielle nodded, trying in vain to conceal her worst fears for the safety of the castle's commander. "I had best leave," she said, knowing she stood in harm's way. "Thank you, Scottie, for your concern. It's an act I won't soon forget."

Scottie returned to fighting his foes, and the Lady Gabrielle fled back down the steps. She crossed the bailey, destined for the keep, when she saw a soldier helping a wounded man to the hospital. She was about to hurry back to her duties but instead ran across the bailey. She raced up the stairs to the southwest tower and reached the summit, her breath coming in gasps.

The men were too busy fighting to notice her standing there much as they had been in the tower she had just left. She saw no sign of Michael Marston, not in the tower or the walls that led to it. She crept closer to the edge, glimpsing the French catapults in the field beyond, the army advancing across the plain. She scanned the faces of the soldiers, those who were mounted on horseback, and at the front of the line with his sword in the air was a man she wasn't prepared to see.

Montague led his men into battle.

Chapter 88

When Trinity reached the cove that Baron Tweed had described, she found a long stone pier jutting into the water and a vessel docked at the far end, its single mast fitted with a square-rigged sail. A flag atop the mast bearing the image of a lion snapped in the breeze. It was different from the symbol the French often used, for the lion had wings, not at all like what she had seen in the camps along the English coast. She suspected it came from a far-off land, which aligned with Tweed's descriptions of his battles in the Holy Land.

Where the pier met the shore, a clearing bisected the forest. A dirt road wound its way upward over the knoll that rose gradually from the shore to a nearby village or a baron's estate. The shoreline was littered with driftwood and rocks, the soft sand stretching in both directions. Six wooden barrels had been stacked along the edge of the dock along with bushels of wheat and several wooden crates. They'd either been recently delivered or were about to be loaded onto the ship, but all was quiet. The area seemed deserted.

Trinity stepped from the shore and onto the pier just as dawn was beginning to break, the eastern sky lit in orange hues, wispy clouds racing across the sun as it rose. She looked up the road and saw no one and then at the ship, which seemed empty though she knew it was not. She started towards it when two men emerged from the shadows cast by the crates stacked on the pier. They wore gray leggings and red tunics and watched her every move as she approached.

She studied them warily, wondering if they waited for Baron Tweed. "I'm here to see the captain," she said when she reached them.

"We look for man," one of the sailors said, his accent thick, Italian or Spanish.

"I came instead."

The sailor looked at his companion and shrugged. "Come," he said. "We take you to ship."

"When do you sail?" Trinity asked as they walked along the dock.

"One hour, maybe more."

"And your destination?"

"Venice," the sailor replied.

Trinity had never heard of such a place. She wondered if it was a city or a country, a land she might like to visit or one torn apart by war like the distant lands Baron Tweed had described.

"Is far away," the sailor continued.

Trinity considered the gold she would get for the Grail, more than she could spend in a lifetime, even if she were to live in luxury. It might be nice to start over somewhere new and live as a foreign noblewoman. It would be one of the easier parts she'd had to play.

"You want to go?" the sailor asked jokingly. "Is nice."

"On the water?"

"Yes, much water. Canals with many boats."

"It sounds lovely," she said as they reached the ship. It was built of massive timbers that were speckled with barnacles at the waterline. A man waited for them on the deck beside a wooden plank that stretched from the pier to the ship, and the crewmen helped Trinity across, carrying her satchels as they, too, climbed on deck.

"Captain Spinoza," the man who was waiting announced, introducing himself.

"Trinity," the seer said. "I'm told you came from far away."

He looked at her curiously. "Your eyes," he said. "Is wrong?"

She smiled. "Just very different."

The captain eyed her suspiciously, not returning her smile. "I was expecting man."

"He sent me in his place."

"You have the Grail?"

"I do," she replied.

"Can I see?"

"Yes, of course," she said. She rummaged through her knapsack and withdrew a worn chalice.

He reached his hand forward. "May I touch?"

She handed it to him, watching closely as he examined it. "Do you take passengers?" she asked.

"Sometimes," he said.

"How much will you pay for the Grail?"

"Much gold," he said, turning the chalice over in his hands.

"May I see how much gold?" she asked.

He squinted at the chalice and then looked up at Trinity. "Just one problem," he said flatly.

She was confused. "What is that?"

The cabin door swung open, and a man stepped out. "I think that belongs to me," said Baron Richard Tweed.

Chapter 89

Trinity's eyes widened; her heart raced. "Baron Tweed," she stammered. "I didn't expect to see you."

Tweed's face contorted with rage, making the large purple bruise on his temple all the more noticeable. "I'm sure you didn't."

"Is she the one?" Captain Spinoza asked.

"She is," Tweed said. "Fortunately, her attempt to dispatch me from this world failed."

"It wasn't me," Trinity pleaded, knowing her life was in danger. "It was Paul the Pure. He forced me to do it."

"Your father?" Tweed asked.

She hesitated. To admit one lie might prove she was guilty of telling many more. "He wasn't my father."

"I'm not surprised," Tweed said with disgust. "There was no truth to the man nor his supposed daughter."

"But he did raise me. We've been together since I was a child," she lied, treading carefully, not knowing how much to admit.

Tweed looked to the shore beyond. "Where is the old fool?" he asked.

Trinity knew she needed sympathy if she hoped to survive. She started to cry. "He's dead," she said, sobbing.

"Dead?" Tweed asked. "May his last breath have been drawn in utter agony."

"It was a horrible death."

"Does Marston live?"

"He does," Trinity said. "It was he who killed Paul the Pure."

Tweed looked at her, his eyes widening, for an instant, with surprise. "Why did Marston kill him?"

"Paul the Pure tried to poison him," she explained. "To honor your request."

"And it didn't work?"

"Marston swapped the goblets."

"And Paul the Pure drank the poison."

She nodded, wiping the tears from her eyes. "He died a few days later."

Tweed started laughing. "The old fool. I cannot say I'm grieved."

"He was the only family I had," she said, forcing tears to once more flow.

Tweed showed no sympathy. "I have no pity for such a man nor for you," he said. "Not after the dark deed you tried to commit."

"I only did what Paul the Pure commanded," Trinity pleaded. "Show me mercy by giving me the chance to make amends." She touched Tweed gently on the arm, hoping to spark his old infatuation.

"Marston still lives? Or did you succeed where your father failed?"

"No, he lives."

"And the castle?"

"When I escaped, it had not been breached."

"Has the battle begun?"

"It has, but the fortress is well defended."

Tweed paused, growing pensive at the news. "Marston will face a grisly death, but only after he has served his purpose. James the Bold will tear his head from his shoulders and mount it on a pike for all to see."

Trinity doubted Tweed's confidence based on what she had seen. "The barons' forces have seen no success. At least not as of yet."

Tweed waved her off. He had no further interest in the castle's fate, knowing victory would soon arrive. He turned to Captain Spinoza. "Do you still desire the Grail?"

"It is real?" the captain asked.

Tweed looked at Trinity. "Unless she has switched it with a fake. And I would not be at all surprised if she did."

"I didn't," she said. "The Grail has never left me."

"Let me see it," Tweed said, taking it from the captain. He examined it closely, assessing the tarnished metal, fingering each of its imperfections carefully.

"Surely your own eyes can see," Trinity said, trying to assure him. "It's the cup that held the blood of Christ."

"No, it isn't," Tweed said. "This chalice is dented and scarred, but it's barely a hundred years old. Where's the real one?"

Trinity looked at him with shock. "That is the real one."

"No, it isn't. You swapped them."

"I didn't," Trinity said. "I swear."

"Somebody did."

"What should we do with her?" the captain asked.

Trinity blinked at the chalice, wondering who had deceived her. The Grail had never left her side.

"Kill her," Tweed said to Captain Spinoza.

"The witch!" Trinity blurted out, the solution to the riddle arriving when she needed it most. "The witch must have taken the Grail."

"What nonsense is this?" Tweed asked. "And why should I believe a word you speak?"

"There's a witch, a powerful sorceress, who lives in the castle," she said. "Her name is Minerva."

Tweed studied her closely, his face filled with doubt. "The Grail is in Marston Castle?"

"I'm sure of it. And I may be able to lead you to it."

"Moments ago, you were sure you held it. I'll get it myself," Tweed said, "when the battle is won, and I'll step over Marston's dead body to do it."

Captain Spinoza stepped forward, grabbing Trinity by the arm. "Do we kill her?" he asked.

"Yes," Tweed replied. "She's of no use to me."

"Wait!" Trinity pleaded. "I can show you how to win the war."

Tweed scoffed. "How? You've done nothing but forestall our victory."

The captain withdrew a long, narrow knife from a scabbard on his belt. "Hold her," he said to two of his men,

"No, wait," Trinity cried. "I've seen what others cannot see."

The two men grabbed her arms roughly as the captain came forward and placed the point of the blade just under her ribcage. He pointed it upward at her heart.

"Stop!" she pleaded. "Please. Don't kill me. I can show you how to breach the castle."

Baron Tweed held up his hand, signaling the captain to stop. "How could a woman as worthless as you undo what's already been done?"

"I know a secret passage into the fortress."

Chapter 90

Richard Tweed squeezed Trinity's right arm savagely as he pushed her forward. They marched up the coast, destined for Marston Castle. When they drew close to the barons' armies' encampment, they were careful to skirt the sentries, hiding in the trees as they made their way forward. At last, they began the climb up the wooded knoll that gave way to the cliff the castle sat upon and approached the French camp. The bulk of their forces were staged on the edge of the plain, and the mood that hung about the cookfires was somber as the men had been defeated in battle.

"Do you want the French to see you?" she asked.

Tweed shook his head. "I didn't come to fight the war nor meet any ally who is."

"I thought you started this war," Trinity said with a smirk.

"I wasn't alone," he said. "Many stand with me."

"None within the castle walls. We should wait until darkness falls to go any farther. Daylight will not be our friend."

"I have no time for your games," Tweed said. "Take me in the way you walked out."

"I cannot. The soldiers are in different positions."

"Then you need to find a way past them," Tweed said.

"But aren't they your allies?"

"It doesn't matter. At least not now."

Trinity was confused. Tweed had spared her life so she could show him the passage, the only means she'd been able to find to breach the fortress. "I thought you wanted to show them the tunnel."

"I do," he said. "But only after I know it myself."

Trinity watched him glaring at her impatiently, almost rabid in his obsession to get the Grail. But she knew he would

309

never again possess it, whether she showed him the passage or not. She had been bold enough to strike him down once, and the next time she would kill him.

"You will lead me right to it," he said, "and once we're inside the castle, you will take me to the Grail."

"If I can," she muttered. She didn't know where the Grail was. Marston could have taken it or Gideon, his advisor. Or it could have been Minerva, the witch that knew all. She shivered at the thought of her.

"Get down," Tweed whispered, pushing her to the ground.

Trinity eyed the French guard who was less than a hundred feet away. She crouched in the underbrush as he scanned the forest for any sign that the enemy had made a move to attack from the rear.

"We have to make our way to the shore," Trinity whispered. "And travel the rest of the way in darkness. It's our only hope."

"I'll wait no longer for the Grail," Tweed hissed. "If you can't show me where it is, a sad day awaits you."

Begrudgingly, Trinity led the baron away from the sentry and toward the shore. They had traveled no more than a few hundred feet when they heard moans of agony, pleas for water, cries of pain—all distant but discernable.

"The wounded," Tweed said. "James the Bold must not be faring well."

Trinity cringed, knowing that many of the men they heard upon the plain would die horrendous deaths. "We've little left to travel," she said. "I'll lead you the rest of the way."

Tweed paused and looked at her sternly. "If you try to deceive me, I will kill you."

"I have no secret I must keep nor any goal except to see the dawn."

As they left the French encampment behind them, a new danger came into view: the hundreds of vigilant archers on the castle walls.

"Don't let them see you," Trinity warned.

310

"Just show me the passage," Tweed demanded, "and don't worry about the archers."

Trinity nodded, and together they began the tedious trek through the maze of rocks that dotted the shoreline. Finally they reached the cliff. Trinity led the baron up through the rocks to the ledge that jutted out above the waves.

"The opening is here," she said, once they'd reached the shelf, careful not to get too close to the deep crevasses on either side.

Tweed cast her a look of mistrust. "I see no secret door," he said. "This had better not be a trick."

Trinity felt along the face of the cliff, searching for the catch that caused the stone door to slide open. At last, she found the trigger and yanked down on it firmly. The stone slid to the side, and the secret entrance was exposed.

There in the gloom stood Minerva.

"Trinity," she said with a smile. "I've been expecting you."

Chapter 91

Jamet galloped back from the wall, leading his men from battle. Covered with dirt and sweat, his tunic tattered and splattered with blood that didn't belong to him, he had been successful at nothing but eluding enemy fire. He watched his men retreat, a sea of green tunics seeking refuge from the unending rain of arrows unleashed from atop the castle walls.

"They show no weakness even after a dozen assaults," he said, breathless, as he approached James the Bold.

The landscape was littered with the broken bodies of men and their weapons, the carcasses of horses scattered about them, a catapult lying in pieces.

"We have suffered enough damage for one day," muttered James the Bold.

Jamet nodded. "May I suggest a potential solution?"

James the Bold glared at the Frenchmen. "If you must," he grumbled.

"We attack a single point with overwhelming force," Jamet said. "Near the northwest or southwest tower. We pummel them with assaults, using all of our forces, the barons' men as well as the French."

James the Bold considered Jamet's suggestion. "We need something daring, an approach not normally taken."

"We can relocate the catapults, focus their blows on the same section of wall. We'll pound it until it collapses."

"We could," James the Bold said, thinking. "Or we can blind them through deceit and take the walls when they least expect it."

Jamet studied the English commander curiously. He wouldn't be surprised by any suggestion he might make. "What tricks might we play?"

James the Bold studied his retreating army. "I've two other options left to employ," he said. "The first involves an ally inside the castle walls, though I don't yet know what he can do."

"If your ally was meant to kill Marston, he failed," Jamet said, "and we don't even know if he lives. He could have been left to rot in the dungeon."

"I have another ally, not as reliable as the first, but he'll still do my bidding."

"Why would he?" Jamet asked, curious why men would betray their king. "Especially if the first has failed."

"Because I hold his family. And whether or not they live will rest with me."

Jamet paled, wondering if there was an end to James the Bold's cruelty. "If he acts when the time is right, there's little Marston's men can do," he said, waiting for the warlord to continue. "And what is the second plan you propose?"

"Do not forget the miners," said James the Bold. "They've been digging tirelessly since we arrived and have only fifty feet more."

Jamet looked at the tunnel entrance, a knoll by the edge of the trees. "What is their path?"

"A straight line across the plain. They will dig beneath the wall where it adjoins with the tower. Then they'll prop it up with wooden beams."

"And set fire to the supports," Jamet said, "so the wall collapses."

James the Bold nodded, casting a cold glare at the castle. "I've just begun the battle in a war Marston will never win. And it only ends when I say it does—with his severed head."

Chapter 92

Montague ordered a retreat, his gaze fixed upon the remnants of battle—arrows, shields, pikes, and ladders littering the plain, red pools of blood staining green grass. The attack had done little damage and had ended far from a castle breach. The keep had never been threatened, and the Lady Gabrielle, who left his thoughts for barely a second, was safe from any harm.

He galloped up to Piers and glanced at the castle. "The north wall was the focus of Marston's defense. He knows the barons' army is twice the size of our own."

"And the west wall is far too strong for us to breach."

"We need to employ a different tactic," Montague said. "I can't permit another assault that takes the lives of so many men."

Piers studied the castle, his gaze scanning the length of the eastern wall. "I know it poses a challenge, but what of the eastern wall?"

"There is little room to maneuver. But it's where an attack is least expected."

"But our troops could be annihilated if the enemy is prepared," Piers said.

Montague considered his probing attack that ran the length of the wall. "We could stage archers at the corner, if only to cover our attack."

"It could work if our archers keep them at bay," Piers said. "But it will be difficult. And many men might die."

"If we do not attack, we're left with a siege," Montague said.

"It would be a lengthy campaign, sire, as you well know, and could last more than a year."

"Then perhaps it will be trickery that wins the war."

Piers looked confused. "And what might you propose?"

"I found the entrance to the passageway that Alaric once described," Montague said. "It's cut into the side of the cliff."

Piers paused to consider how the access could be used. "Hardly a path for an army so visible from the wall."

"Not if I went alone and hid amongst the shadows."

Piers saw the determination etched in his face, having made the suggestion days before. "But, sire, that's far too risky," he said. "As we've already discussed."

"None shall see me."

"But if they do?"

"It's still a worthy prospect," Montague said. "Access to the castle could then be gained without the shedding of blood."

"But it's not worth the risk if we lose you, sire."

Montague looked to his lieutenant with sadness in his eyes. "Not only can we win the battle, but I can save Lady Gabrielle."

Piers frowned but knew what was held in Montague's heart. "If it's what you must do, take a handful of men to protect you."

"Then we shall almost surely be found."

Piers shook his head, knowing he could say nothing that might change his friend's mind. "And if you're killed or captured?"

"The battle will continue," Montague said gravely. "And you will stand in my place."

Chapter 93

Lady Gabrielle spent the day in the Great Hall, having seen the battle that raged outside the walls, horrendous images that weighed upon her. Though she was blind to the carnage the barons' men wrought from deep inside the keep, she gauged the success of the enemy's attack by the number of mattresses that began to fill, one by one, with wounded men, all of them crying for help.

Five assistants, including Mrs. Carney, aided Gabrielle, all of them women she'd trained in the basic arts of healing. Some were assisted by their daughters like Maud. Though unable to treat the wounded, the children fetched ingredients, distributed water to those with parched lips, and kept watch over the soldiers who needed care, which allowed the women to devote their time to healing the critically wounded.

The casualties arrived slowly at first in the arms of their comrades or men from the village. Some of their injuries were minor—burns from vats of oil, arrows that grazed a torso or limb —but many were far more serious. Several had arrows imbedded in bodies, a few had been sliced with lances from an enemy who'd reached the top of the wall only to be killed soon thereafter. Those who could be were helped; those who couldn't were made as comfortable, sometimes only minutes passing before they breathed their last.

"Put cold water on the burns," Lady Gabrielle told her helpmates. "It'll ease the pain."

"And then what should I do" the women asked.

"Wet a cloth with wine and dab the entire area."

"A couple of badly injured men are arriving," Mrs. Carney called across the Great Hall.

Two men were brought in, one with a blood-soaked shoulder where an arrow had gouged him, the second with an arrow stuck in his chest. The latter was carried in by two men, his face pale, his body limp.

"Lay each on a table," Lady Gabrielle directed, and she and Mrs. Carney followed the soldiers to the tables they'd staged for critical care.

"I'll take the man with the shoulder wound," said Mrs. Carney.

The soldiers laid the man on a table, and Mrs. Carney cut away his tunic. She wiped away swaths of blood, exposing the path of the arrowhead that had skimmed his chest, tearing muscle and skin.

"How did you get this wound?' Mrs. Carney asked the soldier.

"I was defending the northern wall and turned to fetch a quiver of arrows," he said, "when this one sliced my chest."

"Good thing you'd turned away," she said. "If you hadn't, the arrow would have hit your heart, and we'd be burying you instead of fixing you."

"Will I be all right?" he asked, his voice trembling.

"You will," Mrs. Carney said. "And back on the wall tomorrow."

They were interrupted by a scream from the man on the next table. Gabrielle and an assistant had cut off the tail of the arrow and yanked the rest of the shaft through the patient's back. It was the only way to remove it.

"Do you need help, my lady?" Mrs. Carney asked.

The patient's wound spurted blood, and Gabrielle moved to staunch its flow. "I'm doing all I can for him."

"He's fainted," Mrs. Carney said.

"Better for him."

"Will he live?"

"That's not a decision for us to make," Gabrielle said. "I'll clean him up and put honey and red root on the wounds. The rest is in the hands of the Lord."

"There's a Frenchman lying out in the hall," one of the women called. "Wounded at the top of the wall."

The Lady Gabrielle turned abruptly, wondering if the man could be Montague. She hurried into the hallway, looking

317

for a pale blue tunic. She found it among a sea of wounded, the man's face not one she had seen before. She sighed with relief, though she didn't know why, and returned to treat the wounded.

Chapter 94

"How many wounded have we?" asked Gideon as he stood with Marston and Carney on the north curtain wall.

"Half the Great Hall is filled," Marston replied. "But they're well cared for."

"How many dead?" Carney asked.

Marston hesitated, briefly thinking of loved ones lost. "Six so far, which is six too many."

"Far fewer than the barons' men," Carney said.

"But they did fight bravely," Gideon pointed out. "And numbered many more than expected."

"It was a trick," said Carney, surveying the battlefield. "Half the army was hidden in the forest."

"They tried to lure us from within the walls," Marston said. "As if we'd be so blind as to launch an attack."

"A lure you wisely let swim away," said Gideon. "Bigger fish will soon be caught."

"Some battles are fought with the mind," Marston said.

"They have no other advantage," said Gideon. "Why not play tricks with the eyes of our men?"

"Even I had doubts," Marston admitted. "And I've fought in many wars."

"And seen many different tactics," Carney said.

"Perhaps it's time to turn the tide and win the game they tried to play," Marston said.

Caney looked at Gideon, and then to his master. "What do you intend, sire?"

"Our eyes should be upon them," Marston said, thoughtful for a moment. "The tunnel we began to dig before the battle began—has it been completed?"

Carney eyed him carefully. "Yes, sire, it has."

"And what route did it take?"

319

"It passes under the north wall," Carney said, "and far into the forest where it emerges from a rock formation by the cliff."

"Can the barons' men find it?" Marston asked.

Carney thought for a moment, envisioning the tunnel and its exit. "I don't think so, sire. It is well camouflaged, and they have no reason to move the rocks that obscure it."

"Once darkness falls and the enemy sleeps, dispatch a band of men through the tunnel to observe what the enemy does," Marston said.

"But we wouldn't want to risk our men, sire," said Gideon. "The enemy can replenish their numbers. We cannot."

"It's a perilous move, I admit, but one that could change the course of the battle," Marston said.

"But if their efforts are unsuccessful, the barons' men might find the entrance to the tunnel," Carney countered. "They then could breach the castle."

"And we would backfill the entrance before they could use it," Marston said.

"And what of the French?" Carney asked.

"They're a much smaller force," Marston said. "We shall focus on the English before we turn our sights upon the French."

"And force them to surrender?" Carney asked.

"Or annihilate them."

Chapter 95

Captain Carney led three men to the tunnel entrance, lighting their way with a torch. Its entrance had been dug just shy of the north wall, past the northeast tower. The passageway to the witch's cave was only a few feet away, but it had remained hidden to those who had dug the tunnel.

Carney and his men descended the wooden ladder perched against the side of the hole. It was six feet in diameter and fenced off so no one would fall in, especially during the turmoil that the battle had brought to the castle. Fifteen feet down, a square room supported by planks and posts sat just below the level of the curtain wall foundation, its ceiling roughly six feet high. The tunnel moved in a northeast direction and was barely large enough for a man to crawl through where it had been carved from the rock. The diameter of the passageway was more generous when the miners had only soil to remove from their path.

Carney and his men crawled much of the way, but at times they could almost walk upright. The tunnel continued northeast, almost meeting the edge of the cliff that rose sharply above the sea. It then ran parallel to the ocean, ending at a unique rock formation almost two hundred feet within the forest.

"Remember, we are to assess the enemy's movements, nothing more," Carney whispered as they crept forward.

"I'm ready to fight if need be, Captain," the man just behind him said.

Carney nodded, impressed by the loyalty of his men. "We are not to strike, not yet."

Carney led his men forward through the gloom, knowing the barons' men were just above them. The tunnel was well-built, and they moved quickly, taking care to not make any loud noises. Scarcely a half hour had passed when they reached the end of the tunnel and the rock formation near the cliff's edge.

The exit was blocked by a pile of massive stones left by nature to confuse both man and beast. Just to the right of the stones a slender corridor, ten feet long and three feet high, led to an opening that was veiled by thick underbrush. Eclipsed by overhanging rock during the day and invisible at night, Marston's men had cut the access point into the rock at an ideal location. Intruders would never happen upon it.

Carney tucked the torch behind an outcropping of stone to hide the light and crawled out of the tunnel. He paused, still on all fours, and looked about him. He could hear the murmur of far off conversation—the men nearer the front and the castle. He saw flames flickering beyond the trees where the barons' men were camped. Slowly, he got to his feet, scanned the forest cautiously, and then motioned for his men to follow. Together they moved quietly through the underbrush.

They hadn't traveled far when one of the soldiers touched Carney's arm and pointed to two men lying on the ground asleep. A sentry stood beside them, looking northward. They were some fifty feet away at the base of a small knoll, barely visible in the inky blackness.

"The rear guard," Carney hissed.

"We can dispatch them to their Maker if you desire, Captain," said one of his soldiers.

Carney weighed the offer. There seemed little to gain by killing the three men.

"Come morning, they might think there's an army behind them if this lot were to be discovered slain," another whispered.

Carney realized tricking the enemy did have its advantages. James the Bold would hold some men back from the battlefield to guard their northern flank, looking for an enemy that didn't exist.

"They'll spend the whole day wondering where the attack came from," another soldier interjected.

Carney glanced toward the castle at the wisps of smoke drifting from the smoldering campfires. The army was at least five hundred feet away, maybe more, closer to the castle than the cliff. He turned and looked at his men.

One of his men withdrew a knife from its scabbard. "Sir?"

"Kill them," Carney said.

Chapter 96

James the Bold and Jamet sat beside a flickering fire, finishing their morning meal. As they watched Marston's men gather atop the walls, silently studying the course that the battle would take, Captain Fletcher approached—the leader of many of the attacks.

"I bear a message you won't want to hear, sire," he said.

James the Bold looked up from a wooden bowl, the last remnants of watery porridge clinging to the bottom. "What is it?"

"The rear sentries have been killed," he said.

Anger flashed across James the Bold's scarred face. He hadn't considered a foe to the rear. "When?"

"Sometime during the night," the captain said.

"Is there an army behind us?" Jamet asked.

"None has made itself known," Fletcher said. "More likely the work of a few roving soldiers."

"Should we delay our attack?" Jamet asked. "If we face an army at our rear, we would be wise to move men toward it."

James the Bold looked at the castle, the waiting prize. He would win this battle no matter how many armies he had to face. "No, we attack the castle."

"But, sire, we run the risk of being squeezed by the enemy from behind," Jamet cautioned.

James the Bold could feel victory in his grasp, and he had no intention of letting it go. "Send a half dozen men to search for an enemy to the north, but not more than an hour's ride."

"Yes, sire," Fletcher said. He left, moving to the nearest campfire, fifty feet away, to speak to the soldiers who surrounded it.

James the Bold summoned another captain.

"Yes, sire?" the captain replied.

"Ready the siege tower," he commanded, then rose and motioned for a soldier to fetch his horse.

"The tower—it isn't ready," Jamet said in protest as he prepared to mount his steed.

"We need a diversion," said James the Bold. "I don't want our men focused on sentries murdered in the dead of night."

"We've gathered logs for the trenches, sir," the captain said. "Although some areas are easier to bridge than others."

"Stage the tower in the most vulnerable location."

Though unfinished, the siege tower was tall and sturdy, made of logs and covered with hides. It contained multiple platforms connected by internal ladders, and fifty men gathered around it and inched it toward the castle wall. Others drug logs behind it to fill the trench, so the tower could be rolled on its wooden wheels right up to the wall.

As soon as the men were within range of the castle's archers, arrows flew through the morning haze, the snap of bow strings singing in the damp air. Most of the arrows dove into the earth or ricocheted off the animal hides that protected the tower's frame, but two men fell, screaming in agony, arrows protruding from their torsos.

Captain Fletcher ordered archers to assume a fighting formation, and they fired back at their foes on the castle wall. Their arrows missed their mark, bouncing off the stone or flying above the heads of Marston's men.

"Launch the catapults," James the Bold directed.

Under cover of catapult fire and a barrage of arrows, the barons' men moved forward, shoving logs in the trenches and pushing the tower across the plain. As men fell victim to the defenders' fire, others were swift to replace them. Soon the ground was littered with arrows, a handful of slaughtered men, and several wounded, crying out in pain.

As the barons' men drew nearer, Marston's men fired oil-filled pouches with slingshots at the siege tower. Their aim was true, and they continually struck the animal hides that protected the tower, drenching them in flammable liquid. When the tower was twenty feet from the wall, and the attackers had begun to climb its internal ladders, the defenders loosed flaming arrows. The first few bounced off the hides, but eventually one of the arrows stuck fast to the frame and ignited the oil-drenched hide and slowly began to spread. Another was quick to follow, and in a matter of minutes the tower was consumed in flames, smoke spiraling into the sky, the men trapped within it screeching as death carried them to heaven.

Chapter 97

Montague and Piers rode to the western face of the castle to survey the attack launched by James the Bold. It was a short battle, and within an hour the siege tower had been destroyed. Dead men lay on the ground beside it, some felled by arrows, others leaping to their deaths when they'd become engulfed in flames.

A messenger approached on horseback. "Word from Jamet and James the Bold," he called.

"What is their command?" Montague asked.

"Attack as soon as you can muster your men," the rider said.

Montague gave Piers a knowing glance and then replied. "We attack within the hour."

As the messenger galloped away, Montague turned to Piers. "We shall probe the eastern wall. Now is as good a time as any."

"But the English will move men to meet the attack," Piers said as they turned their horses to the south and spurred them toward the front line. "Our soldiers will be trapped along the cliff."

"I have a strategy that might prove successful," Montague said. "We'll launch an attack on the southwest tower, using the bulk of our forces."

"But, sire, the western wall boasts the strongest defense."

"We ready for an attack that never will be launched," Montague said.

"Stage the men but beyond the archers' range?"

"Yes," Montague said. "And while the English keep their men at the ready, I'll lead the rest in an attack on the east face."

Piers considered the strategy. "If you breach the wall, and the English divert men from the north and south, I'll launch an attack to keep them pinned where they are."

Thirty minutes later, Piers and the majority of the French forces were ready to advance from their post at the edge of the woods, their target the castle's southwest tower. Meanwhile, Montague and a battalion of men hid in the forest at the other end of the castle, prepared to attack the east wall.

The French commander sat astride his stallion, his sword held high. He waited until he was sure Piers and his men were in position, then signaled the attack. Infantrymen marched forward in a wave of pale blue tunics; archers knocked their arrows, poised to fire. Twenty cavalrymen led the charge toward the castle.

Those on foot bolted forward, carrying ladders and spikes, shields and swords. French archers ran behind them, pausing to fire at the English who stood atop the wall. As they raced across the open field, approaching the trench that rimmed the castle, they met with little resistance, but as soon as they reached the southeast tower, dozens of arrows rained down upon them.

"Forward, men," Montague bellowed, ignoring the arrows that whisked by him.

A group of infantrymen reached the wall and propped up the first ladder. They rapidly climbed to the top, first two and then three men. One soldier climbed over the castle wall and was quickly followed by another. Together they charged the tower.

Marston's men turned, their bows trained on the invaders. They felled both of the French with their arrows as well as a third soldier who'd clambered over the ramparts. But more men followed, replacing the fallen, scaling the rungs of the ladder. Montague's men hoisted a second ladder and then a third, and the soldiers rapidly climbed upward. Marston's archers converged, coming from the north and south, firing mercilessly at the attackers.

Montague realized they would soon be defeated. He ordered a retreat, watching warily as his men fall back. It was another painful lesson that left over a dozen Frenchmen dead or wounded. Although it was clear that the eastern wall was not well defended, Marston's men had been quick to respond when the French began to scale the walls.

As he galloped back to camp, Montague considered the options left him. One was the siege and the time its success required, a massive attack managed with James the Bold which he feared would likely meet with failure, or the second, the secret passage that only he knew for certain existed—a passage which would lead him to Gabrielle.

Chapter 98

Minerva studied the two intruders from the mouth of the secret passage: Trinity, a thief, fraud, and murderer who knew only a fraction of what a true witch would know, and Baron Richard Tweed, a Crusader and the voice of the rebellion, a man intent upon overthrowing King John.

"Stay away, witch," Trinity warned, taking a step backward.

Richard Tweed looked at Minerva, confused. "Who are you?"

"That's the question I should ask of a man who treads where he should not," Minerva said.

"She is called Minerva," Trinity said. "The witch of Marston Castle."

"And you are Baron Richard Tweed," Minerva said, "author of the rebellion."

Tweed looked at her with surprise "How do you know who I am?"

"How do I not?" Minerva asked. "Does not all of England know who you are?"

He paused and studied her for a moment, trying to decide if she posed a threat. "Move aside," he demanded. "We're coming through this passage."

Minerva retreated but only a step. She smiled at the two of them.

Tweed hesitated, unnerved by the witch's gaze. "Come on," he said to Trinity. "Show me the way."

Trinity eyed Minerva warily. "It may be unwise to defy the witch."

"A caution that is as silly as it sounds," Tweed said, pushing Trinity ahead. "Enter."

They took a step forward and then another before stopping abruptly as if they had walked into a wall. They tried to move farther along the corridor, but no matter the effort they made, they could not move an inch.

"I decide who comes and goes," Minerva said as she prevented them from advancing.

Tweed glared at her. "I don't know who you claim to be or what it is you now attempt, but we're going through this passage."

"What is it that you seek?" Minerva asked.

"We seek only what belongs to me," Tweed said.

"And what is that?"

"The Holy Grail," he said, "the chalice that once held the blood of Christ."

"A relic I know well," Minerva said.

"Then you have it," Tweed said angrily.

Trinity reached out to Tweed, touching his arm. "Baron, don't," she said. "You'll only make our task more difficult than it already is."

The baron shook her off and scowled at Minerva.

"Who are you to call yourself keeper of the Grail?" the witch asked.

"Who are you to take it?" Tweed retorted.

He rushed forward and tried to push Minerva out of the way, but when he was within arm's reach of her, she held up her hand, and Tweed stopped abruptly as if bound by an invisible chain. He struggled in vain to continue, but his passage was barred by a magic that made him unable to move, as an angry sea crashed upon the cliffs behind him.

Minerva moved her hand slowly, up and down, back and forth, and Tweed moved with it, standing and then crouching, first to the left and then to right as if she controlled his entire being.

"What devilry is this?" he demanded, turning to Trinity.

"She's toying with you, Baron Tweed," Trinity said, biting back a smirk.

"Was it you who tried, through the deeds of another, to kill Sir Michael Marston, the most glorious knight that England has ever known?" Minerva asked.

Tweed's mouth twisted into an evil grin. "It was I," he said. "And if I make it through this passage and find where he dwells, I intend to steal his last breath."

Minerva shot her hand forward. Though she never touched him, the force shoved Tweed backwards, and he was propelled off the cliff. He soared through the air, waving his arms and legs wildly, before smashing into the sand thirty feet below.

Minerva gazed down at the baron who lay motionless amid the rocks. She turned to Trinity who was quaking with fear. "What am I supposed to do with you?"

"Have mercy," Trinity said. "I beg you."

"Mercy?" Minerva asked. "You were about to betray the secrets of the castle and endanger the lives of all who live within."

"I had to," Trinity said. "I had no choice."

"You had no choice, and neither do I."

Minerva waved her hand back and forth, and Trinity's body was at once under her control, bending and twisting to her every whim, but the witch had no time to savor her revenge. With all her might, she thrust her hand forward, shoving Trinity off the cliff. She sailed backwards, arms and legs flailing, and crashed down upon the sand, lying dead beside Baron Tweed.

Chapter 99

James the Bold stared at the charred ruins of the siege tower, the black embers sending a soft gray smoke spiraling into the sky. The day's battle was coming to a close, a series of disjointed attacks he and his allies had launched against all four faces of the castle. Every one had been thwarted. He huddled with his advisors, discussing what course of action they should take next.

"The best means of attack is one that the enemy cannot see," Blaise said, mysterious as always.

James the Bold studied the warlock but didn't reply. It seemed everything Blaise said or did was wrapped in riddles.

Jamet eyed James the Bold, then the warlock. He turned back to the commander. "The miners are nearing their target," Jamet said, "if it's their efforts Blaise describes."

"They'll reach the foundation in less than a day," said James the Bold, "and then the wall will collapse."

"It gives our men some time to rest after two hard days of battle," Jamet said.

James the Bold considered the impact of the daily attacks both on his men and their morale. "How many men have we lost?" he asked.

Jamet summoned Captain Fletcher who spurred his horse to where they waited. "What are our losses?"

"Fifty dead, forty wounded, six horses killed," Fletcher replied.

James the Bold stared at the castle, strong and defiant as ever. "Stage the catapults," he said. "And throw cadavers over the wall."

"But some of the dead have already been buried, sire," Fletcher protested.

James the Bold eyed him coldly. "Dig them up."

Fletcher bowed slightly, nodding to his commander. "As you wish, sire."

A moment passed before Jamet spoke, eager to dismiss so gruesome an order. "I would suggest any other option that we know exists—your ally in the castle, the miners, a coordinated assault. For history will remember every dirty trick that we've played."

James the Bold eyed him coldly. "Tomorrow we unleash our secret weapons."

"Have you any further needs, sire?" Fletcher asked, sensing the discussion no longer included him.

"Yes," said James the Bold. "Summon the falconer."

The captain called to a soldier who galloped off to a group of men waiting along the forest's edge.

"Divide the army in two," James the Bold said to Jamet. "Half will attack where the miners undermine the wall just east of the northwest tower."

"And the other half?" Jamet asked, confused by the orders.

"They will attack from the west near the drawbridge."

"But, sire," Jamet began to protest.

James the Bold held up his hand, signaling silence.

The falconer ran forward and paused beside the commander. "Yes, sire?"

"It's time to send our message," James the Bold said. "You know what must be done?"

"Yes, sire," the falconer replied. He held his gloved wrist up high, and a falcon that was circling in the clouds swooped down to perch upon it. He stroked the bird's head, smoothing its soft feathers, wrapped a parchment around its talon, and tied it with a string.

"Release him," said James the Bold.

Chapter 100

Montague sat in camp with Piers and watched Jamet approach. "He's not to know of the passage," he said, "or that Gabrielle is within the walls."

Piers nodded. "Of course, sire. But may I know why?"

"He's a man I've never come to trust, and I don't see that changing."

Jamet tethered his horse and came to where they sat. "James the Bold has ordered a full-scale attack," he said. "We strike tomorrow with all the weapons and men at our disposal."

"And is the result expected different from yesterday and today?" Montague asked.

"All forces will be engaged," Jamet said, "and the dawn will bring surprises known only to James the Bold."

"What role are we expected to play?" Piers asked.

"Have you found a weakness in Marston's defense?" Jamet asked.

Montague glanced at Piers. "The eastern wall is manned by no more than thirty men—a force we could overpower—but who knows if tomorrow will show what we found today."

"And if the English divert men to the eastern wall, our men could be slaughtered," Piers added.

"The English will have no men to divert," Jamet said confidently. "Not with the assaults James the Bold will launch."

"Where will the barons' men attack?" Montague asked, surprised by Jamet's confidence.

"They attack the west, at the drawbridge, and to the north just east of the northwest tower," Jamet said.

Montague glanced at Piers, puzzled by Jamet's reply. "Not the locations I would choose, if we've learned anything at all about our foe."

"I don't pretend to know what wisdom James the Bold possesses," Jamet said. "Suffice it to say that he's certain of victory."

"But the western wall remains heavily defended," Montague said.

"James the Bold claims he has two secret weapons that will turn the tide," Jamet replied.

"Just what will these secret weapons achieve?" Piers asked.

"I'm not privy to such details," Jamet said. "Nor is anyone else, but I can tell you that the miners have been digging since the day they arrived."

"And tomorrow they reach the wall?" Montague asked.

"Yes, just east of the northwest tower," Jamet replied.

"At last, the castle is breached," Piers exclaimed.

"One of two fatal surprises James the Bold planned," Jamet said.

"Can you not share the second?" Montague asked.

Jamet paused, wondering if he should indeed divulge James the Bold's secret. "Within the castle is a man loyal to the barons' cause."

"A traitor?" Montague asked.

"So it would seem," Jamet replied.

Montague studied Jamet. "Is he a traitor or not? He can't be loyal to more than one master."

Jamet glanced at the two men, hesitant to continue. "James the Bold holds the man's family hostage."

Montague looked at Piers, a sickened expression on his face. "What has become of the days when men fought with honor?"

"Gone forever, I fear," Jamet said softly.

The French commanders were quiet for a moment, each wrestling with his own conscience. Then Piers spoke. "If the barons are determined to proceed, it improves our chances on the eastern wall."

Montague was quiet, pensive. He knew a massive assault would give him the chance to find the passage and rescue the Lady Gabrielle.

"You're certain?" Jamet asked.

Montague turned to him, confident but careful. "With each attack, the eastern wall was exposed. Marston has had to divert men from north and south to keep our men at bay."

"All of Marston's men will be needed to repel James the Bold's attacks," Piers added.

Jamet looked at his countrymen, wondering whether to share his thoughts. "Let's hope James the Bold delivers all he has promised."

"Or many of our men will die," Montague said somberly.

Chapter 101

Early that evening, Marston and Carney watched from the northwest tower as the barons' men took two catapults from the western face and rolled them to the north. The enemy archers stretched across the plain from the northern wall, small fires built before them.

"Prepare those in the village," Marston said as he watched the planned assault unfold. "I suspect we're about to receive the most sinister attack of all."

"I'll fight this battle from the bailey," Carney said as he hurried away. "And ensure our catapult is set to reply."

Marston left the tower, stood at the edge of the curtain wall, and spoke to his men. "Fire when ready if you're sure they're in range," he called to his archers. "Waste no arrows if it can be helped."

Just as his men let their arrows fly, the enemy replied in kind, hundreds of flaming projectiles streaking across the sky. Some fell short, hitting the wall, while most soared over the top, plunging into the bailey.

Carney stood at the edge of the village with a dozen soldiers and citizens. As each flaming arrow fell to the earth, they quickly moved to combat the blaze. Although many landed in empty fields and were easily extinguished, the thatched roof of the butcher's shop was soon burning, the flames licking along the side and spreading to the remainder.

"Hurry," Carney called, directing the responders. "Form a line to pass the buckets."

The archers poised upon the wall flung one volley after another, and the barons' men began to fall along the line. The toll they took was tremendous as wave after wave of arrows flew, whistling through the heavens and then plunging to the earth.

Marston stood upon the wall as the enemy launched the assault's next phase, firing the first catapult. The men on the wall braced for impact, expecting boulders, but were sickened when a corpse came careening through the sky, arms and legs flailing. It landed in the bailey, splattering upon impact and spewing gore in all directions.

Marston thought he would vomit, so horrendous was the attack. "Pour oil on the cadavers and set them all ablaze," he called from the top of the wall.

The next two catapults were launched, and two more cadavers were flung over the wall. One smashed against the brewery while another struck the walkway that emerged from the central tower.

Marston studied the carnage below, the villagers and soldiers covering their faces with kerchiefs, so powerful was the stench. They hurriedly collected what was left of the corpses, placed them in piles, and threw buckets of oil on the splattered remains.

"Set them ablaze," Carney commanded.

Gideon stood by his catapult, and he ordered his soldiers to fire boulders wrapped in burning rags. The first shot fell short of an enemy machine but caught the grass in front of it on fire. The attackers were forced to withdraw, moving the catapult farther north. But the battle raged on, dead bodies twisting as the enemy flung them through the air, fires raging, catapults splintering. Dusk shadowed the English coast before both sides withdrew.

Marston stood on the wall as the barons' men retreated, keeping a wary eye on the flames that continued to scorch the grass. The air was pungent with the acrid stench of burning bodies, and the cries of the wounded overwhelmed his ears.

"You've left half their army on the ground," Marston called out to his archers, an exaggeration, but a compliment all who fought could hear.

He started to walk down the wall but paused and said a silent prayer for the fallen. He then turned to survey the damage that his own men had sustained. Throughout the bailey, buildings smoldered, wounded men cried out for water, animals wandered the grounds, their stalls and corrals destroyed, and soldiers, tired and hungry from days of battle, made their way through the shadows, fighting fires and scouring the courtyard where the corpses had landed. Villagers manned bonfires stacked with cadavers, the remains smoldering near the east wall. A stiff wind blew the stink out to sea.

Marston hurried down the steps and met Gideon below.

"Intended to destroy our morale," Gideon said as Marston arrived.

"Only the prelude for something far worse," Marston muttered.

He walked throughout the bailey, watching as soldiers and citizens extinguished the flames that still threatened the village. Piles of corpse were yet ablaze. "The end is coming closer," he called to those battling the remnants of the attack. "And victory will soon be ours.

He returned to his chambers and found the Lady Gabrielle sitting by the fire. She was distraught, lines of worry etched across her face. "You must leave tomorrow," he said to her sadly. "Your life is in danger like never before."

"I cannot," she said, a flicker of fear flashing in her eyes. "The wounded need me."

"There are others who can care for the wounded."

"I won't leave without you," she said softly, her eyes trained on the fire. "I would rather die by your side then live a day without you."

"We all could have been killed today," he said, "and I sense tomorrow will be much worse. I won't let you risk your life. I insist. Tomorrow you must leave."

Chapter 102

Marston slept restlessly, his arms wrapped around the Lady Gabrielle.

Just as the sun crept above the horizon, announcing a new day, they were awakened by a harried knock upon the door.

"Sire," Captain Carney called breathlessly. "You must come quickly."

Marston sat up, glanced at a stirring Gabrielle, and climbed from bed.

"What's happened?" Gabrielle asked sleepily, rising with him. She reached for her clothes and started to dress.

"The battle must be about to begin," Marston said as he pulled his trousers on and then his boots.

"Hurry, sire," Carney said in a hushed tone, his message meant for his commander alone.

Marston finished dressing and paused, waiting for Gabrielle to fasten the last of the buttons on her bodice. He strode to the door, securing his belt and scabbard about his waist. "What is it?" he asked as he opened the door.

"Traitors work to sabotage us," Carney said.

It was a message Marston hadn't expected to hear. "Who are they?"

"I don't yet know their faces, but I do know their deeds."

"What have they done?" Marston asked, glancing back at Gabrielle. "And can we undo it?"

"The drawbridge has been lowered and the castle gate raised," Carney said. "Both have been disabled."

"How did this happen?" Marston asked with alarm. "And where were the guards?"

"Three are dead, three unconscious."

"What does the enemy do?"

"We are at their mercy. They already mass at the castle entrance, prepared to launch an attack."

Marston turned to Gabrielle. "I must go, my love," he said. "Before another minute is wasted."

"Do what must be done," she said. "I'll ensure the hospital and all who tend our wounded are fully prepared."

Marston hesitated, looking into her eyes. "You mustn't forget what we discussed," he said. "Take no chances."

"Go," she said. "The enemy will wait no more."

Marston hurried down the hallway, Carney beside him. "Who could have done this?" he asked, unable to think of any to name.

Carney shrugged. "I couldn't name a suspect, even if I tried. But we'll know in minutes, maybe more. Six men lie dead beyond the gate, slain by our defenders."

"How bad is the drawbridge?"

"The windlass has been jammed, the lever is missing, but I think a repair can be easily made," Carney said. "But we race for time with the enemy so near at hand."

"And the gate?"

"Fully opened with pins removed."

Marston frowned. "We are forced to do battle on the enemy's terms," he fumed.

"I've sent for Gideon to make the repairs and provided soldiers to help him," Carney said. "But the enemy is only minutes away."

"Line the walls of the barbican and gatehouse with archers and soldiers armed with hot oil. Reinforce the portcullis and bar the entrance to the bailey with whatever you can find—wagons, timber, even livestock, if you must."

"Yes, sire," Carney said. "But we must hurry. The enemy amasses for the attack."

341

Chapter 103

The Lady Gabrielle collected her belongings and packed them in two leather satchels. She paused, studying the room that had been her home since she'd arrived, though she spent most of her time now with Michael Marston. She stepped into the corridor, her heart aching, for she knew it might be the last time she did so, and entered the library. Her gaze fell upon the many books that lined the shelves, more than she'd ever seen in one collection, and she took one last look at her favorite room in all of Marston Manor.

A cool breeze blew through the window, and she could hear the sounds of the mounting battle: enemy soldiers beyond the castle walls, captains calling out commands, the clatter of weapons being readied, and the creak of catapults the barons' men trundled ever closer to the castle. She knew the battle would be horrendous, beyond anything she could imagine and the very fate of England depended upon who would claim the castle.

She knew Montague, the man who had held her heart for what she thought would be eternity, would be among those storming the walls, assuming he lived, and she wondered if they might cross paths again. Now Marston had eclipsed him, but she couldn't say why. It was a different kind of love, which she could not explain. Still it captured her heart and consumed her soul, linking her life to his.

Gabrielle shied from the window, overwhelmed by the sight of the unfolding battle. She could hear wounded crying out in pain, desperate for any comfort they could find. The women she had trained, she knew, could never care for them all. Lives would be torn apart, families destroyed. How could she desert those who depended on her? How could she run away when she might yet save the life of a husband or son or brother and shield his family from the sorrows she had suffered for so many years herself? No matter how badly she wanted to honor Marston's demands that she save herself, her heart would not let her go.

She placed her bags beside the fireplace and hurried to the door. She had to go back, had to help the sick and dying, the women of the castle whom she'd promised to stand by, no matter what horrors befell them. She hurried down the hallway, unable to ignore those in need. She'd reached the corridor that led to the Great Hall when she saw Marston.

"What are you doing?" he asked. "The attack is about to begin."

"I can't do it," she said softly.

"No, my love. It's too dangerous."

"They need me."

"You have to get out while you still can," he insisted. "Please, before it's too late."

She moved toward him, leaning on him, as he wrapped his arms around her. "I can't leave you," she whispered, a tear drifting down her cheek. "And I can't leave the fallen, not when they need me most."

"But you must," he said, kissing the top of her head. "I can't let anything happen to you.'

Gabrielle shook her head defiantly. "It will be no different from any of the other attacks," she said.

"If only that were true," he said softly. "But you know as well as I that it will be much worse."

"You will prevail."

"We don't know that," he said and gently kissed her cheeks and then her lips.

She pulled away. "It doesn't matter," she said. "I want to be with you."

"But you won't be safe here."

"I must help," she said. "Please, you must understand." She looked up at him again and kissed him on the mouth. "My heart demands that I remain, that I never leave you."

Marston responded by holding her tightly, keeping her close. But then he reluctantly pulled away. "Promise me you'll go."

"I can't make a promise I cannot keep."

343

Marston lifted Gabrielle's chin and looked deeply into her eyes. "If we should be overwhelmed by the attack, if we lose control of the castle, you must leave."

She fought back her tears, unable to think of what might happen to her beloved should defeat find them.

"Promise me," he whispered.

She nodded, unable to speak the words, unable to let him go.

Chapter 104

Minerva stood beside her altar, surrounded by her collection of spices and stones, entrails and herbs, studying a spider that spun its web along a crevice above her head. Her cauldron was still, no mist from its depths, as she turned to sort through a dozen pouches and vials she'd collected from her subterranean stores. She'd stockpiled the rarest of elements for what seemed like centuries, magically replenishing them when her supplies dwindled.

While those above her prepared for the barons' ruthless attack, the witch cared little for the battles fought by man unless her powers were needed to alter fate, creating a future that might not otherwise exist. But wars waged by wizards or warlocks, goblins or ghosts, she was all too eager to fight. She was anxious to prove to her rivals that her powers could not be exceeded, to remind all who deigned rule the mystical world and all the dimensions it now contained that she was the force supreme.

She had never found an adversary as great as Blaise, the English warlock, in the centuries that had passed. He was a danger to her, the castle, and all of mankind, and his presence could not be ignored. Although she was sure she was stronger, she had to contain him, neutralize him, which was much more involved than simply defeating him. She would not kill him because there could be a distant day when he might be needed, whether she wanted to admit it or not.

A crow eyed her from his perch above. "What a surprise I have for Blaise," she said to him with a cackle. "He'll never know what happened, and he won't have any strength to fight."

She filled a wooden pitcher from the stream that sliced the cave in two and poured it into her cauldron. Then she added vinegar, scarcely an ounce, followed by a drop of boar's blood which bloomed across the surface like a frightful flower. Next, she peeled three shriveled figs, extracted their juice, and added it to the mixture. She stirred it for a moment, sniffed the mist that drifted toward the ceiling of the cavern, and placed a crystal underneath the cauldron. Then she chopped the roots from three daisies into pieces with the long, crooked nail of her left index finger and put them into the brew.

"Your eyes know not what they have seen, and soon they will see no more," she muttered, envisioning the warlock in his forest encampment.

She reached for a vial on her altar, the indigo candle flickering beside it casting an unearthly glow, and withdrew three caterpillars. She placed them in a pewter mortar and sliced them with a bronze blade, ensuring each of the parts were equal in length. She tossed them into the simmering brew as a ring of bubbles broke the surface. She added a dash of wormwood next, eyed the mixture, and threw in two dashes more, then stirred the brew three times, waiting nine seconds between each swirl of her crooked spoon. She stepped away to study her progress and smiled, pleased with her creation.

"Forgive me, warlock, but I have to make this particularly strong," she said, cackling. "So you serve me for eternity."

She opened another vial and removed three leeches, bloated with the blood of a dying man, and tossed them into the potion. She closed her eyes and waved her hand above the bubbling brew, and the mixture churned and roiled, turning from a dull red to blue. She cradled the next ingredient in her palm, for it was by far the most potent—a rat's spleen, perfectly intact. Gently, she placed it in the pot where it vanished within the gurgling mixture. Then she added a touch of catnip, mugwort, skullcap, coltsfoot, and valerian root. She held the final ingredient, a water hemlock's shredded leaves, firmly in her clenched fist and then sprinkled it across the surface of the potion. She waited, the temperature rising, bubbles bursting, as the hazy mist upon which she worked her magic gradually appeared.

"Show your face, warlock," she whispered.

Gradually the mist took shape, and the warlock's face appeared. Minerva studied his features closely, reached into the fog, and ran her hand across his cheek.

"You never should have come, warlock," she hissed, "for now you'll never leave."

She took one step backward and muttered a chant, the final link to the perfect spell that could never be broken—not by man nor spirit.

> "I cast a spell so strong and true
>
> It cannot be undone.
>
> I hold your heart in all you do;
>
> I am the only one.
>
> As eons pass and come anew
>
> You shall quit pretending.
>
> For now, what's housed within you
>
> Is a love that's never-ending."

When Minerva had spoken the final word of her incantation, the liquid in the cauldron transformed into a shimmering gray powder, its texture very fine. She poured the residue into a leather pouch and then began to laugh.

"Blaise!" she called. "For all of eternity, your heart belongs to me."

Chapter 105

Captain Fletcher approached Jamet and James the Bold just as they prepared for battle. "The drawbridge is down and disabled, and our forces prepare to attack."

James the Bold was consumed with an evil grin. "I knew if I had enough traitors, success would soon be found," he said. "Today will be the last that Michael Marston breathes."

"There's more, sire," Fletcher said, his excitement not contained.

"What better news could my ears hear?" asked James the Bold, glancing at Jamet.

"The miners have reached the wall," Fletcher continued.

James the Bold was surprised at their success. "Have they shored it with wood and set the fire?" he asked.

"They have, sire," the captain said. "The wall will collapse in no more than an hour."

Jamet envisioned the battle to come. "We attack in the north and west, and the French attack in the east," he said.

"But can they breach the castle?" James the Bold asked.

"They can," Jamet informed him. "They've found a weakness in the castle's defenses."

James the Bold laughed maniacally. "Marston will be dead by day's end, his men completely defeated."

"Shall I lead the attack?" Fletcher asked. "For there's nothing more I'd rather do."

James the Bold paused and studied the castle. "No, I shall lead the attack in the west," he said. "I want to cross the drawbridge and kill all I see."

Fletcher nodded, disappointed. "As you wish, sire. The men are ready and await your command."

James the Bold paused, pensive, trying to coordinate all to come to overwhelm the defenders. "Have them wait," he said quietly, his thoughts not clearly formed.

Fletcher looked at him, puzzled. "The longer we wait, the more they prepare."

"Perhaps not the wisest command," Jamet intervened. "When do you plan to attack?"

James the Bold continued to stare at the castle, the image of its failure formed in his mind. "As soon as the wall collapses," he said. "The dust and debris will cover the plain, and I'll lead the advance right through it."

Jamet glanced at Fletcher, neither prepared to challenge the warlord further.

"Should our forces be halved, west and north?" Fletcher asked.

James the Bold nodded. "Jamet will lead the attack in the north as soon as the wall collapses. You shall come with me."

"I'll ready our army to await your command," Fletcher said, leaving to attend to his duties.

James the Bold turned to Jamet. "No man is better suited than you to destroy Marston's forces," he said. "But I want more than victory."

Jamet shot him a confused look. "What more is there than victory?"

"Total annihilation."

Jamet's eyes grew wide. "We're to show no mercy?"

"None," James the Bold insisted. He studied his French advisor, a man he knew he would likely kill in less than a fortnight. "What's your assessment of the coming day?"

Jamet studied the formidable castle, the mighty towers and long curtain walls. "When first I arrived, I did not think it possible that the fortress could be taken."

"And now?"

Jamet nodded to James the Bold, a sign of his respect. "Now I don't think even Marston can defend it."

Chapter 106

Montague eyed the castle keep as he readied his men for battle. He knew the massive assault that James the Bold planned would likely conquer the castle, and the life of the Lady Gabrielle was threatened just as every man on the battlefield was. He had to somehow find her before the danger heightened. He vowed that as soon as the battle began, he would—either through the secret passage or by scaling the eastern wall.

"The men are ready," Piers said, galloping up beside him.

"This is the day when we shall employ all men," Montague said softly. "The castle falls, or we die trying."

Piers eyed his commander, knowing he was bested by no one. "I'm sure the miners have reached the wall," he said. "And the breach will happen shortly."

"I suspect much more is about to occur if what Jamet told us is true," Montague said. "The barons have traitors within the castle. More than one, most likely."

Montague nodded. "I suspect they'll find a way to lower the drawbridge or disable the gate—anything that gives us the advantage."

"Not the most honorable way to win a war," Piers muttered.

"When a war can't be won with strategy, trickery sometimes stands in its stead."

Piers looked at the castle that rose sharply from the landscape, its towers piercing the early morning mist. "Such a move would complement the miners' efforts."

"And divert forces from the east, so our attack will likely succeed."

A rider approached, careful to stay beyond the range of the archers on the castle walls. Two of Marston's men launched arrows, one after the other, and both fell short, but they served as a warning. If the rider strayed a few more feet toward the walls, his life could easily be lost.

"This must be the courier," Piers said.

"A change of plans?" Montague asked as the soldier reined his horse to a halt. "Or the order to attack?"

"Word from Jamet and James the Bold," he said breathlessly. "The attack is at hand," the courier said.

Montague looked at Piers. "Are we still to target the eastern wall?"

"Yes, sire," the rider said. "Proceed just as you've planned to."

"And the barons' men?" Piers asked.

"A focused attack near the northwest tower," the messenger said, "with the main offensive against the western wall."

Piers glanced at Montague. "Even though it's the strongest position an enemy could take aim at?"

The rider smirked. "Not anymore," he informed them. "A traitor within has lowered the drawbridge."

"The castle entrance is ours to use?" Pier asked, looking at Montague. "Just as you suspected, sire."

"An easy prediction," Montague replied humbly, "and if I can make it, so too can those within the walls. If Marston is the man they say he is, he and his soldiers lie in wait."

"It seems they have made no such preparations," the courier interjected.

"But Marston may yet have a trap that's easily sprung," Montague warned. "If it is, we'll witness a massacre."

"The barons' army is almost in place," the rider said, ignoring Montague. "Jamet orders you to make ready for the charge." He turned and galloped away, avoiding the archers who waited on the wall as he headed for the western side of the castle.

Montague turned to Piers. "Take the majority of the men and attack the southern wall of the southeast tower. I'll take the rest to scale the eastern wall."

"And if the barons' men should find success in the north and west?"

"Then victory belongs to us."

Chapter 107

As Michael Marston prepared for the coming attack, tightening his scabbard around his waist and hooking a battle axe into his belt, he thought of all of the men in his charge. Who among them was a traitor? Who would value the barons and France over king and country? His men had been with him for years; some had spent their entire lives within the castle walls or in its shadow. He couldn't imagine any one of them more loyal to the enemy than they were to him. But that's what traitors and spies did best. They blended imperceptibly into the very worlds they sought to destroy, making sure their lives were intertwined with those they were about to betray.

"We're working to reinforce the gate, but we can't get the drawbridge to function," Carney told Marston when he emerged from the keep.

"Can the windlass be repaired?"

"Gideon claims it can be done, but he'll need time."

Marston watched as soldiers dragged timber, wagons, and refuse from damaged buildings to the castle gate. As roughshod as it was, the barricade would be effective; it would help to keep the enemy at bay while Marston and his men launched a counterattack. They couldn't stop the advance, but they could slow it down. And perhaps they could inflict enough damage to the enemy's forward ranks that the barons would choose to retreat rather than advance.

"We piled what was left of the dead in the barbican," Carney said. "They'll have to climb over the corpses to attack."

"And then they have to get through the barricade," Marston observed, looking through the gatehouse at the barbican walls and down into the entryway.

Carney followed Marston's gaze. "I've readied the archers."

"And the oil?"

"Yes, sire," Carney said. "We'll lay waste to any who approach."

"Have we identified the traitors?" Marston asked with distaste.

"We have, sire," Carney said softly. "And they're men you wouldn't expect."

"All dead, I assume."

"Yes, sire," Carney said. "None made their escape."

"And their leader?"

"Jenks, sire, the blacksmith. The fishmonger claims James the Bold holds Jenks's family captive. He's likely threatened to kill them. Three others were friends, two his brothers."

Marston sighed and slowly shook his head. "If only he had come to me," he muttered, "and allowed for a chance to fix it. We could have attempted a rescue and somehow saved his family."

"I know, sire," Carney said grimly. "But when the heart is pulled, the head sometimes no longer functions."

Marston nodded in agreement. "And how did he receive commands from the barons?"

"Gideon suspects he sent messages using that accursed bird of his."

Marston remembered the falcon always on Jenks's arm. "It's too late to solve the problem now. It's the aftermath we must address."

"Let's climb the wall," Carney said, "so we can see what the enemy brings."

When they reached the top, they could see much of the battlefield on both the north and west sides of the castle, the rolling plain of green grass which met the forest in the north, farm fields and a distant village in the west, the once lush scenery marred by the detritus of battle. Just beyond the field stretched the long lines of the barons' men.

"They advance cautiously," Marston said, scanning their ranks and then his archers. "Almost as if they wait for command. Why not rush the drawbridge while it cannot be closed?"

353

"A mystery, sire," Carney agreed. "But one that gives us all the more time to prepare. Captain Marlowe will defend the bailey. I've ensured he has all he needs."

"The last line of defense will be the keep," Marston said softly, hoping the battle never reached that last bastion of refuge.

A cry echoed across the battlefield, and suddenly the enemy loosed its catapults. From the north, boulders smashed into the curtain wall, just past the tower. From the west, boulders careened into the portcullis and the courtyard. The archers steeled themselves, the boulders crashing down dangerously close to their secondary lines of defense.

"Destroy the catapults," Carney called out to the archers atop the wall.

Seconds later, flaming arrows bore down upon the catapults and men who toiled around them. Some stuck fast to the machines' support beams, oil splattering on impact, flames flaring here and there. The attackers moved quickly to extinguish them. Marston's men loosed more arrows, striking both men and machines.

"Loose!" Carney yelled, urging his men to maintain their advantage. If they were to keep the enemy at bay, the catapults would have to be the first casualty of battle.

Marston ordered his men to maneuver the catapult in the bailey so that it faced the west.

"Fire!" he yelled, and seconds later the massive arm snapped forward, propelling a huge rock into the sky. It came crashing down near one of the enemy catapults, killing three of the barons' men.

"They prepare to attack!" Carney warned.

Marston watched as the enemy advanced slowly and deliberately. Hidden behind their shields, they plodded steadily forward until the first of the English arrows found their mark. Then they erupted with fearsome howls and bolted toward the barbican where the failed castle gates begged entry and the outnumbered English strove, in vain, to stave off defeat.

Chapter 108

James the Bold and Jamet sat astride their mounts, prepared for battle. They watched the castle wall near the northwest tower where the miners had dug vents by the stone to access the air needed to fuel the underground fire. At first only a few wisps of gray smoke filtered through the holes, hugging the stone and fading near the wall. But as the fire raged, the smoke flowed freely, billowing from the vents.

They didn't watch the smoke alone. Marston's men, all veterans of castle warfare, were quick to spy the smoke from the northwest tower. They knew all too well what was about to occur.

"They're scrambling about the wall," Jamet said.

"They know it will soon come down," James the Bold said, waiting impatiently for the stone to collapse.

Minutes passed, and, yet, the wall still stood, sturdy as the day it was built. The archers atop the wall had moved away from the smoke, some farther to the east, others into the northwest tower. They were all distracted, looking down into the bailey below.

Jamet pointed at the castle. "They're preparing their defense for when the wall collapses. Many are now in the tower."

"The longer it takes for the wall to come down, the better prepared they'll be," James the Bold muttered with disgust.

"The breach may not lead to victory as we thought it would," Jamet said doubtfully. "As our men climb over the rubble, the English archers will annihilate them."

"Blaise!" James the Bold called, glancing about for his warlock.

"Here, sire," Blaise replied.

James the Bold turned to find him standing alone at the fringe of the forest, a distracted look upon his face.

James the Bold looked at him curiously. "Blaise, when will the wall come down? My men are ready for battle, and the enemy is better prepared with each second that it stands."

"It'll come down, sire," Blaise said. "In minutes at most."

James the Bold turned to Jamet. "Ready the rest of the men for attack."

"Yes, sire," Jamet said. He mounted his horse and motioned for the advance to commence. Hundreds of men emerged from the forest and lined up along the edge of the plain armed with broadswords and bows, shields and lances.

James the Bold turned to Blaise. "What else do you see, warlock?"

Blaise looked at his master, his face betraying his confusion. His otherworldly vision had been thwarted by Minerva's spell, and he was all but blind, the future no longer his to see. "I know what lies within the walls," he muttered.

"Good," said James the Bold. "Then you go with Jamet."

Chapter 109

Montague mounted his horse and readied his men. He raised his right hand, looked up and down the line to ensure his men were ready, and then dropped his arm.

"Attack!" he bellowed.

Together they surged forward. Row after row of French soldiers marched on the southeast tower, their pale-blue tunics and iron helmets flashing upon the plain. Once they were within range, the archers paused, drawing arrows from their quivers and firing up at the defenders atop the curtain wall.

They advanced a hundred feet and then fifty more, their attack unanswered. But then, when they were clearly within the range of the archers atop the southern wall, a barrage of arrows sailed through the heavens, raining down upon them. They burrowed into the ground, struck the flanks of horses, and pierced some of the soldiers' armor, impaling their chests and torsos. The air was filled with the ragged cries of the wounded, the French captains' commands to attack, and rallying shouts from the defenders.

"Scale the wall," Montague yelled above the din of the battle as he and his soldiers closed in on the castle.

The infantry reached the southern wall, the ground before it strewn with men who were dead, dying, or badly wounded. They swarmed around the southeast tower, raced down the eastern wall another hundred feet, and positioned their ladders against the stone.

The few men posted on the eastern wall, not expecting an attack from that quarter, fought gallantly, firing down upon the enemy soldiers as they scrambled up their ladders, dumping buckets of boiling oil from the ramparts followed by a torrent of flaming arrows. Fire raged along the base of the wall, and the fallen French screamed in agony as they burned to death. A few emerged from the fireball, pitching their bodies to the ground to extinguish their burning clothes.

As the attack wore on, the outnumbered defenders held their own, but soon they were overwhelmed. Too few remained to kick away the ladders or kill those who climbed them. The French tore up the rungs, fighting off the overhead assaults, and reached the summit. The first Frenchman breached the wall, and one of Marston's soldiers ran him through with a lance and pushed him over the edge. But a second followed, climbing over the battlement before the English could land a blow, and ran along the curtain wall. A third and others ran in behind him, and suddenly the French had taken the battle from outside the walls to within.

Montague watched the fight unfold, the stalemate twisting on a torturous path to victory. When Marston's men focused on the soldiers scaling the wall, swarms of Frenchmen moved in from the south side of the castle to join their comrades. Montague peeled away from the battle and led his horse along the cliff back towards the forest, found the narrow path down to the shore, and guided his horse down the pebble-strewn track. Urging his horse forward, he made his way down the beach, past the deserted stone wharf that served the castle.

Keeping watch of the archers on the castle wall, he dismounted and hobbled his horse, careful to remain hidden. Skulking as close to the cliff as he could, studying the terrain, he crept to the mound of rocks where he had seen the woman emerge from the cliff. He skirted the base of the formation, stepping into the sea, and froze when he saw the bodies. The Baron Richard Tweed lay sprawled on his back in the sand, arms and legs extended. A dozen feet away lay Trinity, her body twisted and broken.

Montague turned away and looked up at the castle wall. He would have to be cautious as he climbed the cliff. The bodies were a chilling reminder of the proximity of death, but they assured him he was in the right location.

He found the narrow path that led toward the castle and hurried up to the ledge. Hidden from Marston's men, he made his way to the landing which was tucked among overhanging rocks. He pushed and probed along the cliff face, sticking the point of his sword in various nooks and crannies.

He had searched for almost ten minutes when the point of his sword became embedded in the rock, and a large stone slowly shifted to the left, revealing the opening to a secret passage.

Chapter 110

The Lady Gabrielle knew the barons' men would be streaming through the barbican, intent on killing or capturing all of those within the walls. It was the entrance she had taken when she'd first been brought to Marston Castle, a gift for Michael Marston. It seemed like so long ago, years, but it had been only weeks, and she knew her life, which had so drastically changed, was about to change again.

"The wounded are coming," Mrs. Carney called from the door of the Great Hall.

The women who assisted Gabrielle had made all the preparations. They'd restocked the supply of bandages, salves, and elixirs as well as bottles of wine, which served a variety of purposes, including the treatment of burns.,

Gabrielle watched as the women received the first of the wounded, their devotion to the castle's survival absolute. None of their faces betrayed even a hint of fear. If they had been given the chance, as she had, to escape through the secret passage and run away from the horrors of battle, would they have taken it? She had her doubts.

"Bring him over to this first table," Mrs. Carney said as two villagers brought in a wounded man, limping on an injured foot.

"What happened to you?" she asked as the man settled upon the table.

"I was handling hot oil, dumping it on those who climbed the walls, and spilled some on my leg," he said.

Mrs. Carney fetched a bottle of wine and some salve and began her treatment. "You'll be back in the fight in no time. Just let me put some of this on that burn. Nasty, isn't it?"

Moments later, a second man was brought in and then a third. Soon the women were overwhelmed, and villagers were forced to leave some of the wounded lying in the hallway, their faces pale with suffering, some praying softly to a God who didn't seem to hear.

"Where's the fighting worst?" Gabrielle asked as she and her makeshift nurses hurried through each patient's treatment, knowing many more awaited their care.

"In the barbican," one of the villagers replied. "It faces the fiercest attack."

"And the French just attacked the east wall," added one of the young boys who worked at the butcher's shop.

The wounded continued to stream into the Great Hall and now numbered more than thirty. The women and their young assistants scrambled about, transferring more men to awaiting beds, the tables they used to treat them stained red with blood. The room, which had been quiet only an hour before, echoed with the hectic cries of the women as they toiled over the injured, who wailed in agony and begged for water, the stench of the dead hanging in the stifling air.

"There's another batch coming," Mrs. Carney said as she glanced out the entrance.

Gabrielle looked up from the wounded man she was treating. An arrow had grazed his neck—if it had been much closer to his jugular it would have killed him—and he was bleeding badly. She rubbed an elixir on the wound, a blend of water, vinegar, and a touch of honey. Then she lifted his head and had him drink a healing potion that she and Mrs. Carney had earlier prepared. It contained dwarf everlast, vinegar, garlic, and pine needles and was thought to speed the healing process. Then she helped the man off the table.

"Hold this firmly against your neck," she said, handing him a rag, "and go lie on one of the vacant beds."

"Thank you, my lady," the soldier said once he'd managed to get to his feet. He pressed the rag against his neck, cringing.

"It'll feel better in a few hours," Gabrielle said.

He nodded and smiled grimly. "I don't have a few hours, my lady." He tied the rag around his neck. "I must get back to wall."

"You need rest," Gabrielle pleaded as he turned to leave.

361

"No time, my lady," he replied as he made his way to the door. "If too many of us rest, we'll never win the battle raging outside the door."

Gabrielle's heart clenched, knowing the man would bleed to death in the throes of battle, but she had no time to mourn him. When she turned back to the table, another soldier had already taken his place. An arrow protruded from his torso, close to his heart. His face was gray, his eyes closed. Gabrielle put her fingers on his neck, feeling for a pulse. There was none.

"This one is dead," she said quietly to the villagers who had brought him in.

"We'll take him straight out," an elderly man said gravely. "There are many more to who need your care."

Chapter 111

Marston hurried along the wall to the edge of the barbican, finding Carney commanding the castle's defense.

"The enemy has launched probing attacks," Carney told him. "But now they are massing their forces for a focused assault, the drawbridge their objective."

Marston could hardly hear him above the din of battle. "How does Gideon fare with repairs?" he shouted.

Carney's eyes suddenly grew wide, and he shoved Marston further down the length of the wall, ducking behind him. A boulder from an enemy catapult landed where they had stood, breaking mortar and stone, sending clouds of dust and debris shooting into the air.

"He's almost done with the drawbridge." Carney said, "His efforts are aided by two of my men."

Marston looked up and down the wall and saw an avalanche of arrows flying from the bows of his men. "Our defense seems to be holding," he said. He turned to his men on the barbican walls, pouring hot oil down on attackers. The wagons and timber blocking their path burned brightly, flames raging to the top of the wall, smoke billowing higher.

"As long as the fire rages," Carney said, "the enemy can't advance."

"Look," Marston said pointing at a ladder placed against the wall. Two defenders scrambled upward. "No one sees them."

Carney shouted a harried command, but none of his men heard him. He darted toward the enemy, Marston just behind him. As the first of the enemy soldiers reached the top of the rung, Carney sliced his shoulder. The man cried out and clung to the ladder. Marston bolted forward, and he and Carney pushed the man away from the wall. He fell thirty feet to the ground below. A soldier standing near them turned and launched an arrow into the enemy. They pushed the ladder away, and Marston launched a flaming arrow, hitting the second attacker.

Captain Marlowe, one of Marston's underlings, hurriedly approached. "Sire," he cried above the noise. "The north wall is about to collapse."

Marston faced him, alarmed. "I was just there, and nothing seemed amiss."

"Miners undermined the foundation," Marlowe explained. "The wall is supported only with wood that they've since set ablaze. And they use their catapults to weaken it further."

"How much time do we have?" Marston asked, his mind racing to determine his options.

"It stands for only minutes more," Marlowe said.

Marston looked to the barbican and the men dedicated to defending it. "We barely keep the invader at bay," he said, pointing to the gates. "No men can be spared for another breach."

"There is more, sire," Marlowe said. "The French have scaled the east wall. They threaten our catapult, but we're fending them off."

Marston spun around to find blue tunics far in the distance and knew they stared defeat in the face. "If that wall comes down, we've little hope/ We may have to retreat to the keep."

"I'll muster some archers and form a line in the bailey," Carney said. "When the wall comes down and the enemy comes over the rubble, we'll pierce their hearts with arrows and rebuild the wall with bodies."

Before Marston could respond, a loud roar sounded from the north as the wall collapsed upon itself. Stone, mortar, and debris billowed across the courtyard and the fields beyond as the massive wall buckled, blanketing the area in a cloud of dust. The pile of rubble stood fifteen feet high and, at first glance, seemed impassable, but as soon as the dust began to settle and the barons' men realized their advantage, the cries of advancing attackers resounded up and down the northern front as they streamed toward the ruins.

Chapter 112

James the Bold watched it all with a wicked grin. He sat astride his horse, Jamet beside him. They stared in fascination, amazed by the success the miners had in destroying part of a fortress that had once seemed so formidable.

Captain Fletcher approached, galloping toward them. "Our forces in the west have probed the barbican, and all that blocks the way is ablaze," he informed him. "The men are massed, waiting for you to lead the attack."

"And the French?" Jamet asked.

"They've scaled the east wall and threaten the bailey."

"Marston lives but minutes more," said James the Bold. "Then the castle will be mine."

They waited, watching as the dust plume drifted out to sea and into the forest, blanketing the castle. At first, only the towers were visible. In only a few minutes, the air cleared, and they could see the path forward.

James the Bold turned to Jamet. "It's times like these that men are made. Lead your men into battle."

Jamet nodded and galloped to the front of his waiting army. He waited a moment, raised his right hand, and then issued the command. "Attack!"

The barons' men raced forward, tearing through the veil of arrows launched by the castle's defenders. They had barely gone fifty feet when the first man fell and then another, the defenders as determined to stave off defeat as the attackers were intent on victory.

Within minutes, they'd reached the remains of the collapsed section of the north wall and scrambled over the rubble. Jamet raced to the top of the broken stone, urging his men to follow. He reached the peak, but suddenly his eyes grew wide, not expecting what awaited him. Fifty archers were ready to fire, Captain Carney commanding. Their bowstrings snapped, and arrows flew, the first finding Jamet's right thigh.

"Ah!" he screamed, not expecting the pain. The battlefield becoming blurry as he paused

Stumbling while a second arrow struck, piercing him in the chest. The pain was more than he'd ever known. He fell to his knees, praying to God that he somehow could continue. When he opened his mouth to give a command, however, nothing but blood issued forth. The sky grew dark, and he was about to fall when the third arrow struck his throat. He fell face forward on brick and stone, his eyes now closed forever.

James the Bold, Captain Fletcher beside him, raced around to the west, still thirsting for battle. "I can taste victory," he said to the captain. "Just as Marston can taste defeat."

He took his rightful place before the troops that anxiously awaited his command. He looked at the castle, smothered in dust, the barbican filled with fire and smoke. As his eyes wildly studied the enemy, he craved the combat he'd come to enjoy.

"Forward!" he shouted, racing toward the crippled drawbridge, his sword held high in the air.

He rode into position, pausing just in front of the drawbridge, demanding their attention.

"We've breached the northern wall," he shouted. "And now we take the west!"

The infantry pressed forward, driving into the barbican, climbing over the dead that blocked the way and shoving burning debris aside. A dozen men bolted into the bailey where Marston's archers were poised and ready to strike. Three of the first to break through were felled, followed quickly by two more. As arrows tore past him, James the Bold followed, on horseback, impaling soldiers who ran at his heels.

"Attack!" he screamed, urging his men, forward, brandishing his sword, "and victory will soon be ours!"

Chapter 113

Montague peered into the secret passage, the sunlight at his shoulder casting a faint glow. He wedged the stone door open with rocks, pausing for a moment while his eyes grew accustomed to the darkness. He then tentatively stepped inside and cautiously took a few steps, squinting into the distance where a dim light shone amidst the gloom. From his vantage, there was no way to tell its source.

He withdrew his sword and held it in front of him, pointing at an unseen enemy in the inky blackness. Waving the blade back and forth, ensuring nothing stood in his path, he took one step forward, then another, counting his paces to estimate how far into the side of the cliff he'd traveled. Before long, he reached the light source, a crystal perched on a ledge near the top of the cave.

Montague pictured the lay of the land above him, the width of the plain from cliff to castle, all too aware of the grisly battle his men now waged there. He suspected he was a hundred feet below the surface, perhaps more, but knew at some point the path would ascend, leading him to a hidden exit somewhere in the castle. He continued to make his way slowly down the corridor, wary of traps laid for trespassers, until he thought he might be under the wall or a few feet beyond it.

Guessing how far he had travelled from the cliff's face, he was certain he was beneath the bailey. The passage turned slightly, and he tried to imagine where it would lead. He suspected it ended in the keep if it was truly intended as an escape route for the castle's master where Marston would make his last stand surrounded by faithful followers. But he couldn't imagine just how the tunnel got there.

Believing Lady Gabrielle would be in the keep, just as the wizard Alaric had foretold, he was determined to find her amidst the chaos and rescue her from her captives. They would then escape the way he'd come in. Certain the battle that raged above him wasn't faring well for the English since they faced attacks from three sides, breaches difficult to overcome, he suspected they would soon surrender or try to defend the keep in the hopes of preserving the castle for the king.

Montague quickened his pace as the tunnel ran beneath the bailey, the passage becoming increasingly straight and easier to travel. His vision sharpened, adapted now to the near darkness, and he was less wary of falling victim to a trap.

He came to the end of the corridor and found a narrow, winding stairway inset into the castle wall. Hurriedly, he mounted the stairs, climbing higher and higher until the corridor ended abruptly. A wooden door barred his path. He reached out, running his hand back and forth along the panels and the walls of the corridor, searching for a hidden handle. A moment later, he found a lever tucked in a space between two rocks, and he pushed it with the point of his sword.

The wooden panel began to move, rotating ninety degrees, and exposed a lavish room, its walls ensconced with invaluable manuscripts, a grand fireplace on the eastern wall.

Chapter 114

Blaise stood atop the crumbled heap of stone that had once been the northwest wall of Marston's castle. He studied the courtyard beyond, his gray hood covering his head, his pale face and black eyes veiled in shadow. He was desperate, his breathing coming in labored gasps, beads of sweat dotting the back of his neck. His vision was hazy, the images he beheld distorted, flashes of light marring everything upon which he tried to focus.

He had to find the witch. No more would he attempt to thwart her power by countering spells or playing more games. His intent raced through his mind. I have to kill her, squeeze the life from her body, murder the creature that she is. She is so far from human that she can have been spawned only by the Devil himself. Unless she is dead, my torture will continue every minute of every day for millennia.

As battle waged around him, the barons' men continued swarming over the rubble that had once been a wall. He slid past them, hugging the wall of the bailey and following the path he had seen in his vision that would take him to the witch. He staggered on, light-headed and dizzy as if he hadn't eaten for weeks if not days. His strength was fading, his mind growing more cloudy. He knew he had little time to find Minerva before he had no sense nor strength at all.

The northeast tower beckoned to him, urging him forward. He staggered across the bailey, knowing it led to her. Just as he approached the entrance, an English archer paused on the steps that led to the wall and drew his bow taut, his arrow aimed at the warlock. Blaise turned to meet his gaze, and the archer loosed the arrow, the twang of the bow string ringing in the warlock's ears.

The arrow sliced the air and came toward his chest. Blaise stared unblinkingly as it hurtled toward him, his smile hidden by the hood that cloaked his face. The arrow's path was true, its flight steady, and it whistled in the wind as it coursed straight for his heart.

Just as the arrow was about to strike him, the warlock arched his back and bowed out his chest. The arrow drove into his torso and passed straight through, or at least it appeared to. Slowly, Blaise lowered his hood, exposing his pale face and black eyes, and cast a penetrating gaze at the man who'd fired it. The archer gaped at the wizard, wide-eyed with fear. He knew he had fired a near perfect shot; the arrow should have killed the man standing before him. But as he locked eyes with Blaise, he could see that he was no man at all but some malevolent creature, a subhuman spirit with magical gifts that he could never hope to combat. The soldier threw his bow to the ground and raced across the bailey.

Blaise hurried on to the tower, knowing the witch was far below in a subterranean cavern. He only had to find the entrance. He studied the steps, searching for anything that might hint it did not belong. A stone on the third step was a dull indigo color, not gray like the ones around it. He pushed it firmly, engaging the door that hid the secret passage, stepped tentatively into the corridor, and began his descent.

When he arrived in her den, Minerva appeared from the shadows as if formed from mist. "Blaise, you fool," she said, "so easy to predict."

"Remove the spell you've placed upon me," he muttered as a wave of dizziness overtook him. He could feel the power inside him fading. He tried to lift his foot but couldn't. He moved to raise his arm, and it shifted slightly but then fell limp at his side.

"It can never be undone," Minerva said. "Nor would I ever let it."

"I'll kill you."

The witch threw back her head and cackled. "Never," she said. "Not if you live out the millennium."

Blaise glared at her, willing all of the power that remained in his bones to his fingertips. "You'll soon be nothing more than ashes drifting in the wind."

The witch came towards him, eying him closely as if he were an ingredient for one of her potions. "You can't even move, warlock. How are you going to kill me?"

Again, Blaise tried to raise an arm, but couldn't. He attempted to lift his feet, but they remained planted to the stone.

"Is that all you have left?" she asked with a smile.

"Release me," he tried to shout, but his words escaped his lips as a whisper that made his taunt seem an empty threat.

Minerva began to laugh, softly at first and then with abandon. She came close to her victim, almost brushing up against him. Blaise raised his arm, trying to grab her, but it barely even shifted. The witch sprinkled a turquoise powder over his head and down upon his shoulders, her latest concoction, and his entire body froze. Even his eyes locked in place. He tried to talk, but no sound escaped his lips. Nothing he attempted to do, no command his mind created, was obeyed by the rest of his body.

"I have one more spell to cast, warlock," she said, studying her specimen as if he were a fly in her web. "One more incantation to join those I've already rendered to trick your mind, weaken your body, and ensure your thoughts are consumed with me."

Blaise tried to reply, to rail against her, to claim she could never defeat him, but he couldn't. He could do nothing but stand and wait for what would befall him like a doomed marble statue.

Minerva took another pouch from a fold in her black robe. She reached within and removed a pinch of gray powder. "Bones from the dead," she whispered mysteriously, sprinkling it over the warlock's body.

Blaise recoiled internally, knowing something horrible was about to happen. Powerless to stop it, he watched as Minerva took a vial from her pocket, the liquid it contained deep red like blood. She removed the cork and poured the liquid on top of his head. He could feel it ooze slowly over his skin, through his hair and down his forehead, and then drip past his eyes.

A streak of lightning flashed through the cave, casting a brilliant light like a thousand suns. A profound darkness then descended upon Blaise, blacker than the grave. It enveloped him for almost a minute before it was broken by a gray fog rising from the rocks at the base of the cavern. When the mist lifted, Blaise could see the place where he had stood, but he was no longer there.

He heard Minerva laugh. She raised a slender glass vial to the dim light of a crystal, and he realized he was standing within it, frozen for all eternity, only a fraction of the creature he'd once been. He was nothing more than a child's charm for her to toy with for millennia to come.

Chapter 115

When Marston saw the enemy gather for a massive assault on the barbican, he left the wall and formed a defensive position halfway to the keep. He and his men launched arrows into the barons' soldiers as they came swarming through the gate, the dead and dying gathered on the ground before them.

"Hold them," Marston yelled, his sword held high in the air. "We'll beat them back."

Meanwhile, Captain Carney commanded a hundred men to the north, holding the enemy at bay as they climbed the rubble from the collapsed wall. As the enemy met with failure and more bodies littered the rubble, their advance was stemmed, and a stalemate ensued as they grew weary of the battle.

On the eastern side of the castle, Captain Marlowe had assembled his men near the catapult. The French tried to scale the castle and spread out along the curtain wall, but the English archers picked them off,   and the soldiers fell to the ground below.

The remainder of Marston's men, scattered throughout the bailey, moved where they were needed most, rotating between the northern, western, and eastern breaches, turning attackers into defenders, so vicious was their response. But just as Marston thought the tide had turned and the battle would end in stalemate, the resistance at the entrance began to weaken, and more of the barons' men barged in.

He was about to retreat and form his defense closer to the keep when Gideon raced down the steps from of the barbican and rushed toward him. "Sire," he yelled. "The drawbridge has been lifted, and the gate is being lowered. The enemy is trapped within!"

Marston watched as Goideon hurried across the courtyard, his robe billowing behind him, his black beard bouncing off his chest. He was unarmed, a scholar, not a knight.

"Protect Gideon," Marston ordered two of his men.

"To the keep, sire!" called Gideon. "Your safety should be sacred, not risked amidst the battle."

Suddenly a man on horseback burst through the barbican, squeezing through before the gate dropped down. A giant of a man wielding an enormous sword, he spurred his horse forward, defying the English archers whose arrows failed to find him.

Marston eyed the giant who tore around the bailey, hacking men in half wherever he dared to go. A thick beard hid his face, but not the scar, and Marston knew it could be only James the Bold. The vicious warlord charged toward him while Marston stared in horror, seeing Gideon pinned between them.

"Marston!" James the Bold thundered as he locked eyes with the castle's commander. He urged his horse forward, sword raised high. "No man deserves to die more than you."

"Gideon!" Marston called out, helpless to defend his friend.

James the Bold raced forward, the hapless scholar in his path. The two soldiers beside him wheeled around but were bowled over by the giant's horse. James the Bold leaned to the right and swung his sword downward in a vicious arc, slicing Gideon on his neck. The blow ripped through skin and bone, almost severing his head from his body. Blood gushed from the mortal wound, and he fell, dead before he hit the ground, a red puddle blooming in the soil beside him.

Marston screamed, his eyes clenched closed, his soul crying for his comrade. One of England's greatest minds had been lost in only a matter of seconds.

"I'm coming for you next, Marston!" James the Bold boomed.

Marston cast about for a weapon deadlier than his broadsword. He could never defeat James the Bold in close combat, sword against sword, spear against spear. Any attempt to do so would earn him the same end Gideon had met. He darted to where a fallen soldier lay, his bow and quiver beside him.

James the Bold leaped from his horse, a sword in one hand, a battle axe in the other, and charged toward him.

Marston grabbed the dead soldier's bow and an arrow from his quiver. He stared calmly into the face of James the

Bold, pulled the string as far back as he could, and let the arrow fly.

James the Bold lifted his sword. The arrow pinged as it struck the metal and then was cast aside.

"I'll rip your head from your body!" James the Bold hollered.

Marston fumbled with another arrow and pulled back, aiming hastily.

James the Bold was almost upon him, his blood-slick sword held high.

Marston fired. The arrow sped forward, striking James the Bold in the chest just under his neck.

The giant stumbled forward, hacking at Marston, and then falling to his knees, blood spilling down the front of his tunic and marring the snarling boar's head emblem. He glared angrily at Marston, grabbed the shaft of the arrow, and yanked it from his body with a terrible groan. He got to his feet and staggered forward.

Marston knocked another arrow, his enemy not a dozen feet from him, pulled back the bowstring, and let it fly. It struck James the Bold in the torso just beneath his ribcage, the force of the blow so intense that it bored straight through his body, the arrowhead glinting dully midway down his back. He tried to speak, his lips apart, as blood spurted from his mouth. He dropped the battle axe, but tried to keep advancing slowly, still waving his sword.

Marston withdrew his sword from its scabbard, stepping forward just as James the Bold swung his right arm in a mighty arc. Marston fended off the blow, their swords clanging as they met, surprised by the strength the warlord still possessed. James the Bold fought on with a gaping wound in his neck and an arrow imbedded in his body, eyes afire with rage. Marston landed a shattering blow, the sound of clashing steel echoing throughout the bailey, and leaned up against his foe, staring directly into his eyes. He pushed his sword aside, shoving the warlord off balance.

James the Bold staggered but did not fall. "I'll never let you live," he said, slowly raising his sword over his head, prepared for a fatal blow.

Marston surprised him, his sword downward, using all of his strength to drive the blade into the belly of James the Bold. The warlord's eyes grew wide, surprised at death's arrival. Blood ran down his chin and dripped onto his chest. Marston yanked the sword free, prepared to strike again. He grabbed the handle with both his hands and raised the sword above his head. James the Bold fell backwards.

Marston lowered his sword and looked at the warlord's vacant eyes. "James the Bold is dead!" he shouted.

His cries were met with frenzied cheers from the men under his command and astonished stares from the enemy, tiring of the fight. The attack slowed as the barons' men looked for direction that now could not be found.

Marston left the body lying at the foot of the steps and hurried into the keep. With the battle turning and victory near, he had to find Gabrielle.

Chapter 116

"The barons' men have broken through the front gate," Mrs. Carney said as she hurried back into the Great Hall. "And they're coming over the collapsed wall."

A woman at the first table looked up from the man she'd been treating, an arrow lodged in his leg. "Will defeat find us?" she asked.

"Michael Marston has known nothing but victory," Mrs. Carney declared. "We've no reason to believe today differs from those before it."

"But the French have breached the east wall, too," said a woman at the last table as she wrapped a bandage around a man's head.

"Our defenses crumble on three sides," a third said gravely as she fetched ointments from one of the shelves. "A darker day may never come."

"Our men will fall back to the keep," remarked one of the wounded soldiers.

"May our children never know the hardships that an enemy can bring," Mrs. Carney said with an anxious glance at her daughter Maud.

"We'll persevere," another woman said. "King John will send more men."

Gabrielle heard the desperation in their voices, the fading hope, the fear for the future, and her own heart wrenched, knowing there was little chance victory would be theirs. She knew what Marston wanted of her, the request he had made, and the promise she intended to keep. If they were soon to be under siege, it was time for her to go, to slip away, not frighten the others. She must find the secret passageway and save herself.

Suddenly she was overwhelmed by the feeling she was being selfish. She deserved no other fate than that of the brave men and women who fought beside her in this very room. But she had given her word.

She glanced about, making sure the other women were immersed with treating the wounded, and stepped into the corridor. For a moment, she hesitated, listening for Mrs. Carney to call out to her for help. When she was met with silence, she hurried up the stairs to the highest floor in the keep. She met no one in the hallways, but she could hear the sounds of battle growing ever louder as if Marston's men were retreating, closing in around the keep, trying to preserve their last hope to maintain a defense. The library was only a few strides ahead, and she hurried toward it.

Just as she crossed the threshold, Minerva suddenly appeared before her.

"How did you get here?" Gabrielle asked. She didn't know what the witch might want, and for a moment she was afraid, wondering if escape was no longer part of her plan.

Minerva smiled eerily. "The ways of the witch."

"Please. let me pass," Gabrielle said. "I realize it's wrong to leave the others. I know they need me. But I promised the master I would go."

"Take this with you," Minerva said, handing her a chalice.

Gabrielle hesitated, eyeing the tarnished goblet.

"It's the Holy Grail," the witch said and pressed it into her hands.

Gabrielle gaped at the witch, wondering if what she said was true. But what reason had she to lie? It was a truth that only seemed false, a truth so simple her mind struggled to comprehend it. It was as if she were unworthy to hear it.

"Never let it leave you," Minerva said. "Not even after a thousand tomorrows."

"I'm not deserving to carry such a treasure, let alone keep it," Gabrielle said, the legend and the fate of the cup that held the blood of Christ echoing in her memory. "I will take it to the convent on the coast, not the best resting place for a treasure such as this, but I know not where I am destined to go."

"Ask no questions," Minerva said. "The answers will come when they need to be known."

Gabrielle placed the chalice in her satchel, wrapping it carefully in one of her dresses. She wondered why she, of all the those who might better protect the holy relic, had been chosen to safeguard it.

The sounds of the battle grew suddenly louder as soldiers burst into the keep. She could hear the captains' commands, the clashing of swords, cries of agony—all so distinct they seemed to come from the staircase nearby.

"I must go," Gabrielle said. "Time is not my friend."

"Come, dearie," Minerva said, gesturing for her to follow. "I will take you."

Gabrielle paused. "But why?"

"It's dangerous. And the enemy might have wandered where they shouldn't have."

"The battle is lost and the war with it," Gabrielle said mournfully. "I know it, and so do you." She squeezed her eyes shut, fighting back tears, knowing the life of Michael Marston could be snuffed out that very day.

"The battle is not over," Minerva said. "Nor is it yours to fight."

Gabrielle glanced at the door as the sounds of battle rose and fell, victor and loser not yet known. "What if it isn't?" she asked, wondering if the hospital should be her home, the place where she would fight till the last, no matter what the cost.

"It is true the wall has been breached, and despair infects us all," Minerva said, "but evil never wins. It only delays the victory that the righteous will soon claim."

She took Gabrielle's hand and led her forward, but just as they approached the secret door it swung open. And Montague stepped out.

Chapter 117

Gabrielle stopped abruptly, her eyes wide with surprise. The last face she'd expected to see was Montague's, the man she'd once loved so completely she'd been sure they'd be bound for eternity. Somehow, the love she'd thought wouldn't wane had almost vanished, replaced by a passion for Michael Marston that was just as consuming, and she knew not why. Or so she'd thought. Now, as she gazed into Montague's eyes, she realized her love for him hadn't diminished. It still held her heart captive.

"Gabrielle," he said, rushing toward her.

She hesitated, looking at him curiously, unsure of what to do. Even though her soul was drawn to Montague, she felt a wall around her heart. She shied from his embrace, confused, as if a fog had drifted from the ocean to slowly consume her mind.

Montague froze, shocked by her reaction. "Gabrielle?" he asked tentatively. He looked at the witch, wondering who she was and if she'd played a part in this wicked plan.

"Gabrielle!" a voice called from the corridor.

Gabrielle's heart clenched. It was Michael Marston.

Minerva stepped between Gabrielle and Montague. "The master of the manor," she said.

Marston burst through the door. His sword was drawn, stained with blood. As soon as he saw Montague, he tensed, ready to fight.

Montague stepped back, quickly withdrawing his sword from its scabbard.

"No!" Gabrielle shouted.

Marston lunged forward, the point of his blade nicking the pale blue tunic that Montague wore, as the Frenchman swerved to avoid him. He quickly struck another blow, but Montague blocked him, the clanging of their metal swords echoing through the keep.

"Please, stop," Gabrielle pleaded, watching the fight unfold with horror.

The combatants didn't listen, both taking a more defensive posture, swords drawn, thrusts rebuffed, each seeking an advantage. Montague swung his sword, slicing at Marston. The warlord shifted, averting the blade, and a space opened up between them.

Gabrielle quickly stepped forward. "Enough of death and war," she pleaded. "My heart can take no more. Not now, not ever."

Marston and Montague eyed each other warily, their swords poised and ready to strike.

Minerva intervened. "Stay where you are," she said, holding out her hands to keep them apart.

Marston stared at the Frenchmen and then glanced at Gabrielle. "Do you know this man?" he asked gruffly.

She stood numbly, looking first at Marston and then Montague. She knew she had to make a choice, had to decide which world she would walk in, whose body she would embrace, whose lips she would taste.

Gabrielle?" Marston asked, his eyes boring through his enemy. "Do you know him?"

"He is Montague," she said softly. "My lover."

"Sire!" Carney called from the stairwell. "The enemy retreats. The battle is won."

Marston did not reply. He had saved England and King John, at least for the days ahead. But he took no time to celebrate, the deed at hand all consuming. He kept his gaze locked on Montague, unsure of what to do. He could hear Carney's footsteps in the corridor.

"Come, Gabrielle," Montague said coaxingly. "Normandy awaits."

Marston looked at Gabrielle, his eyes filled with love. He knew her future was better served in France. He had promised her many times, before their love had grown, that he would ensure she was united with her beloved Montague. He knew their own love was fleeting, most likely the work of the witch, but it had come when both had seemed to need it most. Now they would both, perhaps, be released.

"Go," he whispered, a sad smile crossing his face. "Both of you. Hurry. Before they find you."

"Wait," Minerva said. She held up her hand, and an eerie silence filled the keep as if time had somehow been forced to stand still. She withdrew a leather pouch from her robes, opened it, and sprinkled a lavender dust above Gabrielle's head. It fluttered about the air like tiny feathers and then slowly descended. Once it had settled upon her, Minerva began to chant.

"Love once found,

Now will cease,

Tightened bonds

Will now release.

Heart to heart,

No longer tied

So say I,

This spell has died."

She repeated the spell three times, watching Gabrielle closely as she did so.

Gabrielle smiled weakly. She went to Michael Marston, hugged him tightly, her head against his chest, and then kissed him gently on the lips. "Goodbye, my knight."

His eyes moistened, and he nodded with respect. "My lady."

Montague watched curiously, knowing what would forever be left unspoken but willing to pretend he did not. He returned his sword to its sheath but kept a wary eye on Marston.

"Come," the Lady Gabrielle said, taking his hand. "Our life waits to be lived."

They slipped through the secret door just as Carney entered from the hallway. Gabrielle cast one last, loving look at Michael Marston, nodded to the captain, and eased the bookcase closed.

"It's better this way," Michael Marston said, his heart heavy. He turned to look at Minerva. "It's what was meant to be."

Epilogue
A hundred years later
Normandy, France in the year 1316

I told them the tale had come to a close, strummed one last chord on my lute, and looked at those who looked at me. They'd been quiet for hours or more. Soldiers, sailors, merchants and thieves, a few women mixed among them, sat quietly and drank their grog and not a sound was uttered. They watched in silence for a moment more, and then their applause rang through the room, shouts and cheers, cries to continue, even looks of awe. I realized it was the finest tale that I had ever told, one I could tell wherever I went, and all who heard it would understand. I slid off the stool and bowed to the crowd, but the admiration continued. I admit I let it linger, having found a success I had never enjoyed.

The innkeeper, Graves, came to the stage and slapped me on the back. "Please, good friends," he then said to the crowd. "Let the man eat his dinner. He sings for his supper and has traveled so far just to entertain you."

It was only then that the noise died down, and Graves took me to a table. He gave me a bowl of hot stew and placed bread and grog beside it.

"Thank you, good sir," I said, never expecting such a feast.

"Only the beginning," Graves said. "The finest bed I can provide lies waiting for you. A hot breakfast is yours when you awake, and more if you so desire."

"My gratitude cannot be described."

"Yours was the finest performance I've ever seen. And the same for all who heard it."

It occurred to me then, after spending years on the road singing for my supper, that I'd finally found my path to acclaim. My destiny was now determined, and I would perform at the court of the king. My fate promised both fame and fortune, and I

384

knew it as well as I knew the peculiar timbre of my lute. This was the day when it all began.

I slept soundly for the first time in days, rose to a breakfast so immense I could scarcely eat it all, and declined Graves' request to remain. I knew that the "Song of Gabrielle" would travel the country faster than I, reach every inch of the land I loved, working its magic within the hearts of peasant and prince alike.

Once the morning meal had ended and all my farewells had been said, I set off for the village just down the road. As I left the inn and the courtyard around it, I felt compelled to visit the grave of Gabrielle, the woman all of France would soon admire and love. As I walked through the sea of crosses, strange images began to appear, and for a moment I feared I was ill. Somehow the past had become the present, and, as I gazed upon the terrain, I could see where Gabrielle's story had begun a hundred years before.

The coast of Normandy was not much different then, though many years had gone by. The convent sat on the cliff. Today it is unchanged, even if its purpose had been forever altered. The stone cottage remained, huddled before the sea, but the roses that once flanked it had long since withered away. The cliff and the path that winds to the sea were just as they had been long ago, as were the rocks that dressed the shore, though they seemed smaller now from years of battering by angry waves. The village had also persisted, but fewer cottages dotted its fringes, and the faces of the people who lived there were different. I blinked at the vision before me, shivering at the sight of what no mortal man should see, and wondered why I should suddenly possess such a gift.

The cemetery sat behind the convent close to the cottage as it does now. Stone markers and sun-bleached crosses identified homes of the dead. In the corner, overlooking the ocean, lay the grave of the Lady Gabrielle, the woman who had loved two men. I stood before it, knowing our chance encounter had forever altered my fate. I bowed my head, intent upon paying my respects to a woman I would never know but would sing about until my own life ended. The stone had weathered with time, her name little more than a whisper. I ran my fingers across it, and a vision of Gabrielle, shimmering like light cast through a prism, appeared before me and just as suddenly faded away. In an arched recess carved into the top of the stone, hidden from the prying eyes of man, was the aged chalice I had seen the night before. In my story, it had become the cup that had held the blood of Christ, lost to the ages, protected by God.

Humbler graves marked by simple crosses flanked Gabrielle's. To the right, the marker read "Montague of Rouen" and to the left "Sir Michael Marston, Master of Marston Castle." I was startled when I saw their names, for I thought I'd created them for the story I had told—the loves of Lady Gabrielle. How could I have known these men existed?

Terror took hold of my heart, so fearful was I that the Devil had told me every word I'd said, allowed me to glimpse a time not known, and was about to carry me off to the gates of Hell. I swallowed my panic, assuring myself that I must have glanced at the graves, seen the names carved in the markers, and they had come to life in my story even though they breathed no more.

A cold breeze bathed my body, and I turned to see a slender woman wrapped in robes of black, a strange looking pendant around her neck. She had a mass of tangled hair heaped upon her head. Her dark eyes glinted gold in the sunlight, and she nodded at me as if she knew the answer to every question that had ever been asked. She stood quietly beside me, head bowed in mourning and then turned with an eerie smile.

"Her story shall be known for eternity," she whispered, her eyes piercing my body and raking my soul. "Though it never was before."

As the seconds passed, she began to fade and with her the image of the coast from a hundred years past. I stood alone in a graveyard in the shadow of a forgotten convent, shivering as if the witch's breath was still upon my neck. I knew I had met Minerva. It was she who had given Gabrielle's story to me.

And as autumn after autumn became winter and then spring, armies expanded and contracted, people fled and returned, cities died and were reborn, and the English fought the French just as they always had. But no matter the cause of the wars of men, no matter the lives impacted or lost, the people of this storied coast still found time to laugh and love, enjoying what precious moments of peace life might have to offer. And some, like the Lady Gabrielle, lived far longer than they'd ever breathed, their stories told by friend and foe, repeated throughout the ages.

The

End

About the Author

JohnAnthony Miller was born in Philadelphia, Pennsylvania to a father of English ancestry and a second-generation Italian mother. Motivated by a life-long love of travel and history, he normally sets his novels in exotic locations during eras of global conflict. Characters must cope and combat, overcoming their own weaknesses as well as external influences spawned by tumultuous times. He's the author of seven historical thrillers and mysteries, as well as *Song of Gabrielle*. He lives in southern New Jersey.